BATTLE-MAGIC!

At Joram's command, the Druids sent the forest into battle. Giant oak trees with the strength born of centuries heaved themselves from the ground and lumbered forward to the attack. Mosiah, changing into a werewolf, knocked the strange humans to the ground. With one blow of a massive paw, a were-bear caved in a helmet. Illusionists created gigantic tarantulas that dropped down out of the trees, their hairy legs twitching, their many-faceted eyes burning like flame. Skeletons clutching pale swords in their bony hands rose up out of the ground. Dragons swooped down out of the skies, bringing with them flame and darkness. Perhaps the oddest happening on the field of battle that day was the report by several wizards of seeing a ring of mushrooms suddenly appear in a glade. A band of the enemy, charging into the ring, found that they could not get out. One by one, the strange humans were sucked down into the ground. The wizards reported, not without a shudder, that the last sounds that could be heard were the raucous laughter and gibbering voices of the faeriefolk . . .

THE DARKSWORD TRILOGY

VOLUME THREE

Triumph of the Darksword

MARGARET WEIS & TRACY HICKMAN

BANTAM BOOKS
NEW YORK • TORONTO • LONDON • SYDNEY • AUCKLAND

TRIUMPH OF THE DARKSWORD

A Bantam Spectra Book / September 1988

SPECTRA and the portrayal of a boxed "s" are trademarks of Bantam Books, a division of Bantam Doubleday Dell Publishing Group, Inc.

ISBN 0-553-27406-6

Published simultaneously in the United States and Canada

Bantam Books are published by Bantam Books, a division of Bantam Doubleday Dell Publishing Group, Inc. Its trademark, consisting of the words "Bantam Books" and the portrayal of a rooster, is Registered in U.S. Patent and Trademark Office and in other countries. Marca Registrada. Bantam Books, 1540 Broadway, New York, New York 10036.

PRINTED IN THE UNITED STATES OF AMERICA

OPM   15 14 13 12 11 10 9

Acknowledgments

We wish to gratefully acknowledge the help and support of the following people:

Our agent, Ray Peuchner, who died tragically of cancer in the summer of 1987. A kind and loving man, Ray was our friend as well as our agent and we mourn his passing even as we celebrate his beautiful life.

Laura Hickman, for advice, support, and putting up with Tracy.

Cover artist and friend, Larry Elmore, who makes our visions come to life.

Interior artist, Valerie Valusek, and map-maker, Steve Sullivan, both friends as well and both valued members of our creative "team."

Darryl Viscenti, Jr., for portraying Joram in the cover paintings.

Patrick Lucien Price for sharing his knowledge and advice on the tarot cards and the art of divination.

John Hefter for providing us with our Latin phrases and

for insight into the nature of the quest for spiritual under-standing. It is to John that we dedicate the character of the wise and gentle priest, Saryon.

Our editor, Amy Stout, who will probably remove this credit, but we hope she doesn't because she deserves it.

And finally, to you — our readers — whose continued en-thusiastic support and kind words make this so much fun.

THE FIELD OF GLORY

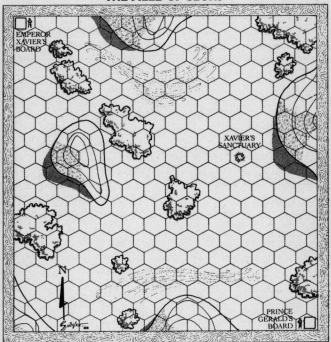

The Watcher

The thirty-foot stone Watcher, posting guard on the Border of Thimhallan, had seen with his eyes of rock many strange sights over the last nineteen years. He had been here only nineteen years, this Watcher. Once a human, a catalyst, his crime had been one of passion. He had loved a woman, committed the unpardonable sin of physically joining with her, and produced a child. He had been sentenced to the Turning, wherein his living flesh was transformed to living stone. He was destined to stand forever at the Border, staring into the realm of Beyond — the realm of death whose sweet peace and rest he would never know.

This Watcher thought back to the first six years of his Turning. Six years of unendurable emptiness, of rarely seeing a human, much less hearing a human voice. Six years of mind and soul raging inside their stone prison. These six years passed, and a woman brought a child to his feet. The child was beautiful, with long black hair and large, dark brown eyes.

"This is your father," the woman told the child, pointing up at the stone statue.

Did the Watcher know this wasn't true? Did he know his child had died at birth? He knew. Deep in his heart, he knew the catalysts had not lied when they foretold that no living issue would come of his union with this woman. Whose child was this? That was something the Watcher did not know, and he wept for the child and still more for the poor woman he had once loved who now stood at his feet, dressed in rags, looking up at him with crazed eyes.

Long years after that, the Watcher remained standing undisturbed without, his soul tormented within. Sometimes he saw others of his Order — the catalysts — changed to stone for some infraction they had committed. Sometimes he watched as a magus of the land was sent Beyond — the punishment inflicted upon those who have the gift of Life. He saw the Executioner drag the victim to the edge of the sandy shore. He saw the victim hurled into the ever-shifting mists that marked the Border of the World. He heard with his stone ears the last horrified scream that came back from those swirling gray fogs, and then nothing. The Watcher envied these victims. He envied them bitterly, for they were at rest, while he must go on living.

But the strangest sight the Watcher ever saw had occurred only a year before. Why should it have touched him? he wondered often in the dark hours of the night that were the hardest to bear. Why should it have left a sorrowful mark upon his stone heart when none of these others had? He didn't know, and he pondered it for days on end sometimes, reliving the scene over and over in his mind.

It was another Turning. He recognized the preparations — the twenty-five catalysts appearing from the Corridors, the mark drawn in the sand where the victim was to stand, the Executioner dressed in his gray robes of justice. But this was no ordinary Turning. The Watcher was surprised to see the Emperor arrive with his wife. Then came Bishop Vanya — the Watcher cursed him silently — and Prince Xavier, brother to the Empress.

At last they brought in the prisoner. The Watcher was stunned. This young man with long black hair and strong, muscular body was not a catalyst! And, so far as the Watcher knew, only catalysts were ever sentenced to the Turning.

Why was this young man different? What was his crime?

The Watcher watched with avid curiosity, thankful for anything that relieved the terrible boredom of his existence. He saw a catalyst arrive next. As the Priest took his place beside the Executioner, the Watcher saw that the catalyst carried a sword, a strange looking sword. The Watcher had never seen one like it before, and he shivered as he gazed upon the black, ungleaming metal.

A hush fell over the crowd. Bishop Vanya read the charges.

The young man was Dead. He had committed murder. Worse, he had lived among the Sorcerers of the Dark Arts and there he had created a weapon of demonic evil. For this, he was to be Turned to Stone. The last sight his eyes would behold, as their vision froze, was the terrible weapon he had brought forth into the world.

The Watcher did not recognize the young man as the child who had crouched at his feet all those years before. Why should he? There was no bond between them. Still, he pitied him. Why? Perhaps it was because a golden-haired girl — not much older than the woman he had once loved — was being forced to stand and watch, as his beloved had once been forced to watch. The Watcher pitied both of them — the young man and the girl; especially when he saw the young man fall to his knees before the catalyst, crying unashamedly in fear and terror.

The Watcher saw the catalyst embrace the young man, and his stone heart wept for them both. He watched as the young man stood — straight and tall — to face his punishment. The catalyst took his place beside the Executioner, sword in his hand. The twenty-five catalysts drew the magic, the Life, from the world, focused it within their own beings, then opened conduits to the Executioner. Magic arced from them into him. The Executioner drew upon it and began to cast the spell that would transform the young man's flesh to stone.

But suddenly the catalyst sacrificed himself, hurling his own body in the path of the magic. The catalyst's limbs began to harden to rock. With his last strength, he tossed the sword to the young man.

"Escape!" he cried.

There was no escape. The Watcher felt the dread power

of the sword even from where he stood, some twenty feet distant. He felt the sword began to absorb the Life from the world. He saw it destroy two warlocks in a burst of flame. He watched it bring the Executioner to his knees, and if his lungs had been able to draw breath, the Watcher would have let out a howl of victory and triumph.

"Kill!" he longed to shout. "Kill them all!"

But there was one thing the powerful sword could not do. It could not reverse the spell of the Turning. The young man saw the catalyst change to stone before his eyes. The Watcher felt his grief and looked forward with a heart filled with hatred to the young man's revenge.

It did not come. Instead, the young man took the sword and laid it reverently in the catalyst's stone hands. The young man bowed his head upon the stone breast of his friend; then he turned and walked into the mists of Beyond. The golden-haired girl, calling out his name, followed him.

The Watcher stared in amazement. He waited to hear the last wail of horror, but in vain. Only silence came from those shifting mists.

The Watcher's stone gaze went to those left behind and saw with grim satisfaction that the young man's revenge was enacted without him. Bishop Vanya fell to the ground as though struck by a thunderbolt. The Empress's body decomposed. It was then that the Watcher realized she must have been dead for some time, existing on magic alone. Prince Xavier ran to the stone statue of the catalyst and tried to wrest the sword from its grip, but the catalyst held it fast.

Soon the living left the Border, left it once more to the living dead. Left it to a new statue—a new Watcher. But it was not made thirty feet tall like the others. Its face was not frozen in fear, or hatred, or resignation as were the faces of its fellow Watchers.

The stone statue of the catalyst holding the strange sword in his hands stared out into the Realm of Beyond, and upon the stone face was a look of sublime peace.

And there was one other unusual thing about this living statue. It had one more, unique visitor. Now, from around the catalyst's stone neck, there fluttered gaily a banner of orange silk.

B O O K O N E

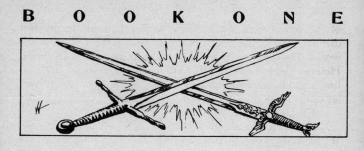

I

... And Live Again

The Watchers had guarded the Border of Thimhallan for centuries. It was their enforced task, through sleepless night and dreary day, to keep watch along the boundary that separated the magical realm from whatever lay Beyond.

What *did* lie Beyond?

The ancients knew. They had come to this world, fleeing a homeland where they were no longer wanted, and they knew what lay on the other side of those shifting mists. To protect themselves from it, they encompassed their world in a magical barrier, decreeing that the Watchers be placed on its Border — eternal, sleepless guards. But now it was forgotten. The tides of centuries had worn away the memory. If there *was* a threat from beyond the Border, no one worried about it, for how could it pass the magic barrier?

The Watchers kept their silent vigil still — they had no choice. And when the mists parted for the first time in centuries, when a figure stepped out of the shifting gray fog and put his foot upon the sand, the Watchers were appalled and cried out their warning.

But there were none, now, who knew how to listen to words of stone.

Thus the man's return was unheralded, unannounced. He had gone forth in silence and in silence he returned. The Watchers shrieked, "Beware, Thimhallan! Your doom has come! The Border has been crossed!"

But no one heard them.

There were those who might have heard the silent cries, had they been attentive. Bishop Vanya, for one. He was the highest ranking catalyst in the land and, as such, it seemed likely that his god, the Almin, would have called His minister's attention to such a calamity. But it was dinner time. His Holiness was entertaining guests and, though the Bishop prayed beautifully and devoutly over the meal, everyone had the distinct feeling that the Almin really hadn't been invited.

Prince Xavier should have heard the warnings of the stone Watchers. He was a warlock, after all — *DKarn-duuk*, a War Master, and one of the most powerful magi in the land. But he had more important matters to consider. Prince Xavier — pardon, Emperor Xavier — was preparing for war with the kingdom of Sharakan and there was only one thing more important to him than that. Or rather, it was all tied together. How to retrieve the Darksword, held fast in the arms of a stone statue. If he possessed this powerful sword — a weapon that could absorb magic — Sharakan must fall to his might.

And so Bishop Vanya sat in his elegant chambers at the top of the mountain fastness of the Font, dining on boar's head and piglet tails and pickled shrimp, discussing the nature and habits of marsupials with his guests, and the warnings of the Watchers were swallowed up with the wine.

Prince Xavier paced about his laboratory, occasionally darting over to read the text in some musty, brittle-paged book, consider it, then shake his head with a bitter snarl. The warnings of the Watchers were lost in his curses.

Only one person in all of Thimhallan heard the warnings. In the city of Sharakan, a bearded young man dressed in purple hose, pink pantaloons, and a bright red silken waistcoat, was wakened from his afternoon nap. Cocking his head toward the east, he cried out irritably, "E'gad! How do you expect a fellow to get any sleep? Stop that fearful racket!" With a wave of his hand, he slammed shut the window.

Beware, Thimhallan! Your doom has come! The Border has been crossed!

The man who stepped out of the mists was in his late twenties, though he appeared older. His body was that of a young man — strong, muscular, firm, and upright. His face was the face of a man whose sufferings might have spanned a century.

Framed by thick black hair, the face was handsome, stern, and — at first glance — appeared as cold and unfeeling as the stone faces of those who watched him. Lines of care and of grief had been chiseled into that face by a Master's hand, however. The fires of anger and hatred that had once burned in the brown eyes had died out, leaving behind cold ash.

The man was dressed in long white robes of fine wool, covered by a wet, mud-stained traveling cloak. Standing upon the sand, he looked about him with the slow and deliberate gaze of one who looks about the home he has not seen in many, many years. The expression of sadness and of sorrow on his face did not change, except to grow deeper. Turning, he reached back into the mists. A hand took hold of his, and a woman with long, golden hair stepped out of the shifting gray fog to stand beside him.

She glanced about her with a dazed air, blinking her eyes in the rays of the setting sun that stared at them from behind distant mountains — its red, unblinking eye seeming to regard them with amazement.

"Where am I?" the woman asked calmly, as if they had walked down a street and taken a wrong turn.

"Thimhallan," the man replied in an even tone of voice that spread like salve over some deep wound.

"Do I know this place?" the woman questioned. And though the man replied and she accepted his answers, she did not look at him or appear to be talking to him but continually sought out and spoke to an unseen companion.

The woman was younger than the man, about twenty-seven. The golden hair, parted in the center of her head, was

tied loosely in two thick braids that hung down to her waist.
The braids gave her a childish look, making her seem younger than her years. Her pretty blue eyes enhanced this childish appearance as well — until one looked into them closely.
Then it could be seen that their eerie brilliance and wide-
open stare were not expressive of the innocent wonder of
childhood. This woman's eyes saw things that could not be
seen by others.

"You were born here," the man said quietly. "You were
raised in this world, as was I."

"That's odd," said the woman. "I would think I'd remember." Like the man's, her cloak was splattered with mud
and wet through. Her hair, too, was wet, as was his, and
clung damply to her cheeks. Both were weary and appeared
to have traveled a long distance through a soaking rainstorm.

"Where are my friends?" she asked, half-turning and
staring behind them into the mists. "Aren't they coming?"

"No," the man said in the same calm tones. "They cannot
cross the Border. But you will find new friends here. Give
them time. They are probably not accustomed to you yet. No
one in this land has talked with them in a long, long while."

"Oh, really?" The woman brightened. Then her face
grew shadowed. "How lonely they must be." Lifting her
hand to her forehead to block out the beaming rays of the
sun, she peered up and down the sandy shore. "Hello?" she
called, holding out her other hand as she might to a wary cat.
"Please, it's all right. Don't be frightened. You can come to
me."

Leaving the woman talking to the empty air, the man —
with a profound sigh — walked up to the stone statue of the
catalyst; the statue that held the sword in its rock hands.

As he stared at the statue in silence, a tear crept from one
of his clear, brown eyes, disappearing into the deep lines that
cut into the stern, clean-shaven face. Its mate slid down the
other cheek, falling in the thick, black hair that curled upon
the man's shoulders. Drawing a deep, shuddering breath, the
man reached out his hand and gently caught hold of the
orange silk banner — now tattered and torn — that fluttered
bravely in the winds. Taking it from the statue, he smoothed
the silk in his hands, then folded it and placed it carefully in a

pocket of the long, white robes he wore. His slender fingers reached out to stroke the statue's careworn face.

"My friend," he whispered, "do you know me? I have changed from the boy you knew, the boy whose wretched soul you saved." His hand pressed against the cool rock. "Yes, Saryon," he murmured, "you know me. I feel it between us."

He smiled, a half-smile. This smile was not bitter, as his smiles once had been. This smile was sad and filled with regret. "Our situations are reversed, Father. Once I was cold as stone, warmed by your love and compassion. Now it is you whose flesh is icy to my touch. If only my love — learned too late — could warm you!"

He bowed his head, overcome by grief, and his tear-dimmed gaze fell upon the statue's hands that held the sword in their stone grip.

"What is this?" he muttered.

Examining the statue's hands more closely, the man saw that the stone flesh of the palms on which the sword rested was cracked and gouged as though it had been struck by hammer and chisel. Several of the stone fingers were broken and twisted.

"They tried to take the sword!" he realized. "And you would not give it up!"

Stroking the statue's injured hands with his own, he felt the anger that he thought was dead flickering to life within him once more. "What suffering you must have endured! And they knew it! You stood there, helpless, while they gouged your flesh and broke your bones! They knew you would feel every blow, yet they didn't care. Why should they?" he questioned bitterly. "They couldn't hear your cries!" The man's own hands went to the weapon, touching it haltingly. Reflexively, his hand closed over the hilt of the stone sword. "I have come upon a fool's errand it seems — "

The man stopped speaking abruptly. He felt the sword move! Thinking he might have imagined it in his anger, he gave the stone weapon a tug, as though to draw it out of its rock scabbard. To his amazement, the sword slid out easily; he nearly dropped it in surprise. Holding it, he felt the cold

stone warm at his touch and, as he watched, astonished, the
rock turned to metal.

The man lifted the Darksword to the light. The rays of
the dying sun struck it, but no flame blazed from its surface.
Its metal was black, absorbing the sun's light, not reflecting
it. He stared at the weapon for long moments. One part of
him was attentive to the woman's voice; he could hear her
moving farther down the beach, calling to person or persons
unseen. He did not watch her. He knew from long experience that, although she never acknowledged his existence,
she would not stray far from him. His gaze and his thoughts
focused on the sword.

"I thought I had rid myself of you," he said, speaking to
the weapon as if it were alive. "Just like I thought I had rid
myself of life. I gave you to the catalyst, who accepted my
sacrifice, then I walked — walked gladly — into death." His
eyes shifted to the gray fog that rolled upon the white sand
shore. "But death is not out there. . . ."

He fell silent, his hand gripping the hilt of the sword
more firmly, noticing how much better it suited him, now
that he was older, with a man's strength. "Or maybe it is," he
remarked as an afterthought, his thick, black eyebrows
drawing together in a frown. His gaze came back to the
sword, then his eyes shifted to meet the unseeing eyes of the
statue. "You were right, Father. It is a weapon of evil. It
brings pain and suffering to everyone who comes in contact
with it. Even I, its creator, do not understand or comprehend
its powers. For that reason alone it is dangerous. It should be
destroyed." The man's gaze turned once again, frowning, to
the gray fog. "Yet now it has been given to me again . . ."

As if in answer to some unspoken question, the leather
scabbard fell from the statue's hands and landed in the sand
at the man's feet. He bent down to pick it up, then started as
something warm dropped on his skin.

Blood.

Aghast, the man looked up. Blood oozed from the cracks
in the statue's hands, dripped out of the deep gouges in the
stone flesh, ran down the broken stone fingers.

"Damn them!" the man cried in fury.

Standing up, he faced the statue of the catalyst, seeing
now not only blood running from the hands but tears falling
from the stone eyes.

"You gave me my life!" the man cried. "I can't return that to you, Father, but at least I can give you the peace of death! By the Almin, they won't torment you anymore!"

The man lifted the Darksword and the weapon began to glow with an eerie, white-blue light. "May your soul rest in peace at last, Saryon!" the man prayed, and, with all the strength of his body, he drove the sword into the statue's stone breast.

The Darksword felt itself wielded. Blue light twined and twisted along the blade, surging up the man's arms as the weapon thirstily drank the magic of the world that gave it life. Deep, deep into the rock it plunged, striking the statue's stone heart.

A cry escaped the statue's cold, unmoving lips — a cry heard not so much with the ears as with the soul. The stone around the sword began to shatter and crack. Jagged lines spread through the statue's body with snapping, rending sounds that obliterated the catalyst's pain-filled voice. An arm broke at the shoulder. The torso split into shards and toppled from the trunk. The head cracked at the neck and tumbled to the sand.

The man yanked the sword free. Blinded by his tears, he could not see, but he heard the shattering of the stone and he knew the man he had learned too late to love was dead.

Hurling the Darksword to the sand, he pressed his hands against his eyes, fighting to stop the tears of rage and pain. He drew a deep, shuddering breath.

"They will pay," he vowed thickly. "By the Almin, they will — "

A hand touched his arm. A voice, deep and low, spoke hesitantly, "My son? Joram?"

Lifting his head, the man stared.

Saryon stood amidst the ruins of the stone body.

Reaching out a trembling hand, Joram grasped the catalyst's arm and felt warm, living flesh beneath his fingers.

"Father!" he cried brokenly, and was clasped fast in Saryon's embrace.

2

And In His Hand . . .

The two men held each other close, then separated. Each regarded the other intently. Joram's eyes went to the catalyst's hands, but Saryon hastily folded them one over the other, keeping them hidden in the sleeves of his robes.

"What has happened to you, my son?" The catalyst studied the stern face that was familiar, yet vastly different. "Where have you been?" His puzzled gaze went to the deep lines carved near the firm mouth, the fine lines around the eyes. "I have lost track of time, it seems. I could have sworn that only one year has passed — only once has the winter chilled my blood, only once the sun beaten down upon my head. Yet I see the marks of *many* years upon your face!"

Joram's lips parted to speak, but a wail interrupted him. Turning, he saw the woman slump down in the sand, frustrated and disconsolate.

"Who is this?" Saryon asked, following Joram as he walked toward the woman.

Joram glanced at his friend.

"Do you remember what you told me, Father?" he asked harshly. "About the groom's gift. 'All I could ever give her,' you said, 'was grief.'"

"Blessed Almin," Saryon breathed in sorrow, recognizing now the golden hair of the woman who sat, weeping, on the shore.

Walking over to her, Joram leaned down and placed his hands upon her shoulders. Despite his grim expression, his touch was gentle and loving and the woman yielded to him as he lifted her to her feet. Raising her head, she looked directly at the catalyst, but there was no recognition in her wide, too-bright eyes.

"Gwendolyn!" Saryon murmured.

"Now my wife," said Joram.

"They are here." Gwen spoke sadly, seeming to pay no attention to Joram. "They are all around me, yet they will not speak to me."

"Who is she talking about?" Saryon asked. The beach was empty, except for themselves and, in the far distance, another stone Watcher. "Who is all around us?"

"The dead," Joram answered, holding the woman to his breast and soothing her as she leaned her golden head upon his strong chest.

"The dead?"

"My wife no longer communicates with the living," Joram explained, his voice expressionless as though he had long ago accustomed himself to this pain. "She talks only with the dead. If I were not here to watch her and care for her," he added softly, stroking the golden hair with his hand, "I think she would join them. I am her one link with life. She follows me, she seems to know me, yet she will not speak directly to me or call me by name. She has not spoken to me — except once — in these past ten years."

"Ten years!" Saryon's eyes opened wide, then narrowed as he studied Joram intently. "Yes, I might have guessed. So wherever you have been, ten years have passed for you to one of ours."

"I did not know that would happen," Joram said, his thick, black brows drawing together. "Yet I might have, if I had considered it." He added, after a moment's thought,

"Time slows here in the center, moving faster and faster as it expands outward."

"I don't understand," Saryon said.

"No." Joram shook his head. "And neither will many others. . . ." His voice died. Absently, he smoothed Gwendolyn's hair, his brown eyes staring far off into the land of Thimhallan. The sun had disappeared, leaving behind only a rapidly fading pale light in the sky. Shadows gathered on the beach, hiding those who stood there from the view of the Watchers, whose silent, frantic shouts were going unheard anyway.

No one spoke. Gazing intently into the distance, as if endeavoring to see beyond the sands, beyond the plains, the forests, and the rims of the mountains, Joram appeared to be mulling over some decision.

Saryon kept quiet, fearing to disturb him. Though many questions crowded into his mind, one question alone blazed with the bright light of a fiery forge, and he knew it would shed light upon all the others. But that question Saryon dared not ask, fearing as he did the answer.

He waited in silence, his eyes on Gwendolyn, who looked around the gathering gloom from the shelter of her husband's strong arm, her face sad and wistful.

Finally, Joram shook his head, the black hair falling about his face, his thoughts returning from whatever world in which he had been wandering to the beach where they stood.

Feeling Gwendolyn shivering in the chill night air, Joram drew her wet cloak more closely around her. "Another thing I might have known, had I thought about it," he said, speaking to Saryon, "was that the Darksword would break the spell holding you prisoner. I didn't, however. I wanted only to give you rest. . . ."

"I know, my son. And I welcomed it. You cannot imagine the horror —" Saryon shut his eyes.

"No, I cannot!" said Joram, anger burning his voice. At the sight of his dark face scowling in the gloom, Gwen shrank away from him. Seeing her fear, he made an obvious effort to master himself. "I am thankful that you are here with me, Saryon," he added in cold, measured tones. "You will stay with me, won't you?"

"Of course," Saryon said firmly. His fate was bound up in Joram's. No matter what he intended.

Joram smiled suddenly; the brown eyes warmed, his shoulders relaxing as though a burden had been lifted from them. "Thank you, Father," he said. Looking down at Gwen, he put his arm around her and, hesitantly, she huddled against his side. "I ask this favor of you, then, my old friend. Watch over my wife. Take her in your care. There is much I must do and I may not always be able to stay close by her. Will you do this for me?"

"Yes, my son," Saryon said, though inwardly he asked fearfully, *What must you do?*

"Will you stay with this Priest, my dear?" Joram said gently to his wife. "You knew him once, long ago."

Gwendolyn's blue eyes went to Saryon, a mystified expression clouding them. "Why won't they talk to me?" she asked.

"My lady," the catalyst said helplessly, not knowing quite how to reply, "the dead of Thimhallan are not accustomed to talking to the living. No one has been able to hear them in many hundreds of years. Perhaps they have lost their voices. Be patient."

He smiled at her reassuringly, but it was a sad smile. He could not help thinking of the merry, laughing girl of sixteen who stood before him at the gates of Merilon, a bouquet of flowers in her hand. Looking into the blue eyes, he remembered the dawn of first love that had made them radiant. Now the only light in Gwen's eyes was the eerie light of madness. Saryon shuddered, wondering what terrible thing had happened to her to cause her to retreat from the world of the living into the shadowy realm of the dead.

"I think they're frightened of something," she said, and Saryon realized she was not talking to him or to her husband but to the empty air, "and they want desperately to tell someone, to warn them. They want to speak, but they can't remember how."

Saryon glanced at Joram, somewhat taken back by the earnestness of her discussion.

"Does she really —"

"See them? Talk to them? Or is she insane?" Joram shrugged. "I was told by" — he paused, the dark brows coming together — "by someone experienced in these matters that she might be a Necromancer, one of the ancient wizardesses who had the power to communicate with the dead. If that is true, it's fitting" — Joram's lips twisted in a bitter half-smile — "since she married a Dead man."

"Joram," said Saryon, at last able to give utterance to the terrible question burning in his mind, "why have you come back? Have you returned to . . . to . . ." He faltered, seeing by the expression in Joram's brown eyes that the question was anticipated.

But Joram did not answer. Leaning down, he lifted the Darksword from the sand and carefully slipped it into the leather scabbard. His hands lingered on the soft leather, caressing it, thinking undoubtedly of the man whose gift it had been.

"Your Grace," Saryon thought he heard Joram murmur, shaking his head.

"Joram?" Saryon persisted.

Still Joram did not answer the unspoken question that echoed all around them like the silent cries of the Watchers. Stripping off his robes and his wet cloak, he strapped the leather scabbard around his bare chest, positioning the sword on his back where it would remain hidden beneath his clothes. When it was comfortably in position — the magic of the scabbard causing the sword to shrink in size — Joram drew his white robes back on, secured them tightly with a belt at his waist, and flung his cloak over his shoulders.

"How do you feel, Father?" he asked abruptly. "Are you well enough to travel? We have to find shelter, build a fire. Gwendolyn is chilled through."

"I am well enough," answered Saryon, "but —"

"Fine. Let's be off." Joram took a step forward, then stopped as he felt Saryon's hand on his arm. He did not turn around, and the catalyst was forced to draw near to see his averted face.

"Why have you returned, Joram? To fulfill the Prophecy? Have you come to destroy the world?"

Joram did not look at the catalyst. His eyes were on the mountains before him.

Night had fallen. The first bright evening stars sparkled in the sky and the jagged peaks were visible against them only by their darkness. Joram stood in silence so long that the moon rose from behind the black rim of the world — its single, white, uncaring eye glaring down at the three figures standing on the shores of Beyond.

At the sight of the moon, Saryon saw the twisting half-smile darken Joram's lips.

"Ten years have passed for me, my friend, my father, if I may call you such?"

The catalyst nodded, unable to speak. Reaching out, Joram grasped Saryon's hands in his own, though it seemed the catalyst would have stopped him if he could. But Joram gripped them firmly. Looking down at the hands held fast in his, he continued. "For ten years I have lived in another world. I have lived another life. I never forgot this world, but when I looked back on it, I seemed to see it as through a mist. I remembered its beauty, its wonder and I came back to . . . to —" He stopped abruptly.

"To what?" Saryon urged, trying unobtrusively to withdraw his hands.

"No matter," Joram answered. "Someday I'll tell you. Not now."

His eyes were on Saryon's hands.

"How does that Prophecy read, Father?" he asked softly. "Doesn't it say something like this — 'And when he returns, he will hold in his hand the destruction of the world'?"

Suddenly, without warning, Joram roughly shoved Saryon's sleeves back. Fushing, Saryon attempted to cover his hands, but too late. The moonlight shone on long white scars on his wrists and his palms, on the broken fingers that had healed crooked and misshapen. Joram's lips pressed together grimly.

"Nothing has changed. Nothing will change." Releasing the Priest from his grasp, Joram walked away, moving across the sand, heading inland toward the mountains.

Saryon remained standing beside Gwendolyn, who was calling on the night to talk to her.

"The destruction is not in my hand," Joram said bitterly. The darkness closed around him, the rising wind obliterating all trace of his footsteps in the sand. "It is not in my hand but in theirs!"

Half-turning, he glanced behind him. "Coming?" he asked impatiently.

3

The Anniversary

Cardinal Radisovik?"

The Cardinal raised his head from the book he was reading and turned to see who called him. Blinking in the bright sunlight of early morning that beamed through the intricate patterns of the shaped glass window, he saw only a dark figure silhouetted in the doorway of his study.

"It's me, Mosiah, Holiness," the young man said, realizing the catalyst did not recognize him. "I hope I'm not disturbing you. If I am, I can come back another —"

"No, not at all, my son." The Cardinal closed his book, beckoning with his hand. "Please, come in. I haven't seen you around the palace lately."

"Thank you, Holiness. I'm living with the Sorcerers now," Mosiah replied, entering the room. "It was easier to move in with them, since my work keeps me at the forge most of the time."

"Yes." Cardinal Radisovik nodded, and if there was a slight darkening of his face at the mention of the forge, its shadow quickly passed. "Just yesterday I was in the new part of the city the Sorcerers have built. I am impressed with the work they have accomplished in such a short length of time. Their homes are snug and comfortable. They can be shaped quickly and at a reduced cost of Life expenditure. What is the name of the stone of which they are built?"

"Brick, Holiness," Mosiah said, smiling inwardly. "And it isn't stone. It's made of mud and straw, formed in a mold, then baked hard in the sun."

"Yes, I know," the Cardinal replied. "I saw them forming these . . . bricks . . . when I was in their village last year with Prince Garald. For some reason, the term *brick* refuses to stick in my head." His gaze went from Mosiah to the palace garden outside his window. "You will be interested to know," Cardinal Radisovik continued, "that I have advised the nobility to utilize this method to build homes for their Field Magi. Several of the *Albanara* were with me yesterday, inspecting the dwellings, and at least two have agreed with me that they are far superior to existing structures."

"What about the others, Holiness?" Mosiah asked. As a former Field Magus himself, who had lived with father, mother, and numerous brothers and sisters in the magically enlarged trunk of a dead tree, he knew what a blessing warm, dry brick buildings would be for those forced to endure the vagaries of natural weather patterns.

"They will agree, I believe," Radisovik said slowly. Rubbing his eyes, which were overstrained from reading, he shook his head, smiling wryly. "I will be honest, Mosiah. They were . . . shocked . . . at the sight of the so-called Dark Arts of Technology and found it difficult to accustom themselves to thinking of it rationally. But with the Sorcerers dwelling now within the city walls of Sharakan, their skills on display for all to see, the people will become more accustomed to technology in time, I believe, and will accept it as a part of man's nature."

Mosiah saw the Cardinal frown again as he said these words, and they were followed with a sigh.

"A part of man's nature that leads to war. Is that what you are thinking, Holiness?" Mosiah said softly. His hand absently opened the covers of another book that lay near him on a table magically and lovingly shaped of walnut.

"Yes, I was," Radisovik said, glancing sharply at Mosiah. "You are a perceptive young man."

Mosiah flushed, pleased but embarrassed. He closed the book, smoothing the leather binding with his hand. "Thank you, Holiness, though I don't deserve the compliment. I've thought the same thing myself . . ." He faltered, unaccustomed to speaking his feelings. "Especially when I'm working. I forge the tip of a spear and I think, as I'm making it, that it will . . . will kill someone.

"Oh, I know Prince Garald says not," Mosiah added hurriedly, fearing that his words might imply criticism of his ruler. "The spears are intended to intimidate or — at most — to be used against centaur. Still, I can't help but wonder."

"You are not alone in your wondering, Mosiah," Cardinal Radisovik said, rising to his feet and walking over to stare, unseeing, out the window. "Prince Garald is a fine young man. The finest I know, and I speak from the vantage point of one who has seen him grow from child to manhood. He is all that is best and noble in the *Albanara*. He has an immense amount of wisdom for one so young. Sometimes I forget he is only twenty-nine. I often think" — the Cardinal's voice softened — "of the light he brought to the dark soul of that friend of yours. What was his name?"

"Joram," said Mosiah.

Hearing the pain in the young man's voice, the Cardinal turned from the window. "I am sorry," he said gently. "I did not mean to reopen old wounds."

"No, it's all right, Holiness," Mosiah said. "I know what you mean. Joram could never have done . . . what he did if it hadn't been for Garald showing him the true meaning of honor and nobility."

"Garald showed him that, yes. But it was the catalyst who opened his heart to love and sacrifice. A strange man, Father Saryon," the Cardinal said, speaking more to himself than to Mosiah. "And a strange and tragic turn of events. I am not satisfied yet that I know the truth about Joram. Are you, Mosiah?"

The question was asked quietly. It was unexpected and caught Mosiah unaware. He answered that yes, of course he was satisfied, but his voice was low and he kept his eyes averted from the Cardinal's penetrating gaze. Nodding to himself, Radisovik looked back out into the beautiful garden.

"But we have strayed off the original path," he said, resuming the conversation and smiling to himself at the sound of nervous, restless shifting behind him. "We were talking of Garald and of this war. If my prince has one fault, it is that he glories in this upcoming battle — to the point even of forgetting the goals we are fighting to obtain. To marshal his troops, to place his warlocks at their correct stations, to train them and their catalysts, to pour over the Board of Contest — this is all that occupies his mind these days.

"Yet wars, when they are ended, are either won or lost, and plans must be made for the eventuality of either victory or defeat. He refuses to discuss the subject with His Majesty, however." Radisovik frowned, and Mosiah realized with a start that he was hearing things never intended for the ears of a lowly subject of Sharakan. "The king is blind when it comes to Garald. He is proud of him — deservedly so — but he cannot see the real man for the radiant halo. Garald plays happily with his shining toy soldiers, refusing to stop long enough to consider such mundane issues as what we will do with Merilon if we manage to conquer it. Who will rule the city? Will it be the now-deposed Emperor, although I've heard rumors that he is mad? Who is to take Bishop Vanya's place as head of the Church? What will we do with those nobles who refuse to extend their allegiance to us? The other city-states have kept carefully clear of this war, but what if they — seeing us grow more powerful — decide to attack us?

"You understand the problems?" Cardinal Radisovik demanded, turning around to face the discomfited Mosiah. "Yet whenever I try to talk to Garald about them, he waves his hand and says, 'I don't have time for this. Discuss it with my father.' And the king tells me brusquely, 'I have worries enough with this realm. Refer all matters of war to my son!'"

Mosiah shifted from one foot to another, wondering if he had Life enough to sink quietly through the floor. Seeing the young man's discomfort and realizing what he had been saying, Radisovik checked himself. "I do not mean to burden you with my problems, young man," he said.

Leaving the window, he crossed the room to stand near Mosiah, who watched him with a kind of awe. Everything

about the minister spoke of court intrigue; even the skirts of
his gold-trimmed robes appeared to whisper secrets as he
walked. "With the help of the Almin, these things will work
themselves out. Now, you came here for a reason and I have
kept you talking of inconsequential matters. I apologize.
What can I do for you?"

It took Mosiah a moment to gather his thoughts, all the
while noting and appreciating Radisovik's skillful handling of
what could have been an awkward situation. Very neatly, the
Cardinal reduced his criticism of his Prince to an "inconsequential matter" and dumped it in the lap of the Almin, sub-
tly instructing Mosiah to forget what he had heard and put
his trust in god.

This Mosiah was only too willing to do. Sharakan was
not a dangerous court, as was Merilon rumored to be these
days. Still, no royal court was truly safe and Mosiah had
learned early on that it did not pay to know either too much
or too little.

"I apologize in advance for bothering you with something
so trivial as what I'm about to ask, Cardinal Radisovik," the
young man said. "But . . . it's important to me . . . and no
other catalyst will perform it without obtaining your clear-
ance, since we are in a state of war."

"What is it you want, my son?" Radisovik asked in a mild
voice that had yet grown suddenly cool and cautious.

"I . . . I came to ask if you would open a Corridor to me,
Holiness."

"You want to leave Sharakan," Radisovik said slowly.

"Yes, Holiness."

"You are aware that travel outside the magical boundaries
of this city is forbidden for the good of our citizens. All travel
is perilous these days, especially for the citizens of our city.
Our own *Thon-li* currently control our Corridors, with the
help of the *Duuk-tsarith*, of course. But it is possible that the
warlocks of Merilon may always attempt to gain entry."

"I know, Holiness," Mosiah said respectfully but firmly.
"This trip is important to me, however, and I am willing to
take the risk. I've informed Prince Garald," he continued,
seeing Radisovik hesitate. "He gave me his permission to
leave. I have a message from him." Fumbling in his tunic,
Mosiah produced a small crystal globe that, when activated

by a spoken word of magic, would produce the image of the young and handsome prince of Sharakan.

"That will not be necessary," Radisovik said, smiling. "If you have discussed this with Prince Garald and he has given his permission, then I will certainly open a Corridor and wish you godspeed. Now, where is it you want to go?"

"The Borderlands," Mosiah answered.

Radisovik started, looking at the young man with a mystified expression. "Why do you —" Then his brow cleared. "Ah," he said softly. "Today is the anniversary."

"Yes, Holiness," Mosiah replied in a low voice. "I've never been there. When the Sorcerers found me in the Outland, I was more dead than alive. I didn't hear what had happened until . . . long after. I wanted to go, but I couldn't make myself." He looked at the floor, ashamed. "I know I should have, but I couldn't bear to see Saryon . . . to see him changed. . . ." Coughing, he cleared his throat.

"I know, my son. I understand." Radisovik laid his hand upon the young man's shoulder. "I heard about your ordeal and it must have been a terrible one. None can blame you for not wanting to travel to that awful place until you were stronger."

"I must go. I need to go," Mosiah said stubbornly, as though arguing with himself. "I need to make myself realize that it was real. That it all truly happened. Then maybe I can accept it, or understand it."

"I doubt if we will ever understand," said Radisovik, watching the young man intently, his eyes noting every nuance of expression in the open, guileless face. "But certainly we must come to accept what has passed, lest rage and bitterness gnaw at us and prevent us from living out our own lives."

He paused, waiting to see if Mosiah said anything more. The young man, struggling with his emotions, appeared incapable of speech, however. The Cardinal shrugged imperceptively and, speaking a word of prayer, caused a Corridor to open in the room, creating an oval void of nothingness in the air.

"Go with the Almin's blessing, Mosiah," Radisovik said as the young man, with a flushed face, mumbled and coughed his thanks. "May you find the peace you seek."

The Corridor elongated. The young man stepped inside, and the pathway through space and time formed by the ancients long ago closed around him. Mosiah vanished from the room.

Staring after him, his brow creased, Cardinal Radisovik shook his head. "What secret gnaws at your heart, young man?" he murmured. "I wonder. . . ."

The Corridor closed around Mosiah with its familiar squeezing effect, as though he were being dragged through a small, dark tunnel. The young man experienced a terrifying moment of panic, recalling with horrible vividness the last time he had traveled this route. . . .

Her face expressionless, the witch spoke a word and Mosiah caught his breath in fear as the thorns began to grow on the Kij vines again, this time merely pricking his flesh but not digging into it.

"Not yet," said the witch, reading his thoughts. "But they will grow and keep on growing until they pierce right through skin and muscle and organs, tearing out your life with them. Now, I ask you again. What is your name?"

"Why? What can it matter?" Mosiah groaned. "You know it!"

"Humor me," the witch said and spoke another word. The thorns grew another fraction of an inch.

"Mosiah!" He tossed his head in agony. "Mosiah! Damn it! Mosiah, Mosiah, Mosiah. . . ."

Then their plan penetrated the haze of pain. Mosiah choked, trying to swallow his words. Watching in horror, he saw the witch become Mosiah. Her face—his face. Her clothes—his clothes. Her voice—his voice.

"What do we do with him?" the warlock asked in subdued tones.

"Throw him in the Corridor and send him to the Outland," the witch—now Mosiah—said, rising to her feet.

"No!"

Mosiah tried to fight the warlock's strong hands that dragged him to his feet, but the tiniest movement drove the thorns into his body and he slumped over with an anguished cry. "Joram!" he yelled desperately as he saw the dark void of the Corridor open within the foliage. "Joram!" he shouted, hoping his friend would hear, yet knowing in his heart that it was hopeless. "Run! It's a trap! Run!"

The warlock thrust him into the Corridor. It began to squeeze shut, pressing in on him. The thorns stabbed his flesh, his blood flowed warm over his skin. Staring out, he had a final glimpse of the witch — now himself — watching him, her face — his face — expressionless.

Then, she spread her hands.

"It's all the rage," he saw himself say.

What happened after that, Mosiah couldn't be certain. Mercifully, he lost consciousness in the Corridor. When he came to, days later, he was in the Sorcerer's crude town in the Outland. Andon, their elderly, gentle leader, was with him as was a *Theldara* — a healer — and a catalyst who had been sent to the Sorcerers' village by Prince Garald himself. Mosiah begged to know the fate of his friends, but none in the secluded village could — or would — tell him.

The following weeks were ones of pain when he was awake and terrible dreams when he sank into the magically induced sleep. Then he heard, in a whispered conversation not intended for his ears, what had happened to Joram and Father Saryon. He heard about the catalyst's tragic sacrifice, about Joram's voluntary walk into Beyond.

Mosiah himself drew near death. The *Theldara* tried everything but told Andon that the young man's magical Life was not working to save him. Mosiah didn't care. Dying was easier than living with the pain.

One day Andon told him he had visitors, two people who had been brought to the village by orders of Prince Garald. Mosiah couldn't imagine who they could be and he didn't much care. . . . And then his mother's arms were around him, her tears bathing his wounds. His father's voice was in his ears. Gently, tenderly, his parents' rough, work-worn hands led their son back to life.

The memories of his pain and his despair overwhelmed Mosiah and he felt as though the Corridor were smothering him. Fortunately, the journey was short. The feeling of panic subsided as the Corridor gaped open. But the terror was replaced by feelings more profound yet no less painful — feel-

ings of sorrow and of grief. Stepping from the Corridor,
Mosiah gritted his teeth, nerving himself. Although he had
never visited the Borderlands, he had familiarized himself
with them and he knew what to expect.

A shoreline of fine white sand, dotted here and there
with patches of tall grass that eventually, near the shifting
mists of gray leading to Beyond, died out completely, leaving
a beachline as stark and bare as a picked bone. Upon this
beach would stand the Watchers and here, as well, would be
Saryon — his flesh transformed to stone.

"The sight is not dreadful as you might expect," Mosiah
had heard Prince Garald tell a group gathered around him
during a party one evening not long ago. "There is a look of
peace on the man's stone face that makes one almost envious
of him, for it is a peace that no living man can know."

Mosiah was skeptical. He hoped it was true, he hoped
Saryon had found the faith the priest had lost, but he didn't
believe it. Radisovik had said Garald had one fault — he
gloried in warfare. That was true, and if he had another it
was that he tended to see in people and events what he
wanted to see, not necessarily what was there.

Saryon's stone form would be staring perpetually into
Beyond, the shifting, ever-changing mists of the magical
Border that turned in upon themselves in endless swirls and
whorls.

"It is a calm and peaceful place, the Borderland," Garald
told the crowd in a grim voice. "To look at it, no one would
ever suspect the tragedies that take place upon that Shore of
Death."

Calm. . . .

Peaceful. . . .

Stepping from the Corridor onto the sand, Mosiah was
knocked off his feet by a tremendous gust of wind.

He couldn't see. Sand stung his face and made it nearly
impossible to open his eyes. The force of the wind was un-
believable, like nothing he had ever seen before in his life and
he had once experienced a thunderstorm conjured up by two
warring groups of *Sif-Hanar*. He struggled to stand, but it
was a losing battle and he would have been tossed along the
beach like the uprooted plants that were flying past, entan-

gling themselves in his legs, had not a strong hand reached out and grasped his own.

Knowing he wouldn't be able to endure much more of this, Mosiah quickly activated a magical bubble that surrounded him and the person who had saved him. Instantly, the protective shell enveloped both of them, shutting out the wind, encasing them in quiet and calm.

Rubbing the sand out of his eyes, Mosiah blinked, trying to see who had come to his rescue, wondering what anyone else would be doing on the Border. Catching sight of a flutter of orange silk, his heart sank.

"I say, old chap," came an all too familiar voice, "thanks awfully. Don't know why I didn't think of that shield myself, except I was having a rollicking good time getting tumbled about like those jolly plant things that never take root but go bounding along the sand. And I've got a new style. I call it *Cyclone*. Do you like it?"

4

I Call It Cyclone

Mosiah glared in displeased astonishment at the figure standing next to him in the magical bubble.

"Simkin," he mumbled, spitting sand out of his mouth. "What are you doing here?"

"Why, it's Almin's Day. I always come here on Almin's Day. What did you say? This is Thursday? Well"—he shrugged—"what's a day or so between friends." Raising his arms, he exhibited his clothes. "What do you think?"

Mosiah glanced at the bearded young man in disgust. Everything Simkin wore—from his blue brocade coat to his purple silk vest to his shimmering green trousers—was inside out. Not only that, but he was wearing his undergarments on top of his clothes. His hair stood straight up on his head and his normally smooth beard stuck out in all directions.

"I think you look a fool, as always," Mosiah muttered. "And if I'd known it was you I would have let you sail off until you smashed headfirst into the mountains!"

"It was *I* who saved *you* from sailing off, remember?" Simkin said languidly. "What a foul humor you're in. Your face will freeze like that, I've warned you before. Puts me in mind of the corpse of the Duke of Tulkinghorn who didn't die but just nastied away. I can't think *what* you have against me, dear boy." Conjuring a mirror, Simkin gazed at himself with pleasure, ruffling up his beard to heighten the effect.

"Oh, can't you!" Mosiah snapped viciously. "There were only a few people who knew we were to meet in the Grove that night — myself, Joram, Saryon, you, and, as it turns out, the *Duuk-tsarith*! I suppose that's just the sheerest coincidence?"

Lowering the mirror, Simkin stared at Mosiah incredulously. "I can't believe it!" he cried in tragic tones. "All this time you have suspected me of betrayal! Me!" Dashing the mirror to the sand, Simkin clutched at his heart. "Break! Break!" He moaned. "Oh, that this too, too sullied flesh would wilt."

"Stop it, Simkin," Mosiah said coldly, barely able to control an urge to grab the young man around the neck and choke him. "Your games aren't funny anymore."

Glancing at Mosiah from beneath his fluttering eyelids, Simkin suddenly straightened, smoothed his hair, and changed his clothes to a very proper and conservative ensemble of gray silk with white lace, pearl buttons, and a tasteful mauve cravat. Adjusting the lace at his wrist, he said casually, "I had no idea you were harboring this resentment. You should have spoken out earlier. Saryon was the traitor, as I've told you before. Surely Prince Garald has his sources for discovering the truth? Ask him, if you don't believe me."

"I don't and I have," Mosiah said, scowling. "And no one knows anything . . . if there's anything to know — "

"Oh, there is," inserted Simkin.

Mosiah shook his head in exasperation. "As for the catalyst betraying us, I've heard that wild story you concocted about Saryon and Joram and I don't believe it. Father Saryon would never have betrayed us and — "

" — I would?" Simkin finished calmly, smoothing his hair. With a wave of his hand, he pulled a bit of orange silk from the air and dabbed at his nose. "You're right, of course," he continued imperturbably. "I might have betrayed you, but only if things got dull. As it turned out, I didn't need to. You must admit, we had rather an exciting time of it back there in good old Merilon."

"Bah!" Angrily turning his gaze from the primping Simkin, Mosiah peered out from the shelter of the shield into the flying sand and howling wind. "I didn't know storms like this struck the Borderland. How long will it last?" he asked coldly, making it clear he was talking to Simkin only because he needed information. "And keep your answer brief!" he added bitterly.

"They don't, and a long, long time," replied Simkin.

"What?" Mosiah demanded irritably. "Say what you mean."

"I did," retorted Simkin, offended. "You told me to make it brief."

"Well, maybe not that brief," Mosiah amended, feeling more and more uneasy the longer he stayed here. Although it was nearly midday, it was almost dark as night and growing increasingly darker. Though protected by the shield, he could tell that the force of the wind was rising, not abating. It was costing him more and more of his Life energy to keep the magical bubble around them. He could feel his strength beginning to drain and he knew he wouldn't be able to hold it in position much longer.

"Are you going to insult me anymore?" Simkin demanded loftily. "Because if you are, I won't say a word."

"No," muttered Mosiah.

"And you're sorry you accused me of treachery?"

Mosiah didn't answer.

Simkin, placing his hands behind his back, gazed out into the raging wind. "I wonder how far one would get out there before being hurled into something large and solid like an oak. . . ."

"All right, I'm sorry!" Mosiah said sullenly. "Now tell me what's going on!"

"Very well." Simkin sniffed. "They *never* have storms on the Borderland. Has to do with the magical boundaries or some such thing. And therefore as to how long this particular storm will last, I have a presentiment that it will last a long, long time. Much longer, I imagine, than any of us would care to consider."

This last was spoken in low tones, Simkin's face growing increasingly more solemn as he stared out the magical shield into the wind-driven sand.

"Can we walk in this thing?" Simkin asked suddenly. "Can you move it and us with it?"

"I . . . suppose so," Mosiah said reluctantly. "Although it will take a lot of energy and I'm feeling pretty weak as it is —"

"Don't worry. We won't be here long," Simkin interrupted. "Head over in that direction." He pointed.

"You know, you could help me keep this shield in place!" Mosiah said as they floundered through the sand. He had absolutely no idea where they were going, being completely unable to see anything.

"Couldn't possibly," Simkin said. "Far too fatigued. Having your clothes blown off, then blown back on inside out and upside down takes a great deal out of one. It's not far."

"What isn't?"

"The statue of the catalyst, of course. I thought that was what you came to see?"

"How did you know — ? Oh, skip it," Mosiah said tiredly, stumbling as the sand shifted out from beneath his feet. "You said you come here a lot. Why? What do you do?"

"I keep the catalyst company, of course," Simkin said, regarding Mosiah with a self-righteous air. "Something you are too busy to do. Just because the poor man's been turned to stone doesn't mean he doesn't have feelings. Must get frightfully boring, standing there all day, staring out into nothing. Pigeons landing on your head, that sort of thing. Might be different if the pigeons were interesting. But they're such wretched conversationalists. Then I should think their feet must tickle, don't you?"

Mosiah slipped and fell. Reaching down, Simkin hauled him upright. "Not far," the young man said reassuringly. "Almost there."

"So, what do you . . . uh . . . talk about?" Mosiah asked, feeling unaccountably guilty. He knew that those sentenced to the Turning were, in actuality, still living, but he had never considered that it might be possible to talk to them or to provide them with some measure of human involvement.

"What do we talk about?" Simkin asked, pausing a moment as if to get his bearings, though how he could tell where he was in the blinding storm was more than Mosiah could figure. "Ah, yes. We're headed in the right direction. Just a few more steps. Now, where was I? Oh, yes. Well, I regale our statuesque friend with the latest gossip from court. I exhibit my newest fashions, though I do find it depressing that his responses to them are definitely what one might call stony. And I read to him."

"What?" At this startling statement, Mosiah stopped floundering through the sand, partly to catch his breath and recover his strength and partly to stare at Simkin in amazement. "You *read* to him? What? Texts? Scriptures? I can't imagine you—"

"—reading anything so boring?" Simkin lifted an eyebrow. "How right you are! Gad! Scriptures!" Growing pale at the thought, he fanned himself with the orange silk. "No, no. I read him jolly things to keep up his spirits. I found a large book of plays written by this frightfully prolific chap back in the old days. Quite entertaining. I get to act out all the characters. Listen, I have some of it memorized." Simkin assumed a tragic pose. "'But soft, what light through yonder window breaks? It is the east, and Juliet has fallen through the glass. Oh, pardon me, thou bleeding piece of earth. . . .'" He frowned. "Is that how it goes? Doesn't quite scan." Shrugging, he continued. "Or, if we're not in a scholarly mood, I read him this."

With a wave of his hand, he produced a leather-bound book and handed it to Mosiah. "Open it, any page."

Mosiah did so. His eyes widened. "That's disgusting!" he said, slamming the book shut. He glared at Simkin. "You don't mean you read that . . . that filth to . . . to—"

"Filth! You peasant! It's art!" Simkin cried, snatching the book away from Mosiah and consigning it to the ethers. "As I said, it *helped* keep up his spirits—"

"Helped? What do you mean 'helped'?" Mosiah interrupted. "Why past tense?"

"Because I am afraid our catalyst is now in the past tense," Simkin said. "Move the shield over a fraction of an inch. There, at your feet."

"My god!" Mosiah whispered in horror. He glanced back up at Simkin. "No, it can't be!"

"I'm afraid so, dear boy," Simkin said, shaking his head sadly. "There is no doubt in my mind that these blocks, these stones, these worse than senseless things are all that is left of our poor bald friend."

Mosiah knelt down. Protected by the magical shield, he brushed away the sand from what appeared to be the statue's head. He blinked back sudden tears. He had been hoping, praying that Simkin had made a mistake, that this was one of the other Watchers, perhaps. But there was no denying that it was Saryon—the mild, scholarly face; the gentle, loving expression he remembered so well. He could even see, as Garald had said, the look of infinite peace carved forever in the stone.

"How could this happen?" Mosiah demanded angrily. "Who could have done such a thing? I didn't know it was possible to break the spell—"

"It isn't," said Simkin with a strange smile.

Mosiah rose to his feet. "It isn't?" he repeated, regarding Simkin suspiciously. "How do you know? *What* do you know about this?"

Simkin shrugged. "Simply that this spell is not reversible. Stop and think. The Watchers have been here hundreds of years. During that time, nothing and no one has been able to alter them or return them to life." He gestured at the broken pieces on the sand. "I've stood here and watched while Xavier and his merry band hacked and hammered at the rock hands of our friend, trying to free the Darksword. All they got for their pains was gravel. I saw the warlock shoot spell after spell at Saryon, and beyond setting fire to a few pigeons—nothing. And yet we find the stone statue now, shattered into pieces when not even the most powerful spells of one of the strongest warlocks in the world could touch it."

Mosiah shivered. Despite the magical shield, he could feel the temperature of the air dropping. His mouth was parched and dry and the longer he stayed the stronger his feelings of uneasiness grew. "What else do you—"

"Over there. I'll show you," Simkin said, gesturing insistently.

"How far away is it?" Mosiah asked hesitantly. "I'm not sure how much longer. . . ."

"You're doing fine. The shield's holding. Just a ways. Keep going, straight ahead."

Mosiah walked forward, trying as best he could to avoid the sand-covered mounds that he assumed were parts of the broken stone statue. That Saryon was dead, he had no doubt. He supposed he should feel grief or relief, but right now all he felt was a numbness and a growing fear that something was terribly wrong.

"There," Simkin said, coming to a halt, his hands on his hips.

Mosiah followed his gaze, staring straight ahead of him and his blood congealed in his veins, the chill causing him to shudder from head to toe.

Garald had described the Border as gently shifting, swirling patches of mist. Mosiah saw a whirling mass of ugly greenish black cloud. Lightning flickered on the fringes, the wind sucked the sand up in twisting funnels, then spewed it out of its boiling maw, alternating inhaling and exhaling like a living thing. Mosiah felt his magical shield begin to give way.

"My Life's drained!" He gasped. "I can't hold the shield much longer!"

"Corridor!" Simkin said coolly. "Run for it!"

Turning, they stumbled back through the sand; Simkin leading the way or Mosiah would have been instantly lost in the storm.

"We're nearly there!" Simkin cried, grasping hold of Mosiah as the young man collapsed onto the beach. With Simkin's help, Mosiah staggered to his feet, but the shield vanished. Sand blasted them. The wind roared and shrieked around their ears, beating at them with gigantic fists, tugging them backward into the maw, then pitching them forward onto their knees.

Mosiah couldn't see, he couldn't hear. All was noise and tumult, darkness and stinging sand.

And then there was blessed quiet.

Opening his eyes, Mosiah looked around him in astonishment. He hadn't even experienced the sensation of being in the Corridor and here he was, back in Radisovik's study along with Simkin, looking particularly ludicrous with the orange silk tied around his nose and mouth.

Rising from his seat, Cardinal Radisovik stared at the two in amazement.

"What is the matter?" he asked, hurrying forward to help Mosiah, pale and trembling, to a chair. "Calm yourself! Where have you been? I'll send for some wine. . . ."

"The Border . . . Borderlands!" Mosiah stammered, trying unsuccessfully to stop shaking. He jumped to his feet, rebuffing the Cardinal's attempts to soothe him. "I must see Prince Garald! Where is he?"

"In the War Room, I believe," said Radisovik. "But why? What's wrong?"

"This cravat," said Simkin, regarding himself critically in a mirror on the Cardinal's wall. "The mauve . . . absolutely wretched with gray. . . ."

5

Sharakan Prepares For War

The War Room was, in actuality, a large ballroom located in one wing of the king's palace in the city-state of Sharakan. Unlike the magnificent floating Crystal Palace of Merilon, the palace at Sharakan stood on firm ground. Constructed of granite, it was as unpretentious, stalwart, and matter-of-fact as its citizens and their rulers.

The castle had once been a mountain — a small mountain but a mountain nonetheless — that had been magically altered by stone shapers of the *Pron-alban* class of wizards into a sturdy, exceedingly grim fortress. Later rulers of Sharakan had added their own touches to the palace, softening the harsh lines of the battlements, adding a garden in the center courtyard that was considered one of the loveliest in all of Thimhallan, and generally making it a more pleasant place in which to dwell.

But the palace was a fortress still; its one major distinction in the world being that it had never fallen in battle, not even during the terrible and destructive fights of the Iron Wars, which had leveled the palaces of Zith-el and Merilon, among others. Thus it had been an easy matter for Prince Garald to convert the palace of Sharakan into an armed camp, bringing in warlocks and catalysts from the city and its surrounding environs to train them in the art of warfare. Into the city of Sharakan itself he brought the Sorcerers from their exile in the Outland, setting them to work manufacturing weapons, siege machines, and other dark, technological implements of destruction.

The inhabitants of Sharakan were gearing up for war as well. The Illusionists ceased wasting their energies creating living paintings or enhancing the colors of the setting sun and turned their attention to creating illusions more terrifying and horrible; illusions that would penetrate the mind of the enemy, causing as much or more destruction than an arrow tip penetrating the body.

The Guilds of the *Pron-alban*, including Stone Shapers, Wood Shapers, Fabric Shapers, and so forth, turned their attention from mundane domestic duties to war. The Stone Shapers strengthened the walls of the city in case the unthinkable happened — that Xavier should break his sworn word and refuse to accept the decision determined on the Field of Glory, in which case he would undoubtedly attack the city itself. The Wood Shapers joined forces with the Sorcerers of the Dark Arts to create spears, arrows, and the siege engines.

Working thus closely with the Sorcerers proved difficult for some of the Shapers to accept. Although more liberal in their views of Technology than most people in Thimhallan (carts with wheels could actually be seen in use in the city), the magi of Sharakan had been raised to believe that the extensive use of Technology was the first step on the path to the realm of Death. Only their love and loyalty for their Prince and King and their belief that this war was necessary for the continuance of their life-style caused the people of Sharakan to grit their teeth and perform what was considered a mortal sin — give life to that which was Lifeless.

The Guildsmen worked with the Sorcerers, therefore, many discovering with a certain amount of pleasure and astonishment that Technology had definite advantages and that, when combined with magic, it could be used to create many functional and useful objects — the brick houses that so impressed Cardinal Radisovik, for example. While the Guildsmen and the Sorcerers worked, the *Sif-Hanar* made certain that the weather in the city was generally fine, while still providing rain for the crops in the outlying farming villages to insure a bountiful harvest. In case the city itself was besieged, the warlocks and catalysts would have no energy to spare conjuring food.

The nobility of Sharakan — the *Albanara* — were preparing for war in their own way as well. Those who owned and managed the farmlands made certain that their Field Magi were working to the fullest. Those with some smattering of skill in Shaping volunteered to assist the Guildsmen at their work. This notion quickly caught on and became much the fashion in Sharakan. Soon it was not unusual to see a Marquis expending his magical energies repairing a crack in the city wall or a Baron merrily pumping the bellows of the forge. The nobles had an extremely good time, working at these arduous tasks for an hour or so each week, then returning home to collapse with fatigue, soak in a hot bath, and congratulate themselves on contributing to the war effort. Unfortunately, they were more of a hindrance than a help to the Guildsmen, who, however, could do nothing but put up with it and endeavor to repair the bungled jobs as best they could after the nobles tired of them.

The aristocratic ladies of Sharakan were no less enthusiastic than their husbands about supporting the war, many contributing their own catalysts and House Magi to the cause. This involved considerable sacrifice. To have "done one's own hair" became quite the rage, whereas the Baroness who could sigh and say she "simply did not have Life enough to play Swan's Doom today as her catalyst had been summoned to the palace to learn to fight" was looked upon with envy by those less fortunate ladies whose catalysts had been pronounced unfit for duty and sent home.

Prince Garald knew of these absurdities and overlooked them. The Marquis who had spent three hours shaping one small rock had contributed half his wealth to the war. The bellows-pumping Baron gave enough food to keep the city stocked for a month. Garald was well satisfied with the way his people were preparing for the forthcoming conflict. He himself worked untiringly at it, spending long hours in either training or study.

If Garald had one secret wish in his life, it was his desire to be a warlock. Since he could not — having been born *Albanara* — he did the next best thing, throwing himself into the war body and soul. Having studied warfare extensively, he was nearly as knowledgeable in it as were the War Masters, those warlocks who spent their lives training for battle. Garald garnered the respect of these men and women — not an easy task — and, unlike some kingdoms where the War Masters were only too happy to hustle the king out of their way, those of Sharakan were only too happy to have the Prince's help and advice. Prince Garald worked with them to teach the novice warlocks and their catalysts how to fight. He developed a strategy for the war and announced that he would take on the role of Field Commander at the Gameboard when the battle started — a decision that was not disputed by the War Masters, who recognized natural talent when they saw it.

Cardinal Radisovik knew exactly where to find Prince Garald, therefore. His Grace had — for all practical purposes — moved into the hall known now as the War Room. The three men searching for him found him easily. Approaching the building, Mosiah, the Cardinal, and Simkin (in a pink cravat) could hear Garald's voice echoing among the high, ornately painted ceilings.

"All catalysts will now take up their positions either to the left or right of his or her warlock, depending on which side the wizard prefers." A pause, during which a murmur of voices rose in the air, warlocks explaining that they were right- or left-handed. Then Garald's voice rose above the hubbub. "You catalysts, stand about five paces to the side and five paces back." There were sounds of shuffling and some confusion. Arriving at the great doors of the ballroom, the three could see the catalysts and wizards moving about, taking up their positions preparatory to practicing their own type of dance upon the polished marble floors that had once, not so long ago, gleamed beneath the feet of less deadly couples.

When all had assumed their fighting positions, the Prince walked up and down the long rows of red-robed warlocks and gray-robed catalysts, inspecting them with a critical eye. Two black-robed *Duuk-tsarith* — the Prince's own guards — paced solemnly behind him, their hands folded before them.

"The positioning of the catalyst is crucial in the battle." The Prince continued the lecture as he moved among the ranks, moving a catalyst forward a step here, motioning one to stand farther off there. "It is the catalysts' responsibility to grant Life to his warlock during the fighting. That much you know. Thus he stands near enough to his warlock to open a conduit and let the magic flow from him into his partner. Since this requires the catalyst's complete concentration and attention, the catalyst has no means of defending himself. Therefore he positions himself slightly behind his warlock so that his partner may use whatever magical shields or other means he chooses to protect his catalyst.

"An intelligent opponent will, of course, endeavor to knock out his enemy's catalyst at the first opportunity, thus severely weakening the warlock. All of you warlocks have learned standard defenses against this, which we will practice later.

"Today I want to concentrate on an ability of the catalyst that is sometimes overlooked. Not only are you catalysts able to grant Life to your wizard, you have the ability to drain the Life of your opponent and utilize this additional magical energy to feed to your partner. This involves great skill in judgment and a keen eye, for you must know that your own warlock has sufficient Life to be able to carry on the fight without requiring your assistance and you must also know when an enemy warlock is so preoccupied with battle that you can strike him unawares. The inherent danger in this is, of course, that the enemy will immediately sense the Life being drained from him and will act at once to stop the catalyst attacking him. Therefore you must strike quickly, concentrating all your efforts on the job at hand."

Having finished his inspection, Garald floated up in the air above the heads of his troops so that he could look down upon them. "The two front rows face each other. The rest of you take your places against the wall. You there! Pay attention. You'll have your turn soon enough. I expect those now watching to perform perfectly the first time, since they will have had the advantage in seeing others do this first. Warlocks — skip to third and fourth round combat spells. Go ahead and rehearse your chants; the room is protected with a dispersion spell. You catalysts, see if you can successfully drain the Life from the 'enemy' opposite."

Sounds of numerous voices rose into the air, casting fire, raising windstorms, calling forth lightning as the warlocks went into action. Standing in position next to them, the catalysts began the difficult task of attempting to drain Life instead of giving it. Most of the catalysts were less than successful at this. Although each had been taught the technique at the Font, few had ever seen it done and no one in the room had ever attempted it, there having been no warfare on Thimhallan for countless years. Some mistakenly drained Life from their own warlocks. Many couldn't remember the correct words of the prayer that gave them the power, and one poor young catalyst was so flustered that he accidentally drained himself, passing out in a dead faint on the floor.

Mosiah watched, open-mouthed, so fascinated that he nearly forgot the reason he'd come. He had never seen a training session before and, up until now, the talk of war had been just that to him — talk. Now it became reality, and a tingle of excitement shot through his blood. Like Garald, he, too, longed to be a War Master, but — again like his Prince — although a skilled magus, Mosiah was not born to the Mystery of Fire, the gift of the Almin necessary to excel in the art. Garald had promised Mosiah, however, that the young man would be among the archers, since he was already trained in the use of the bow and arrow. The archer's practice sessions were due to start any day now and suddenly Mosiah couldn't wait.

But if the young man had forgotten the reason for his visit, Cardinal Radisovik had not. He had interrogated Mosiah and Simkin on the way. The two described what they had seen on the Borderland, the Cardinal listening with outward calm to their recital of the strange and unnatural happenings. He was so calm, in fact, that Mosiah grew ashamed and embarrassed, receiving the distinct impression from the minister that he was being frightened by — as Simkin said — a cyclone in a teapot. But Radisovik was far more disturbed and worried than he let on to the two young men, and, when a halt was called in the training session to remove the catalyst who had passed out, the Cardinal took advantage of the lull in the proceedings to approach Prince Garald, beckoning to Mosiah and Simkin to follow him.

Seeing the Cardinal, Garald immediately and respectfully descended to the floor where the catalyst stood. The Prince was attired in the tight pants and white, flowing-sleeved shirt he normally wore in practicing his swordsmanship — an art in which he was known to be highly skilled. Although he approached them with the winning smile and the grace and poise that came naturally to the handsome man, it was obvious from the dark line between the feathery brows that he was irritated. Whether this irritation stemmed from the fact that the Cardinal had interrupted him in his work or whether he was irritated by his students was difficult to determine.

His first words soon cleared up the matter.

"Well, Cardinal Radisovik," Prince Garald said, frowning at the head of the Church in Sharakan. "I am not at all impressed with your brethren."

Radisovik, preoccupied with more important matters, merely smiled. "Be patient, Your Grace," he said soothingly. "The catalysts are beginners at this. They will learn. I seem to recall a time when you yourself were a beginner in the art of fencing."

Prince Garald glanced at Radisovik out of the corner of his eye, seeming a bit chagrined. "Come now, Radisovik, I wasn't that bad."

"I seem to recall Your Grace entering the classroom, tripping over your sword, and falling flat on your —"

"I did no such thing!" Garald denied, his face flushed. Seeing Radisovik regarding him with a stern gaze, he shrugged. "All right, I *did* stumble over the sword, but I did *not* fall. . . . Oh, have it your way!" Grinning ruefully, he relaxed, his frown easing. "And you are correct, Cardinal, as always. I am being too impatient. Mosiah, it is good to see you again." He made a point to recognize the young man with a warm smile, extending his hand not to be kissed but in friendship. "You are well, I hope? How are things at the forge?"

Having known the Prince for some months, Mosiah had recovered from his awe of this man sufficiently to be able to take his hand and reply to his question without having to untangle his tongue. Though the initial feeling of awe was gone, it had been replaced by respect, admiration, and love. It was easy for Mosiah to understand why all of Sharakan was following their handsome Prince to war. They would have done the same if Garald had announced his intention of leaping into the sea.

"Simkin," said Garald, turning to the bearded young man, "I find your attire strangely depressing. Aren't you feeling well?"

"Matters of grave consequence, Your Grace," said Simkin in a doleful tone that might have served the head pallbearer in a funeral procession.

Garald raised his eyebrows at this, a laugh playing about his lips, prepared to hear the rest of the joke. But a glance at the grave face of Radisovik warned the Prince instantly that the matter was of an important and serious nature.

"Send the people to their luncheon," Garald ordered one of the War Masters who floated in the air nearby. "Call them back in half an hour. If I have not returned, have them repeat this drill."

"Yes, Your Grace," said the War Master, bowing, his hands hidden in the sleeves of his flowing red robes.

Prince Garald led the Cardinal and the two young men from the War Room that was now echoing with relieved sighs and cheerful voices. The castle at Sharakan was a warren of rooms and it was not difficult for the Prince to find one vacant, suitable for private conversation.

Long unused, the chamber was empty and windowless. Waving his hand, Garald caused globes of light to flicker among the shadows of the high ceiling. The light was bright as the sun, gleaming warmly from the walls and sparkling on the shaped, inlaid, decorative tiles that graced the floors in intricate patterns of flowers and birds. There was no furniture in the room. Garald obviously didn't expect to be here long and he waited for the Cardinal to speak, standing before him with an expectant, impatient air.

"I believe you should seal this chamber, Your Grace," said Radisovik.

Looking somewhat surprised and also annoyed at the waste of time, Garald ordered the two *Duuk-tsarith* who accompanied him everywhere to perform the task. When the room was secure — both from intrusion and from curious ears and prying eyes — he turned to the Cardinal.

"Very well, Radisovik. What is on your mind?"

Cardinal Radisovik gestured to Mosiah to speak.

Unaccustomed to commanding the complete attention of both Prince and Cardinal, and having to deal with Simkin's intermittent and irrelevant insertions — "Underwear wrapped around my neck! . . . I assure you those pictures are art of the highest form!" — Mosiah haltingly told what he had seen and experienced on the Borderlands.

Prince Garald's face grew increasingly solemn as the tale unfolded. When Mosiah told of finding Saryon's statue smashed and desecrated, the Prince flushed in anger.

"I presume you know what this means?" he demanded of Radisovik, interrupting Mosiah's description of the storm raging on the beach.

"I'm not certain that I do, Your Grace," Radisovik said gently, reprovingly. "I think you should hear the young man out."

"Mosiah understands that I am not being rude," the Prince answered impatiently. "He knows the seriousness of this information —"

"But the storm —"

"Storms! There are always storms!" Pacing about the room, the Prince brushed aside the matter with a wave of his hand.

"Not on the Borderlands," Radisovik said quietly.

"That isn't important!" Garald cried, his fist clenching. His voice had risen almost to a shout and the Cardinal was regarding him with a worried look. Drawing a deep breath, the Prince mastered himself. "Don't you understand, Radisovik! This means he has it!"

"Who has what?" Simkin asked with a yawn. "I say, you all can march up and down if you like, but I've had an exhausting day. Beastly tired. Mind if I sit down?"

Making a fluttering motion with the orange silk, the bearded young man caused a fainting-couch to appear in the room and languidly stretched himself full length upon it, blissfully ignoring the Cardinal's glare of stern disapproval, for no one sat in the presence of the Prince unless given permission.

Glancing at Mosiah, Garald said in low tones, "Thank you, my friend. I am deeply indebted to you for this information. Now, if you will excuse us, I would like to discuss this privately with the Cardinal — "

"No, keep them here, Your Grace," Radisovik said unexpectedly, moving closer to the Prince. "They know as much about this as we do, Garald. *Or more,*" he added in an undertone.

The Prince regarded Radisovik dubiously a moment, then glanced at Mosiah who, aware of the scrutiny and perhaps aware of what the Cardinal had whispered, shifted uncomfortably beneath the penetrating gaze. Garald's eyes went next to the languishing Simkin. The Prince frowned.

"Very well, Radisovik," he said in low tones. "What I am about to say must not leave this room, young men!"

Mosiah muttered something unintelligible, aware now of the unseen eyes of the black-robed *Duuk-tsarith* upon him.

"You may trust me implicitly, Your Grace," said Simkin, with a flutter of orange silk. "Cross my heart and hope to die, though not quite as suddenly as the Duchess of Malborough, who toppled over on the spot. She always took things so literally. . . ."

Garald cast an irritated glance at Simkin, who immediately snapped his mouth shut. "Mosiah, did you see the sword — Joram's sword — anywhere in the sand near Saryon?"

Mosiah shook his head. "No — "

"You see!" Garald interrupted, speaking to Radisovik.

" — but there was so much sand flying around, it could have easily been buried, Your Grace," Mosiah continued.

"Yes," struck in Simkin cheerfully. "The catalyst's poor old bald head had been covered up to the eyebrows. Had to dig for it. Beastly task. Felt a bit like a grave robber."

Mosiah made a strangled, choking sound, covering his face with his hand.

"I am truly sorry, Mosiah," Garald said sternly. "I share your grief. But this is a time for action and revenge, not for tears."

"Revenge?" Mosiah looked up, startled.

"Yes, young man," Garald said grimly. "Your friend Saryon was murdered."

"But . . . why?" Mosiah gasped.

"Isn't it obvious?" Garald said. "The Darksword. I think we may safely assume that now it is in the hands of our enemy. Xavier finally succeeded in obtaining it." The Prince resumed his pacing. "Fool that I was!" he muttered to himself. "I should have kept watch! But I didn't think there was any way for him to —"

Mosiah opened his mouth, then checked himself, remembering that he was in the presence of his sovereign. To his amazement Cardinal Radisovik caught his eye and — with an urgent gesture — indicated to the young man that he should speak.

"But what about the storm, Your Grace?" Mosiah asked finally, after a second imperative gesture from Radisovik. "It's . . . it's awful!" he said helplessly, unable to find a word powerful enough to describe the terrible sights he had witnessed. "I was frightened, Your Grace! More frightened than I've been of anything, even when the *Duuk-tsarith* caught me in the Grove! It was a fear that came from deep inside" — he pressed his hand against his heart — "and went through me like ice."

"One of Xavier's spells, no doubt."

"No, Your Grace!" Mosiah cried. Realizing from Garald's reproachful glance that he had contradicted his sovereign, Mosiah flushed. "I am sorry, Your Grace. I know that the possibility of Emperor Xavier obtaining the Darksword is serious, but it is nothing to what might be truly happening. I didn't believe Simkin at first, but now —" He stopped.

Simkin, lying back on the couch, was engaged in blowing the orange silk up into the air and letting it settle back down over his face. Seeing the triumphant smile upon the young man's bearded lips, Mosiah paled in shame and anger. Staring down at the floor, he missed the swift exchange of glances between Garald and Radisovik.

"What do you know of this, Simkin?" Garald asked slowly.

"Oh, quite a number of things, actually," Simkin said airily, blowing the orange silk high above his head, watching as it floated down, spiraling round and round like a dead leaf in the unmoving air. "Among which is the interesting and little known fact that our beloved and sadly missed Joram is destined to return from the dead and destroy the world."

6

The Prince Frog

Prince Garald cast the Cardinal a reproachful glance. "I have serious matters to attend to," he said coldly, turning on his heel. "Since Xavier now has the sword, our plans for war must be accelerated before he learns—"

"Your Grace," said Radisovik, "I suggest you take the time to hear this out."

Though he spoke quietly, the Cardinal's tone was firm and not to be questioned. A man well into his middle years, Radisovik had watched his Prince grow from child to man, taught him his lessons, presided over his later schooling, guided him along life's path. Mosiah saw, with a sudden flash of insight, that it was this priest—not the doting father—who had played a major role in shaping Garald's nature. As a druid lovingly and carefully nurtures a growing tree, Radisovik had taken an undoubtedly spoiled and willful child and, through love and by example, shaped him into a forceful, disciplined prince. It was the voice of the teacher—

the shaper — who spoke now, and it was the pupil who turned in reluctant, yet respectful, obedience to listen.

"Very well, Simkin," Garald said coldly, "tell your story. It's a pity there are no children present," he added but only under his breath. If Cardinal Radisovik heard, he kept a straight face.

"Pardon me, Your Grace," said Radisovik, his voice once more mild, "but I should like to inquire first why Simkin or Mosiah never told us this before. You must have known," he said, turning to Mosiah — who flushed uncomfortably and looked down at his boots — "that we found it difficult to accept the official pronouncement that came out of Merilon."

"What official pronouncement was that?" Simkin asked, sending the orange silk skyward with a puff.

His face grim, Garald reached over, snatched the orange silk out of the air, and stuffed it into the sash he wore around his waist. "Sit up and behave yourself," he commanded in such grating tones that even Simkin apparently realized he had gone a bit too far. Changing the fainting-couch to a straight-backed, uncomfortable chair, Simkin flew it into a corner of the room. Garbing himself in a child's sailor suit, he sulkingly pressed his forehead against the wall and began to suck his thumb.

Prince Garald took a step toward him, but Radisovik hurriedly intervened.

"There would have been no official pronouncement at all, I am certain," the Cardinal said, "had it not been for the bizarre events that were so strange they could not be hushed up. Vanya and Xavier held the trial in secret and scheduled the Turning immediately afterward. It was obvious — the world was intended never to know this took place. Their plans might have worked, but the death of the Empress could not be denied. Neither could Bishop Vanya's near fatal stroke or the deposed Emperor's disappearance. Too many people had witnessed all this.

"The official statement went out from the palace of Merilon, therefore, that Joram had been sentenced to the Turning because he was Dead. The catalyst, Saryon, through some misguided fanaticism, chose to martyr himself, and Joram took the opportunity to try to escape. Seeing that he was surrounded by *Duuk-tsarith*, Joram could not escape and cast himself into Beyond, rather than face his just punishment."

"I think I did hear something along those lines." Simkin's voice was muffled, due to his having his head in the corner and his thumb in his mouth.

"That's not how it happened?"

Simkin shook his head.

"How do you know?"

"I was there," he replied, removing his thumb with a pop. "Third palm tree to the left."

Prince Garald gave an impatient sigh, but was checked by Radisovik's upraised hand. "Go on."

"I'm not certain I will," said Simkin, pouting. "After all, Garald won't believe me. . . . Well, if you insist," he added hastily, hearing an ominous growl behind him. Scooting his chair along the floor, he wriggled around to face his audience. "You see, our Joram was a prince in frog's clothing." Seeing a perplexed expression on the Cardinal's face, he explained. "The Empress's baby son. Reports of the child's death, highly exaggerated."

"Of course!" Garald muttered, startled. "I knew Joram reminded me of someone. That hair, the eyes — his mother's!"

Simkin was warming up. "Stolen from his royal crib by migrant workers, the tadpole was spirited away to a small midwestern farming community. Raised up to be a wholesome young frog, he was led astray by unsavory companions" — Simkin cast a reproachful glance at Mosiah — "and traveled the dark path to murder and metallurgy.

"Sword in hand, unaware of princely blood, our frog journeyed to Merilon where he was saved by the love of a good woman, betrayed by the love of a wretched catalyst, and delivered into the chubby hands of Bishop Vanya. When kissed soundly upon the head by His Tubbiness, our warty youth turned to dangerous prince and was subsequently sentenced to life as sculpture — "

"*That* part doesn't make sense," Garald interrupted, turning to Radisovik.

And the rest of it does? Mosiah asked silently, glaring at Simkin.

"I'm not finished!" Simkin said loudly, but Garald wasn't listening.

"If Joram *were* the real prince of Merilon, it would have been much safer for Xavier to have him put to death. Why the Turning?"

"Ah, you see," explained Simkin, exasperated, "if you'd only been patient, I was coming to that. It's all tied up with the Prophecy —"

At the sound of this word, the hooded heads of the two *Duuk-tsarith* turned silently toward each other, the gaze of the unseen eyes meeting, unspoken conversation flowing between them.

"If only I can remember . . ." Simkin frowned. Lost in thought, he apparently sought to find his way out again by thumping his head against the wall. "This is such a muddle. Ah, I've got it! This is the Prophecy. 'A royal child will be born and then die and live and then die and then live and then die and keep on doing this interminably until everyone is sick and tired of the whole business when they will promptly throttle him and chuck him down a well.'"

Turning on his heel, Prince Garald headed for the door. "Remove the seal," he commanded.

"Begging your pardon, Your Grace." One of the *Duuk-tsarith* stepped forward. "But I may be able to assist with this matter."

The Prince turned to look at the warlock in astonishment. The silent, watchful guardians of the law in Thimhallan rarely spoke at all and when they did it was generally only in response to a question. Garald had never in his life known one to volunteer information.

"Do you warlocks know something about this?" the Prince demanded. "I questioned you once before following the incident, and you claimed you knew nothing!"

"At the time, all we knew about Joram was what you knew, what was given out in the official statement," replied the *Duuk-tsarith* coolly, untouched by the Prince's anger. "As you are aware, Your Grace, our Order takes strict oaths of loyalty and fealty to those we serve. The members of our Order who were in attendance at the execution serve Bishop Vanya and Emperor Xavier. They would no more betray them than we would betray the secrets of His Majesty and yourself."

"Of course," Garald said, flushing, knowing he deserved the rebuke. "Forgive me."

"But we do know something of this Prophecy of which the young man has spoken."

"That child's tale? Live and die and live and die—"

"No, Your Grace. The Prophecy is, I fear, no child's tale. Given in the dark days following the Iron Wars by the Bishop of Thimhallan, the Prophecy actually runs thus: *There will be born to the Royal House one who is dead yet will live, who will die again and live again. And when he returns, he will hold in his hand the destruction of the world—*"

"I was close." Simkin sniffed.

"May the Almin protect us!" Radisovik prayed, making a sign of blessing.

"May He indeed!" remarked Garald fervently. "How do you know this?" He turned upon Simkin.

"E'gad, I was there!" Simkin said languidly.

"Where?"

"There, with the catalysts. Several hundred years ago it was. We were gathered around the Well of Life, waiting for the Almin, who is—by the by—a remarkably shabby dresser. Considers Himself above clothes, no doubt, but that doesn't excuse—"

"Bah!" Garald interrupted angrily, turning back to the warlock. "Who else knows? I never heard it mentioned."

"No, Your Grace. It is—or was—" the hooded head moved slightly in Simkin's direction—"the most carefully guarded secret in all of Thimhallan. For obvious reasons, as Your Grace can readily understand."

"Yes." Garald shivered, then paled as the consequences occurred to him. "No royal child would be safe!"

"Precisely, Your Grace. Therefore the Prophecy was put into the keeping of the *Duuk-tsarith*, who reveal it to one person outside their Order and that is the current, reigning Bishop of Thimhallan. If this Joram was truly the son of the Empress and if he was Dead—"

The warlock paused. Prince Garald, after a moment's profound consideration, acquiesced to both with a nod.

"—then you see why it would be impossible to have him put to death. The Turning would be the ideal solution, for it would keep him alive, yet rendered harmless. Apparently, that didn't work. Knowing himself near to being captured, he chose to die by casting himself into Beyond — thus fulfilling the beginning of the Prophecy."

"Captured? But he wasn't! If you'd only listen!" Simkin struck in. "I keep telling you I'm not finished —"

"But, surely, he *is* dead, then, isn't he?" Garald interrupted in a low, shaking voice. "No one has ever returned from Beyond!"

The *Duuk-tsarith* did not reply. It was his duty to impart information, not speculate on its veracity.

"Your Grace," Simkin tried again.

"Do you believe this, Radisovik?" Garald asked abruptly, ignoring Simkin who, with a sigh, folded his arms and sat languidly back in his chair.

"I'm not certain, Your Grace," said the Cardinal, obviously shaken. "The matter needs further study."

"Yes," said Garald. He was silent, pacing back and forth. Then he shook his head decisively. "Well, I don't believe it. One man — with the power to destroy a world? Bah!"

"Your Grace —"

"And even if I did give credence to this faery story," the Prince continued over Simkin's interruption, "I can't let it interfere with our plans for war. The fact that something like this could occur at all is simply further proof that Vanya and Xavier must be overthrown! And I must operate on the assumption that Xavier has the Darksword, not some ghost from Beyond. I am returning to the War Room."

The Prince had spoken and, it was obvious, would not be gainsaid this time. Radisovik bowed in silence and Garald motioned to the *Duuk-tsarith*, who lifted the seal from the chamber and drifted silently after their Prince as he stalked out of the room. Radisovik remained standing, staring after him, shaking his head. Then, with a sigh and a rueful smile at Mosiah, the Cardinal left the room as well.

"As usual, you botched things nicely." Mosiah turned on Simkin. "Lucky for you that warlock stepped in. I think Garald was ready to chuck *you* down a well —"

Simkin didn't answer. He remained seated in his chair, his arm thrown negligently over the back. The ridiculous sailor suit he was wearing vanished, replaced by the conservative gray silk suit.

"You know, my dear Mosiah," he said, staring into nothing with casual intensity, "there's one thing that appears to me to be of the utmost importance and no one will listen to me."

"What's that?" Mosiah asked moodily, thinking about the storm on the Borderland.

"I kept trying to tell Garald, but he's so hungry for war he refuses to eat anything else that's set before him. Xavier knows, and he's afraid. That's why he kept trying to take the sword. Vanya knows, that's why he had the stroke. The late and unlamented Emperor — Joram's real father — knew, that's why he vanished. Joram didn't flee into Beyond because he was trying to escape the *Duuk-tsarith*. He didn't need to."

"Why? What do you mean?" Mosiah looked up apprehensively, the cold fear creeping over him again.

"Joram had the Darksword. . . . Joram was winning . . ."

7

A Discourse On The Rules Of War

Fearful that Prince Xavier had the Darksword and hoping to strike before the warlock learned to use its full powers, Garald accelerated his country's preparations for war. The catalysts and warlocks began their drills early in the morning and did not end until far late into the evening; many so exhausted that they slept where they collapsed on the floor of the War Room.

The forge of the Sorcerers glared into the night with bright eyes; the gnashing of its metal teeth and the breath of its bellows made it seem as though a monster had been captured and chained up in the center of the city. The Sorcerers as well as the warlocks were learning to work with catalysts; having had only one — Saryon — in the last dark years of their history. Combining magic and Technology, they were able to construct their weapons easier and faster — a fact that not all took as a blessing.

Finally, Garald deemed his city-state ready for war. In a formal, centuries-old ceremony that involved the donning of red robes and odd-looking hats (a source of considerable suppressed merriment and speculation among the nobility for no one remembered where the hats had come from or why), Prince Garald and the high ranking of the land came before their King, read the grievances against Merilon, and demanded war.

The King agreed, of course. There was a grand party that night in Sharakan and then everybody prepared for the next step — the Challenge.

There were strict rules of warfare in Thimhallan, dating back to the time when the people first came to this world. It was hoped by those early residents that a people driven from their birthworld by prejudice and violence could have lived in peace in this new one. Such was not human nature, however, as the wisest of the new inhabitants knew. Therefore they set down Rules of War that had been strictly followed and obeyed (for the most part) throughout the centuries, the exception being the destructive Iron Wars.

It was due to the breaking of these very Rules that the Sorcerers had been driven from the land. According to the catalysts (who maintained the histories), the Sorcerers slipped the leash held by their masters — the War Masters — and attempted to take over the world by force. Refusing to accept the outcome on the Field of Glory — the outcome decided by War Masters utilizing the Gameboard — the Sorcerers brought real, deadly war to the land. Prince Garald's use of Sorcerers in this war, therefore, was raising cries of outrage throughout Thimhallan, despite the fact that the Prince patiently reassured his allies (and his enemy) that he had them under complete control.

The Rules of War as drawn up by the ancients were rather like the rules of dueling — considered a civilized means of settling disputes between men. The affronted party aired his grievances publicly, then issued the Challenge — tantamount to tossing a glove in the face of one's enemy. There were two responses to the Challenge. It could be Taken Up — which meant war — or the party so challenged could issue an Apology, in which case the city-state then negotiated terms for surrender. There was no fear of an Apology in this instance; plans for war were being made in Merilon as well as Sharakan.

There are advantages and disadvantages to being the Challenger as opposed to the Defender. If the Challenge is impressive, the Challenger is considered to have gained the psychological upper hand. In return, the Defender is allowed to choose his position on the Field of Glory and is granted the opening move on the Gameboard.

The long-awaited day of the Challenge finally arrived. All Sharakan had been up throughout the night in preparation for the event, which was to begin at midday with the ceremonial battle between the *Thon-li* — the Corridor Masters — and the forces of the Prince.

In the ancient days, this battle had been a real one — fought between the War Masters and those who built the Corridors, the Diviners. But those magi gifted with divining the future had been wiped out during the Iron Wars, leaving only the catalysts that had assisted them — the *Thon-li* — to maintain the pathways by which the people of Thimhallan traveled through time and space.

Since the *Thon-li* were merely catalysts, with little magical Life of their own, the War Masters — the most powerful magi in Thimhallan — could have literally blown them off the face of the earth. This would have meant destruction of the transportation system in Thimhallan, however, something not even to be considered. Therefore, the *Thon-li* were permitted by the Rules of War to surrender after a token resistance, opening the Corridors to the armies of Sharakan.

Prince Garald put on a grand show for his people that day. The battle began with the stirring music of trumpet and drum, calling the people to war. Out they came, dressed in their best clothes, clutching wildly excited children by the hand. Surging into the streets, the citizens gathered around certain predesignated locations throughout the city where the War Masters and their catalysts, dressed in accoutrements of war — red robes for the magi and gray with red trim for the catalysts — stood waiting.

The martial music ceased. Silence fell. The crowd held its breath. Then the call of a single trumpet, blown by a bugler standing beside Prince Garald upon the palace battlements, rang through the clear, crisp air (the *Sif-Hanar* outdid themselves that day). At this signal, Prince Garald raised his voice in a shout that was echoed by his War Masters around the city, demanding in the name of the King of Sharakan that the *Thon-li* open the Corridors.

One by one, Corridors opened, forming gaping voids in the center of the streets. Standing within them were the *Thon-li*, the Corridor Masters.

"In the name of the King of Sharakan and his loyal subjects, we call upon you to grant us safe passage to the city-state of Merilon, that we may issue the Challenge to war," cried Prince Garald to the *Thon-li* who faced him. The demand was repeated by all the War Masters throughout the city to all the *Thon-li* who faced them.

"In the name of the Almin, who watches over the peace of this world, we refuse," answered the *Thon-li* to the Prince in return. A high-ranking member of the catalysts and chosen especially for this important part, she threw herself into her role, glaring at Garald as fiercely as if he truly meant to take her post by storm.

Though somewhat taken back by the catalyst's vehement defiance, the Prince signaled for the trumpet to sound again. His War Masters came forward, their catalysts at their sides, and the "battle" began.

The catalysts opened conduits to their wizards; the Life that they gathered into their bodies arcing into that of the magi with a blue light. Suffused with magic, the War Masters cast their spells. Balls of fire exploded in the skies. Cyclones appeared out of clear air, spinning in the palms of the warlocks who threatened to unleash their fury upon the *Thon-li*. Lightning crackled from fingertips, fiery hail sizzled on the street. The children shrieked in excitement, and one young War Master was so carried away by the spectacle that he accidentally caused a crack to open in the earth, frightening the populace as much or more than the *Thon-li*.

Fortunately, the Corridor Masters surrendered immediately at this show of power, even the fierce catalyst who continued to glower at Prince Garald with wounded dignity. Stepping out of her Corridor, she held her hands in front of her, wrists together. The other *Thon-li* followed her example. The War Masters bound the wrists of the catalysts loosely with silken cord. The trumpet rang out in victory and a great cheer went up from the populace.

Then the *Thon-li* returned to their Corridors, the citizens returned to their homes, and the Prince and his forces set forth to issue the Challenge.

What the people of Sharakan did not know was that their Prince wasn't playing a grand game. Garald believed secretly — and he had not shared this with anyone, either his father or the Cardinal, although he was fairly certain Radisovik suspected — that Xavier would not be content with winning on the Gameboard if he won. He would certainly not be content if he lost. No matter what the outcome on the Field of Glory, Prince Garald believed that once again war — true war — had come to the world.

His heart swelled with excitement. Dreams of deeds of bravery done on the field of battle, of the glories of victory won over an evil foe set his blood burning. Looking into the heavens, the Prince gave fervent thanks to the Almin that he had been born to right the wrongs of this world.

8

The Challenge

The Crystal Palace of Merilon outshone the sun in the early morning dawn. This was not a difficult task. Yesterday, the *Sif-Hanar* had spent most of the day practicing their war spells against the shining orb — covering it with black clouds, turning it ghastly colors, once attempting to obliterate it from the sky completely. Today the sun edged up over the mountains, appearing pale and sulky, seeming ready to set again in an instant if it caught sight of the weather magi.

The pallid sun couldn't hold a candle, therefore, to the brilliance of the Crystal Palace, whose lights had been burning all night. At dawn, the tapestries covering the transparent walls of every room in the palace were rolled up, curtains were opened, shades and shutters raised. Magical light spilled out, beaming down upon the city below.

In the days of the old Emperor and his enchanting Empress, this brilliant splendor would have meant night-long revelry and merriment. In the old days, beautiful women and elegant men would have thronged the palace, filling the rooms with laughter and perfume. In these days of the new Emperor, the brightly burning lights meant night-long plotting and planning. In these days, red-robed warlocks lurked about the halls, filling the rooms with grim discussion and the faint smell of sulphur.

On this morning, the morning of the Challenge, Emperor Xavier hovered in the air near the transparent wall of his study in the Crystal Palace, staring down at the city below his feet. To all appearances, he was waiting impatiently for his enemy. A glance showed him his War Masters at their posts, observing from vantage points both within the Crystal Palace and without. Xavier and his ministers planned to be able to gauge Sharakan's military strength by the Challenge. In particular they expected to get some hint of how Garald intended to utilize the Dark Arts of the Sorcerers in his battle formations. Not that Xavier expected Prince Garald to reveal all his secrets. No, the Prince was far too intelligent a military strategist for that. Still, Garald would have to exhibit some of his military might in order for his Challenge to be taken seriously and, according to old custom, "frighten" Merilon into surrender.

Xavier knew, of course, from his spies in Sharakan, that the Sorcerers had taken up residency in that city and that they were working day and night developing weapons. But his spies had been unable to penetrate that closed society, whose years of persecution made them wary of strangers. The DKarn-Duuk had no idea what weapons they were developing and how many. Worst of all — as far as Xavier was concerned — he had no idea if the Sorcerers had discovered how to use darkstone or whether the Darksword — forged by Joram — was the only weapon in existence made of the magic-absorbing ore.

An Ariel, one of the winged messengers of Thimhallan, appeared outside Xavier's wall, the mutated man's gigantic wings beating slowly in the morning breeze, allowing him to rest on the air currents that swirled gently about the Palace.

Dissolving the wall with a wave of his hand, Xavier motioned the Ariel to fly inside.

"The Taking of the Corridors has just been completed, my lord," the Ariel informed his Emperor.

"Thank you. Return to your post." Dismissing the messenger, Xavier absently replaced the wall, then gave the prearranged signal. Red smoke filled the sky. His War Masters ceased talking among themselves and crowded near the walls, watching expectantly.

The DKarn-Duuk himself was prepared to witness the event from the best possible vantage point, having had his study magically transported to the topmost turret of the crystal-spired Palace. Looking down, he could see the people of Merilon jostling to gain the best views of the proceedings. The wealthy rode in their splendid winged carriages or drifted lightly among the clouds of City Above. The middle-classes flowed into City Below, gathering around the Gates, crowding into the Grove, massing around the perimeter of the protective magical dome.

There was a festive air about the crowd. Not even the oldest among them could remember the last time a Challenge had been issued. It was an historic occasion and excitement was widespread. Lavish parties were being given by the nobility this night following the Challenge. Military garb of every day and age was the style; the city looked somewhat like an encampment of Julius Caesar's that had been overrun by the combined forces of Attila the Hun and King Richard the Lion-Hearted. But amid all this heady excitement, there ran a single thread of disappointment. One tiny cloud cast a shadow over an otherwise perfect day.

There was to be no party held at the Crystal Palace.

People wondered at this. Emperor Xavier was known to be a serious-minded man (some even used the term *dour* to describe him — but only in whispers). Everybody believed it perfectly right and proper that he treat this war seriously. But a party in honor of the momentous event had been expected and, when it was not forthcoming, when word went out that the Emperor specifically demanded not to be disturbed, people exchanged dark looks and shook their heads. Such a thing would not have happened under the old Emperor, they said wistfully (again only in whispers). And more than a few began to speculate that perhaps this war wasn't going to be the easy victory The DKarn-Duuk had been predicting.

Xavier knew the people were disturbed by his refusal to celebrate tonight. His Minister of Morale had spent the last two days informing him of nothing else. The DKarn-Duuk didn't care. Moody and restless, he flitted back and forth in front of the vast expanse of crystal wall, his hands twisting together behind his back. Xavier indulged himself in this unusual outward display of agitation only because he was alone in his study. Though the walls were transparent in order that he could see out, he had cast a Mirror Image spell upon them, thus keeping others from seeing inside. A highly trained and disciplined warlock, Xavier appeared to the rest of the world to be enigmatic and imperturbable. Indeed, he was, most of the time. But not on this particular occasion. Not with what he had on his mind.

And it wasn't the Challenge.

The entrance of someone into the Emperor's study brought Xavier's pacing to a halt. The person had traveled the Corridor that opened silently to admit him; the rustle of heavy robes and the grunt of labored breathing were the first indications of the man's arrival. Xavier knew who it was — only one man in this world had access to him through the Corridors — and so he merely glanced over his shoulder to see the expression on the face, more interested in that than the face itself.

At the sight of that expression, Xavier scowled. Biting his lip, he turned back to staring intently out at the panorama of city spread beneath him. There was nothing to see yet. The Challenge hadn't begun, and he wasn't truly watching anyway; his thoughts and his vision ranged far afield. Pretending to be preoccupied with the forthcoming event provided him with the opportunity to conceal his face from his visitor.

"I take it the news is bad, Eminence?" Xavier said in a cold, even voice. He had ceased his airborne pacing and stood perfectly still now, his hands held quietly before him — the Almin alone knew by what effort of will.

"Yes," puffed Bishop Vanya.

Although the stroke had left the Bishop paralyzed in his left arm and had immobilized the left side of his face, Vanya had been able — with the help of the *Theldara* — to overcome these handicaps and lead a fairly normal life. Certainly his power in the realm had not diminished. If anything, it had grown under Xavier's new regime.

The elderly Bishop tired easily these days, however. Even the few steps that he had taken from the desk in his office in the Font to the Corridor and out of the Corridor into the study of the Crystal Palace of Merilon had exhausted him. Collapsing into a chair, Vanya gasped and wheezed for breath while Xavier stood waiting, outwardly calm, inwardly seething with suppressed impatience — and fear.

When he had recovered somewhat, Bishop Vanya shot a sharp glance at the warlock from beneath half-closed eyelids. Seeing that The DKarn-Duuk was staring intently out the wall and, apparently, not looking at the Bishop, Vanya hurriedly lifted his paralyzed left hand with his right, and placed it upon the arm of the chair, carefully arranging the limp fingers so that he might hide all signs of paralysis. Everyone knew the Bishop did this, of course, and everyone deliberately kept their eyes politely averted until Vanya had managed to arrange himself. These were a people accustomed to dissembling. After all, they had pretended the corpse of their Empress was alive for a year.

Hearing the Bishop finally settled in his chair, Xavier half-turned, glancing over his shoulder. "Well, Eminence?" he demanded abruptly. "What kept you? I expected you last night."

"The *Duuk-tsarith* did not return until early this morning," Vanya said, leaning back cautiously in the chair, careful not to disturb the placement of his arm. He spoke clearly and distinctly, with only a slight slurring due to the paralysis of the left side of his face, a disfigurement barely noticeable (through the help of magic) by a downward slant to the corner of his lips and an almost imperceptible droop of the left eyelid. The Bishop would have considered this intolerable, had not the *Theldara* who treated him assured Vanya that he should thank the Almin he was alive, and not complain about such mundane matters.

"I know from your expression the news isn't good," Xavier said, turning back to glare down upon the city. "The Darksword is gone."

"Yes, Highness," Vanya replied, the fingers of his good hand crawling spiderlike over the arm of the chair.

"What took them so long to discover that?" Xavier demanded bitterly.

"The storm on the Border is worsening," Vanya said, moistening his lips. "By the time the *Duuk-tsarith* arrived, the statue of the catalyst had been completely covered by sand. The entire landscape has changed, Highness. They could not even recognize the Borderland and they were present during the Execu —"

"I am aware of when they were there, Eminence," Xavier interrupted impatiently. The man's hands, clasped correctly before him, were white from the strain of maintaining this semblance of outward calm. "Get on with your report!"

"Yes, Highness," Vanya muttered. Irritated at the imperious tone, he took advantage of the man's turned back to glower at him in hatred. "It took the warlocks some time even to discover the location of the statue, then they had to remove the mounds of sand covering it. The *Duuk-tsarith* were forced to work under magical shields to protect themselves from the storm that blew fiercely about them. It took two warlocks and four catalysts alone just to maintain the shield so that work could proceed. Finally, they dug down to the remains of the statue. . . ."

"Is the catalyst — that Saryon — dead?" Xavier asked.

Vanya paused to mop his sweating forehead with a white cloth. He was either too hot or too cold these days. There never seemed any in-between.

When he finally spoke, it was in a low voice. "Certainly the spell was broken, the spirit fled. But whether to the realm of the dead or the living, no one is certain."

"Damn!" Xavier muttered beneath his breath, the fingers of one hand clenching. "And the sword is gone?"

"Sword and scabbard."

"You are certain?"

"The *Duuk-tsarith* do not make mistakes, Highness," Vanya replied acidly. "They combed a wide area around the site of the statue and found nothing. What is more important is that they *felt* no trace of the sword's presence as they surely must have if it had been there."

Xavier made a snarling sound. "The sword was quite capable of concealing its owner from the eyes of the *Duuk-tsarith* before —"

"Only when it had lost itself and its owner in the crowd. When isolated, the Darksword can be sensed by the *Duuk-tsarith* due to the minute draining effect it has — even unwielded — upon their magic. At least, that is what the witch tells me, Highness. They had little time to test the sword, she says, before it was turned to stone in the arms of that wretched catalyst.

"No," Vanya continued gloomily, "the Darksword is gone. . . . What's more, the *Duuk-tsarith* say that only *its* power could have been used to break the spell surrounding Saryon."

The DKarn-Duuk stood in silence, staring out the wall. The Challenge had started. The Corridors surrounding the invisible, magical walls of Merilon gaped open. (Few Corridors provided entry into the city itself. Those that did were located in the Gates, guarded normally by the *Kan-Hanar* alone. Now, in time of war, the *Duuk-tsarith* and The DKarn-Duuk — the War Masters — also stood guard over the Gates of Merilon. This was really a formality, however. Besides being an infraction of the Rules of the War, any attempt by the enemy to enter the city through the Corridors would precipitate a magical battle that would endanger both the city and its inhabitants; something neither side wanted — at least at this early stage. The only other Corridors that led into and out of the city were the secret Corridors that connected the palace to the Font.)

The army of Sharakan — hundreds of warlocks, resplendent in their red robes of war, followed by their catalysts — emerged from the Corridors. The warlocks arranged themselves at intervals surrounding the city, their catalysts at their sides. When all were in place, a single trumpet sounded and Prince Garald himself appeared, riding out from the Corridor in a golden chariot drawn by nine black horses. Flame breathed from the nostrils of the magic animals, lightning flickered at their hooves as they pawed the air. The animals' shrill cries were so loud they could be heard through the magical dome.

Holding his fiery steeds in check, Prince Garald was a magnificent sight, accoutered in silver armor that had been handed down among his family for generations; some said it came from the ancient world and that it was endowed with spells of victory and protection for the wearer. He carried his helm beneath his arm, his chestnut hair ruffled in the wind. Making a formal bow to the residents of Merilon, he turned his horses' heads and began to drive his chariot around the walls of the city. As he galloped past, he caused banners of the kingdom of Sharakan to unfurl from out the air, until Merilon was ringed round by the sparkling colors of its enemy. So handsome was the Prince, so awesome was the sight of the black, fire-breathing steeds, and so beautiful were the banners that the inhabitants of Merilon gave the spectacular sight a rousing cheer.

Arriving back at the front Gate of the city, Prince Garald brought his chariot to a halt. Raising his hand, he caused the trumpet to sound again. Suddenly, savage centaur — their half-human, half-bestial faces twisted in rage, their hooves striking the ground — poured out from the Corridors. They rushed straight for the domed city, death burning in their eyes. In their hands they held spears — weapons of the Dark Arts.

Above them flew dragons, tearing the air with their talons, poisoning it with their foul breath. Giants appeared next, their huge heads on a level with City Above, leering at the tiny people below them with dumbfounded grins. Griffons, chimeras, satyrs, sphinxes — all manners and types of magical beasts — burst out of the Corridors, howling in rage, eager to taste human blood.

No one in Merilon applauded now. Children wailed in terror. Mothers grabbed their shrieking babes, men leaped to guard their families. The noblemen, furious at this effrontery, shouted out oaths; their lady wives rose to the occasion by decorously fainting dead away.

When the centaurs were within spear's throw of the walls, when the giants were reaching down their huge hands, when it appeared that the dragons were prepared to crash through the magical dome, Prince Garald ordered the trumpet call to sound a final time.

One by one, with brilliant, multicolored starbursts and roaring explosions that shook the ground, the illusions vanished. Left behind, the exhausted warlocks and their equally weary catalysts who had created the illusions had just strength enough to bow proudly to the stunned people of Merilon.

Lifting his banner above his head, Prince Garald shouted in a voice that could be heard throughout the city.

"I call upon you people of Merilon to overthrow your evil leader and his toad of a Bishop. You live in a dream as tragically dead as your late Empress, a dream as sadly insane as your late Emperor. Destroy the dome that hides you from the real world. We, in Sharakan, offer you life. Return to the land of the living.

"If you refuse to rid yourself of these parasites that feed on your blood, then we will do so ourselves, in order that they do not infect the rest of the world. There will be war between our kingdoms.

"What is your answer?"

"War! War!" shouted the people of Merilon in a high state of excitement. "War! War!" the nobles chanted. The fainted ladies roused themselves in time to cry, "War!" Mothers coaxed their babies to crow the word, "War!" which they did with mimicking, uncomprehending delight. Children shrieked, "War!" and conjured up pointed sticks on the spot, imitating the spears they had seen the centaurs holding. University students yelled, "War!" and vowed to a man to enlist in the army as soon as possible. Several young catalysts chanting "War! War!" were rebuked by a passing Deaconess, who reminded them sternly that the Almin was opposed to bloodshed. But since the Deaconess was in a hurry — on the way to offer her aid to the warlocks — she did not have time to watch over the culprits, and the catalysts resumed their cries the moment she was gone.

"So be it!" Prince Garald shouted grimly, but his words went unheard in the tumult. With one final, coldly formal bow, the Prince drove his chariot back into the Corridor and vanished from sight, his warlocks and their catalysts disappearing as well.

It was noon. Bells pealed out in Merilon, the *Sif-Hanar* — in a fit of patriotic frenzy — colored the clouds to match Merilon's own banners, making it appear as if the sky were draped with flags. The nobles flew to their parties, hymns of battle and Merilon's national anthem on their lips. The people of City Below held an impromptu street dance and lit bonfires. The city was ablaze with light, the parties and gaiety would last far into the night.

Standing silent in his crystal-walled study high above the tumult and the merriment, the Emperor of Merilon looked down upon it unseeing, unhearing. For him, the Challenge had come and gone and he had missed it, though it had spread out before his eyes. In his vision, there walked only a single figure and in its hand it held a weapon of darkness.

The parties in Merilon were just reaching their height, the sunlight was fading sulkily to twilight, the first of the evening stars could be seen flickering dimly overhead before The DKarn-Duuk stirred or spoke. Behind him, the Bishop sat, breathing heavily. Occasionally mopping his forehead with a cloth, he was thinking it was well past time for his dinner and he started nervously when Xavier broke the long silence.

"Joram has returned from the realm of the dead," The DKarn-Duuk said in a soft voice. "If we do not stop him, the Prophecy will be fulfilled. Alert the *Duuk-tsarith*. If they find Joram, he is to be killed on sight. This time he can — and must — be destroyed!"

9

To Victory!

A week following the Challenge, on a day determined by negotiation between representatives of the warring nations, the battle between Merilon and Sharakan began.

Early in the morning, long before dawn, Prince Garald and his entourage arrived on the Field of Glory to set up the Gameboard. His enemy, Emperor Xavier and his entourage, arrived at nearly the same time, doing the same thing several miles distant.

The Field of Glory was located in the approximate center of the world of Thimhallan. A large tract of land, relatively flat, dotted here and there with clumps of trees and covered overall with thick, smooth, green grass, the Field of Glory had been set aside in ancient days for the purpose of settling disputes between nations. No one ever came here for any other reason. The Field was consecrated, both by prayers and by blood — the latter being the unintentional result of the Iron Wars.

Before and after that time, warfare in Thimhallan was fought in a civilized manner as befit the higher order of magically gifted humans who fought it (as opposed to the lower order of Dead humans left behind in the old world). The primary feature of the Field of Glory was the Gameboards. Made of the holy stone of the mountain fortress of the Font — granite taken from around the Well of Life, the source of magic in the world — the Gameboards were located at opposite ends of the Field. Each Board was shaped into a perfect square, nine feet long by nine feet wide. When the Field was not in use, the flat and featureless Boards lay upon the ground. The druids saw to it that the Boards were carefully tended; the grass around them was shaped trimly and neatly, spells of shielding kept animals and birds from desecrating the Boards' surfaces.

On the day of battle, as was happening this day, the leaders of the combatants, accompanying nobles, War Masters, and high-ranking catalysts arrived at the site of the Gameboards and performed the Ceremony of Activation and Blessing just as the first rays of dawn lit the Field.

Prince Garald took his place with Cardinal Radisovik at the head of the Board, which faced north. His companions — the noblest of the nobility of Sharakan — gathered around the Board, nine on each side. Each nobleman's catalyst stood by his side. At a signal from Prince Garald, the Cardinal began the prayer.

"Almighty Almin," he prayed, acutely aware that several miles away his words were being echoed by Bishop Vanya, "look down upon our contest this day and bless it. May we who fight this battle be judged worthy by You and granted victory, for we fight to find glory in Your eyes and to chastise a foe who has broken Your Commandments and brought turmoil and strife to our peaceful land."

There followed a redress of the grievances of Sharakan against Merilon (vice versa at the opposite end of the Field), in case the Almin had forgotten the acts of aggression, attempts at enslavery, and other heinous crimes committed by the foe.

"Grant us victory this day, Almin," continued Radisovik earnestly, "and we of Sharakan promise that we will improve the conditions of the peasants living beneath the iron yoke of the greedy nobles of Merilon."

("We of Merilon promise that we will destroy the evil Sorcerers who now hold the people of Sharakan in thrall.)

"We of Sharakan will destroy the magical dome that surrounds Merilon, opening it to your blessed light and air."

("We of Merilon will bring enlightenment and culture to the people of Sharakan, encasing their city in a magical dome.")

"We of Sharakan will depose the evil man who rules Merilon."

("We of Merilon will depose the evil man who rules Sharakan.")

" — overthrow his Bishop, proclaimed a heretic by the Church."

(" — overthrow his Cardinal, proclaimed a heretic by the Church.")

". . . and bring peace to the world of Thimhallan in Your Name. Amen."

(". . . and bring peace to the world of Thimhallan in Your Name. Amen.")

At this point in the ceremony, many of the spectators began to arrive, their fantastic flying carriages glittering in the air overhead. Cardinal Radisovik, concluding his prayer, had the strangest, fleeting impression of the Almin arriving, too, sitting somewhere up above them, drinking a glass of wine and munching on a chicken leg. The vision was startling, and Radisovik hurriedly banished it, inwardly begging the Almin's forgiveness for the sacrilege.

Prince Garald nudged his catalyst, engrossed apparently in watching the arrival of the guests and forgetting that the Ceremony was not complete. Flushing, Cardinal Radisovik granted Life to his liege lord. Each of the catalysts in attendance did the same to their own lords. Most of the magi assembled were *Albanara*. There were, however, two members of the *Sif-Hanar*, one member of the *Kan-Hanar*, and a Sorcerer — the blacksmith, who was now leader of his people. Bowing their heads, each man reverently accepted Life from his catalyst and, at another signal from Prince Garald, the magi in turn used their Life to activate the Gameboard.

The gigantic slab of granite began to glow with a blue light. Slowly, the magi raised their hands and the Gameboard began to rise from the ground. Higher and higher it rose under the guidance of the magi until it hovered four feet above the earth. Prince Garald made a commanding gesture, and the magi ceased their spells. The Board remained floating in the air at a level convenient for play; its plain, featureless surface sparkling in the sunlight.

Then Prince Garald, who up until this time had not participated in the magic, laid his hands upon the Board and began to chant a ritual ancient as the rock itself. This was the Activation. At his command, tiny magical figures — scaled-down miniatures of the real people and animals participating in the battle — took their places upon the Gameboard at the same time as their real life counterparts were taking their places upon the Field of Glory.

First appeared the War Masters and their catalysts, taking up positions on the Gameboard that now began to divide itself into hexes to render the movement of pieces easier. Occasionally asking for advice from those near him but more often acting on his own, Prince Garald arranged the tiny, living pieces on his Board — instructing a War Master to move several hexes to the north, for example, or calling back one who had inadvertently drifted over into enemy territory.

Once the War Masters were arranged to Garald's satisfaction, he next brought in the *Sif-Hanar* — the wizards who controlled the weather — and placed them at various intervals (determined by long-standing tradition) around the Board. Finally, when all was in readiness, he began to move in his troops; those people or beings who would be under the command of the War Masters.

Bands of savage centaurs — captured in the Outland and held in thrall by the *Duuk-tsarith* — surged onto the Field of Glory. Kept in check by the warlocks, the centaur units were each under control of a War Master, who would unleash them either at his own discretion or upon a direct command from the Prince. The winged Ariels stood at Garald's side, ready to carry his orders to anyone on the Field.

Along with the centaurs came the giants — mutated humans who, like the centaurs, dwelt in the Outland. Unlike the centaurs, however, who lived to kill, the giants were actually gentle creatures with the intellect of small children. Ordinarily peaceful, the giants were goaded into fighting by such stratagems as bolts of lightning shot into their flesh or other pain-inducing measures, such being the one thing that could drive the overlarge humans into a rage.

Next appeared the dragons, griffons, and a host of magical beasts, including some created by magic specifically for the battle: giant rats that stood six feet tall on their hind feet, giant cats to fight the rats, and so on depending on the magus's creativity and level of skill. Particularly dangerous were the werebeasts — men and women transformed by the War Masters into savage animals while retaining the intelligence and skills of humans.

Finally, taking their places at the edges of the Board were the *Theldara*, the druid healers, who would immediately go to the aid of any human of either side injured in the fighting.

As Prince Garald worked, he could see the armies of Emperor Xavier materializing on the opposite side of the Gameboard. Keenly Garald studied the disposition of the forces of his enemy, knowing his opponent was doing the same. Occasionally he made changes, shifting a piece here or there depending on how Xavier was setting up his men. But Garald did not allow what he saw to influence him overmuch. He had his strategy planned out. He was confident in it, in his War Masters, and in his people.

Finally, all was in readiness. Looking down at the Gameboard — now populated with wizards, warlocks, catalysts, howling centaurs, grinning giants, flying dragons, snarling werewolves, and a host of other combatants — Prince Garald smiled in pride and satisfaction. Raising his hand in which appeared, suddenly, a glass of wine, Garald called for a toast.

His guests immediately followed suit, raising their own glasses in the air. The toast was shared by the spectators, many of whom were gathered in the sky above the Gameboard, waiting eagerly for the battle to begin.

"To victory!" Prince Garald shouted. "This day, it is ours!"

The toast was heartily drunk, the noblemen regarding each other and particularly their Prince with pride. Garald had never looked so handsome or regal as he did this day, dressed in his pure white robes trimmed with red and gold — the robes of the commander. His face flushed with excitement, his clear eyes gleamed with the sincere belief in the righteousness of his cause and his eagerness to engage his enemy in conflict. Once again, he lifted his glass, the red wine flowing into it through his magic. Radisovik, watching, was reminded vividly of blood flowing from a wound and, shuddering, made a hasty sign against evil, wondering as he did so why he was being plagued with these disturbing and unwelcome thoughts.

"To our secret weapon," Garald said, turning to the Sorcerer and toasting him.

"To our secret weapon," the others replied, all eyes on the blacksmith, who was so flustered with pride and confusion that he swallowed his wine at a gulp, choked, and had to be pounded on the back by the Baron standing next to him.

All eyes went to a section of the Board shrouded in a magic cloud. Prince Xavier had a similar, cloud-hidden section on his side of the Board as well. Although the laws of warfare demanded that the majority of the combatants' forces be in plain sight, players were allowed to keep certain forces hidden, waiting in reserve.

It was these reserves that could tip the scales of battle for either side, and the eyes of both commanders — Garald and Xavier — were on those cloud-shrouded hexes, trying to deduce from the position on the Board, the reports of spies, and a hundred other factors what menace lay concealed within the fog.

Xavier knew this must be the army of Sorcerers, but what weapons did they carry? What was their plan of attack? Most urgent question of all, did they carry the Darkstone?

Prince Garald little doubted what lay beneath Xavier's cloud. A warlock, armed with the Darksword. The Prince had given his most powerful War Master a regiment of men armed with special weapons and one single instruction — at all costs, capture the Darksword.

Garald would have been astonished to know that Emperor Xavier had provided his own most powerful War Master with a regiment and the same instruction.

Capture the Darksword.

One other Order was searching for it as well. Prompted by fear of the Prophecy, the Order of *Duuk-tsarith* had come together in a rare, secret conclave the night prior to the battle, meeting in caverns far below the world, caverns whose whereabouts were unknown to kings and emperors.

The black-robed figures, faceless in the eternal night of the caverns, gathered in silence deeper than the darkness around a nine-pointed star embedded in the stone floor. One of their Order rose into the air above them, unseen by the eye, visible in their minds. She asked a question.

"Does the Darksword fight with the armies of Sharakan?"

"No." The answer came from many voices on one side of the cavern chamber.

"Does the Darksword fight with the armies of Merilon?"

"No." Again, many voices answered, this time from the other side.

"Has the Dead man, Joram, or the catalyst, Saryon, been seen in this world?"

"Yes." This time, only one voice replied, coming from the back of the circle.

Instantly, the witch dissolved the Conclave. The black shadows slipped into the night, returning to their duties. All except one. The witch summoned him.

"Where is Joram?"

"I do not know. The Darksword shields him well."

"But he has been seen. By whom? What is your source?"

A name formed in the man's thoughts. He did not speak it, afraid, perhaps, to let even the night share the secret.

The witch, perceiving his thought, nodded in satisfaction.

The man appeared dubious. "Is that source to be trusted?"

"Absolutely," said the witch.

10

Out Of The Fog

Mosiah sat upon a small, grass-covered knoll, his shoulders hunched against the thick, oppressive fog that wrapped itself around him like a chill, clammy hand. He had no idea what time of day it was or how long he had been sitting here. It might have been a half-day since his unit had been ordered to take up its position. It might have been a half-month. He had lost all sense of time in this cloud-shrouded world and he appeared close to losing his other senses as well.

He could see nothing through the impenetrable mist, not even the shapes of the others of his unit. The fact that the enemy could not see him was, he supposed, some sort of comfort. But it did not make up for the growing uneasiness he was experiencing — something deep inside whispering that the rest of humanity had long ago departed, leaving him behind, the only person left in this world.

He knew that wasn't true. He could hear sounds, for one thing. Although distorted by the fog, the noises took on an eerie, unnerving quality almost worse than silence. Were those cold and hollow voices the voices of humans or ghosts? Were those footsteps? Was it the enemy, creeping up on him from behind?

"Who goes there?" Mosiah questioned the fog in a quavering voice.

There was no answer. Winding his words in its web, the mist dragged them away.

Was that a hand on his shoulder . . . ?

Drawing his dagger, Mosiah leaped to his feet, whirled around, and skillfully stabbed a tree.

"Numskull!" he muttered. Sheathing his dagger, he shoved the clawed branch that had brushed across his neck out of his way. He glanced around hurriedly, hoping no one had seen him, then let out his breath in relief and sat back down on the hummock, nursing a cut on his hand; the branch having been able to gain some revenge upon its assailant by digging several small twigs into his flesh.

Had the battle started? Mosiah thought it likely, having convinced himself that he had been sitting here for several hours at least. Perhaps it was over? Maybe his unit had been called up and he hadn't heard? The thought of this was so alarming that he picked up the heavy, metal crossbow and walked a few steps, peering into the fog, hoping to find somebody who knew what was going on.

Then he stopped, irresolute.

His orders had been specific. Remain silent and unmoving until the fog lifts. Prince Garald had emphasized the importance of obeying this command to the letter.

"It is you Sorcerers who hold the key to our victory," he told them in the dark hours before the dawn when they had assembled near the Corridor preparatory to being transported to the Field of Glory. "Why? Because you do not rely upon magic! When our warlocks have drained Xavier's warlocks of Life, when the enemy's catalysts are so exhausted that they can no longer draw the magic from the world, you will come forth and the enemy will be at your mercy. Xavier will be placed in check, he will be forced to surrender the Field to us."

Sighing, telling himself that he hadn't been here five weeks but more probably five hours, Mosiah turned back to resume his seat on the grassy knoll, only to find that the grassy knoll had disappeared. Standing absolutely still, he tried to retrace his steps in his mind. He had risen from the knoll and turned to his left, he was certain. He had taken only four or five steps. Therefore, if he turned back to his right, he should locate his position easily.

Twenty steps later, he had not found it. Worse than that, he was thoroughly confused, having turned right, left, and every other conceivable direction in the fog.

"Now you've done it!" spoke a peeved voice right in his ear. "You've gotten us completely lost."

Mosiah leaped straight into the air, his heart climbing in terror up his chest and into his throat. Dagger in his shaking hand, he whipped around to confront nothing.

"You're *not* going to attack a tree again, are you?" queried the voice sternly. "I've never been so humiliated. . . ."

"Simkin!" Mosiah hissed furiously, searching this way and that, trying to calm his heart, forcing it to return to some semblance of beating normally. "Where are you?"

"Here," said the voice in aggrieved tones. It came from somewhere near Mosiah's ear. "And a more boring few hours I've never spent in my entire life, not even the time the former Emperor recounted his life's story, from the womb up . . . or out as the case may be."

Unslinging the quiver of arrows that he wore on his back, Mosiah flung it on the ground.

"Ouch!" cried the voice. "I say, that was completely uncalled for! You've ruffled my feathers!"

"How about scaring me half to death!" Mosiah said in a seething whisper.

"Well, I will, if you insist," remarked the arrow in puzzled tones, "though why you want me to scare you again is — "

"No, you fool!" cried Mosiah, kicking at the quiver in his rage. "I meant you already *did* scare me half to death." He clutched at his chest, feeling his heart pounding. "I think I hurt something," he muttered, sinking down — weak-kneed — on a nearby tree stump.

"Frightfully sorry," said an arrow, slowly working its way out of the quiver. Mosiah, watching it grimly, saw that it was bright green with orange feathers — a remarkable contrast from the plain, metal arrows he carried. "You could help me, you know," remarked the arrow, twisting and turning in its efforts to drag itself onto the grass.

Not only did Mosiah make no effort to assist the arrow, he told it in no uncertain terms what it might do with itself.

"A simple no would have sufficed," the arrow commented, sniffing. With one last wriggle, it wormed its way out of the quiver and in a blur of green and orange, Simkin — large as life — stood stiffly before Mosiah, arms at his sides, feet pressed together. "I'm stiff as the late Empress and I've lost all feeling in my toes," he complained gloomily. "I say, do you like my ensemble? I call it *Lincoln Green*. There was this jolly group of bandits whose leader took to frolicking about the woods in silk hose and pointy hats with feathers. He was caught doing funny things to the deer. Complaints were made to the local sheriff and as a result — "

"What are you doing here?" Mosiah grumbled, looking about in the fog, trying to see or hear something. He thought he could detect confused sounds coming from his left, but he wasn't certain. "You know Garald said he didn't want to see so much as the hem of that orange silk scarf of yours on the battlefield."

"Garald is a dear boy and I love him to distraction," remarked Simkin, stretching luxuriously, "but you must admit that there are times when he's a pompous ass — "

"Shhh!" whispered Mosiah, scandalized. "Keep your voice down!"

"I hate to tell you this, old bean," said Simkin cheerfully, "but we're undoubtedly miles from the Field right now. Don't look so glum. Whole thing's a complete bore anyway. Bunch of aging warlocks, casting spells at each other, when they can remember the words that is. Catalysts snoozing in the sun. Oh, sometimes you get a young hothead who livens things up a bit by tossing a centaur or two into the fray. Rather a fun thing to see the old fellows hiking up their robes and beating a swift retreat into the shrubbery. But I assure you, it's dreadfully dull. No one's getting killed or anything."

"Well, no one's supposed to!" Mosiah muttered, wondering uneasily if Simkin was right and he had wandered off the Field.

"I know. But I was rather hoping a centaur would get loose or a giant run amuck. But, no such luck. I found myself growing quite bored. To make matters worse, I was sharing the carriage of the Baron Von Licktenstein, who generally provides the most marvelous cold luncheons. He had a large hamper of food with him from which the most delectable smells were rising. But it was still an hour or so until noon, the Baron was a crashing bore, insisting on describing all the plays to me. I told him I was growing faint with hunger, but he missed my delicate hints that a snack would help me revive my flagging spirits. I finally decided to find you, dear boy. Had something important I wanted to tell you anyway."

"Not nearly noon. What time is it now?" Mosiah asked, wishing Simkin hadn't mentioned food.

"About one-ish or two-ish, I should say. By the way, deucedly clever of me, sneaking in amongst your arrows like that, wouldn't you agree—"

Mosiah interrupted again. "What do you mean, you have something important to tell me?"

Simkin raised an eyebrow. "Yes, indeed," he said with that strange, half-mocking yet wholly serious smile that never failed to send shivers through Mosiah. "I ran into an old acquaintance of yours in Merilon."

"Mine?" Mosiah glared at Simkin suspiciously. "Who?"

"Your friend, the witch. Head of the *Duuk-tsarith*."

"My god!" Mosiah paled, shuddering.

"Almin's beard, dear boy!" Simkin said, watching him in amusement. "Don't carry on so. You look quite guilty and you haven't done anything—that I know of, at least."

"You don't know what it was like!" Mosiah swallowed. "I dream sometimes that I still see her face, leering down at me . . ." Mosiah stared at Simkin, suddenly realizing what he'd said. "What were you doing in *Merilon* last night?"

"I've been there the past week," said Simkin with a yawn. Glancing with distaste at the stump on which Mosiah was sitting, he conjured up a couch with a wave of his hand and lay down on it, hands behind his head. "The parties there have been quite marvelous."

"But Merilon is the enemy!"

"My dear boy, I *have* no enemies," Simkin remarked. "But you've completely unlinked my chain of thought. It was important, too." He frowned, stroking his beard. The thick fog rolled over and around him, partially blotting him from view,

until all Mosiah could see was the bright orange hat Simkin
wore with his green outfit and the tips of his orange shoes.
"Ah, yes. The witch asked me, quite casually, if I had seen
Joram lately."

"Joram!" Mosiah repeated, aghast. Standing up nervously, he moved nearer Simkin and laid his hand on the
couch in the forest, relieved to touch something solid and
real. "But . . . that doesn't make sense! Maybe you heard
wrong, or she didn't mean . . ."

"Precisely what I said. I was quite floored. Literally.
Tumbled down, plop, right out of the air. 'Bit of fluff in my
ear,' I said to the witch. 'Didn't hear well. Thought you asked
if I'd seen Joram.'"

"'I did,' she replied. Straightforward, these *Duuk-tsarith*.
No beating about the old bush.

"'Joram?' I repeated. 'Chap with the remarkable sword
who . . . er . . . passed on about a year ago?'

"'The same,' says the witch.

"'Are we speaking ghostly manifestation, here?' I in-
quired further in what I fear was a trembling voice. 'Rattling
bones, clanking chains, things going bump in the night,
Joram seen stalking the halls in his nightshirt?'

"She did not answer, but stared at me like this." Simkin
imitated the piercing dagger gaze of the witch so well that
Mosiah shuddered again and nodded hurriedly.

"I understand," he muttered. "Go on."

"Then she said, 'I will be in touch,' which — with them —
means exactly that. I swear," continued Simkin solemnly
with a shiver of his own that was not entirely affected, "that I
have felt icy fingers lingering near my ear. . . ."

"Don't say things like that!" Beads of sweat dotted
Mosiah's lip. "Especially not now." He glanced about. "I hate
this wretched fog! Did you hear something?" He paused,
listening. A strange sound — a low humming noise — was
coming from out of the mist. "What's going on? Why don't
we do something?"

"Well, you understand, of course, what all this means?"

"No," Mosiah snapped, cocking his head, trying to figure
out the direction of the odd sound. "But I suppose you're
going to tell me. . . ."

"It means, dear boy," said Simkin loftily, "that Xavier doesn't have the Darksword. Not only that, but either he or the *Duuk-tsarith* or both believe Joram has returned. And with Joram — the Prophecy."

Mosiah said nothing. He couldn't hear anything anymore and assumed it must have been his imagination. Staring out into the fog, he shook his head. "Xavier's right, you know," he said finally, reluctantly, in a low voice. "Joram *is* back. I knew it in my heart when I stepped on that beach and saw Saryon lying there. Joram's the only one who could have broken that spell. . . ." He paused, then said heavily. "We have to convince Garald — "

"Hush! The fog's lifting!" cried Simkin, raising his head and starting to his feet.

The note of a single trumpet sounded. A sharp, crisp wind sprang up, blowing the fog to wispy shreds that curled about the ground, then fled completely. The noonday sun shone full upon them.

Blinking in the bright light, feeling it warm his blood, Mosiah hurriedly grabbed his crossbow and slung the quiver of arrows over his shoulder.

"There's my unit!" He pointed to a band of men forming into ranks under the leadership of one of the blacksmith's sons. "Not twenty feet away! I didn't lose them! I'm over here!" Mosiah began to shout, waving his arm, when he heard the weird humming sound again, much nearer and louder. Turning, he glanced around behind him.

Mosiah gasped in horror. Fear impaled him on its sharp-honed point, driving deep, draining him. He could not move, he could not think. He could only stare.

"Simkin!" Mosiah cried out wretchedly, praying for the touch of living flesh, needing it to reassure him of his own reality in the midst of the blinding terror that was closing over him, thicker and more chill than the fog. "Simkin!" he moaned, frozen in fear. "Don't leave me! Where are you?"

There was no answer.

II

The Invisible Foe

Prince Garald could not understand what was happening. He stared down at his Gameboard in bewilderment, unable to comprehend.

On his northern flank, gamepieces were under attack. They were fighting desperately, fighting for their lives.

They were dying. . . .

And there was nothing there! No enemy within sight!

"What is this?" Garald cried hoarsely. Grasping the edge of the Board with his hands, he gripped it tightly, as though he might somehow squeeze the answer from the unspeaking stone. "What is going on?" he demanded of his commanders, who stared back at him blankly.

"Cardinal?" Garald glared at his minister. But the catalyst's face was ashen, his lips moving in prayer. Looking at his Prince, he could only shake his head.

"I do not know," he managed to murmur.

"Xavier!" Garald snarled in fury, his fingers digging into the stone. "He is responsible! The Darksword! Yet—"

"No, Your Grace," Radisovik answered, pointing at the Board with a trembling hand. "Look! Whatever is attacking us is attacking Xavier, too."

Garald turned his gaze back to the Gameboard. His eyes widened, his voice choked.

Emperor Xavier's gamepieces were apparently battling the same unseen foe, for they had broken off their attack of Garald's gamepieces and were now fighting for their lives as well.

Gamepieces! Garald groaned. Those were real men and women dying out there, their living bodies represented by the tiny images that populated the magical Board. Watching in helpless confusion, the Prince saw the ranks of the War Masters on the northern part of the Board begin to crumble and break apart. The small figures were turning and fleeing, some of the red-robed warlocks dropping to the ground as though struck from behind by an unseen force, their bodies fading away on the Board as the life left them. Other warlocks and witches were apparently attempting to stand and fight the enemy that Garald could not see, but these tiny figures, too, soon disappeared, leaving no trace behind.

As for the catalysts — they were not being struck down, their bodies did not fall lifeless to the Board. The catalysts were simply and suddenly vanishing.

"What is happening? What is going on?" Garald raved. Wrenching his hands from the Board, he clenched them into fists. "The Ariels from that sector! Where are they?" he cried suddenly, scanning the skies. "Why don't they report?"

Cardinal Radisovik raised his eyes, too, and clutched at the Prince.

"Your Grace! The spectators," the Cardinal said urgently. "They don't know what is happening. You must remain calm, or you will start a panic."

Prince Garald looked at the glittering carriages circling or parked in the skies above him, their wealthy occupants enjoying their midday meals. Faintly, mingled with the murmur of voices and laughter, he could hear the tinkling sounds of clinking champagne glasses.

"Thank you, Radisovik," the Prince said, drawing a deep breath. Straightening, he clasped his hands firmly behind his back and tried to assume a nonchalant attitude. "Move in closer around the Board," he ordered his commanders crisply. "Block it from their view. We've got to get them out of here!" he added in a low voice as the nobles gathered close, crowding around the Board, their faces pale. "But under what pretense —"

"Perhaps a storm, Garald," suggested Radisovik, the catalyst's fear evident in his use of the Prince's given name in public. "The *Sif-Hanar* —"

"Excellent idea!" Garald motioned to one of the Ariels, who was standing by. "Fly to the *Sif-Hanar*," the Prince ordered the winged man. "Tell them I want storms to sweep across this entire Board! Rain, thunder, hail, lightning. That might help stop whatever is attacking us from the north as well," the Prince added, glancing back at the Board, his brow furrowed with concern. "Send additional messengers to warn the spectators" — Garald gestured upward — "both here and in other parts of the Field, that storms are imminent."

The Ariel bowed, spread his wings, and soared into the air, motioning others of his kind to follow him. Gazing after them, Garald saw several suddenly swerve out of their course, flying over to a dark object that appeared between two carriages.

"It's an Ariel," Garald reported in carefully emotionless tones. "They are bringing him in. I think he's been injured."

Two Ariels — one flying on either side of their comrade, holding him gently by the arms — returned to the Prince while the others continued on to carry out their orders. The Ariels flew slowly, bearing their burden between them. Waiting impatiently below, trying to remain calm, Garald was acutely aware of the sudden silence falling among the crowd of spectators, then the slow murmur of voices as they caught sight of what was transpiring. As the Ariels neared, Garald saw the man they carried and he caught his breath in horror, hearing similar reactions from those gathered around him.

The Ariel's body was burned, the feathers of the giant wings singed and blackened. His head slumped, he hung limply in the gentle grasp of his comrades.

"My lord, we caught him falling from the air," one of the Ariels reported as they alighted on the ground before their Prince, easing the wounded man down on the grass.

"Send for the *Theldara*!" Garald ordered, his heart wrenched with pity for the wounded man and the thought of the courage it had taken to fly in that terrible condition.

Someone hastened away in search of a healer, but Garald, kneeling by the winged man's side, saw that it was too late. The man was unconscious, obviously dying. The Prince gritted his teeth. He had to find out what was happening! At a word, he caused water to appear in the palm of his hand. Moistening the Ariel's burned lips, he sprinkled the cooling substance on the cracked and blackened flesh of the face.

"Can you hear me, my friend?" Garald asked in a low voice. Cardinal Radisovik, kneeling by his side, began to quietly perform the ritual rites granted to the dying.

"Per istam Sanctam. . . ."

The Ariel's eyes fluttered open. He did not seem to know where he was, but gazed around wildly and cried out in terror.

"You are safe, my friend," Garald said softly, touching the lips with water. "Tell me, what happened?"

The Ariel's eyes focused on the Prince. Reaching out a bloodied hand, the winged man grasped hold of Garald's arm. "Monstrous creatures . . . of iron!" The man gasped for breath, clutching Garald tightly, painfully. "Death . . . crawls. . . . No escape!" The Ariel's eyes rolled back in his head, the lips parted in a scream that was never heard, the voice died in the throat with a rattle.

". . . Unctionem indúlgeat tibi Dominus quidquid deliqústi. . . ."

The hand on Garald's sleeve slid from its convulsive grasp. The Prince remained kneeling, staring unseeing at the stains upon his robes, the blood a dark black against the crimson red of the velvet.

"Creatures of iron?" he repeated.

"The poor man was delirious, Your Grace," said Cardinal Radisovik firmly, closing the vacant, staring eyes of the corpse. "I would pay little attention to his ravings."

"Those weren't the ravings of a delirious man," Garald said thoughtfully, when he felt the Cardinal's hand close tightly over his arm. Glancing up, he saw Radisovik shake his head ever so slightly, with a warning look in the direction of the commanders, who were watching them intently, faces pale, eyes wide.

"Perhaps you are right, Holiness," the Prince amended lamely, licking his dry lips.

Above them, the bright blue sky was darkening rapidly as storm clouds materialized, surging and boiling like the confused thoughts in Garald's mind. Though not consciously aware of it, he heard the voices of the spectators — shrill with irritation or deep with anger — demanding to know what was going on. He heard the stern voices of the Ariels in answer, urging the spectators to return to their homes before the full fury of the storm broke.

The full fury. . . . Creatures of iron. . . . Death . . . crawls. What an odd expression. Death crawls. . . .

Voices clamored. Everyone was talking at once, demanding his attention.

"Shut up! Leave me alone! Let me think!" The words swelled in his throat, but — with an effort of will — he swallowed them. They would reveal to everyone that he was losing control of the situation. *Losing* control? Garald smiled bitterly. He had no control to lose! He had absolutely no idea what was going on. He was still inclined — perhaps wanted desperately — to believe this was some trick of Xavier's. But another glance at the Gameboard was enough to convince him that this was not so. The forces of Merilon were being routed, destroyed, along with the forces of Sharakan.

Routed and destroyed by an unseen foe. . . .

Creatures of iron. . . .

Death crawls. . . .

"I'm going out there to see for myself," Prince Garald said abruptly.

Clouds darkened the sky, massing thicker and blacker. A sudden gust of wind flattened the tall grass and set the limbs of the trees creaking. Heralded by a forked tongue of lightning and a sharp thunder crack, the storm broke around them. Driving rain soaked clothes through in an instant, hail stung their skin painfully. The release of the storm released the tensions within each man as well. Chaos erupted, as panic swept among the entourage like the wind over the grass.

Some tried to dissuade their Prince from going, pleading that he return to Sharakan. Others insisted that he go and take them with him. One faction decided it was a clever ploy of Merilon and were arguing that they should hurl everything they had against Xavier's forces. Several pointed accusing fingers at the blacksmith.

"Creatures of iron!" cried one. "It's the accursed work of these Sorcerers!"

Suddenly all fears had a focus.

"The Dark Arts!" cried several. "The Sorcerers are taking over the world!"

"Emperor Xavier said this would happen," came an angry shout.

"My lord, I swear!" The agonized voice of the Sorcerer blacksmith boomed over the cracking thunder. "It isn't us! You know we would never betray you —!"

Creatures of iron. . . .

Ignoring the pleas and the arguments and the clutching hands as he ignored the rain in his face and the hail that was pelting him, Garald shoved his commanders aside. Cardinal Radisovik had just drawn his own cloak over the body of the Ariel and was rising to his feet as the Prince approached him.

"Open a Corridor to me, Radisovik," Garald demanded, glaring at the catalyst sternly, expecting further opposition.

To Garald's surprise, the Cardinal nodded in acquiescence. "I will do so, Your Grace, in a moment." Laying his hand upon Garald's arm, Radisovik looked intently at his Prince. "What are your orders in your absence?" the Cardinal reminded him gently.

Garald's first impatient impulse was to rebuff the catalyst, to shove him aside as he had the others. But the Cardinal's touch on his arm was firm and reassuring, his minister's voice calm and steady. Although there was fear on the face of the older man, it was being held in check by wisdom. Garald saw his own face reflected in Radisovik's eyes, he saw his own eyes, wild and staring, he saw the beginnings of panic.

The Prince made himself relax. Rational thought returned.

"My orders," he repeated, running his hand through his wet hair, noticing as he did so that though the rain was falling around him, it was no longer falling on him. Someone — he supposed it was a *Duuk-tsarith* — had cast a magical shield over the group and the Gameboard, protecting them from the elements. Garald cast a shield over his mind in much the same way, creating a tiny calm in the center of the mental turmoil. Slowly, he turned back to the Gameboard.

"Pull all the warlocks and their catalysts back from areas near that front immediately," he said, indicating the eastern flanks that were not yet under attack. There were no signs of fighting there yet, no one was fleeing or dying in those sectors. Whatever was happening was spreading westward from the north. "Bring them down south, near where we stand now. Cover their retreat with centaurs, the giants, the dragons." He indicated other areas on the Board. "These creatures appear to be having some effect in stopping" — he paused — "whatever is out there. . . ."

"There is also a pocket of strong resistance here, Your Grace," said one of the commanders, calling everyone's attention to an area on the far northwestern corner of the Board.

"Yes," said Garald, recognizing it as did everyone else there. It was Emperor Xavier's position around his own Gameboard. Silently, the Prince watched the small group of figures fighting . . . what? Garald roused himself. "Do nothing further until you hear from me," he added, turning and walking swiftly from the Board. "Radisovik, open the Corridor. I place you in charge —"

"I'm going with you, Garald," interrupted the Cardinal, coming to stand beside his Prince.

"Thank you, Radisovik," Garald said in a low undertone, "but I think it would be better if you stayed here." He looked about at his commanders, noting their nervous, darting glances at the Board and at each other. "Let me take one of the other catalysts. Your wisdom and cool thinking —"

"— will be needed by my hot-headed Prince," finished Radisovik with a slight smile. Leaning near Garald so that the Prince alone could hear, Radisovik added softly, "Remember what we heard about the Borderlands?"

Puzzled, Prince Garald stared intently at Radisovik, wondering what he meant, silently interrogating the catalyst with his eyes. But the Cardinal — casting a meaningful look around at the others — said no more. Radisovik's face appeared to age visibly beneath the Prince's gaze, however, answering Garald more eloquently than words.

The Prince suddenly understood. The Prophecy. . . .

"Very well, Radisovik," Garald said, keeping his voice under control though he felt that his heart might have turned to iron, so heavy was it with this new burden of fear.

Radisovik caused a Corridor to open, a void of quiet nothingness set against a background of storm-tossed trees and slashing rain. The Prince, his Cardinal, and two *Duuktsarith* prepared to step inside.

"I will send Ariels back to report," Garald said, turning to his commanders who were gathered around him. "Sorcerer, I leave you in command in my absence," he added, silencing protesting murmurs with a glance. This was one decision of which he felt secure. He had already considered that this might be a plot by the Sorcerers to take over the world and he had discounted it. He knew these people, he trusted in their loyalty. More important, he knew their capabilities and their limitations.

Creatures of iron.

Garald brought forth a mental image of the blacksmith, summoning demons from the forge fire.

No. It made no sense. He had seen them, working day and night, fashioning spear tips and crude daggers. . . .

Creatures of iron. It was almost laughable.

"What is your destination, Your Grace?" asked Radisovik as Prince Garald entered the Corridor.

"Take me to Emperor Xavier."

12

Creatures Of Iron

Life is magic. Magic is life. Magic poured from the heart of Thimhallan, flowing from the Well of Life within the mountain fortress of the Font to every object in the world. Each pebble, each blade of grass, each drop of water was imbued with magic. Every person in the world — even those declared Dead — was gifted with magic. There had been only one truly Dead man on Thimhallan, and he had been driven beyond its borders.

But now, it was as if the well of magic had been poisoned, the magic laced with a fear that sprang from a source so deep and dark that it had — for centuries — been forgotten. As the Watchers screamed their unheard warnings from the border, so now the rocks of Thimhallan cried out in terror, the trees swayed their limbs in frenzy, the very ground shook.

Mosiah could not move. A Nullmagic spell could not have robbed him of life more thoroughly than did his fear, its chill fingers stealing reason, breath, and energy, leaving him unable to think, to react when the clouds of fog parted and he saw the horror that had come to Thimhallan.

It was a creature of iron; Mosiah, who had worked for months in the forge, recognized the shining scales of metal as would few other magi in Thimhallan. The creature's squat, toadlike body was as big as that of a griffin, but it had no wings, it could not fly. It had no legs either, and was forced to crawl along the ground on its belly. The head swiveled like the head of an owl, and Mosiah thought it must be blind, for it appeared to blunder forward aimlessly. Oblivious to anything in its path, the creature smashed into trees, mowing them down, wrenching their living roots from the earth. It crushed rock and churned up the ground, leaving marks of its clumsy passage in the trampled grass and mud.

Mosiah watched it in helpless terror, wondering what hideous being this was and how it came to be loosed upon the world. Then he discovered, horribly, that the creature was not blind. It had eyes. Like the basilisk, it used them for seeing . . . and for killing.

Hidden in a clump of trees about twenty feet from the creature, Mosiah saw suddenly a warlock fly toward him, fleeing the lumbering monster. Hurtling in wild panic through the air, his red robes streaming behind him, the War Master was easily outdistancing the slow, awkward creature.

The creature's head revolved; it appeared to be hunting its prey, sniffing it out. Suddenly, a single eye — hollow, dark, and empty — winked open in the head and focused on the flying wizard. The eye blinked, shooting forth a thin beam of light that flashed on and off so swiftly Mosiah wasn't even certain afterward that he had seen it.

The eye beam struck the warlock in the back, causing the man to plummet to the ground. The momentum of his frantic flight carried him forward. He rolled near Mosiah, who stared at the warlock hopefully. At last, he wasn't alone! Surely this War Master would know what was going on. Mosiah waited for the warlock to stand up, for the fall had not been particularly severe. But the warlock didn't move.

"He's not dead," Mosiah told himself, swallowing the fear that was a choking bile in his throat. Glancing up, he saw that the creature had momentarily come to a halt, its head staring forward. "How could he be dead? There's no wound,

nothing but a hole burned in his robes. . . . He must just be
stunned. I've got to help. . . ."

But it took several seconds to grapple with panic's de-
bilitating grasp. Finally, keeping one eye warily on the creature, seeing the head start to swivel around again — probably
in search of its downed prey — Mosiah crept from the shelter
of the trees and, grabbing the warlock by the collar of his
robes, dragged the man back into the shadows.

Mosiah turned the warlock over on his back, but he knew
even before he saw the staring eyes and gaping mouth that
the man was dead. A tiny wisp of smoke curled upward from
the wizard's breast. Mosiah's breath caught in his throat and
he backed away from the corpse.

The beam of light that had flashed for less than a split
second had burned a hole through the wizard's body as a red-
hot poker burns a hole through soft wood.

The ground shook beneath Mosiah's feet. The creature
was coming in search of its victim. Mosiah wanted to run,
but all feeling left his legs; the sight of the dead warlock and
the swift and sudden manner of the man's death completely
unnerved him. Raising his gaze from the corpse, Mosiah
stared at the great beast as it approached, knowing it must
see him when it came in search of the wizard it had felled.
But still he couldn't move.

The creature drew nearer. Mosiah could smell its foul
odor, poisonous fumes spewed out from its underbody, rob-
bing him of breath. Choking and coughing, cowering amidst
the trees, he had no thought of escape, no thought of anything except his fear.

Undoubtedly, this saved his life.

The creature swerved and rumbled past him, as a wolf
passes by the rabbit sitting frozen in the presence of its enemy, knowing instinctively that movement draws unwanted
attention.

Mosiah watched the thing lurch away from him, its hideous head — now seemingly blind again — turning this way
and that in search of more prey, crawling past the body of the
warlock without a look, without so much as a sniff.

A centaur kills out of hatred and mutilates the body.
Dragons kill for food, as do the griffin and the chimera. A
giant kills out of ignorance, not understanding its own

strength. But this thing had killed purposefully, coldly, without apparent reason or even interest.

Though the fog had lifted and Mosiah could now find and join up with the rest of his unit, he huddled within the sheltering grove, afraid to move, scared to stay. The creature of iron was still within sight and sound, its foul breath poisoning the air, its blind head turning this way and that as it blundered through the vegetation.

Were there more of its kind around? Mosiah wondered, leaning weakly against a tree. He was starting to shake, a reaction to his terror. Unwillingly, his gaze went to the body of the warlock, lying some distance from him. What monstrous being was this that Xavier had created? Mosiah quickly averted his gaze from the pale, astonished face of the corpse, the tiny curls of smoke rising from the charred fabric of the robes. . . .

The robes.

Mosiah looked back at the body, his eyes widening. The warlock wore the robes of Merilon!

"Blessed Almin!" Mosiah whispered, his eyes going back to the creature, which was just vanishing out of sight beyond a small hill. "Is that . . . ours? Is that why it didn't attack me?"

The Sorcerers! was his next thought. He put a trembling hand to his lips, wiping away chill sweat. Hastily, he glanced about, hoping to see other members of his unit. Many of them were true Sorcerers, people who had been born and raised in the hidden Coven of those who practiced the Dark Arts of Technology. They would know. Perhaps they had been building this thing secretly, intent on taking over the world. He had heard them talk of that often enough.

Closing his eyes, Mosiah pictured the creature — its metal scales, its breath reminding him of the fumes that rose from the forge.

Yes, he thought with swift anger and hatred. Yes! They must have done it. I never trusted them, never. . . .

But even as he reached this decision, some cold part of him that was thinking rather than panicking said no. Mosiah looked down at the crossbow he held clutched in his hand. (He had completely forgotten in his terrified state that he even held a weapon.) He saw its crudeness, its misshapen lines. He thought of the time it had taken to fashion this tool, of the men hammering and sweating in the forge hours upon hours. He recalled the creature of iron — the shining metal scales, the way it crawled smoothly over the uneven ground. Even in days of their power and glory the Sorcerers had not been able to construct anything like that. How could they now? They could barely build a working crossbow. . . .

Drops of rain struck Mosiah's cheek, rising wind blew cold against his already shivering body. A magical storm was brewing; the sky was darkening with thunderclouds. Jagged lightning tore through the air, thunder rumbled around him, making his heart stand still, reminding him of the creature. He looked again at the body of the wizard. . . . Suddenly, Mosiah started to run.

Panic drove him from his hiding place. He admitted that to himself as he stumbled over the uneven ground, dragging the heavy crossbow with him, his gaze constantly darting fearfully around him. Panic and a desperate need to find other people, someone, anyone who could tell him what was going on. His need for information — his need to know — was greater than his fear of the creature. This horrible panicked feeling would leave as soon as he knew for certain what was happening!

The storm lashed out at him, driving him forward with whips of wind and rain and stinging hail. Water streamed into his eyes; he could see nothing, yet still he ran, caroming off trees like some crazed gamepiece, slipping in the wet grass, entangling himself in clutching weeds.

Finally, bruised and battered, he stopped, huddling in a small grove of trees. Slumping back against a tree trunk, gasping for breath, he thought suddenly, "Simkin!"

In his terror, he had forgotten all about his erstwhile companion. "Simkin would know what's happening. Simkin *always* knows," Mosiah muttered bitterly. "But where the devil did he get to?" Unslinging the quiver of arrows, Mosiah dumped it on the ground and kicked at it with his foot. "Simkin?" he yelled above the storm, feeling incredibly stupid, yet hoping against hope to hear that insipid "I say, old chap!" in reply.

There was no green and orange feathered arrow among the metal ones, however. Angrily, Mosiah kicked the quiver again. Only silence.

"Why should I want that fool around anyway?" he mumbled, wiping the rain from his face — rain that mingled with his tears of fear and frustration and the knowledge that he was now completely lost. "He's only trouble. I — "

Mosiah hushed, listening.

The thunder boomed around him, lightning lit the gray gloom until it was nearly bright as day. But through the noise and confusion of the storm, he thought he had heard . . . yes, there it was again.

Voices!

Weak with relief, Mosiah nearly dropped the crossbow. Shaking, he set it carefully on the ground and peered out from the cover of the dripping foliage. The voices were near him, coming apparently from another small grove of trees only a few yards away. He couldn't understand what the voices were saying; it was difficult to understand their shouts over the noise of wind and rain and thunder. Perhaps it was centaurs. Mosiah hesitated, listening closely. No, it was unmistakably human speech! Warlocks, undoubtedly.

Mosiah moved forward cautiously. He planned to call out when he was close enough. The last thing he wanted to do was to startle some nervous warlock and find himself mutated into a frog. He could hear the voices quite plainly now; it sounded as if there were several men in the small grove, shouting orders of some sort. Words of glad relief were on his lips, words of thankfulness at finding friends, but Mosiah never spoke them.

Reaching the outer trees of the grove, the young man slowed his pace. Why? Mosiah didn't know. His mind urged him to leap forward, but some deeper instinct kept his voice silent, his steps quiet. Maybe it was because — even though he couldn't hear clearly above the storm — he *didn't* understand the speech of these men. Maybe the bad experience with the *Duuk-tsarith* in the Grove long ago had taught him a bitter lesson in caution. Or maybe it was the same animal instinct for self-preservation that had kept him safe from the creature of iron.

Padding softly around a tree, knowing that he himself couldn't be heard above the storm; knowing, too, that he would be difficult to see in the driving rain, Mosiah crept near the source of the voices. Gently parting the wet leaves, he saw them.

He held perfectly still — not out of fear or caution. He felt no emotion whatsoever. It was as if his brain had left him, had said, "I've had enough, let someone else cope with this for a while. Good-bye."

Those speaking were humans. But they were like no humans he had ever before seen or imagined.

There were six of them. They were male, from the sound of their voices and the muscular appearance of their bodies. At first Mosiah thought they had heads of iron, for he could see the lighting reflecting off their shining scalps. Then one of them removed his head, wiping sweat from his brow, and Mosiah realized that the strange humans were wearing helms, similar to the bucketlike contraption Simkin donned on infrequent occasions.

In addition to their helms, the strange humans were dressed alike in suits of shining metal that fit them like their own skin. In fact, it might have been their skin, for all Mosiah knew, except that he saw one yank a glove from a hand, revealing flesh like his own. The man had taken off the glove to toy with an object he held in his hand — an object that was oval-shaped and fit neatly in the palm.

The man showed the object to a companion, saying something in his unintelligible language, apparently with regard to it, for he sounded disgusted and shook the object. The companion shrugged, barely glancing at his partner. He was keeping watch, staring out from the grove of trees, and he was obviously tense and nervous.

The man with the object in his hand continued to shake it until one of the other men made a hissing sound. Reacting hastily, the man pulled the glove on over his hand, turning to face the same direction as his other five companions. All of them crouched low in the wet brush, and now Mosiah could see through the driving rain that each man held one of the oval-shaped objects in his hand and that they pointed them forward, in front of them.

Mosiah kept watch with them, wondering what had drawn their attention. He still felt no fear, not even curiosity. He was numb, in shock. If the men had turned around and faced him, he could have done nothing but stand and stare at them. Once one did happen to glance behind him, but he did so quickly and nervously, obviously more worried about what was ahead. Mosiah, well concealed by the brush and the cover of the heavy rain, remained hidden, unnoticed.

A warlock, a witch, and their catalysts emerged from another small grove of trees some distance from the one in which Mosiah and the strange humans were hiding. The magi moved cautiously and—from the wild-eyed, terrified expressions upon their pale faces, expressions that Mosiah knew must reflect his own—it was apparent that they had suffered similar, frightening experiences. Their black robes marked them *Duuk-tsarith*, and at the sight of the magi, the metal-skinned humans in the brush crouched down even further.

A lost child catching sight of his parents could know no greater joy and thankfulness than Mosiah experienced at the arrival of the *Duuk-tsarith*. Flattening himself against the tree trunk, he hoped fervently he was out of range of the spell he knew the warlock would cast on the strange humans and waited for the inevitable. The metal-skinned humans moved quietly, sinking down into the brush with a skill that indicated that they had been well trained in the art of concealment and ambush. But they did not move quietly enough. The *Duuk-tsarith*—it is said—can detect a rabbit's presence by the sound of its breathing.

The warlock reacted instantly. His black robes swirling around him, he faced the grove. Pointing toward it, the warlock cast a spell, a Nullmagic spell that is the *Duuk-tsarith*'s first form of attack. The warlock was exceptionally powerful; in addition, he must have been suffused with Life by his catalyst, for Mosiah felt a slight draining effect of his own magic even though he stood some distance from the enemy. Expecting to see the metal-skinned humans fall writhing to the ground, helpless as the spell bereft them of Life, Mosiah started to leave his own hiding place, hoping to be able to question the *Duuk-tsarith* and find out what was going on.

But he halted, stunned. The strange humans were not affected by the Nullmagic. Seeing the warlock aware of their presence, realizing that concealment was no longer necessary, they rose to their feet. Mosiah, watching, saw in his mind another man who had not been affected by the Null-magic — Joram.

These strange humans were Dead!

Raising his right arm, one of the Dead pointed at the warlock. A beam of blinding, intense light streaked out from his palm. The air hummed and sizzled, the warlock collapsed, dying without a cry, leaving his catalyst to stare at him in astonishment. A thin wisp of smoke rose up from the man's black robes and Mosiah recalled with awful clarity the death he had witnessed earlier; the hole burned through the man's flesh.

Mosiah glanced from the warlock to his fellow *Duuk-tsarith*, but the witch had vanished. Her disappearance appeared to disturb the Dead, who remained crouching in the trees, their metallic heads turning this way and that as had the great metallic head of the iron creature Mosiah had seen earlier. After a moment, the Dead man who stood in the center of the group shrugged his shoulders. Pointing to the warlock's catalyst, who was kneeling over the body of his master, performing the Last Rites, the Dead man began to walk forward.

Pressed against the tree, Mosiah waited, cringing, for them to kill the helpless catalyst. The Dead man walked toward the Priest. The catalyst heard them coming, but he did not look up. With the steadfast courage of his faith, he anointed the head of the dead warlock with oil and spoke the ritual words, *"Per istam sanctam unctionem indúlgeat . . ."* in a firm voice.

The Dead man kept his hand raised, the light-beaming object trained on the catalyst. To Mosiah's astonishment, however, the strange humans did not murder the priest. One of the men reached out (gingerly, it seemed to the watching Mosiah) and grabbed hold of the catalyst by the arm.

Angrily, having still to complete his rite, the catalyst shook off the Dead man's grip. The Dead glanced at another of the strange humans, as if for instructions.

This man, whom Mosiah was beginning to realize must be the leader, spoke in the unintelligible language of the Dead and made a motion with his hand. The metal-skinned human backed off slightly, allowing the catalyst to complete his rite in peace.

A mistake, Mosiah counseled them silently from his hiding place. Of course, being Dead, they could not sense the heightening tension in the air, the magic that was beginning to build and boil around them. They couldn't know that the witch was still near.

". . . *quidquid deliquísti. Amen.*" The catalyst came to the end of the rite. Reaching out, he closed the warlock's staring eyes and began, slowly, to rise to his feet.

Mosiah heard one of the Dead cry out — a shout of fear and terror that echoed weirdly from the metal head. Pointing at the corpse of the warlock, the metal-skinned human began to scream in terror. The corpse was changing into a gigantic snake. The warlock's eyes that had just been closed in death now opened wide, burning with a red, unnatural life. The warlock's body elongated and grew, becoming a reptilian body bigger around than an oak. Rearing up out of the wet grass, its flat oscillating head swaying slightly, the dead warlock — now a huge hooded cobra — towered over the metal-skinned humans, its forked tongue flicking in and out of its venomous mouth.

The leader of the Dead fell back in terror. He aimed the deadly beam at the snake, but his arm shook visibly and the beam missed its target, striking a tree branch and setting it aflame. Lunging swiftly, the giant snake sank its fangs into the Dead man's shoulder, easily piercing the metal skin. The Dead man's cry of pain and terror echoed through the forest, causing Mosiah to grit his teeth until it ended in a high-pitched wail of death.

Wrenching its fangs loose from its victim, the snake reared back to focus on its other enemies. The Dead were fleeing in panic, however, crashing blindly through the woods. Standing near the snake, the catalyst watched them run away. When they were gone from sight and when the sound of their screams could no longer be heard, the snake shimmered in the air and collapsed to the ground. Bereft of its magical Life, the cobra was once more the corpse of the warlock.

Mosiah, realizing he had quit breathing, drew in a shivering breath. Sweat beaded on his forehead, he was shaking violently and uncontrollably. The sudden appearance of the black-robed witch hovering beside him made his heart lurch wildly in his breast. He very nearly ran away himself, but her strong hand reached out and grabbed hold of him.

"I told you I'd find him!" said an aggrieved voice coming from a bit of orange silk the witch wore tied around her wrist. "I brought you straight to him!"

"You are Mosiah?" said the witch, her eyes glittering from the depths of the black hood, staring at him intently. "Yes," she answered her own question. "I recognize you."

Mosiah recognized her as well, and the recognition robbed him of his ability to speak, for this was the witch who had captured him and nearly sent him to his death.

The orange silk disappeared from the witch's wrist, coalescing in the air to become the tall, thin body of Simkin. But it was a changed Simkin—a pale, distraught Simkin, a Simkin whose normally elegant, fashionable attire appeared to have been flung on without care or thought. He wore breeches of coarse cotton, such as might have been worn by the meanest Field Magus. A slovenly tunic of leather covered a drab silk shirt with a torn sleeve. The bit of orange silk still fluttered bravely in his hand, but the next instant he stuck a corner of it into his mouth and began chewing on it distractedly.

"What's going on?" Mosiah managed to gasp weakly, looking from Simkin to the witch.

"Precisely the question we would ask you!" the witch hissed at him, reminding him forcibly of the snake. He glanced nervously at the warlock's body and saw the catalyst hurrying in their direction.

"We cannot stay!" the catalyst called softly. "One of the creatures of iron is coming this way!"

"The Corridor!" the witch said, and the catalyst caused one to gape open instantly. Simkin leaped inside, almost before the Corridor was open, and the catalyst followed.

Mosiah hesitated. He could hear the low humming noise of the iron creature, he could feel the ground shake beneath his feet. Yet he would almost have chosen to take his chances with the blind monster than the witch, whose presence and touch brought back the pain of the binding vines and their flesh-piercing thorns.

"You fool!" The witch's hand closed over his arm. "You will not survive in its path an instant. It has no eyes, but it is not blind. It kills with unerring accuracy. I will take you with me, whether you choose to go or not. But I would prefer that you came voluntarily. We need your help."

The humming grew louder. Mosiah remembered the wizard, fleeing. . . . The hole burned in the flesh. . . . Yet still he hesitated—a man stranded on a sheer cliff face with a great boulder crashing down on him from above, his one hope a leap into a dark chasm below.

"Where?" he asked through lips so stiff they would barely form the word. The Corridor was already starting to close.

"Emperor Xavier's," said the witch, the hands holding Mosiah tightening with an ominous grip.

"Don't," he said softly, swallowing. "I'll come."

The Corridor opened, sucked him inside, and squeezed shut around him.

13

Death Crawls

It was all so quiet.

Garald, stepping cautiously from the Corridor, wondered briefly if the *Thon-li* — who were in a pitiable state of confusion — had made a mistake and sent him to some distant, peaceful part of the world. But it took the Prince only a moment to realize that he had reached his destination, only a moment to realize that the quiet was not the quiet of peace.

It was the quiet of death.

The Corridor closed hastily behind Garald. He was dimly aware of Cardinal Radisovik covering his eyes with his hand, murmuring a prayer in a broken voice. Garald was also aware of his bodyguards — the *Duuk-tsarith*, trained from childhood to the discipline of silence — gasping aloud in shock and anger. Garald was aware of this, yet none of it touched him. It was as if he stood alone upon this world and, looking around, saw it for the first time.

The sun shone brilliantly, a startling contrast to the stormy weather they had just left. Flaming in the slate blue sky, the orb blazed with fierce energy, as though trying to burn away all evidence of the horrors it had witnessed. Garald could see, looking southward, his storm clouds surging in this direction. By all the rules of warfare, this weather attack by Sharakan's *Sif-Hanar* should have prompted Xavier to order his own *Sif-Hanar* to counterattack, leading to a rousing, thunder-clapping battle in the air. But this had not happened. The sun was out, the day was fine. The reason was obvious.

Merilon's *Sif-Hanar* lay dead beneath their Gameboard, their bodies among several sprawled on the scorched and blackened grass.

The Board itself had been destroyed, chopped completely in two. Made of massive stone, an exact copy of the one used by Prince Garald, half of it leaned at an unlikely angle, propped up by the bodies beneath it. The other half lay on the ground. Staring at it, Garald could not imagine the tremendous blow it must have taken to shatter the magical stone.

Slowly, looking around him cautiously, Garald walked over to the Board. Kneeling beside it, he touched its smooth surface, cool beneath his fingers. Like the stone, the Board's magic was broken. No miniature dragons breathed their flame into the air from its surface, no small giants tromped across it, no tiny figures of warlocks and witches fought their enemies in enchanted battles. The Gameboard of Merilon was empty and lifeless as the eyes of the bodies that lay crumpled beneath it.

Lifting his gaze from the Gameboard, Prince Garald saw the true field of battle.

It was strewn with bodies. The Prince could not begin to count the number of dead. Cardinal Radisovik walked among them, his red robes of office fluttering about him in the winds of the approaching storm — a bitter wind that blew across the Field of Glory, sucking up the warmth of the sun and returning it with a breath of ice.

"If you are searching for those who might yet live, Radisovik, you are wasting your time," Prince Garald started to advise the catalyst. Nothing lives out there. . . . Nothing. . . .

It was only after watching Radisovik for several moments — moments that seemed to Garald to be increments of
time that he could literally see and touch as they slipped by
him — that the Prince realized the Cardinal was not searching
for the living. He was granting the final rites to the dead.

The dead. Garald gazed out over the sunlit meadow that
stretched before him. Once smooth and well-kept, the green
grass had been torn and uprooted by some powerful force,
blackened and burned as though the sun itself had dipped
down and licked it. The dead lay all over the field, their
bodies in various poses and attitudes according to the manner of their dying. On each face, however, there was the
same frozen expression: fear, horror, terror.

Suddenly Garald cried out in anger. Stumbling across the
grass, he slipped and fell in a pool of blood. Instantly the
Duuk-tsarith were at his side, helping him stand, warning him
to be careful, that the danger might still be present. Thrusting aside their hands, heedless of their words, Garald ran to
Radisovik, who was murmuring a prayer over the body of a
young woman in black robes. Grabbing the Cardinal by the
arm, Garald jerked him to a standing position.

"Look!" the Prince cried hoarsely, pointing. "Look!"

"I know, milord," Radisovik answered softly, his face so
altered and aged by anguish and grief that Garald almost
didn't recognize the man. "I know," the Cardinal repeated.

One of the fancy carriages that belonged to the wealthy
of Merilon had crashed to the ground, its charred, smoldering ruins scattered over a wide area. The team of magical
swallows that had once pulled it lay dead nearby, the birds
still tied together by strands of gold, the smell of burnt feathers tinging the air.

A glimpse of blue fluttering silk caught Garald's eye. Ignoring Radisovik's remonstrances, he hurried over to the carriage. Grasping a piece of smoking wood that may have once
been a door, he hurled it aside. Buried beneath it was a young
woman, her burned and broken arms wrapped around a
child as though she had tried, in her last moments, to shield
the baby from death with her own fragile body. The pitiful
attempt had not worked. The baby lay limp and lifeless in his
mother's grasp.

Near the woman was the body of a man, lying facedown amid the wreckage. From the manner of his dress and the elegance of his clothes, Garald judged him to be the owner of the carriage, a noble of Merilon. Hoping bleakly to find some spark of life, Garald turned the man over.

"My god!" The Prince recoiled in horror.

The grinning mouth and eyeless sockets of a charred skeleton stared up at the Prince. Clothes, skin, flesh, muscle — the entire front part of the man's body — had all been burned away.

The world turned upside down. The sun fell from the sky, the earth slid out from beneath Garald's feet. Strong hands gripped him, holding onto him tightly. He felt himself lowered to the ground and heard Radisovik's voice coming from wherever it was the winds came from, somewhere far distant . . . .

"*Theldara* . . . fetch one quickly."

"No!" Garald managed to croak. His throat felt swollen, talking was painful. "No. I am all right. It was . . . that poor man! What kind of fiend could possibly —"

Creatures of iron.

"I'm . . . all right!" Thrusting away the hands of his minister, Garald forced himself to a sitting position. Lowering his head between his knees, he drew in deep breaths of the chill air. Sternly he reprimanded himself, using the pain of his own stinging criticism to obliterate the horrors he had witnessed. What kind of ruler was he? When his people needed him most desperately, he had given way to weakness. This middle-aged man — a catalyst — had more strength than he — a Prince of the realm.

Garald shook his head, attempting to bring order to his chaotic thoughts. He had to decide what to do. My god! Was there anything he *could* do? His unwilling gaze was drawn back by a horrid fascination to the body of the nobleman. Shuddering, he hastily averted his face. Then he stopped and, gritting his teeth, made himself stare fixedly at the gruesome sight. As he hoped, it kindled anger within him and he used the anger to warm his fear-chilled blood.

"Garald," said Radisovik, kneeling at his side, "Emperor Xavier is not among the dead, nor are any of his War Masters. I believe your original intent was to seek him out. Do you still want to do so?"

"Yes," said Garald, grateful to the catalyst for seeing his weakness and tactfully guiding him. Hearing his voice crack, he swallowed in an attempt to moisten his aching throat. "Yes," he repeated more firmly. Putting his hand to his brow, he called up an image of his own Gameboard in his mind. Once again, he could see that small pocket of resistance. "Their location . . . is more to the east."

"Yes, Your Grace," said Radisovik. "To the east."

The Cardinal's tight, constrained manner of speaking caused Garald to glance up at him quickly. The Cardinal's eyes were on the eastern horizon, where a column of smoke was just beginning to rise above the trees.

"Should we take the Corridor, milord?" Cardinal Radisovik asked, once more offering guidance without seeming to. "It could be dangerous. . . ."

"Undoubtedly," Garald answered, thinking swiftly, anger and the need for action lending him strength. Refusing assistance, he stood up and began to walk with firm, assured tread back to the broken Gameboard. "We were foolish to have used the Corridor the first time. We could have emerged right into the middle of . . . of this"—he faltered and grit his teeth—"unprepared, defenseless. But we have no other means—" He paused, forcing himself to consider the matter coldly and logically.

"I believe we should—" Garald began, but one of the *Duuk-tsarith* interrupted him, silencing him with a swift movement of the hand. His companion spoke one word and in an instant a magical shield surrounded the Prince and Cardinal; the black-robed warlocks rose immediately into the air, one guarding the front, one guarding behind.

Surrounded by the magical force, Garald strained to hear what had attracted the attention of his sharp-eared warlocks. Eventually he felt it more than heard it—a shivering of the ground as though a large, heavy object was moving nearby.

Creatures of iron.

Like most mortals, Garald had thought about dying. He had discussed death philosophically, speculating about the afterlife with his tutors and the Cardinal. When he heard of Joram's death, Garald had wondered deep within himself if he possessed the courage needed to walk into those shifting mists. But, never, until now, had death been close to him. Never had it appeared to him in such a hideous, horrifying aspect.

He saw the terror on the faces of the corpses, he saw the pain that not even the peace of dying could erase from their features. Fear welled up from deep within him, cramping his stomach, weakening his legs.

Hearing the Cardinal whispering a prayer, Garald envied the man his faith. The Prince had supposed himself to be devout in his beliefs, but he realized now it hàd been lip service. Where was the Almin? Garald didn't know, but he certainly doubted He was here.

The movement of the ground became more pronounced, and Garald could hear a thudding sound. His stomach wrenched, he thought he might be sick from fear. The vision came clearly to his mind—the Prince of Sharakan vomiting on the Field of Glory.

Garald could hear it passed down in legend and song and he laughed suddenly, shrill laughter that drew a look of concern from the Cardinal.

He thinks I'm hysterical, Garald realized, and drew a shuddering breath. His sickness eased, the fear subsided, no longer threatening to master him. So this is courage, he said to himself with grim amusement. Thinking to the end how we will look in the eyes of others.

The thudding grew louder and more pronounced. Movement drew Garald's attention. He grasped Radisovik's arm, pointing, releasing his breath in a heartfelt sigh of relief.

The top of a huge head appeared over the rim of a hill. The head was followed by massive shoulders; a vast expanse of body draped with animal skins came into view, propelled forward by two thick legs.

"A giant!" murmured Radisovik, giving thanks to the Almin.

His thanks may have been premature. Although this was not the monster they had feared, the *Duuk-tsarith* maintained the magical shield in place around their Prince, since giants—though normally gentle—were unpredictable in their behavior. This particular giant appeared hurt and befuddled and, as he drew nearer, Garald saw that he had been injured.

The giant nursed his left arm and there were streaks of tears down his filthy face.

A wounded giant was even more dangerous, and one of the *Duuk-tsarith* moved to stand directly between the giant and the Prince. The other bodyguard, after an exchange of a few brief words with his companion, turned to talk to the Prince.

"My lord," said the *Duuk-tsarith*, "this could be an ideal means of transportation to reach Emperor Xavier."

Startled by the suggestion and suffering a reaction to his fear, Garald at first stared blankly at the black-robed warlock, unable to think coherently enough to make a decision. The man was looking at him expectantly, however, and Garald prodded his numb mind to working.

He had to admit, it seemed a good idea. The giant — with his great strength and ground-eating strides — could carry them to the location where Xavier was battling the unknown foe. Not only could the giant carry them there faster than they could fly, but they would be able to see, from their lofty perch atop the massive shoulders, what was transpiring a long time before they reached it. In addition, once under the control of the *Duuk-tsarith*, the giant would be a valuable ally in case of attack.

"Excellent idea," Garald said finally. "Do what you must."

But the *Duuk-tsarith* had already gone into action. Leaving his companion to guard their charges, the warlock — who was about one-tenth the giant's size — lifted into the air and flew near the mutated human. The giant watched him warily, suspiciously, but did not appear openly hostile.

"So it wasn't a warlock who attacked it and injured it," Garald reflected aloud. "If it had been, the giant would have lashed out instantly at the sight of the warlock or would have fled in terror."

"I believe you have guessed correctly, milord," said Radisovik. "This giant was probably trained by warlocks for the battle and still trusts them. Some *one* else — or some *thing* — must have hurt it."

The warlock spoke soothing words to the giant, as a parent talks to an injured child, offering to heal the injured arm. Its tears flowing faster now that it was receiving attention, the giant approached the warlock readily, holding up its arm for inspection and blubbering incoherently. Seeing the fiery red burn that covered the massive arm, Garald again tried to imagine what force existed on this world that could have inflicted such damage.

The same force that could break a massive stone in two halves, that could fell a carriage from the skies and burn the flesh from a man's body. . . .

Creatures of iron.

The *Duuk-tsarith*, with a wave of his hand, caused a salve to appear on the giant's arm, spreading over it with soothing effect to judge by the smile on the tear-stained face. Conjuring up a roll of fabric, the warlock next hastily wrapped the giant's arm in a bandage, more because these childlike beings were fond of such ornamentation than because the bandage would be particularly useful in healing the wound. This task completed, the warlock made a gesture in the air above the giant's forehead, then flew back to report.

"I have laid a geas on the giant," said the *Duuk-tsarith*, as his companion removed the magical shield from around the Prince and the Cardinal. "I told the thing that it must hunt down whatever it was that hurt it. Since this geas goes along with the giant's natural inclination, we should have no trouble with it."

"Excellent," Garald replied. He glanced to the east, where the columns of smoke were growing larger, thicker, and more numerous. "We must hurry."

"Certainly, milord." Speaking a series of words, the warlock used his magic to lift the Prince and Cardinal into the air and set them down gently upon the giant's huge shoulders.

Settling himself as best he could, Garald wrinkled his nose at the smell of the giant's unwashed body dressed in animal hides. The giant was intensely curious about its riders, and there was several moments' delay as it twisted its head this way and that in an effort to get a close look at them. Its breath was even more foul smelling than its skin. Garald gagged and Cardinal Radisovik covered his nose with the sleeve of his robes when the grinning, broken-toothed mouth turned in his direction.

At last, however, the *Duuk-tsarith*, with a sharp command, was able to goad the giant into lumbering motion. Pointing toward the smoke to indicate the direction in which they wished to travel, the warlocks flew ahead of the giant, guiding its clumsy footsteps.

Garald had been somewhat afraid that, despite the geas, the giant would refuse to go anywhere near smoke, considering the painful burn it had sustained. Perhaps, however, the giant did not connect smoke with fire, for it stomped forward without hesitation, gabbling away in its unintelligible language that sounded very much like the prattlings of a toddler in a state of wild excitement.

Only half-listening to it, Garald realized suddenly that the giant was attempting to tell them what had happened. Repeatedly, it gestured to its hurt arm — once with such force that the Prince was nearly thrown off. Clinging precariously to his seat, both hands tangled in the giant's matted, filthy hair, Garald regretted bitterly that no one had ever attempted to communicate with these oversized humans. Mutated for the purposes of war, they had been abandoned by their masters, left to roam the wilds until needed again. Locked in this huge head were the answers to Garald's questions, for he had no doubt that the giant had been attacked by whatever it was that had massacred the people of Merilon.

They covered the miles of territory between the broken Gameboard and the columns of smoke swiftly, the giant hurrying forward with such enthusiasm and excitement that the *Duuk-tsarith* were forced to order it sternly to slow down or risk losing its passengers.

Inspecting the Field of Glory from his observation point, Garald saw more bodies, and his lips tightened grimly as his anger grew. He also saw additional indications of the foe — long snakelike tracks of churned-up earth that led overland, heading toward the east. The enemy stopped for nothing, apparently. Large trees had been uprooted and pushed aside, smaller ones snapped in two, vegetation plowed down or set afire. It was mainly on either side of these tracks that the bodies of his people could be seen.

At one point, near what was left of a smoldering grove of trees, Garald caught sight of a bright flash — metal gleaming in the sun. He turned to examine it, risking a fall from his precarious perch on the shoulder of the giant. It appeared to be a body of a human and, if it had not seemed too fantastic, the Prince could have sworn that the body had skin of metal.

Garald's first thought was to stop and investigate, but he was forced to abandon this idea. The giant — under the influence of the geas and its own mounting excitement — would be difficult to bring to a halt and would probably charge off on its own if left by itself. By the time the Prince reached this decision, the giant had carried them far past the thing; Garald, looking back, couldn't see any sign of the grove of trees, let alone a body lying beneath it.

"I'll probably find out what is going on soon enough," he said to himself grimly, noting that they were drawing nearer the thickest columns of smoke. Suddenly Garald could hear — above the giant's babblings — a low humming sound, combined with explosions like those created by Illusionists to startle children on holidays. Once again, he experienced the cramps in his stomach, the dryness of his throat, and the weakness in his knees. But this time his fear was laced by a strange excitement, a curiosity, a strong desire to know what lay ahead of them.

At that moment, the *Duuk-tsarith*, flying in front of the giant, topped a steep hill. Suddenly, their forward motion slowed. Garald, watching them closely, saw the hooded heads turn to look at each other. Though he could not catch a glimpse of the warlocks' faces, he could sense a shared incredulity and awe, emotions foreign to this well-disciplined sect.

Frantic to see what they saw, Garald half-rose to a crouching stance on the giant's shoulder as it clamored up the hill. Staring ahead, Garald and the giant both saw the enemy at the same time. Bellowing in rage, the giant came to a sudden halt, and Garald lost his footing. Slipping, he fell backward off the shoulders. His magic was enough to sustain him, however. Using his Life force, he kept himself afloat in the air, hovering just above trees at the hill's crest.

Looking down, he saw the enemy.

Creatures of iron.

14

Legions Of The Dead

They crawled over the face of the earth, seemingly blind as moles, leaving death and desolation to mark their passing. They spared no living thing. Garald watched, stunned and aghast, as the heads of the creatures of iron swiveled this way and that, and wherever the heads looked, death followed, swifter than the blink of an eye.

Their movements were coordinated, purposeful. Twenty or more of the monsters were converging, coming from various positions to the north. Once they met up, they traveled in a straight line, separated from each other by about a distance of thirty feet. Walking behind the creatures were humans, hundreds of them. At least Garald assumed they were human. They had legs and arms and heads, they walked upright. But their skin was metallic. He could see them gleam in the sun and he recalled the body he had seen among the trees.

At least they can be killed, was his first thought. His second, and more terrifying, was that the enemy — the creatures

and these strange humans—was heading in one direction—
south. Tearing his gaze from them, Garald looked ahead, to
the south. He could see the storm clouds of the *Sif-Hanar*
that marked his lines. In his mind's eye, he could see his War
Masters, the warlocks and witches, standing unknowing,
waiting for death to rumble over them. He remembered the
carriage, now shattered on the ground, and he thought of the
hundreds of spectators, with their wicker baskets of fruit and
wine. Certainly the storm would have prompted some of
them to leave, but they had probably just moved off to the
borders of the Field of Glory, where it was dry. Some, perhaps, might even be traveling in this direction where they
could undoubtedly see the sun shining. . . .

"Milord!" One of the *Duuk-tsarith* touched his arm, something that Garald could not ever remember occurring, and a
certain sign that these trained and disciplined warlocks were
shaken. Garald looked back down and ahead several miles
distant to where the warlock indicated.

A natural formation of rock had been hurriedly shaped
into a crude fortress of stone. Within that fortress, the Prince
could see figures moving, their red robes and black marking
them as warlocks and witches. The varying shades of red
denoted the side of the war they had been on before the new
threat made all things equal. As Garald watched, he saw a
figure dressed in crimson stride across the compound of the
hastily conjured fortress, waving his arm, obviously giving
orders, though he could not be heard from this distance.

"Xavier," Garald murmured.

"Milord, they are directly in the path of those things!" the
Duuk-tsarith said, the tightness of his voice indicating his
struggle to maintain control.

Did Xavier know that? Did he know the creatures were
coming and intend to make a stand here? Or had he simply
retreated to this place, unaware of the forces massing against
him?

And what were these creatures of iron? These men of
iron? Garald wondered, his gaze returning to them in terrible fascination. Where had they come from? Was it possible
that another city-state in Thimhallan had somehow gained
knowledge and power enough to create these things? No.
Garald rejected the idea. Nothing like this could have been

kept secret. Besides, the creation of these things must have
been undertaken by Sorcerers whose knowledge and power
were beyond anything even the ancients had dreamed.

Yet another question. Why hadn't they shown up on the
Gameboard? Why hadn't he been able to see them. . . ?

The answer was there, so obvious he realized he'd known
all along, surmised it from the very beginning.

They were Dead. Every one of them — the creatures of
iron, the strange humans with the metal skin. Dead.

The *Duuk-tsarith* was touching him again. "Milord, Cardinal Radisovik, the giant. . . . What are your orders?"

Garald tore his gaze from the monsters. Glancing one
final time at the stone fortress of Emperor Xavier, he turned
away. As he did so he saw one of the creatures pause before a
gigantic boulder that blocked its path. A beam of light shot
from its eye and the boulder shattered into a thousand tiny
pieces.

So much for the stone fortress.

Garald moved quickly now. His mind, no longer tormented by shadowy fears, was active.

"We're going to warn Xavier," he said, "and get him to
pull back. He can't face these things with that small con-
tingent of people. And I'll need messages carried back to our
lines."

Talking to himself, he sped through the air, returning to
the giant, having forgotten about it, the Cardinal, and nearly
everything else in his first paralyzing glimpse of the creatures.

Cardinal Radisovik waited for him on the ground, having
been carried down by the *Duuk-tsarith*. The enraged giant
was barely being held in check by the warlock, and Garald
felt a twinge of remorse when he realized that Radisovik had
undoubtedly been in some peril and that his Prince had left
him — a weak catalyst — to fend for himself. The feeling
passed quickly, however, trampled underfoot by the need for
action.

"You saw?" Garald asked his Cardinal grimly as he
neared the stretch of scorched grass on which he and the
giant stood.

"I saw," Radisovik replied, pale and shaken. "May the
Almin have mercy on us!"

"May He indeed!" Garald muttered, his sarcastic tone drawing a look of concern from the Priest. But there was no time for worrying about faith or the lack of it. Gesturing to the *Duuk-tsarith* who had accompanied him — the other warlock was keeping the giant in hand — Garald began issuing his orders.

"You and Cardinal Radisovik enter the Corridors —"

"My lord! I believe I should stay —" interposed the Cardinal.

" — and return to my headquarters," Garald continued coolly, overriding the Priest's objections. "Use whatever means you must, but get the civilians out of the area. Take them all . . ." He hesitated, then continued with a twisted smile, "even our people, to Merilon. It's the closest city and the magical dome protects it best. I wonder who Xavier left in control?" he muttered. "Probably sent Bishop Vanya back. Well, it can't be helped. Cardinal Radisovik, you must go to the Bishop. Explain what is happening and —"

"Garald!" Radisovik said sternly, his brows coming together in a manner that the Prince had not seen since he was a young boy caught in some misdeed. "I insist that you listen to me!"

"Cardinal, it is *not* for your own safety that I am sending you back! I need you to talk to His Holiness —" Garald began impatiently.

"My lord," interrupted Radisovik, "there are no bodies of catalysts!"

Garald stared at the Priest, uncomprehending. "What?"

"On the field near the Gameboard, on the Field of Glory we have passed over —" Radisovik waved his hand — "there are no bodies of catalysts, milord! You know as well as I that they would never abandon their masters to death, or leave their bodies without the final rites. Yet none of the dead back there near the Board had been given the rites. Where are the bodies if the catalysts are dead? What has happened to them?"

Garald had no answer. Of all the strange things he had seen, this seemed the strangest. It was inexplicable, it made no sense. Yet, what did make sense? Creatures of iron, destroying everything in their path, killing for no reason. Killing everything except catalysts.

"I therefore must insist, milord," continued Radisovik coldly and formally, "that — as a high-ranking member of the Church — I be allowed to stay and do what I can to resolve this mystery and find out what has become of my brethren."

"Very well," Garald said confusedly, trying to grasp the tail-end of his thoughts that had hurried on ahead of him. He turned to the *Duuk-tsarith*. "You . . . explain to Vanya. Merilon needs to be fortified. Send messengers, the Ariels, to the farm settlements and begin transporting the people into the safety of the city's dome. Contact members of your Order in other cities and find out if they are being attacked."

The *Duuk-tsarith* nodded silently, his hands clasped in front of him as was proper, disciplined and under control once more. Perhaps, like Garald, the warlock felt better now that he had something to do.

"The War Masters are to remain until the last possible moment. I'm going to try to convince Xavier to withdraw, to retreat to our lines. You must get word to my father. Tell him what is happening and that Sharakan must be prepared to withstand an assault as well. Although how they will defend themselves against these things . . ." His voice broke. Garald coughed, clearing his throat, angrily shaking his head.

"You have your orders? You understand?" he said gruffly.

"Yes, milord."

"Then go. But first, instruct your companion to lose the giant."

"Yes, milord."

Was it Garald's imagination, or did he actually see the flicker of a smile on the pale face that was barely visible within the depths of the hood. "That should buy me the time I need," the Prince muttered, watching the warlock fly up to his comrade, who was holding the giant in thrall. He saw the black hood nod. "You'd better open a Corridor, Radisovik. When the spell over the giant is broken, we'll need to get out of here quickly."

A Corridor gaped open. The first *Duuk-tsarith* had already disappeared, carrying out the Prince's orders. The second, with a word, released his hold on the giant. Shrieking a deafening cry of rage, the giant stomped around in uncontrolled, undirected fury, his thudding, kicking feet felling trees and shaking the ground. Ducking into the Corridor, the

Prince and the Cardinal waited only for the *Duuk-tsarith* to join them before closing the magical gate and beginning their journey.

"It may take some time, but the creatures of iron will kill the wretched thing. You know that, of course, Garald," Radisovik said gently.

"Yes," said Garald, thinking of the boulder he had seen literally disintegrate before his eyes. The thought hurt him and made him angry, and he didn't quite know why. Though he had never hunted giants for sport, as did some of the nobility, he had never — before now — cared whether they lived or died.

Now he cared, he cared a great deal. He cared for the giant, for the mother, and her dead baby. He cared for the *Sif-Hanar,* lying beneath the Gameboard, he cared for the uprooted trees and the burned grass. He cared for Xavier, for his enemy, standing in the path of these things.

Unbidden, unwillingly, he recalled the words of the Prophecy.

There will be born to the Royal House one who is dead yet will live, who will die again and live again. And when he returns, he will hold in his hand the destruction of the world —

The giant's world, that small baby's world.

His world.

15

No Escape

Sharper than the thorns of the murderous Kij vine, the witch's fingernails dug into Mosiah's flesh. Thrusting him out of the Corridor, she followed immediately after him, never once letting loose her grip on his arm. Simkin appeared inclined to remain in the Corridor, but a piercing glance from the witch—a glance as sharp as her nails—brought the young man tumbling out, still chewing nervously on the orange silk.

"Use it to gag yourself, traitor!" Mosiah snarled.

Gazing at him with wounded eyes, Simkin started to reply, choked, and coughed. Spitting out the orange silk, he gazed ruefully at the sodden mass, then consigned it to the air.

"I say, that hurts," he remarked moodily. "State of national emergency, that sort of thing. What could I do?" he asked with a helpless glance at the witch. "She appealed to my better nature."

"This way!" said the witch, shoving Mosiah forward.

The Corridor had brought them to a large fortress. Made of stone, the fortress had obviously been hastily formed from a natural rock formation standing in the center of the Field of Glory. About ten feet high, the walls straggled over the irregular landscape in a roughly circular shape. It was crowded with people — warlocks, witches, healers, and catalysts. "Windows" shaped into the rock allowed the warlocks to cast spells at their enemy, or they could float up into the air and drop back down, using the walls to shield them instead of wasting their own magic. The walls also protected them from being overrun by centaurs. During the "battle," this fortress would have served the same purpose that a child's sand castle serves in games on the beach. Whichever side held the fortress against the enemy won this particular area of the Gameboard.

Looking at the pale faces, the tight lips, and the clenched jaws of the magi crowded into the fortress, Mosiah knew that now the stakes were much greater: life itself.

There was no need to tell Mosiah what enemy the people waited so grimly to face. He could see curls of smoke rising up into the air. The ground trembled beneath his feet, he could hear in the distance the low humming sound.

"They're coming, aren't they?" he said, the image of the sand castle lingering in his mind . . . washed away beneath relentless waves. "The creatures. What are you going to do?" he demanded of the witch. "Just stay here and die?"

For the first time since she had taken him into the Corridor, the witch looked directly at him. "Stay here and die, go somewhere else and die. What does it matter?" she asked softly, turning from Mosiah to address a warlock in crimson robes who stood with his back toward them. "Your Highness," she said crisply, "I have found the young man, Mosiah."

The warlock was speaking to several other War Masters. At the witch's call, however, he wheeled instantly, his crimson robes with their golden emblems flashing in the bright sun.

At the sight of the man's face, Mosiah felt a swift stab of painful recognition. It was not that the man resembled Joram, for he did not. The face was thinner, older, sharper. But he had the black, glistening hair; the clear, brown eyes;

the proud and elegant grace; the same arrogant tilt to the head.

Joram — the Emperor's son?

If Mosiah had not believed Simkin before, he believed him now. The family resemblance was too strong to deny. Mosiah was looking at the former Prince Xavier, now Emperor of Merilon. Joram's uncle.

Xavier smiled, or rather the thin lips expanded into the mockery of a smile.

"I see you recognize me, young man," he said. "You recognize me because of him, don't you?"

Mosiah could not answer.

"He's returned! I know it!" Xavier nodded wisely, the cold eyes probing Mosiah. "He has come back and brought with him the end of the world! Where is he?" the Emperor demanded suddenly. Stretching out his hand, his clawlike fingers clutched at Mosiah's neck. "Where is he! Answer me or by the gods I'll tear the words out of your heart!"

Shocked, Mosiah could not move. If Simkin had not accidentally blundered into the Emperor, nearly knocking him over, Xavier might well have succeeded in his threat.

"E'gad! Is that you, Highness? Allow me to assist. . . . I say! What a beastly expression! Your face will freeze like that someday, you know. Unhand me, you lout!" This to a *Duuk-tsarith*, who had firmly grasped hold of the bearded young man. "It *wasn't* my fault! Chap over there" — he gestured vaguely — "made the most startling remark. Said we were all going to die horribly. A sudden desire to leave came over me, and I mistook His Highness for a Corridor."

"Get rid of this fool!" Flecks of saliva speckled Xavier's lips.

"I'm going. You needn't spit!" Simkin said loftily, plucking the orange silk from the air and dabbing at his face. "But first, don't waste your time with this peasant." He cast a scathing glance at Mosiah. "Why don't you ask me? I can tell you where Joram is. I've seen him."

Xavier stared at Simkin, the wild light in The DKarn-Duuk's eyes flaring with such intensity that it seemed he might burn the young man to the ground. An explosion shook the compound, causing nearly everyone else to start and glance fearfully to the north. The Emperor did not move.

"What do you mean, you have seen him?" Xavier demanded. "Where is he?"

"He is here," said Simkin imperturbably.

"Fool! I have had enough of your—" The DKarn-Duuk made a furious gesture, and Mosiah froze, expecting to see Simkin burst into flames.

Apparently, Simkin expected much the same thing.

"Not *here* here," he amended hastily. "Near here. Somewhere. I—uh— Pick a card!" he said suddenly, producing a deck of tarok cards out of nowhere. "Any card." He held them to the Emperor, whose eyes narrowed alarmingly. "Here, I'll do it. Don't trouble yourself." Simkin held up a card. "Death." He drew another. "Death again." A third. "Death three times. That's Joram, you see. A Dead man. His wife talks with the dead and he walks with the dead Priest."

Xavier clenched his fist.

"You're right. S-stupid game," stammered Simkin, tossing all the cards into the air. They fell to the ground, fluttering around him like gaudy, multicolored leaves. Looking at them, Mosiah saw that every single card in the deck was Death.

The air was hazy with smoke, the smell of burning strong. The humming noise grew louder.

"Your Highness!" called out several voices. War Masters began crowding around, shouldering forward, vying for The DKarn-Duuk's attention.

"I will deal with these young men, Your Highness," offered the witch.

"Swiftly!" said Xavier, fist clenched. His dark-eyed gaze going once again to Mosiah, it stayed with him to the last, when the Emperor finally turned his attention to his ministers.

"I don't know anything about Joram!" Mosiah cried desperately. "You can do what you like to me," he continued, the witch's penetrating gaze staring through his eyes, searching his brain. "I haven't seen him."

"But you know he has returned."

Another explosion shook the ground. Mosiah glanced around fearfully.

"I—I don't know!"

"Of course he's returned!" Simkin stated, exasperated. "I've seen him, I tell you! No one believes me," he continued, sniffing in wounded dignity. "And if you think I'm going to hang around here and die in the company of people who consider me a liar, you have another think coming. No, don't apologize. I find this deadly dull. You will, I'm afraid, simply find it deadly. And therefore I am away."

Gazing at Mosiah, Simkin suddenly burst into tears.

"Farewell, friend of my childhood!" He flung his arms around Mosiah, hugging him close, nearly choking him. "We who are about to flee to a place of safety salute you. Go forth bravely, my son! Come back with your shield or on it!" Simkin raised his hand, the orange silk fluttered wildly in the air. "Once more into our breeches, dear friends, once more!" he cried gallantly.

There was a flurry of orange silk, and Simkin was gone.

"So he's telling the truth." It was not a question. The witch, staring thoughtfully and absently at the place where the young man had been standing, was obviously pondering Simkin's words.

"The truth? Simkin?" Mosiah started to laugh, but it caught in his throat.

A shattering explosion hit the fortress wall, sending sharp fragments of rock skimming through the air. People cried out in fear or pain or both.

"They're coming! We're trapped!" someone yelled, and the crowd began to rush about aimlessly, like mice in a box. Those near the site of the explosion fled to the rear of the fortress. Those who had been standing near the rear wall surged forward to see what was going on. The few *Theldara* in the compound hastened to aid the injured. The War Masters were all yelling at once, Emperor Xavier shouting back at them.

"That can't be the creatures! They're too far away!"

"Besides they're blind. . . ."

"No, they're not! Why I saw one. . . ."

It was all noise and confusion. The witch was gone; Mosiah had no idea where, but he thought he caught a glimpse of her, flying up over the wall to investigate. Standing in the center of the compound, feeling frightened and alone, Mosiah cursed Simkin for getting him here, then leaving him. But the curse was halfhearted.

"I might still be out *there*," he muttered, shuddering. Another explosion rocked the stone work. People cried out in pain and terror; the confusion within the compound became general. "Trapped!" He felt suffocated. Suddenly, he *wanted* to be out there, anywhere but trapped inside these walls, waiting to die.

Looking around wildly, searching for a way out, Mosiah's gaze chanced on Xavier, who stood nearby with his War Masters. Mosiah stopped, staring. A change had come over the warlock. Having been in a state of near frenzy when demanding to know the whereabouts of Joram, now Xavier stood calmly, his face pale but composed. He was listening to his ministers who, as nearly as Mosiah could figure out from the snatches of heated conversation he overheard, were arguing about the most effective means of destroying the creatures.

"It kills with its eyes, like the basilisk, Your Highness," argued one. "So we attack it the same way. One distracts it from the front and the other attacks the creature from the rear. A Sleeping Death spell—"

"Begging your pardon, Highness, but it is the light beam cast *from* the eyes of the creature that kills. A simple Darkness spell and—"

"Reptile. The creature is obviously a reptile, Your Highness. It has scales like a dragon. Freeze its blood with an Ice spell."

It is hopeless, Mosiah told them silently. I've seen them. I've seen the head that can turn in all directions. I've seen the scales and they are made of iron. I've seen the Dead men with silver skin who serve these monsters, men who can kill with the palms of their hands.

Watching the Emperor, Mosiah realized suddenly that Xavier thought the same thing. The DKarn-Duuk was listening to the arguments but with a singular air of detachment, his mouth twisted in a wry, bitter smile, as though he found the warlocks entertaining but nothing more. His eyes were flat, empty, uncaring. He did not react to anything around him. A nearby explosion that caused everyone standing around him to fling up their arms, shielding their faces, did not affect him at all. Xavier didn't even blink.

There came another explosion, then another. Beams of light from the monster's eyes shot into the compound, striking their victims with unerring accuracy. There seemed to be no escape from death, no way to avoid it. Those who flung themselves on the ground died. Those who sprang into the air died. No one knew where the deadly light would strike next. The beams never missed. A druid standing near the wall crumpled over without a sound, a hole burned through his head. An Ariel who had been watching from the skies crashed to the ground almost at the young man's feet, his feathery wings on fire.

Those watching from the walls cried that the creatures were in sight, others shouted that a giant could be seen walking among them. Judging from sporadic bursts of lightning and flame, a few warlocks had rallied together, attempting to halt the monsters' approach.

"I should be doing something," Mosiah said to himself, but he had no idea what. He had no weapon, he'd lost the crossbow. Not that it would have been much use anyway. Mosiah felt despair envelop him in its winding sheets, wrapping him up tightly, depriving him even of the will to live.

"Go!" said Xavier suddenly, and Mosiah heard his despair echoed in the Emperor's voice.

"Go," Xavier ordered his War Masters, accompanying the command with a nonchalant wave of his hand. "Cast your worthless spells. Die in whatever manner amuses you."

Stunned — he had caught most of them in midargument — the War Masters swallowed their words, staring at their Emperor in disbelief. Xavier gestured again, a frown of irritation creasing his brow.

The War Masters turned to gaze at each other in helpless confusion and growing fear when a clear baritone voice rang out, shouting over the wails of the dying, the cracking of rock, and the low hum of the approaching monsters.

"Emperor Xavier!"

The Emperor turned, so did Mosiah, so did everyone in the compound. Prince Garald, Cardinal Radisovik, and a warlock in black robes appeared, stepping out of a Corridor. The appearance of the Prince — their enemy — sent a ripple of confusion and interest through the crowd, momentarily quelling the panic. A tiny flicker of light glimmered through Mosiah's dark despair and he hurried forward with the rest, anxious to hear. The *Duuk-tsarith* acted immediately to keep an area around the Emperor clear. Xavier and Garald faced each other, surrounded by an ever growing circle of tense, strained faces.

"So you have come crawling to me at last, Prince of Sorcerers!" Xavier said. "Is this surrender?"

This unexpected question took Garald completely by surprise. He stared at the Emperor, perplexed. "Do you have any idea what is heading your way, Xavier?" the Prince asked in a low voice. Glancing at the crowd, he drew nearer to the Emperor. "We must speak privately."

Xavier stepped back, haughtily drawing his robes out of the way of Garald's touch. "Say what you have to say, Demon Prince, then be gone."

Mosiah, pressing close with the rest of the crowd, saw Garald's face flush in anger and the Cardinal lay a restraining hand on the Prince's arm.

"Very well," Garald said, his lips tightening grimly, and a hush fell over those standing near; a hush broken by blasts of exploding rock or the screams of the injured. "I asked to talk to you alone, Xavier, because I did not want to start a stampede."

Glancing at those standing near, the Prince continued gravely, "But your people are too well trained for that. You've got to evacuate this position, Emperor, and you must do so now!"

Xavier shook his head. "This is your fault, you know," he said softly. Folding his arms across his chest, he stared at the Prince with flat, cold eyes. "You had him, and you let him go."

"Let who go? What are you talking about?" Garald demanded in apparent confusion, though it was obvious to Mosiah that the Prince knew exactly what Xavier meant.

"Joram, of course. Now you pay the piper."

"Joram! Have you gone mad? Joram is dead!"

Mosiah heard the slight tremor in Garald's voice as he spoke those last words, and undoubtedly The DKarn-Duuk did too, for he smiled bitterly and, shrugging, turned away.

Exasperated by the man's coolness, Garald glared at the warlock's back in anger and frustration. The ground shook. Every few minutes, someone else died in the compound as the deadly eyes of the monsters pierced another victim. The Prince pointed toward the north.

"Xavier, listen! There are twenty or thirty of those monsters coming straight for this place! You don't stand a chance! You've got to get your people out of here!"

The magi stared at each other. Mosiah sucked in his breath, trying to visualize thirty of the iron creatures.

"You can't fight them!" Garald shouted, and his cry echoed among the crowd.

"We can't fight them! We must flee!"

"Open the Corridors!"

The panic Garald had feared burst into flame, its fires fed by the flashing beams of killing light. Mosiah, like everyone around him, had one clear, coherent thought in his mind: "Escape!" When a Corridor opened near him, he dove for it, fighting anyone who stood in his way. The magi turned on each other, fear driving them mad as they struggled to reach the safety of the Corridors, which only a few could enter at one time.

An enraged shriek rose above the clamor.

"Stop!" Xavier screamed in fury. "Seal the Corridors, you *Thon-li*! Do you hear me? Seal the Corridors by my command! No one is to leave!"

Mosiah caught a quick glimpse of several pale catalysts, peering out from the magical Corridors. Their eyes wide and frightened, the *Thon-li* obeyed the Emperor instantly. The gaping Corridors slammed shut, leaving people stranded in the compound, wailing frantically, some even scrabbling at the empty air with their fingers, endeavoring to force the Corridors back open. Others stood as Mosiah stood — numb, appalled.

"You're insane, Xavier!" Garald cried. Breaking free of the restraining hands of the Cardinal, the Prince lunged at the Emperor — whether with the intention of shaking sense into him or choking the life out of him, no one knew, perhaps not even the Prince himself.

Xavier, watching him with a sneer, raised his hand, and Garald slammed up against a wall of ice. Dazed, the Prince staggered backward, the Cardinal hurrying to help him.

"Why do you run, fools?" Xavier shouted and his voice — amplified by magic — rose above the chaos. "Why put it off? Die quickly, here and now. This is the end of the world!" Extending his crimson robed arms, he slowly turned a full circle within his cold, glistening barrier. His eyes stared up into the heavens. "The Prophecy is fulfilled!"

"No, uncle," came a voice in answer. "The Prophecy is not fulfilled. I have come to stop it."

16

The Destruction Of The World

Once, when Garald was young, he had been caught in an open field during a weather fight between rival groups of *Sif-Hanar*. A lightning bolt struck near him; so close that Garald smelled it sizzle on the air. He could still remember quite clearly the dazzling, paralyzing thrill surging through him, the concussion of thunder that slammed into him a split second after, knocking the very breath from his body.

"The Prophecy is not fulfilled. I have come to stop it."

The voice that spoke those words had the effect of that lightning bolt on him. Its rich timbre — familiar, yet different — sent a thrill through him that tingled in his blood; his entire being seemed to glow with a dreadful, powerful aura.

"Joram!" he cried, turning.

As the voice was familiar — yet wasn't — so Garald recognized the man who stood before him — yet didn't.

Thick, luxuriant black hair glistened in the sunlight. Garald remembered that hair, falling in long, tangled curls around the face of an eighteen-year-old youth. But now the black curls were cut short, worn shoulder-length, combed smooth and sleek. A shock of pure white hair sprang from the brow, framing the left side of the man's face.

The face itself was familiar in its dark, finely carved beauty. But here and there the Master Hand wielding the chisel had slipped, marring the visage with lines of grief, age, and a strange, undefinable sorrow. The man's face was so changed, in fact, that if it hadn't been for the eyes, Garald would have doubted his first impression. But he knew those eyes. The eyes were Joram's. Garald could see the fire of the forge smolder in them still—glowing coals of pride, bitterness, and anger.

Prince Garald recognized something else as well—the scabbard the man wore strapped about his body; the scabbard that had been a present, his present to Joram. Carried in that scabbard, Garald knew, was the Darksword.

"Joram?" the Prince repeated softly, staring at the man dressed in plain, white robes who stood in the center of the compound.

Cardinal Radisovik fell to his knees.

"Yes, Cardinal," Xavier sneered. "Pray to the Almin for His mercy. The Prophecy is fulfilled. The end of the world is come." With a wave of his hand, he dispelled the ice shield around him, then, striding ahead, he pointed his finger at the man. "And this demon brings it! Kill him! Kill—"

A flash of blinding light, and the Emperor's words broke off in a horrible, gurgling sound. Through an afterimage of red streaking across his vision, Garald saw The DKarn-Duuk pitch forward onto his face, felled like a lightning-struck tree.

Stunned, shocked, no one dared move or speak.

One of the *Duuk-tsarith*, coming to her senses, knelt swiftly beside her Emperor. Turning over the body, she started to call for the *Theldara*. The words died on her lips.

A charred and blackened hole—a horrible mockery of what had once been the man's mouth—was burned completely through the skull. Hurriedly the witch covered the gruesome wound, drawing the red hood of Xavier's robe over what was left of the face.

But it was too late. Those who had seen the ghastly sight began to mill around in a frenzy of terror, some dropping to the ground, others flying up into the air, still others shrieking for the Corridors to open. The Emperor's last words—"the end of the world"—were being cried out in an anthem of hopelessness and despair.

Xavier's bodyguards sprang toward the white-robed man. Reaching behind his back, he drew the Darksword and held it before him. The weapon began to glow with a blue light.

"Stop!" Garald cried out. The warlocks reluctantly halted. The Prince stared at the corpse, then looked back at the man holding the blue-flaming sword.

"Listen to me!" the man said, his eyes intent upon the menacing *Duuk-tsarith*. "You will all be dead, just like my uncle, unless you act at once." Holding the sword poised between himself and the *Duuk-tsarith*, he took a step nearer the Prince.

"Don't come any closer!" Garald cried out, raising his hand as though to ward off a spirit from the grave. "Was Xavier right? Are you a demon? Did you bring this destruction down upon us?"

"You brought it on yourselves," the man answered grimly.

Reaching out suddenly with his left hand, he grasped hold of Garald's arm. The Prince gasped, flinching at the touch, and the *Duuk-tsarith* instantly closed on the man. His sword flared, and they halted again uncertainly. They could feel the magic-absorbing Darksword draining the Life, their magical powers seeping out of them.

The man squeezed the Prince's arm tightly, painfully. "I am flesh and blood! I have been Beyond and I have returned. I know this enemy and how to fight it! You must listen to me and follow my orders or this *will* be the end, as my uncle said!"

Garald stared at the hand clutching his arm, doubting his senses, yet knowing he felt the touch of a living person. "Where have you come from?" he asked in a hollow voice. "Who is this enemy? Who are you?"

"There is no time for questions!" the man cried impatiently. "The giant has stopped the tanks for the moment, but the wretched thing is dead now and the enemy is moving swiftly. Within minutes, there will be no one left alive in this fortress!" Suddenly, he thrust the Darksword back into its sheath. "Look," he said, spreading his arms wide, "I am unarmed—your prisoner, if you choose."

As the *Duuk-tsarith* sprang forward, a blast shook the ground.

"The stone wall is breached!" someone shouted. "We can see them! They are coming."

"Death crawls. . . ." Garald murmured.

Tears of frustration and anger and fear blurred the vision of the corpse lying at his feet. Confused, shaken, horrified, scared, he put his hand to his eyes to hide them, cursing himself for his weakness, knowing he must not give way. Another explosion rocked the fortress. The people cried out to the Prince, begging him to save them. But how could he? He was as lost and desperate as they. . . .

Near him, he could hear the Cardinal, praying to the Almin. Was this Joram? Was·this salvation or destruction?

Did it matter. . . .

"Let him go!" he ordered the warlocks finally. Drawing a deep breath, he turned to face the white-robed man. "Very well, I will listen to you, whoever you are," he said harshly. "What do *you* say we should do?"

"Gather the magi and their catalysts together. No, Cardinal, there is no time for that," the man said to Radisovik, who looked up from where he was kneeling beside the Emperor's body. "The living need you now, not the dead. It will take you and all of the catalysts to grant the magi Life enough to cast this spell. We must build a wall of ice around this entire complex, and we must do it without expending all of our magical energy."

"Ice?" Garald stared at him incredulously. "I've seen those creatures shatter rock with their light beams! Ice—"

"Do as I say!" the man commanded, his fist clenched, the imperious, arrogant voice ringing like a hammer blow through the chaos around him. Then, suddenly, the stern face relaxed. "Do as I say, *Your Grace*," he amended, a dark half-smile twisting his lips.

A vision came to Garald, a vision from long ago, himself and an arrogant, hot-tempered youth. . . .

"Fine words!" Joram retorted. "But you're quick enough to lap up 'Your Grace' and 'Your Highness!' I don't see you

dressed in the coarse robes of the Field Magi. I don't see you rising at dawn and spending your days grubbing in the fields until your very soul starts to shrivel like the weeds you touch!" He pointed at the Prince. "You're a wonderful talker! You and your fancy clothes and bright swords, silk tents and bodyguards! I—" Choking on his anger, Joram turned and began to walk away.

Garald caught hold of him by the shoulder, spinning him around with his strong hand. Joram shook free, his face distorted by rage, and struck back, swinging his fist wildly. The Prince countered the blow with ease, catching it on his forearm and, with practiced skill, forced the young man to his knees on the ground. Joram struggled to rise.

"I can keep you here with a spoken word of magic!" Garald hissed, his arms holding the young man in a strong grip.

"Damn you, you—!" Joram swore, spitting filth. "You and your magic! If I had my sword, I'd—" He looked around for it, feverishly.

"I'll give you your sword," the Prince said grimly. "Then you can do what you will. But first, you will listen to me. More important, you will listen to the voice of your own soul! It is true that in order to do my work in this life, I must dress and act in a manner befitting my station. Yes, I wear fancy clothes and bathe and comb my hair, and I'm going to see to it that you do these things, too, before you go to Merilon. Otherwise you will be laughed out of the city. Why? Because, unfortunately, people judge by appearance. As for my title, people call me 'milord' and 'Your Grace' as a mark of respect for my station. But I hope it is a remark of respect for me as a person as well. Why do you think I don't force you to do it? Because it is empty for you. You don't respect anybody, Joram. You don't care for anybody. Least of all yourself! . . ."

"My god!" Garald whispered. "It can't be! It can't. . . ."

"You *are* Joram!" Mosiah shoved his way through the crowd, staring at the white-robed figure with wide eyes. "For once, Simkin was telling the truth! It *must* be the end of the world," he muttered.

"Trust me, Your Grace. Give the order!" the man urged.

Garald tried to study the man's face, but he found it too painful and unnerving to look at for long. Averting his gaze, he glanced at the pale and shaken Mosiah, then silently interrogated the Cardinal, who could only shrug and raise his eyes heavenward.

Faith in the Almin? Well and good, but what he needed was faith in himself, in his instincts.

"Very well," Garald said suddenly, with a sigh. "Mosiah, spread the word. We are going to encompass this fortress in a wall of ice."

Mosiah hesitated one last moment to look at the man — who was regarding him with an expression of sadness and regret — then he dazedly stumbled off to carry out his orders.

But it seemed it might be too late. The magi — even the well-disciplined members of the *Duuk-tsarith* and The DKarn-Duuk — appeared too disorganized to come together. Those who had not succumbed to panic were acting on their own, fighting as they'd been taught to fight. Floating above the wall, they were casting balls of flame at the creatures. The fire had no effect on the iron scales of the monsters. It did nothing except call attention to the warlocks themselves. The blind eyes turned in their direction, the beams flared, and the magi fluttered to the ground like dead leaves.

Others were working frantically, trying to repair the breach in the stone wall. Summoning the rock up from the earth, they hastily shaped it to fit the hole. But the creatures of iron blew apart sections of wall faster then the magi could shape it, and soon those standing near the wall fled before the coming of the humming, foul-breathed monsters.

One person acted on Garald's instructions. Having been the one who captured Joram in the Grove of Merlyn, the witch — head of the Order of *Duuk-tsarith* — recognized him immediately. When Joram put away the Darksword, the witch was able, by using the mind-searching skills of her kind, to probe the man's mind. Though the witch understood little of what she saw there, she learned enough about the creatures in the brief span of time she shared Joram's thoughts to comprehend his plan.

Moving through the crowd, speaking calmly and forcefully, the witch gathered around her the members of the *Duuk-tsarith* and any others who were standing nearby. All the magi obeyed her without question; some because they were accustomed to doing her bidding, most because she was authority, a focal point of reality in a horrifying nightdream.

The witch organized the catalysts and, mumbling their prayers, the Priests drew the Life from the world around them, sending it arcing into the bodies of the warlocks, the witches, the wizards, even those few sorcerers who, like Mosiah, had strayed here from their disbanded or destroyed units. Concentrating their thoughts upon a single spell, the magi caused a wall of ice to rise, shimmering, into the air, completely surrounding the fortress.

Almost instantly, the lethal beams of light ceased. The killing stopped.

The wizards stared in amazement. The frosty breath of the ice was visible in the warm air. Swirling about the feet of the magi, it cooled their fevered blood, bringing calm and order where there had been only moments before panic and chaos. Silence fell upon the crowd inside the fortress, as they blinked, half-blinded, at the ice wall gleaming in the sunlight.

A light beam shot through the ice, but it was aimless, directionless. The creatures had no targets now, apparently, and though they continued to fire the light at the ice, most of the beams passed harmlessly through empty air.

"It worked," said Garald, mystified. "But . . . how? Why?"

"The tanks — the 'creatures' as you call them — kill by focusing their laser weapons — their 'eye' — on anything that moves or gives off heat," the white-robed man replied. "Using that, they lock onto their targets. Now they can no longer sense the body heat of those in the fortress."

Shading his eyes against the glare of the reflected sunlight, the Prince peered through the ice at the creatures.

"So we are safe." He let out his breath in a sigh.

"Only for the moment," the man said grimly. "This will not stop them, Your Grace. It will merely slow them down."

"It will give us time enough to contact the *Thon-li* and force them to open the Corridors again," Garald stated briskly. "You have saved us! We will begin the retreat —"

"No, Your Grace." The man caught hold of Garald's torn, bloodstained shirt as the Prince was starting to move away.

"You cannot retreat, not yet. You must fight. My uncle was right about one thing, there is no escape, nowhere to run. If you don't stop them here, they will take over the world."

"Fight them? How? It is impossible!"

Garald's gaze returned to the creatures. Evidently at a loss for coping with this new and unexpected situation, several of the iron monsters had come together and were focusing their light beams on the ice, intent on melting it away. This had little effect — the magi simply used their magic to replace it. Other creatures kept up random firing, occasionally cutting down a victim but generally doing little harm. The shining bodies of the strange humans could be seen moving among the creatures now, keeping close to them as if for protection.

But Garald knew his people couldn't maintain their defense for long. Already, the magi were growing weak, the Life needed to keep the huge wall of ice in existence was slowly being drained off. When their strength gave out, they would be at the mercy of the creatures of iron and the metal-skinned humans.

"Our magic is helpless against them!" Garald persisted. "You've seen that —"

"Only because you do not know them, Your Grace!" the man interrupted impatiently. "You don't know how to fight them!"

"Then you must tell me what is going on! I need to know before I can make this decision."

The man clenched his fist in frustration, and Garald was strongly reminded of the impatient, arrogant youth. The man checked himself, however, swallowing hot words. Fighting some internal battle for control, he rubbed his fingers over the leather that crisscrossed his chest, perhaps feeling a soothing comfort in the touch. When he spoke, his voice was calm.

"Look into my face."

Reluctantly, the Prince did as he was asked. Staring into the face that he knew yet didn't know, he realized that he had been avoiding looking at this man, avoiding dealing with the inexplicable, fearful change.

"Who am I? Say my name."

Garald tried to withdraw his gaze, but the brown eyes held him fast. "Joram," he said at last, reluctantly. "You are Joram," he repeated again.

"How long is it since I left this world?" Joram asked softly.

"A year," Garald faltered.

Reality struck a telling blow. He was forced to confront the fact that only a few hundred days before he had walked in the wilderness with a youth. Now he faced a man as old or older than himself.

"I don't understand!" he cried, frightened.

"*Ten* years have passed for me," answered Joram. "There is not time enough for me to explain everything. If I do not survive this battle, seek out Father Saryon, who is in Merilon. I have left in his keeping a record of my life. What I am going to tell you now you must accept on faith. If not faith in the thankless boy you knew and helped"— Joram paused, sighing—"then faith in what I thought would be my final act: the renunciation of this sword I created, the voluntary walk into death."

Joram's face was anguished as he spoke; the hand closed over the leather straps, pressing them into his heart.

Garald recalled all that he had heard of the final, terrible day in Joram's life on this world, and his last suspicions vanished. He tried to say something to this effect, but the words would not come. Joram saw and understood, removing the need for words by reaching out and grasping hold of the Prince's hand.

"I walked into what I thought was death, but there is not death Beyond, Your Grace," Joram continued quietly. "There is life! In our conceit, we imagined ourselves safe, protected from the rest of the universe by our magical Border. When we left the ancient world to come to this one, we thought—we hoped—the Old World would forget us as we forgot them."

Joram looked away, staring beyond the wall of ice into realms that had been revealed to his eyes alone. "They did not forget," he said softly. "They missed the magic and they searched for it, knowing that somewhere it still lived." Joram smiled, but it was a dark smile and it sent a shiver through Garald. "I said before that there was not death Beyond. I was wrong. Actually, there is nothing out there *except* Death. Those worlds that lie Beyond are populated by the Dead. Some Life, some magic exists, but it is scattered throughout the universe like atoms in deep space."

"Atoms . . . deep space." The words were strange, meaningless. Garald's gaze turned, like Joram's, to the heavens. His confusion was not dispelled, but rather was growing, as was his fear. The ancient world, the world they had fled in terror, was searching for them? He almost expected to see faces leering at him from the cloudless sky.

"I am sorry. I know you don't understand." Joram's gaze returned to Garald and it was pleading in its intensity. "What can I say?" He gripped the Prince's hand harder, as though he could communicate through touch what he was failing to communicate with words. "They — the Dead, if you will —" there was a bitter irony in Joram's voice that made Garald wince — "call this an 'expeditionary' force. It has been sent to investigate this world, to conquer and subdue it, and prepare the way for occupation."

"What?" Gerald repeated, stunned. Conquer, subdue, occupation: these were words he knew, he understood. He forced himself to attend, urging his brain to let loose of its grasp of what he had known this morning as reality. "You say, *they* — the Dead" — he stumbled over the word, his mind still stubbornly disbelieving, although all he had to do was look out beyond the wall of ice to see the evidence of his senses — "want to conquer us? Why? What then?"

Removing his hand from that of his friend, Joram thrust it in the sleeves of his robes. The temperature inside the ice-bound fortress was gradually falling, growing colder and colder.

"They plan to destroy the barriers, release the magic back into the universe," he replied. "They will take you prisoner and carry you back to their worlds."

"But if such is their object," argued Garald, with the strange sensation that he was debating a point in a meaningless dream, "why are they killing everyone they encounter, including civilians?" He gestured. "They're not taking prisoners! Or, if they are," he added, remembering Radisovik's observation, "they're only taking catalysts!"

"Are they?" Joram appeared startled, his gaze shifting swiftly to Garald.

"Yes! I saw — the nobles, their wives, their children, riding in their glittering carriages, coming with their wine and their lunches to watch a game. These creatures murdered them!" Once again, Garald was turning over that body, seeing the grinning face of the skeleton. "Is this how they fight in Beyond?" he demanded angrily. "Do they slaughter the helpless?"

"No," said Joram, appearing grave and troubled. "They are not savage like the centaur. They do not love to kill. They are soldiers. They have rules of warfare, handed down through centuries. I don't understand. They wanted prisoners." He paused, his face darkened. "Unless. . . ." He did not continue.

Garald shook his head. "Make some sense of it for me, Joram."

"I wish I could!" It was a murmur, spoken almost to himself. "I thought I knew them. Yet I have proof now that they betrayed me. Are they capable of more . . . ?"

Garald looked at him intently, hearing again the old, familiar bitterness in Joram's tone and now something else as well — an echo of pain and loss.

"All the more reason we must fight them," Joram said suddenly, his voice as cold as the chill breath blowing from the ice wall. "We must show them that they will not take this world as easily as they anticipated. We must make them fear us so that when they leave they will never return."

"But what will be our weapons?" Garald asked helplessly. "Ice?"

"Ice, fire, air. The magic, my friend," Joram said. "Life — Life will be our weapon . . . and Death."

Reaching behind him, he drew the Darksword from its scabbard. "Long years have passed since I made this. Yet I've often dreamed of that night — the night in the blacksmith's when I forged the metal and Saryon gave it Life." Joram turned the sword, studying it. His man's hand fit it better than had the boy's, but it was still heavy and awkward and unbalanced, difficult to wield. "Do you remember?" he asked Garald, the half-smile touching his lips, "the day we met? When I attacked you in the glade? You said this sword was the ugliest of its kind you had ever seen."

Joram's gaze went to the sword the Prince wore at his side. The sun sparkled off the ornately carved hilt of shining silver. By contrast, it did not even flicker in the beaten metal of the Darksword. He sighed.

"Though I didn't know about the Prophecy, I knew I was bringing something evil into the world with this sword. Saryon knew it — he warned me to destroy it, before it destroyed me. I've thought about it since then, and I've come to understand that I wasn't the one who brought the evil into the world with the sword." He gazed down upon the weapon, running his fingers over the crude, misshapen hilt. "The sword *is* the evil in the world."

"Then why keep it?" Garald glanced at it, shuddering.

"Because, like any sword, it cuts two ways," Joram replied. "Now, the Almin willing, I can use it to save us. Will you fight, Your Grace?"

Still the Prince hesitated. "Why are you doing this for us, Joram? If, as you say, we brought this fate upon ourselves, why do you care? After what we did to you —"

"You call me Dead! . . ." Joram murmured, repeating the last words he had said before he walked into Beyond. "But it is you who have died. It is this world that is dead."

He stared at the sword, dark and unlovely in his hand.

"I was gone ten years. I came back, hoping to find the world changed, intending to —" He stopped abruptly, scowling. "But never mind that. It isn't important now. Suffice it to say that I returned to find that you — this world — had *not* changed. In an effort to gain power, you had tortured and tormented a helpless being. I abandoned my project, my hopes, and walked the land in bitterness, seeing everywhere the signs of tyranny, injustice.

"In my anger, I planned to return to Beyond when I discovered that it, too, had betrayed me." The dark half-smile twisted his lip. "I had no world, it seemed. I was willing to leave you, all of you" — his bitter glance included the creatures of iron attacking the wall of ice — "to your fate, little caring whether either of you won or lost.

"Then a man, a very wise man, reminded me of something I had forgotten. 'It is easier to hate than to love.'" Joram fell silent, his gaze going to the sparkling wall of ice, to the trees, the surrounding hills, the blue sky, the fiery sun. "I realized that this world is my home. These people are my people. And therefore I cannot speak of it in the second person. I say 'you' tormented Saryon, but I should say 'I' tormented that good man. Had it not been for me, he would not have suffered."

Absently, Joram ran his fingers through his dark, tangled hair. "And there is one other reason," he said, an inexpressible sadness shadowing his face. "Not a day passed during those ten years in another world that I didn't dream of the beauty of Merilon."

He looked quizzically at Garald. "It is easier to hate than to love. I've never done anything the easy way. Do we fight for this world . . . Your Grace?"

"We fight," said the Prince. "And call me Garald," he added with a wry smile. "I still hear those words 'Your Grace' stick in your throat."

17

The Angel Of Death

They said afterward — those that survived — that they were led into battle by the Angel of Death.

Confused rumors about Joram began to spread among the magi fighting for their lives inside the fortress of stone and ice. Few knew his true history — Mosiah, Garald, Radisovik, and the witch. Many more knew fragments of it, however, and it was these fragments that were hastily whispered to companions during the brief lull in the battle following the raising of the ice wall. Emperor Xavier had said enough prior to his death to enable people to piece these fragments together as they might have a broken stone statue. Unfortunately, it was like putting together a statue that they had never seen whole in the first place.

Several of the catalysts fighting in the fortress had been present at the Judgment of Joram. Those who had been standing near Prince Garald heard him pronounce that name, and they remembered it. Xavier's words, *The Prophecy is fulfilled. The end of the world is come,* were repeated in hushed tones, as was each catalyst's version of what had occurred that dreadful day on the beach when they had all witnessed this man — this Joram — step into Beyond.

"He is Dead. . . ."

"He carries a sword of darkness that sucks the life out of its victims. . . ."

"He murdered countless numbers, but only the wicked, or so I heard. He was falsely accused and now he has come back from the dead to seek his revenge. . . ."

"Xavier fell at his feet! You saw it! What more proof do you want? The old Emperor dropped out of sight opportunely for The DKarn-Duuk, didn't he? What does it matter who hears me now? Xavier's dead now and I'll wager *he* won't come back. . . ."

"The Prophecy? I heard a tale once that had to do with a Prophecy, something about the old wizard, Merlyn, and a king with a shining sword that would come back to his land and save them in their hour of need. . . ."

A sword Joram bore, but it did not shine. When he called for battle and the people gathered around him, it seemed to those watching that he held a fragment of the night in his hands. His face was dark and unyielding as the metal of the weapon he carried. There was no call to glory in his words or the grim tone in which they were spoken.

"This will not be a day celebrated in legend and song. If we fail, there will be no more songs. . . ."

He was dressed in the white robes of those who escort the dead to their final rest — the white robes of a pallbearer. The magi and the catalysts who heard his words that day knew that they went forward without hope, even as he had gone forward into Beyond.

"You are fighting an enemy who is not of this world. You are fighting an enemy who is Dead, an enemy who can deal death with the swiftness of a lightning bolt. Your only advantage is your Life. Use it wisely, for when it is gone you will be at their mercy."

When Joram's voice ceased, there were no cheers. Silence shrouded the magi, silence broken only by the hissing of the light beams cutting through the ice and the fearsome rumblings of the creatures of iron. When the magi went forth into battle, they went in silence.

According to Joram's orders, the wall of ice came down. Spells had to be cast, and the wall was draining the Life from the magi and their catalysts. Each warlock, witch, and wizard from that point on was responsible for his or her own means of protection from the deadly light beams.

Acting on Joram's advice, some became invisible. Though this would not protect them from death should a beam strike them, he said, they were not obvious targets and they could sneak up upon the enemy unobserved. Others protected themselves from the heat-seeking "eyes" of the monsters by surrounding themselves with their own ice walls or causing their body temperatures to drop drastically. Still others turned themselves into were-animals, fearsome beasts who attacked their prey before the victims knew what was upon them.

As in the ancient days, catalysts were changed into familiars — small animals who traveled with the magi, able to hide easily in bushes or the limbs of trees or beneath rocks.

Using the Corridors that Prince Garald forced the *Thon-li* to open, the magi took the field, dividing up, spreading out, fighting in small groups. There had not been time to plan complex strategy. Joram ordered hit-and-run tactics designed to confuse the enemy and keep him off-guard. Once on the field of battle, he and Prince Garald traveled the Corridors, going from group to group, advising them on the best means of fighting.

Joram showed the *Duuk-tsarith* how to cast lightning so that it would kill the creatures of iron, not strike their iron scales harmlessly as it had done before.

"See that part of the creature where the head is attached to the body? Like the soft underbelly of the dragon, that is the place where it is most vulnerable. Cast the lightning bolts there, not against the scales."

The warlocks did so and were astounded to see the creatures of iron explode, catch fire, and burn.

"Use the Green Venom spell," Joram counseled the witch. "The creatures have a vulnerable spot on top of their heads. Cover that with the poisonous liquid and watch."

Though this seemed absurd — after all, the poison affected living flesh, not metal — the witch did as she was ordered. A gesture of her delicate hand caused the green, burning liquid to coat the top of the creature of iron as it would coat the skin of a human victim. To her amazement, the witch saw the head of the creature burst open. Screaming in pain, the strange humans flung themselves out of it, their skin covered with the green poison that had apparently seeped through the top of the creature's head, dripping on the humans concealed inside.

At Joram's command, the druids sent the forest into battle. Giant oak trees with the strength born of centuries heaved themselves from the ground and lumbered forward to the attack. Catching one of the creatures of iron, their huge roots wrapped around it, cracking it like one of their own acorns. The stone shapers caused the ground to gape beneath the iron monsters, swallow them whole, then close over them, burying their enemy inside. The *Sif-Hanar* called down rain and hail upon their enemy, plunged him into night, then blinded him with daylight.

"When you fight the metal-skinned humans, remember that the metal is not skin," Joram told his people. "It is a type of armor, such as that worn by the knights in the old House Magi tales. There are gaps in this armor — the largest between the neck and the helmet."

Mosiah, changing into a werewolf, knocked a strange human to the ground and sank his sharp teeth into the unprotected throat. With one blow of a massive paw, a werebear caved in a helmet. A were-tiger dug her claws through the silver skin, shredding and mauling.

"These humans know little of magic. They are frightened of it. Use their fear against them, particularly their subconscious fears, which are similar to our own," Joram instructed.

Illusionists created gigantic tarantulas that dropped down out of the trees, their hairy legs twitching, their many-faceted red eyes burning like flame. Blades of grass turned into swaying, hissing cobras. Skeletons clutching pale swords in their bony hands rose up out of the ground.

"Call upon the creatures of *our* world to come to our aid."

A force of centaurs was summoned. Consumed by the wild excitement of bloodlust, they attacked and killed the strange humans, then rent the bodies limb from limb and began feasting on their victims' raw, mangled flesh.

Dragons swooped down out of the skies, bringing with them flame and darkness. Basilisks and cockatrice used their own lethal stares to freeze the deadly eyes of the creatures of iron. The serpentlike tail of a chimera swept the strange humans to destruction. The snapping heads of the hydra caught up its victims and devoured them whole.

Perhaps the oddest happening on the field of battle that day was the report by several wizards of seeing a ring of mushrooms suddenly appear in a glade. A band of the enemy, charging into the ring, found that they could not get out. One by one, the strange humans were sucked down into the ground. The wizards reported, not without a shudder, that the last sounds that could be heard were the raucous laughter and gibbering voices of the faeriefolk. . . .

When their attack began in the morning, the creatures of iron must have been certain of victory. By late afternoon, the magi had turned the tide. But they had not managed to stop the flood. The iron monsters kept coming, the armies of silver-skinned humans threatening to drown the beleaguered wizards in sheer numbers. The magi were weakening, their Life draining from them, their catalysts dropping insensible. The creatures of iron rolled on without the need for rest or food, crawling over the land, breathing their poison fumes, casting their deadly light beams.

It was then that the miracle occurred, according to later tellings and retellings of this great battle. The Angel of Death himself took the field, or so it was said. In his hands, he wielded a sword of death, and it was this sword that eventually brought the enemy to its knees.

In actuality, no one was more astounded by what happened than the Angel of Death himself, but that part of the story was never told, it being known only to Joram and Prince Garald.

The two had just finished destroying one of the iron monsters when their position was overrun by a squadron of the strange humans. Garald's magic was nearly gone. Drained of Life, he drew his sword and faced his enemy with grim hopelessness, knowing he could never survive the beams of deadly light that these silver-skinned humans were capable of shooting from the palms of their hands. Joram, too, drew his sword, prepared to die beside his friend. He, too, knew that to fight this enemy with a sword was a ludicrous, futile gesture. They would be dead within seconds, without even the chance to strike back. But, at least, they would die with weapons in their hands. . . .

As Joram drew the Darksword, however, the metal began to glow blue-white, burning brighter and brighter in his hands. He stared at it in wonder. The only time he had seen the sword flame like this was at the Judgment, when it had drawn the Life cast by the catalysts to the Executioner into itself. It was reacting the same way, drawing Life from something around it. But from what? Certainly not the enemy who were as Dead as Joram himself. There were no catalysts. Prince Garald had ordered Radisovik to stay behind with the injured in the fortress. Whose Life was it draining?

A silver-skinned human raised his hand, aimed his deadly beam at Joram and Garald, and fired.

The beam of light streaked from the human's palm, but it did not strike its target. The light streamed into the metal of the Darksword, causing it to glow with a radiance so bright that Joram could not see for the blinding light. The sword vibrated in his hand, electric shocks jolted through his body. He had all he could do to hold onto the weapon, much less try to wield it. He couldn't see a thing, and it was Garald who told him later that the strange humans, shielding their eyes, tried everything in their power to fire the light beams at their victims. It proved impossible.

The Darksword sucked up the energy from the weapons of the Dead as it sucked the Life from the world. The beams of light died and the Darksword lived, flaring fiercely and humming with an eerie sound. Throwing down their useless weapons, the strange humans turned and ran.

Those who witnessed that battle from a distance spread the report that the Angel of Death possessed the power to put out the sun if he chose.

When night — true night — came to Thimhallan at last, the battle was over. The magi had won, or at least it seemed so. The creatures of iron and the strange humans who came with them retreated, withdrawing to some place unknown — confused reports came in of having seen the iron monsters entering the bodies of still larger monsters and that these enormous creatures of iron had then flown straight up into the heavens and disappeared.

No one believed these fanciful rumors, however. No one except one man — Joram — who looked up grimly into the sky, and shook his head. He said nothing, however. Time enough for that later. Now there was much to be done.

The cost of victory had been grievous.

Mosiah, changed back from his form as a werewolf, was returning to the fortress when he came across the body of the witch. Her enemies lay scattered around her, but in the end there had been too many. Gently Mosiah covered the pale and beautiful face with the black hood. Lifting the body in his arms, he carried her back to the fortress.

Here the dead — and there were many — were buried beneath piles of stone; Cardinal Radisovik spoke the words over them in a voice that was choked with tears and anger. The bodies of those who had died upon the field of battle were left where they had fallen. The surviving magi protested against this, but Joram held firm. He knew — no one knew better, having lived in the Outland — what terrible desecration the centaurs and other beasts would commit upon the bodies, but he also knew that finding them, bringing them back, and burying them would take too much time.

The only ones allowed to return to the battlefield were the *Duuk-tsarith*. They had an interest in the dead. Not their own dead — the dead of the enemy. Working swiftly and silently under the cover of night, they stripped the bodies of everything from weapons to personal artifacts, never touching any of the objects but handling each with powerful spells of levitation, transporting them to their secret chambers for future study.

The warlocks carried out their task efficiently, then they, too, were ordered by Joram to leave the field and return to Merilon.

"What is there to fear?" Garald asked wearily, so tired he could barely stand. "We drove them away—"

"Perhaps," Joram replied. "We have no way of knowing for certain until our spies return with their reports."

"Bah! They've left the world."

"I don't think so. Their retreat was orderly, well planned, and swiftly carried out. It wasn't a rout, by any means. My guess is that they fell back to assess the situation and reevaluate their strategy."

The two stood in the center of the compound, talking together in low voices. Traveling the Corridors, the magi were returning to Merilon. The injured and dying had been sent through the Corridors first, then the catalysts, then the wizards. Some were so exhausted they staggered inside and collapsed. Others couldn't walk at all but had to be carried.

They evacuated the fortress under the cover of darkness, the weary *Sif-Hanar* working until the end; Joram refused to allow even starlight to shine down upon them.

Joram's grim tone, his precautions, and his ceaseless searching of the skies made Garald increasingly uneasy. "At least we did what we set out to do," he said. "We have made them afraid of us. We have proved to them that they cannot sow the seeds of death without reaping its bitter harvest as well."

"Yes," Joram agreed, but he remained grave and his eyes continued their watchful vigil.

"What will they do now?" Garald asked quietly.

"Hopefully they are confused, frightened, perhaps even arguing among themselves," Joram replied. "They may—if we are lucky—leave this world. But if not, the next time they attack, they will know what to expect. They will be prepared. And so we had better be prepared ourselves."

Eventually, the magi were gone. Joram and the Prince were alone now, standing in the rubble of the blasted and ruined fortress of the Field of Glory.

We are alone—if you don't count the dead, Garald thought. Looking at the huge cairn that had been made of stones taken from the shattered walls, he thought back on the beginning of this day, remembering with bitter pain his dreams of the glories of battle, his delight in the silly game he had been playing.

Some game. If it hadn't been for Joram, he would be lying beneath that pile of stones. No he wouldn't. There would have been no one left alive to bury him.

"Please, please let this be ended!" he prayed fervently. "Please grant us peace and I promise I . . ."

But even as he spoke, he saw a dark figure emerge from the Corridors. Coming up to stand before Joram, the *Duuk-tsarith* gestured, pointing toward mountainous country to the north. Joram nodded wordlessly and glanced at Garald. Turning away, weary and despairing, the Prince pretended he didn't notice. He knew without hearing what the warlock had reported. The enemy hadn't fled, they had done what Joram predicted and gone into hiding.

Now what? Garald wondered bleakly. Now what?

A hand touched his arm. Turning, he saw Joram at his side. Together, in silence, the two entered the Corridor and disappeared, leaving the fortress to the night and the dead.

Beyond

I leave this record with Father Saryon to be read in the event that I do not survive my initial encounter with the enemy. . . .

The enemy.

I call them this, yet how many of them have become my friends over these past ten years? I think back on them, especially those who have ministered so gently to my wife and who helped me through those first few terrible months when I, too, feared I might lose my sanity. If word reaches them of what I am doing, I know they will understand, however. For they have fought him — the one known as the Sorcerer — far longer than I.

I am going to tell you everything, you who read this. I wonder, as an aside, who that will be. My old friend, Prince Garald? My old foes, Xavier, Bishop Vanya? It doesn't matter, I suppose, since you will all find yourselves on the same side in this conflict. Therefore I will set down everything that has happened to me as best I can explain it. It is imperative that you understand this enemy in the event that you are forced to fight him alone, without my aid.

I will start at the beginning, or perhaps I should say the end.

I can tell you little of my thoughts and feelings when I walked — as I suppose I did — into death, into Beyond. There is a darkness that comes over me sometimes that I cannot control. This darkness has been diagnosed by those in the world that I shall now call Beyond as a form of *psychosis* — a word they use to describe a mental disorder that is not physical in its cause.

Shortly after my return to Thimballan, Father Saryon asked me if I was thinking consciously of the Prophecy when I made my decision to walk into death. Was I actively working to bring it to its fulfillment as a kind of revenge upon the world?

Once more, I consider the words of the Prophecy. They are, as you might imagine, graven upon my heart as Bishop Vanya once threatened to carve the image of the Darksword upon my stone chest.

There will be born to the Royal House one who is dead yet will live, who will die again and live again. And when he returns, he will hold in his hand the destruction of the world —

It would be to my credit, I suppose, if I could answer yes to Saryon's question. At least it would show that I was thinking clearly and rationally. Unfortunately, I wasn't. Looking back, I see myself as I was then — arrogant, proud, self-centered — and I find it miraculous that I had the mental and physical strength to survive at all. That I did, I owe more to Father Saryon than to myself.

I spent the hours before the Turning alone in a prison cell. There, my mind fell victim to the darkness that lurks within me. Fear and despair claimed me. To have suddenly discovered my true parentage and the strange accident of my upbringing, to know the terrible fate that was to be mine in order to keep me from fulfilling the Prophecy — these drove me almost to madness. When I stood upon the sand that day, I was aware of very little going on around me. I might well have been turned to stone already.

The terrible, noble, loving sacrifice made by Father Saryon was a shining light into the darkness of my soul. By its bright radiance I saw the evil that I had brought upon myself and those I loved. Overwhelmed by grief for a man I had come too late to love and admire, sickened by the corruption I saw in the world — a corruption I knew was reflected in me — my only thought was to rid the world of the evil I had brought into it. I gave the Darksword into Saryon's lifeless hands and I walked into death.

I did not know at the time — so lost was I in my own despair — that Gwendolyn had followed me. I remember hearing her voice as I stepped into the mists, calling me to wait, and I may even have hesitated at that point. But my love for her, like everything else in my life, was a selfish love. I cast her from my thoughts as the chill fog closed over me, and I did not think of her again until I found her, lying unconscious, on the other side.

The other side.

I can almost see the parchment in your hands tremble as you read this.

The other side.

Long I walked. I don't know how long, for time itself is warped and altered by the field of magic that surrounds this world and keeps it cut off from the rest of the universe. I was conscious of nothing except the fact that I was walking, that there was solid ground beneath my feet, and that I was lost and wandering in a gray nothingness.

I don't recall being frightened and I think I must have been in shock. I have heard, however, from others I have met in Beyond, others who passed through the magical boundary, that it was not frightening to me because I was Dead. To those with magic, it is a fearful experience. The ones who survived with their sanity intact (and there are not many) cannot talk of it without difficulty. And I will never, to my dying day, forget the look of terror and horror I saw in Gwendolyn's eyes when she first opened them.

I think it probable that, in my despairing and unreasoning state of mind, I might have continued to walk uncaring through the gray and shifting mists until I sank down and died. Then — with a suddenness that literally took my breath away — the mists ended. As one can walk out of a patch of dense fog and find oneself standing in broad sunlight, so I emerged from the realm of death (so I thought) and found myself standing in an open field of grass.

It was night, a perfectly clear and lovely night. The sky above me — yes, there was sky — was smooth, deep black, and every possible inch of it sparkled with stars. I never knew there were so many stars. The air was crisp and cold, a full, bright moon poured silvery light down upon the land beneath it. I drew in a deep breath, let it out, drew in another, let it out and — for I don't know how long — I just stood there, breathing. The blackness lifted from my soul. I considered what I had done and knew for the first time in my life that I had done something right, something good.

My religious training had been neglected in my chaotic childhood. As I grew older, I had no faith in mankind or in myself; consequently I had no faith in the Almin either. I had given little thought to a life after death, except possibly to fear it if it existed. After all, for me, life itself was a daily burden. Why should I want to prolong it? At that instant, however, I believed I had found heaven. The beauty of the night, the peace and solitude that surrounded me, the sense of blessed aloneness. . . .

My soul was content to take flight and slip away into the night. My body, however, stubbornly persisted in living and in reminding me — by its weakness — that I was alive. A chill wind blew through the grass. I had no shirt. I was clad in nothing but some cast-off trousers that the *Duuk-tsarith* had given me in prison. I began to shiver with cold and with, undoubtedly, a reaction to my recent experiences. I was thirsty and hungry, too, having refused all food and drink during my captivity.

It was at that moment I began to wonder where I was and how I got here. I could see nothing in any direction but broad expanses of empty, moonlit grassland and — strangely — a small red, flashing light about one hundred feet from me. I suppose the light had been flashing all that time, but my spirit had been floating with the stars and had paid no attention to it.

I began to walk toward the light with some vague idea, I recall, that it might be the coals of a fire, which only goes to show that I was still not thinking clearly or I would have realized no fire would flash on and off in that persistent manner. It was while I was walking toward the light that I discovered Gwen.

She lay in the grass, unconscious. I knelt beside her, caught her up in my arms, and pressed her close all before it occurred to me to wonder how and why she was here. At that moment I recalled having heard her voice as I stepped into the mists and a confused impression that I saw a fluttering of her white gown. Perhaps we had been within a few feet of each other and never knew it, so thick was the fog. It didn't matter. It seemed so right, somehow.

At my touch, she awoke. I could see her face clearly in the moonlight and it was then I saw the madness in her eyes. I knew it for what it was — how could I not? I had lived with it all my childhood. It was many months before I could admit it to myself, however. Certainly, I did not in that instant.

"Gwendolyn!" I whispered, cradling her in my arms.

At the sound of my voice, the eerie glint in her eyes faded. She looked up at me with the same look of love I had been so blessed to receive — a blessing I had changed to a curse!

"Joram," she said softly, reaching up with her hand to touch my face.

I saw my reflection in her eyes and then it began to waver and grow dim as the horror and madness banished me from her vision. I held onto her tightly, as though she were physically leaving me. Her body remained in my arms, but I could not prevent her spirit from running away.

The wind was rising. White fire lit the night and there came a thunderous crash. Looking up, I saw darkness swallowing the stars like some great monster crawling across the heavens. Lightning streaked from sky to ground. Even though the storm was some distance from us yet, the force of the wind nearly blew me over. The clouds swept toward us, the moon vanished as I watched, and I could smell the rain and feel its mist blowing against my face.

I could not believe the swiftness or the power of this storm. I looked around in panic. There was no shelter anywhere. We were stranded out in the open. A bolt of lightning struck near enough that its concussion deafened me. I saw huge chunks of earth fly into the air. The wind increased, screaming shrilly in my ears. The rain began, slanting down out of the sky with the force of lightning itself. In an instant, both Gwen and I were soaked through, though I did what I could to shield her with my body.

I had to find help! The lightning danced around us, the wind grew stronger. Pellets of ice stung my face, bruising and cutting my flesh. All was total darkness now, except for the brief intervals of terrible day when the lightning lit the sky. And then I saw through the slashing rain the flashing red light, blinking on and off, apparently unaffected by the storm. Perhaps there were people there, gathered around a fire, using their magic to keep it alive. Lifting Gwen in my arms, I carried her toward the red light, praying the first unselfish prayer I probably ever uttered — that the Almin would send someone to save her.

Who was I expecting to find by that fire? I didn't know. I wouldn't have been much surprised to see angels or devils. I would have welcomed either one. We could not survive this storm long. It was increasing in ferocity, and I had the dim, almost dreamy thought that comes sometimes in the midst of terror that it was battering against the Border of the world, trying to break it down.

There were times I literally could not move against the tremendous force of the wind; times when I had to use all my strength just to stand, clasping Gwen's cold, motionless body close to my own as the wind buffeted me and the rain and ice drove like sharp needles into my skin.

By sheer effort of will, I struggled on. Eventually, I came to the red light. It was not a fire. There was no one around — devil, angel, no one. The red flashing light came from an odd-looking object sticking out of the rain-soaked earth, and it was not even warm to the touch. Frustration and despair overwhelmed me. The strength in my legs gave way, and I sank, with Gwen in my arms, to the ground.

At that moment, above the noise of the storm, I heard a rumbling sound. It grew louder as I listened. I could feel the ground shake. The lightning was almost incessant now. Peering through the rain, I saw — illuminated by brilliant flashes — a huge monster crawling toward us. It had a squat, angular shape with two great flaring eyes in front, and it was bearing down on us with incredible speed!

So this is how it ends, I thought. Torn to bits by some foul beast. I gave myself up to the darkness inside me. My last remembered thought was one of thankfulness that Gwen was unconscious and would slip into death without knowing these final moments of terror.

They tell me I was conscious when they found me. They said I spoke to them and it appeared to them — for they could not understand me — that I was prepared to fight. They tell me — and they smile to recall it — that I couldn't have fought a child. My struggles were feeble, and I fainted.

As for me, I remember nothing until I woke to the sound of voices. Terror assailed me, then I calmed myself. It was a dream! My heart beat rapidly in hope. The trial, the sentencing, the execution, the storm . . . it was all a dream and when I opened my eyes I would find myself back in the house of Lord Samuels. . . .

I opened my eyes and stared into a glaring light, so bright it hurt. My bed was hard and uncomfortable and I realized suddenly that I was inside something made completely of iron. It seemed we were moving, for we rocked back and forth with a sickening, swaying motion. My dream had been all too real.

Yet, I still heard voices. Sitting up, I tried to see, shielding my eyes from the light.

The voices were very close. Dimly I saw two figures, standing near me, walking unsteadily with the motion of the iron thing. They noticed me as I sat up and one came over to my side.

He spoke in a language I could not understand and it seemed he realized this, for he kept patting my shoulder while he spoke, in a reassuring manner, as one comforts a frightened child.

I was not frightened. By the Almin! After what I'd been through, I didn't think I could ever be frightened of anything again. My only thoughts were for the poor girl who had given up everything for my sake. Where was she? I looked around, but I couldn't see her. I tried to get up, but the man held me down — he was very gentle. It was not difficult to keep me from moving, I was too weak even to sit up long.

All the while, the other figure inside the iron thing was talking to someone else — someone who spoke in a crackling voice.

I know now, of course, that he was talking into a communications device, located inside his landrover (a type of vehicle similar to a carriage except that it operates by the Dark Arts of Technology, not by magic). I can still hear the man's words quite clearly, though at the time I didn't know their meaning. Months after that, in my struggles against madness, his words came to me over and over in my night-dreams.

"We've checked out the alarm. There's two of them on the Border this time — a man and a woman."

I remember nothing after that. The man who knelt beside me pressed something cold against my arm, and I sank into sleep.

When I awoke, I found that Gwendolyn and I had been transported to a new world — or perhaps you might consider it a very old one — to begin living a new life. I married my poor Gwen — to keep her safe and secure — and part of every day I spent with her in the quiet, loving place where she stayed while the healers of Beyond endeavored to find some means to help her.

It has been ten years . . . ten years in our new world . . . since she has spoken a word to me or to any living person. She talks only to those her eyes alone can see. She talks to the dead.

I came to know many people in this world of Beyond, including a man who was not of that world but is of our own. His name is Menju, but he calls himself Sorcerer, and I have spent much of my time during those ten years learning his true nature and doing what I could to thwart his rise to power.

I do not have the time, nor is it the intent of this document, to describe the world Beyond. Suffice it to say, the world Beyond is a world of Technology, a world beyond your comprehension. You would understand little and believe less of what I could tell. Alas, you may come to know it all too well. . . .

In closing, I will leave you with some thoughts regarding our world and how it relates to the universe. One of you, I pray, will have wisdom enough to understand and accept, not shut your eyes to it as you have done for so many centuries.

The ancient magi, finding themselves persecuted for being "different," fled what they considered a dying world — a world that was becoming too dependent on technology, a world that denied and even feared the magic. Seeking a place where they might live in peace, the ancients traveled through time and space. Their coming to this world was no accident, for here is contained the source of magic in the universe. The magi were led here by the magic's siren call. Once they arrived on these friendly, welcoming shores, the ancients burned their ships and vowed never to leave.

Not only did they cut off all contact with their old world, they built a barrier around this one so that there was no possible way anyone from Outside could enter. So powerful was this magical barrier, however, that it not only shut the universe out, it sealed the magic within.

In their ardent desire to secure their present, the ancients destroyed their past. Instead of keeping memories of the old world alive — and thus reminding themselves that it was still out there — they destroyed the records and banished the memories until now it has become, for you, a House Magi's tale, less real than the realm of the faerie.

And because you forgot there was a land outside, distant and remote as it might be, you felt safe and secure — safe and secure enough to cast out those you believed did not belong in this world — even in death. Thus evolved the custom of sending people into "Beyond." It is a neat and simple means of dealing with those who are different. It rids the world of them quickly and efficiently. The punishment is so awful that it serves as a fairly effective deterrent. What you did not realize was that you were sending these magi out, not to death, but to life.

Though we forgot about them, the world Beyond has never forgot about us. The majority of the magic was shut up, sealed off from them, that is true. But tiny bits of it escape, now and then, seeping through cracks in the barrier. The world Beyond is hungry for Life, and — when it had the means through its advanced uses of Technology — the people of Beyond went in search of the magic.

They found it, of course, but they could not reach it. The magical barrier was too strong for them to penetrate. They did, however, find those who had been cast out, wandering — as did Gwen and I — in the land across our Border. It is a dreadful land, swept almost hourly by terrible storms such as I experienced. There are few people here. It is an outpost, the men who run it have only one objective — to search for a way to gain the magic.

Thus they found us, thus they found others. Alarms — those red flashing lights — are set along the Border, detecting anything that moves. Whenever possible, they have rescued magi, and now these outcasts live in the world Beyond.

Most are insane — as is my poor Gwen. But some are not. Some — one in particular, this man known as "Sorcerer" — are quite sane. He tried, countless times, to get back across the Border. According to him, the barrier is an energy field composed of the magical energy within this world and within each of the Living. The Living who are cast out cannot get back in due to their own energy force. Much as two like magnetic fields repel each other, the magic of the world repelled his magic. All these years, he has waited for this world to make a mistake, a mistake that would let him back inside.

I was your mistake.

A Dead man crossed the magical boundary. The spell was shattered, the lock broken. I myself, having no magical energy, would not be repelled. I could come back. And if I did, it was theorized that I would disrupt the field. I would leave the door open behind me.

As I said, Sorcerer came to this conclusion after months of study. We were not always enemies, you see. Once I trusted and admired him —

But that is another story.

Those in power managed to convince me that the two worlds must meld, become one. I thought this would prove a blessing for Thimhallan. I believed that a blending of the two worlds would bring about a new order in the universe. My dreams were bright. The dreams of others, however, were twisted and distorted.

I came back . . . and they followed me, bringing war.

They deceived me and betrayed me. I realize now that they mean to conquer this world as they have conquered others.

Will the Prophecy be fulfilled? Are we hurtling to our own destruction as rocks tumbling down a cliff face? The thought is a terrifying one. And it is made all the more frightening because it seems we have no choice in our own destiny; that some all-knowing and uncaring Master controls our puny lives and has controlled them from time immemorial.

Is there no escape? I am beginning to think there is not. The only two right and good things I have ever done in my life — choosing to leave this world and choosing to return to save it — have apparently only brought the Prophecy that much closer to fulfillment.

If this is true, if our lives are dealt to us like the cards of the tarok, if we are thrown down to take a trick or be lost as our Player deems and there is nothing more to life than that, then I begin to understand Simkin and his way in this world.

The game is nothing, the playing of it everything.

B O O K   T W O

The Enemy

Major James Boris, commander, fifth battalion, Ma-
rine Airborne, was known among his men affectionately (if
unofficially, and never when he was within hearing) as
Stump. In build he was short, thick-bodied, and well mus-
cled—physical qualities that undoubtedly helped earn him
this nickname. Thirty years old, he kept his body in top condition, and yearly, during the base's annual inspection by the
brass and top government officials, Major Boris invited as
many young recruits as wanted to endanger their skulls to
rush him in a group and attempt to knock him off his feet.
(According to legend, a recruit once stole a tank and drove it
straight at Major Boris. Legend has it that, when the tank
struck him, James Boris remained standing rooted to the
spot, and it was the tank that flipped end over end.)

Those who served with James Boris from his early days
as a young recruit knew the true derivation of his nickname,
however. It came from the classroom, not the locker room.

"James Boris, you have all the imagination of a tree stump!" remarked an instructor caustically.

The name stuck.

The comment — and the nickname — didn't bother James Boris one bit. He wore it proudly, in fact, as he wore his many medals. This lack of imagination was, he considered, one factor that had enabled his swift rise through the ranks. Major Boris was a by-the-book commander. His roots were deeply mired in the firm ground of rules and regulations, a comforting and reassuring thought to those he led. There was never any need to wonder where James Boris stood on any issue. If it was covered in the rules and regulations, then Major Boris stood squarely on top of it and nothing — not even the legendary tank — would move him. If it wasn't covered in rules and regulations . . .

Well, that point was moot. James Boris had never encountered anything that wasn't.

Until now.

This particular aspect of Major Boris's personality — the fact that he had no imagination — had been one of the major factors involved in selecting him for the expeditionary force to Thimhallan. Top government officials had descriptions of this bizarre world, descriptions provided by two men: one known to casino audiences as Sorcerer and another known only to certain secret government agencies as Joram. The top officials, many of whom could scarcely believe what they heard, decided that it would take a man of nerve and cold, hard logic to survive in Thimhallan without losing his senses.

It was easy to see how they reached this decision and it undoubtedly had some merit. Unfortunately, the decision proved disastrously wrong. Although any person sent from the safe, secure world of technology into the strange and terrifying world of magic must have been shaken to his core, a commander with imagination might have been flexible enough to cope with the mind-boggling situations. Major Boris, on the other hand, felt that — for the first time in his life — his solid, sturdy stump had been blasted clean out of the ground. Now he lay helpless, his roots exposed, a pathetic sight.

"You want to know what I recommend, Major?" muttered Captain Collin. "I recommend we get the hell out of here!"

The Captain, a man of forty-five and a veteran of one of the most grueling tank campaigns ever fought on the Outer Fringes, took out a cigarette with a trembling hand, dropped it, took out another, accidentally snapped it in two, and finally stuffed the case back in his pocket.

Major Boris looked gloomily at his other captains and received emphatic nods from the rest, except for one, who wasn't paying attention, but sat huddled in a chair, shivering.

"You're suggesting we retreat—" James Boris growled.

"I'm suggesting we get out of here before we're all dead or looney as—" Captain Collin bit his words off with a vicious snap, letting a glance at the shivering captain sitting beside him complete his sentence.

Major Boris sat behind a standard-issue metal desk, facing his company commanders who sat before him in standard-issue metal folding chairs, meeting inside Major Boris's standard-issue field headquarters, a dome of plastic made in the latest geodesic design. A series of other domes—some larger (supply domes, mess domes) and many smaller, living-quarter domes—dotted the landscape for miles about. The domes could be dismantled in a matter of minutes; the entire battalion could be aboard ship and out of this nightmare world in a matter of hours.

Resting his hands firmly on the metal top of the desk, the Major felt reassured by its coolness, its stolid, unyielding . . . what? James Boris groped for a word. Metalness? Stolid, unyielding metalness? He didn't suppose *metalness* was a word, but it said what he meant. He could be out of here by 0300 hours, back in a world of metal. . . .

His hands clenched on the desk top. He looked around it carefully, taking in everything from a green teapot with a bright orange lid that he couldn't recall having ordered—tea was the last thing James Boris wanted to drink right now—to the papers stacked neatly in a pile next to his standard-issue field computer. Nervously, unaware of what he was doing, the Major began to drum his knuckles softly on the metal, his gaze switching to a small transparent plastic window set into the side of the plastic dome.

It was night, dark as hyperspace, with no moon or stars visible. James Boris wondered, his gloom deepening, if this was *real* night or one of those terrifying, magic nights that had been dropped over him and his men like some huge, smothering blanket. A quick glance at his watch reassured him of the time, however: 2400. They'd been here only forty-eight hours.

Forty-eight hours. That was the length of time the brass had figured it would take to intimidate the population of this world. A populace that, according to reports, was living somewhere just south of the Middle Ages. Forty-eight hours and Major Boris was to have sent back word that the situation was well under control, his forces were occupying the major capitals, negotiations for peaceful coexistence could begin. . . .

Forty-eight hours. Half his men dead, over half his tanks destroyed or out of commission. Of those men surviving, probably a third were in little better shape than the shivering captain. Major Boris made a weary, mental note to turn the man over to the medics and declare him unfit for command.

Forty-eight hours. They were safe enough here, he supposed, hidden in the mountains, but he kept having the eerie feeling he was being watched, unseen eyes observing him.

Staring out the window, Major Boris heard his captains talking. They were going over the incidents of the last forty-eight hours, describing them for the hundredth time in tight, tense voices, as though daring anyone to dispute what they had seen. James Boris floated on top of their sea of words, seeing occasionally in his mind the fragment of a rule or a regulation drift by. Floundering, he sought to grasp it, to hang onto it. But it always sank, and he was left helpless, drowning. . . .

So lost in this dark sea was the Major that he never noticed the silent entrance of another man.

Neither did any of the others. This was due, perhaps, to the fact that the man did not enter through the headquarters' door, but simply materialized inside the dome. A tall, broad-shouldered, handsome man, he was dressed in an expensive cashmere suit, a silk tie at his throat. It was odd apparel for a battlefield and, if his dress was odd, his demeanor was odder. He might have been lounging at the bar, waiting for a table in a fine restaurant. Calmly, he straightened the cuffs of his white shirt; a jeweled cufflink sparkled at his wrist. Calmly, he regarded Major James Boris. A plastic laminated identity card adorned with his picture was tucked carefully into his suit pocket. Stamped across it in red was his name, Menju, and the single word: *Advisor.*

Although the man made no sound to draw attention to himself, he did nothing to try to conceal his presence either. The captains sat with their backs to him. Major Boris, wrapped in his own problems, was still staring at his desk. The newly arrived man listened to the captains' reports with interest, occasionally stroking the identity card he wore with the tips of fingers remarkable for their length and delicacy of touch. When he toyed with this placard with the single word, *Advisor,* he smiled, as though he found it all highly amusing.

"It was when we were attacking that stone fortress where we had, so we were told" — Captain Collin's tone was bitter and ironic — "the creeps trapped. One of my tank crews had one of them, a woman, a *woman,* mind you" — the Captain's tone grew dark — "in their sights when this green goo starts oozing through the hatch. Before they know what's happening, this . . . this slime is eating into their skin! They start to glow, like, and within seconds they're a quivering mass of green jelly. . . ."

"Kid turned into a wolf right before my eyes! Leaped on Rankin, knocked him down, and tore his throat out before I could move. God help me! I'll never forget Rankin's scream. . . . What could I do? Run? Hell yes I ran! And the whole time I was running I could feel hot breath on my neck, hear that thing panting behind me. I can still hear it. . . ."

"We fired at this thing, but he must have been thirty feet tall. We coulda been tossin' matches at it instead of lasers for all it cared. Lifted one foot and smash! That was the end of Mardec and Hayes. We couldn't even get the bodies outa the wreckage. . . ."

"A man in white robes, like some damn picture in a Sunday school book, jumps up and attacks my boys with a sword. Yeah, a sword. They get ready to cut him in two with their phaser guns and — wham! They fire and the sword —"

" — deflects the light?"

"Deflects, hell! It sucks up the damn light! I saw those weapons. Every one was completely drained, and they'd all been recharged right before battle. We shoulda been able to shoot those things for a month without recharging. Not only that, but the guy in the robes did the same thing to a tank, too."

"Naw —"

"I saw, I swear! The crew reported their instrument readings going wild, and then everything went dead. But this sword and the guy in the robes stood in front of them, glowing with this weird blue light and the last thing the crew reported was this bright flash. . . . There was an explosion . . . and then this hole in the ground; the tank blown halfway to hell —"

The shivering Captain suddenly spoke, "Halfway. Half-man, half-horse. Hair covers their faces, but I see their eyes, horrible eyes and hooves — sharp hooves. . . ." The Captain leaped to his feet. "They're trampling Jamesson! Stop them! Oh, my god! They've got him . . . tearing his arms off. He . . . he's still alive! My god! His cries! Shoot him! Make him stop! Make him stop!" The Captain clamped his hands over his ears, sobbing.

"Get him out of here," Major Boris ordered, raising his head, his attention caught at last.

The rest of the commanders ceased their argument and fell silent, carefully avoiding looking at their broken comrade. The Major opened his mouth to call for the sergeant, whose office was in another, smaller geodesic dome attached to the main one, and it was at this point that James Boris became aware of the presence in the room of the man with the word *Advisor* attached to his expensive suit.

Major Boris went cold all over, shivering nearly as violently as the poor Captain. Noting their commander's fixed and rigid stare, seeing the hands clenched upon the desk suddenly go limp, the captains looked around behind them hastily. When they saw the man watching them, they all turned back — some slower than others, Captain Collin in particular — casting uneasy glances at their Major.

They're losing confidence in me, James Boris realized bitterly. How can I blame them? I'm losing confidence in myself, in everything around me! His gaze went reluctantly yet inexorably to the weeping Captain. I'll be as mad as Walters next. . . . I've got to pull myself together.

Forcing himself to sit upright, setting his thick jaw rigidly, and thrusting out his chin, Major Boris bellowed for the sergeant.

The door opened, the Sergeant entered. "Sir?"

"I gave orders no one was allowed inside. What is this man doing here? Did you leave your post?"

The Sergeant looked at the visitor and his eyes opened wide, his skin took on a sallow tinge. "No, sir! I didn't let him in, Major, I swear! I — I haven't left my desk all night, sir."

The man labeled *Advisor* smiled.

James Boris tensed, longing to shove the white, even teeth of that smile down the silk-necktied throat. His hand twitched in anticipation, and he was forced to clench it tightly. The Major knew well enough how Menju had gained entry; he'd seen him perform this trick earlier, just a few hours previous. Only this was no trick, James Boris reminded himself. This was no grand illusion to leave children gasping and adults shaking their heads in wonder. This wasn't done with mirrors. It was real, at least it was as real as anything in this unreal world.

"Never mind, Sergeant," Major Boris muttered, noticing that his captains were growing increasingly nervous. "Send for the medics." He made a gesture toward the hysterical Walters. "Have him declared unfit for command. I'll promote Lieutenant . . . Lieutenant . . ." James Boris flushed. He had always prided himself on remembering the names of the officers under his command, as well as most of the enlisted men, too. Now he couldn't recall a lieutenant, a man who'd served under him for over a year. "Confound it, whoever's next in line, have him report here to me in" — he glanced at his visitor — "half an hour," he concluded coldly.

"Yes, sir," said the Sergeant, starting back out the door.

"Sergeant!" yelled Major Boris.

"Sir?" The Sergeant turned.

"Get rid of that damn tea! I never drink the stuff. You know that. Why did you bring it?"

The Sergeant looked at the teapot with surprise. "I didn't bring it, sir," were the words that were on his lips. A look at his grim-faced Major, however, and he simply removed the teapot, mumbling, "Sorry, sir," as he picked it up by its handle and carried it into his outer office.

"Thank you, gentlemen, for coming," James Boris said wearily. It was Rules and Regulations talking, not him. If he had to consciously think about what to say, he couldn't have spoken a word. "I will take your recommendations under advisement. Dismissed."

There was the sound of metal scraping against the plastic floor as the captains rose and began to file out. They did so in silence — a bad sign, James Boris knew.

Flicking on the computer, he pretended to be absorbed in reading something on the screen, although in reality he hadn't the vaguest idea what he was looking at. He didn't want to talk to any of them anymore; he didn't want to have to face them or look into their eyes. He felt more than saw the sideways glances they gave him and he knew that they were exchanging looks with one another. Questioning, wondering.

What will he do? Will he send for the ships? Retreat? And what *were* his orders anyway? Already, of course, the rumors were starting; the Major was no longer in command of the battalion. . . . They were being led by Menju the Sorcerer, who had seized control when the battle turned sour.

Major Boris could hear the voice of the sergeant shouting into the field phone, attempting to raise the medics. They'd been having trouble with the phones, something about this weird, energy-laden atmosphere the techs told him. One of the captains, probably Collin, had grabbed hold of poor Walters and was leading him out. When everyone was gone, the Sergeant — still on the phone — kicked the door firmly shut.

"Well, what do you want?" Major Boris growled, his eyes on the computer screen, refusing to look at the visitor.

Menju crossed over to stand before his desk. The magician's eyes were large and gleamed with disarming charm. His skin was tan, his face clean-shaven. His hair was full and thick. Combed back stylishly from a peak in the center of his forehead, its silver gray color contrasted well with his richly tanned skin. State lighting set it off most effectively. Placing the tips of his fingers on the metal, he stared down the length of his handsome nose at the thick-necked and square-jawed Major.

"Rumor has it that you are intending to withdraw," the man said. His voice matched his appearance — a deep, rich baritone cultivated over years of performing before live audiences.

"And what if I do? I am still in command here!"

Major Boris shut off the computer with an irritated motion, realizing as he did so that he had been staring at a memo he had written several months ago regarding an infraction of the military dress code by female officers. He swore softly to himself. Turning to face Menju, he burned his hand on something hot, and the swearing became louder.

"What the devil — Sergeant!" he roared furiously.

There was no answer. Heaving himself out of the chair, James Boris strode angrily across the floor and threw open the door. "Sergeant!" he thundered. "That damn teapot —"

There was no one there. Lifting the field phone, he held it to his ear. The static and other strange noises it was making nearly deafened him. Apparently, communications were dead now, too. The Sergeant must have gone off in search of the medics. Major Boris started to swear again, but checked himself. Swallowing his hot words, he could feel them burn all the way down, at least that's what it seemed. Pressing his hand against his hurting stomach, he stomped back inside his office, flung himself down in his chair — without a glance at his visitor — and glared at the green teapot with the bright orange lid.

"Damn it all to hell and back again! I thought I told him to take that thing out of here!"

"So you did," said Menju, known on theater marquees in all the major systems as the Sorcerer. Sitting casually on the desk, he was now eyeing the teapot with extreme interest. "So you did," he murmured. "No, don't touch it." Reaching out a quick, slender-fingered hand, he intercepted James Boris as he was about to grab hold of the teapot and do something with it — just what the Major wasn't certain, but he'd been considering the window. . . .

Menju's strong hand closed over Boris's wrist.

"Let us discuss this rash retreat you are planning," the Sorcerer said pleasantly.

"Rash —"

"Yes, rash. Not only in terms of your future career in the military — I am not without influence as you well know — but in terms of your life and the lives of your men. No, don't try it, Major."

James Boris, his face flushed with rage, made a quick move to free himself of the Sorcerer's grip. The smile never left the magician's face. A sound of crunching bone brought a gasp of pain from the Major.

"You are strong, but now I am stronger." Menju's hand continued to tighten on James Boris's wrist. Furious, the Major grabbed the magician's arm and tried with all his legendary strength to pry the man's hand loose. He might as well have tried to bend the steel laser gun of one of his tanks.

"Forty-eight hours ago I could have snapped your chicken-leg bones in two!" James Boris grunted through clenched teeth, staring up at the Sorcerer in anger that was — he hoped — concealing his fear. "Is this more of your . . . your magic!" He spit the word.

"Yes, Major James Boris. Just as this is more of my . . . magic!"

Speaking a word in a strange language, Menju lifted the Major's hand.

James Boris screamed, snatching his hand — or what had been his hand — free of the Sorcerer's grasp. Laughing, the magician let go, and Major Boris fell backward in his chair, staring in horror. His hand was gone. In its place was the clawed foot of a chicken.

A gurgle, coming apparently from the teapot, caused Menju to glance at it swiftly. But the teapot hushed instantly, though a wisp of steam coiled up lazily from its spout.

"Change it back!" James Boris clutched his wrist, the chicken foot that was his hand twitched convulsively. "Get rid of it!" His voice rose to a shriek, and he choked.

"There will be no more talk of retreat," the Sorcerer said coldly.

"Damn it!" Sweat beaded on Boris's forehead. "We're beat! We can't fight this . . . this . . ." He sought for words, failing. "You heard my men! Werewolves, giants! Some guy with a sword that can suck up energy. . . ."

"I heard them," Menju said grimly. With a motion of his hand, he gestured a folding chair to come scurrying forward and position itself behind him. Sitting down comfortably, he smoothed out a wrinkle in the cashmere pants and continued to watch the Major, who had never taken his eyes from his mutated hand. "I heard about the man with the sword. Frankly, that was the only thing I found the least bit interesting, much less frightening."

With a wave of his delicate fingers, the Sorcerer spoke another strange word and the Major had his hand back again. Shuddering in relief, James Boris examined it feverishly, rubbing the skin as though to assure himself of its reality. Then, wiping the sweat from his upper lip, he stared at Sorcerer with narrow, fear-filled eyes.

"Pull yourself together, Major," the magician snapped. "You know, of course, the identity of the man with the sword."

Elbows on the desk, the Major let his head, with its regulation military haircut, sink slowly into his hands. "No," he muttered in hollow tones. "I don't . . ."

"Joram."

"Joram?" Major Boris looked up. "But they told me he'd stay neutral —" The Major stopped, his mouth twisting bitterly. "Oh, I see. He would have remained neutral if we hadn't started slaughtering his people!"

"I suppose." Menju shrugged. "Frankly, I always doubted whether he would allow us to conquer this world without reacting in some way to stop us. He played his role well, however, and he can be dealt out of the game. He has, in fact, increased the stakes immeasurably!"

The Sorcerer slid his bottom lip beneath his two white upper teeth, a habit that gave a sinister cast to his handsome face, or so James Boris thought, staring at the magician with a morbid fascination.

"Joram has been able to retrieve his Darksword," the Sorcerer said, after a pause, during which he put the tips of the index fingers of each hand together, tapping them on his cleft chin. "Blast it!" Though he spoke with emotion, his voice was still soft and controlled. "We must get hold of some of that ore to analyze! Darkstone! According to him, it drains the magical energy from this world. Now it seems it has the capability of draining the physical energy used in our world as well.

"Think of it, Major!" Menju lowered his hands, straightened his tie, adjusted his shirt cuffs in a preoccupied, obviously habitual gesture. "An ore that can drain energy from one source and convert that energy to its own use! Get hold of that weapon, and the battle is won. Not only in this world, but on any other we might choose to invade. Now, Major, how soon will it be before reinforcements arrive?"

"Reinforcements?" Major Boris blinked glazed eyes. "There are no reinforcements! We are an expeditionary force, our mission is . . . or was" — his voice cracked — "peaceful."

"Yes, it was peaceful. We attempted to negotiate, but we were viciously attacked, our people mercilessly butchered," the Sorcerer said coolly.

"So *that's* your game, is it?" James Boris responded in lifeless tones.

"That's the game." Menju spread his hands. "Led by this Joram — who tricked us into coming here in the first place — the people of this world were lying in wait for us and attacked us without warning. We fought back, of course, but now we are trapped here. We need help, to save ourselves."

"And once these reinforcements come, they'll fall under your control, just like my men, just like me," James Boris continued in the same dull and uncaring voice.

"And on my orders they'll kill every man, woman, and child in this world, except the catalysts, of course, who — as you can see for yourself — are helping me increase my magical powers."

"That's genocide!" The Major gasped, his face flushed red with anger. "By god, you're talking about wiping out an entire population! Why?"

"Why?" The Sorcerer smiled the charming smile that caused audiences worlds over to believe in the fabric of illusions he wove before their dazzled eyes. "Isn't it obvious? I alone will possess the magic. I and my sons and daughters. Which reminds me, I need several young women for breeding purposes. I'll take charge of that personally. With the magic, my family and I will rule the universe! And there will be no magicians left alive with the power to stop me!"

"I won't obey you! I'll denounce you! I'll break you —" James Boris swore viciously. The words stopped cold on his lips as the Sorcerer, rising slowly to his feet, pointed casually — with one finger — at James Boris's right hand.

Turning deathly white, the Major snatched his hand back and hid it beneath the desk.

"When we talk of breaking people, Major, I suggest you remember that simply by speaking a few arcane words I can break you, quite literally, bone by bone. There are what — over two hundred bones in the human body? I forget, biology was never an interest of mine. But it would be, I fancy, an extremely painful way to die."

"My men will not murder innocent — "

"Oh, but they already have, Major Boris," the Sorcerer interrupted with a shrug. "Your men are terrified of the people of this world. What is that quaint saying of Joram's? 'What they do not understand, they fear. What they fear, they destroy.' A few more battles like the one they've been through today and they will be more than willing to exterminate these wizards. Now, I asked you a question about reinforcements. How long?"

Major Boris ran his tongue over his lip. He had to swallow several times before he could speak. "Seventy-two hours, at least."

The Sorcerer shook his head thoughtfully. "Seventy-two hours! That won't do, I'm afraid. That's too long. The magi will attack us before that. Joram will push them to it."

"Not even your magic can make it any quicker, Menju!" James Boris said with a bitter smile. "We have to get the message through and we're having trouble with the communications link-up. The starbase is on alert, but the men will have to draw supplies and board the ship. Then there's the jump. Turn me and all my men into chickens, if you want," he added, seeing the magician's tan, handsome face flush in anger. "It won't help speed matters any."

The Sorcerer stared intently at James Boris, but Major Boris stared just as grimly back. There are limits you can push a man — even a shattered man. The magician had apparently reached them. "We need to stall for time then," Menju said smoothly, turning away from the sweating, tight-lipped Major. "And, above all, we need that sword!"

James Boris, sighing, put his elbows on the table and rested his aching head in his hands.

Frowning in thought, the Sorcerer stared down, unseeing, at the teapot that was, under the man's scrutiny, suddenly very quiet and subdued. No steam rose from its spout, the gurgling noises inside it had ceased.

The magician began to smile. "I have a plan," he murmured. "Peace . . . we came here in peace . . . just as you said, Major Boris." Reaching down, Menju lifted the green teapot with the bright orange lid in his hands. "Now, all we need is someone to carry our message to the one man — a pious holy man — who will undoubtedly — if we play our cards right — be most eager to help us."

2

Of Great Price

It was no longer spring in Merilon.

Winter had come to the domed city, as it had come to the lands outside the city's magical cover. It was not that winter had been decreed to occur that day, or that the *Sif-Hanar* were derelict in their duties. Winter had come to Merilon because there were too few *Sif-Hanar* left to alter the season. Those who had survived the battle at the Field of Contest were so weak that they barely had breath enough to mist the icy air, let alone attempt to conjure the pink and fluffy clouds of spring.

It was snowing inside the city for the first time that even the oldest resident could remember. It had started out as rain; the heat from thousands of living bodies combined with the heat and moisture given off by the trees and plants within the Grove and gardens of Merilon had been enough to over-burden the air trapped within the city. Without the *Sif-Hanar* to govern it, the humidity level within the dome rose until the air itself began to weep — crying for the dead, or so the story went. With the coming of night, the rain changed to snow and now the city lay buried beneath a blanket of white —

"—like a corpse," said Lord Samuels heavily, staring out a window.

The frozen, snow-shrouded garden that he contemplated sorrowfully was not the same garden where his Gwendolyn had loved to walk. It was not the garden where her love for Joram had grown and blossomed. It was not the same garden where Saryon, nursing his dark secret, had sought to protect the blossom by uprooting the plant. No, this garden was far grander, far lusher than the one that had nurtured so many dreams in its dark soil.

The garden was grander and so was the house, being, like the garden, built on a magnificent scale. Lord Samuels and Lady Rosamund had finally attained their dream. They were, at last, nobility. The cost had been nothing more than they had been prepared to spend — their daughter. Too late they realized they had exchanged a pearl of great price for a mere bauble.

Shortly after his daughter's disappearance, Lord Samuels had taken to haunting the deserted sands of the Borderland searching for her. Every day, following his work at the Guild, he traveled through the Corridor to that desolate, barren place, roaming up and down the beach crying out her name until it became too dark to see. Then, exhausted and despairing, he would return to his home.

His sleep was restless, sometimes he woke up and insisted on returning to the Border in the middle of the night, saying he had heard Gwen calling to him. He ate little or nothing. His health began to suffer. The *Theldara* — the same blunt woman who had tended Father Saryon — told Lady Rosamund that her husband was in a dangerous state of body disharmony that could cause his death.

At this juncture Lady Rosamund had received a visit from Emperor Xavier. The Emperor was all kindness and understanding. He had heard that Lord Samuels was behaving in a most peculiar manner, a manner that was — the Emperor sought to phrase this delicately — causing renewed public attention over a deeply regrettable incident. No one felt for the grief of the bereft father and mother more than

Xavier. But it was time Lord Samuels viewed this tragic incident in its proper perspective. It had happened, nothing could change that. The Almin works in mysterious ways. Lord Samuels must have faith.

Xavier said this last with a grave voice, his hand patting Lady Rosamund's. Why it should have filled her with terror was unknown to her. Perhaps it had been the expression of the cold, flat eyes. Removing her hand from the Emperor's disturbing touch, she pressed it against her palpitating heart and murmured distractedly that the *Theldara* had recommended a change . . . a change of scene.

Excellent idea! the Emperor had remarked. Precisely what he'd had in mind. It was in his power to bestow a small estate upon some fortunate man. Lord Samuels would be conferring the greatest favor upon the Emperor if he would accept this trifling gift. The estate consisted of a small Field Magi village, a castle in an outlying district, and a house in the city. It was falling to rack and ruin since the death of its owner — a Count Devon — who had left no heirs. It behooved Lord Samuels, as a loyal subject of the crown, to take it over and make the estate properous once more. There was a small matter of back taxes, but a man in Lord Samuels's position . . .

Lady Rosamund had managed to stammer out that she was certain this was exactly what her husband needed to take his mind off his grief. She thanked the Emperor most profusely. Xavier had accepted her thanks with a gracious inclination of the head and had said, as he rose to leave, that he presumed her husband would henceforth be much too busy to make those nightly journeys to the Borderlands. He had further added that he trusted her husband's new duties would provide him with more cheerful subjects to discuss other than whatever it was he might have heard or witnessed concerning the young man called Joram.

Xavier left Lady Rosamund with a little homily: A man who walks backward, staring into the past, is likely to trip and hurt himself.

That night Lord Samuels's visits to the Border ceased. The following week, he and his family journeyed to Devon Castle, returning to the Devon townhouse in Merilon only for holidays and during the winter season as was customary with the rich and the beautiful. They had everything they had ever wanted: wealth, position, acceptance by their betters, who were now their peers.

Gwendolyn was spoken of no more. Her things were given to her cousins, but these simple girls could never look at the pretty dresses and jewelry without weeping, and soon put them away. The little brother and sister were taught not to ask for their Gwen.

Lord Samuels and Lady Rosamund attended all the important court functions and parties. If the joy appeared to have gone out of their lives — and it often seemed that they did not truly care where they were or what was transpiring around them — they were merely exhibiting the proper attitude of noble indifference. They fit in perfectly with their new peers.

Lord Samuels and his family had only last night arrived in their house in Merilon, having been forced to leave Devon Castle when news of war was brought to them by the Ariels. It was to Lord Samuels's credit that he had not fled his lands until assured that the peasants who worked for him would be protected. Remembering what he'd heard from Joram of the life of the Field Magi and witnessing the appalling conditions in the village when he'd taken over the estate, Lord Samuels had done what he could to improve the living conditions of his people, spending his own money and magical energy. It was now one of the few pleasures in his barren, empty life to see the people's formerly dull, lackluster stares replaced by gratitude and respect.

"Do you think what we've heard is true?" Lady Rosamund asked him softly, glancing about to make certain the House Magi were out of hearing.

"About what, my dear?" he asked, turning to look at her.

"About . . . about the battle yesterday, the death of the Emperor? You've been locked in your study all forenoon. I heard you talking to someone and then the Ariels came. What messages did they bring?"

Lord Samuels sighed. Taking his wife's hand, he drew her near to him. "The news is not good. Yes, the reports are true. I was going to tell you, but I wanted to wait until Marie and the children and the servants were settled for the afternoon."

"What is it?" Lady Rosamund's face was pale, but her manner composed.

"The person I spoke to this morning was Rob."

"Rob?" Lady Rosamund looked at him in wonder. "Our overseer? Did you go back to the castle? After they warned us —"

"No, my dear. Rob is here, in Merilon. All our people are here. The *Duuk-tsarith* brought them into the city this morning. And it is not only ours, but they brought in the Field Magi of the surrounding villages as well."

"Name of the Almin!" Lady Rosamund moved closer to her husband, who put his arm around her comfortingly. "Such a thing has not happened since the Iron Wars! What is going on? Sharakan agreed to the Field of Contest. Why did they break their solemn vows —"

"It is not Sharakan, my dear," said Lord Samuels.

"But —"

"I know. That is what Bishop Vanya would have us believe. There are too many who know the truth, however, and who have returned to report it. The enemy is rumored to have come from Beyond. It is said that Prince Garald of Sharakan, who, you know, my dear, is reputed to be a man of honor and valor, fought side-by-side with Emperor Xavier against this new menace."

"Then why is Bishop Vanya lying to us?"

"That, my dear, is what a great many of us would like to know," Lord Samuels said gravely, frowning. "He won't even admit publicly that Xavier is dead, though witnesses have come forward giving their accounts. The Bishop — may the Almin forgive me — is old and infirm. This responsibility is too much for him, I fear. That is my belief and the belief of others, according to the messages they sent me. There will be a meeting this night at the Palace to consider what is to be done. I plan to attend."

Lord Samuels looked intently at his wife as he spoke. She gripped his arm more tightly.

"Who has called this meeting?" she asked, seeing a troubled expression in his eyes.

"Prince Garald, my dear," Lord Samuels answered calmly.

Lady Rosamund caught her breath, her lips parted to protest, but her husband forestalled her.

"Yes, I know Vanya will probably consider this treason. But something must be done. There is growing unrest in the city, particularly in City Below. Temporary quarters for the Field Magi have been established in the Grove, but those poor people are crowded in there like rabbits in a warren. There has always been dissatisfaction and rebellion among them. Now they have been dragged from their homes and brought here, to be held like prisoners. There is talk among them that they are going to be mutated and sent to fight, as were the centaurs in the ancient days. They plan to revolt —"

"Merciful Almin!" Lady Rosamund murmured.

"The lower classes of Merilon are in much the same state. Wild rumors fly among them. I have heard that they are gathering in front of the Cathedral, crying out for Bishop Vanya to show himself. Even among the nobility, families who have lost loved ones are angry and demanding answers. But the Bishop has shut himself up in his chambers in the Cathedral and refuses to see anyone, not even Duke d'Chambray or the other high-ranking nobles. Prince Garald and his retinue are staying with the Duke —"

"With the Duke?" Lady Rosamund gasped. "Here, in Merilon? A guest?"

"My dear," said Lord Samuels. "The situation is serious, I may even say desperate. I don't want to alarm you, but you must be prepared to face the truth. According to the message I received from the Duke, Merilon itself is in danger."

"That's ridiculous," said Lady Rosamund crisply. "The city has never been taken, not even during the Iron Wars. Nothing can penetrate the magic —"

Lord Samuels appeared about to remonstrate his wife when they were interrupted by the sound of a bell ringing in a distant part of the large house.

"The front door," said Lady Rosamund, inclining her head to listen. "How very strange. Someone has come out in this storm! Were you expecting anyone?"

"No," replied Lord Samuels, puzzled. "Not even the Ariels have been able to fly in this weather. They used the Corridors — I wonder . . ."

The two said nothing more but waited nervously and impatiently for the House Magus to appear.

"My lord," said a wide-eyed and flustered servant, flinging open the door to the parlor. "P-Prince Garald of Sharakan and a catalyst named Saryon to see you on a matter of extreme urgency."

"Show them in, please," said Lady Rosamund faintly. Prince Garald! Here, in her house! She had time enough to exchange a swift, questioning glance with her husband, who mutely indicated that he knew nothing more than she, when the guests were shown in. The Prince was attended by the ever-present black shadows of the *Duuk-tsarith.*

"Your Highness." Lady Rosamund sank into a curtsey but not as deep as she would have made to the late Xavier; after all, Prince Garald was the enemy. At least, he had been an enemy forty-eight hours ago. This was all so confusing, so frightening. . . .

"Your Grace." Lord Samuels bowed. "We are honored —"

"Thank you," replied Prince Garald, cutting off milord's speech. He did not do so rudely or even intentionally, but simply out of weariness. "May I present Father Saryon?"

"Father," murmured both milord and milady.

But when the catalyst withdrew his hood from his head, Lord Samuels recoiled, staring at him in shock and horror.

"You!" he cried in a hollow voice.

"My lord, I am truly sorry!" Saryon's face was drawn and anguished. "I forgot that you would recognize me from . . . from the Turning. I would not have come upon you in this sudden way had I known —"

Lady Rosamund went deathly pale. "My lord, who is this man?" she cried, clutching her husband.

"Lord Samuels, Lady Rosamund," said Prince Garald gravely, "I suggest that you be seated. The news we bring you will be difficult to bear and you both must be strong. It is unfortunate that we have to spring it on you in this abrupt manner, but our time is short."

"I don't understand!" Lord Samuels said, looking from one man to the other, his face suddenly grown pale. "What news?"

"It's about Gwendolyn!" Lady Rosamund cried suddenly, with a mother's instinct. She swayed where she stood and Prince Garald moved to help her to a couch; her husband — still staring at Saryon in a dazed manner — being totally incapable of coming to his wife's assistance.

"Send for the House Catalyst!" Garald said aside to one of the *Duuk-tsarith*, who did as he was instructed. Within moments, Marie was at the side of her mistress with a bowl of aromatic, restorative herbs. Ordering chairs to come forward around the fire, the Prince persuaded Lord Samuels to be seated as well.

A sip or two of brandy restored milord's composure — though he continued to stare at Saryon — and milady was recovered enough to flush deeply at the sight of the Prince waiting on them. She begged His Grace to be seated near the fire and dry his wet robes.

"Thank you, Lady Rosamund. We took a carriage here," said Prince Garald, noting the color returning to his lordship's face, yet still deeming it wise, for the moment, to keep the conversation general. "Despite that, I am soaked through. The Duke's conveyances are not equipped to deal with snowstorms, and there was no one in the manor this morning with magical energy enough to alter them. By the time we arrived, there was an inch of snow in the bottom of the carriage." He glanced ruefully down at his elegant, wine-colored velvet robes. "I fear I am dripping water on your carpet."

Milady begged the Prince not to concern himself in the slightest degree. The storm was certainly dreadful. Their garden had been ruined. . . . Her voice died. She could not continue. Lying upon the couch, holding tightly to Marie's hand, she stared at the Prince.

Garald exchanged glances with Saryon, who nodded slightly. Rising to his feet, the catalyst walked across the floor to stand before Lord Samuels. In his hands, he held a scrollcase.

"My lord," Saryon began, but hearing his voice, Lady Rosamund made a choking sound.

"I know you!" she cried, half-rising, thrusting aside Marie's gentle hands, "You are Father Dunstable! But your face is different."

"Yes, I am the man you knew as Father Dunstable. I was in your home in disguise." Saryon bowed his head, flushing in shame. "I beg your forgiveness. I took the face and body of another catalyst when I came to Merilon because — had I appeared in my own form — I would have been recognized and seized by the Church. How . . . how much of my history and of . . . Joram's do you know, my lord?" Saryon asked Lord Samuels hesitantly.

"A great deal," Lord Samuels replied. His voice was steady now. He gazed fixedly at Saryon, the horror gone from his eyes, replaced by hope, mingled with dread. "I know too much, in fact, or so Xavier thought. I know about Joram. I know his true lineage. I know, even, about the Prophecy."

At this, Garald's face became grave. "Are there many who know about that?" he asked abruptly.

"About the Prophecy?" Lord Samuels transferred his gaze to the Prince. "Yes, Your Grace. I believe so. Although it is never discussed openly, I have caught — now and then — oblique references to it among several of the higher ranking nobles. There were, you remember, many catalysts present that day. . . ."

"The Font has ears and eyes and a mouth," murmured Saryon. "Deacon Dulchase knew. He was present at that mockery of a trial Vanya held for Joram." The catalyst smiled faintly, turning the scrollcase over in his hand. "Dulchase was never noted for his ability to hold his tongue."

"This makes matters easier, Lord Samuels," Prince Garald remarked, "at least as far as you are concerned. What it may mean to us later is difficult to tell, so many knowing of the Prophecy."

He stared thoughtfully into the fire. The flickering flames did not brighten the Prince's face. They only made it seem darker, etched with deep shadows of worry and care. He made a gesture to the catalyst. "I am sorry for the interruption. Continue, Father."

"Lord Samuels," began Saryon gently, withdrawing a sheaf of parchment from the scrollcase and holding it out to the man, who stared at it but did not take it. "A great shock lies ahead of you. Be strong, milord!" The catalyst placed his hand over the trembling hand of the nobleman. "We have considered the best way to prepare you and, after much consultation, Prince Garald and I decided that you should read this document I now hold in my hand. The one who wrote it agrees with us. Will you read it, Lord Samuels?"

Lord Samuels reached out his hand, but it shook so that he let it fall back in his lap. "I can't! You read it for me, Father," he said softly.

Saryon glanced questioningly at the Prince, who nodded again. Carefully unrolling and smoothing the document, the Priest began reading aloud:

I leave this record with Father Saryon to be read in the event that I do not survive my initial encounter with the enemy. . . .

As he read Joram's description of his entry into Beyond, Saryon glanced up now and then to observe Lord Samuel's reaction and that of his wife. He saw upon their faces first perplexity, then growing comprehension, and, finally, unwilling, fearful understanding.

I can tell you little of my thoughts and feelings upon walking—as I suppose I did—into death, into Beyond.

A moan escaped Lady Rosamund at these words, accompanied by soothing, whispered words from Marie. Lord Samuels said nothing, but his expression of grief and sorrow and confusion touched Saryon deeply.

He glanced at Garald. The Prince was staring into the flames. He had read the document; Joram had given it to him on their return from the battlefield last night. He had read it many times and Saryon wondered if he fully comprehended it, fully understood. The Priest didn't think so. It was too much to grasp. He knew it to be true. After all, he had seen the evidence with his own eyes. Yet it was so unreal.

I did not even know—so lost was I in my own despair— that Gwendolyn had followed me. I remember hearing her voice as I stepped into the mists, calling me to wait. . . .

Lord Samuels groaned—a deep, wrenching sob. His head sank into his hand. Saryon ceased reading. Rising swiftly, Prince Garald came to kneel by the man's side. Resting his hand upon milord's arm, he repeated gently, "Be strong, sir!"

Lord Samuels could not reply, but he laid his hand gratefully over the hand of the Prince and seemed to indicate, by a weak nod, that Saryon was to continue. The catalyst did so, his own voice breaking once, forcing him to stop and clear his throat.

When I awoke, I found myself in a new world, living a new life. I married my poor Gwen—to keep her safe and secure—and part of every day I spent with her in the quiet, loving place where she stayed while the healers of Beyond endeavored to find some means to help her.

It has been ten years . . . ten years in our world . . .

"My child!" Lady Rosamund cried brokenly. "My poor child!"

Marie held Lady Rosamund close, her own tears mingling with those of her mistress. Lord Samuels sat quite still; he did not raise his head or even move. Saryon, after glancing at him a moment in concern, continued reading without interruption to the end.

The game is nothing, the playing of it everything.

Saryon fell silent. Sighing, he began to roll the parchment in his hand.

Outside the window, the falling snow deadened all sound. It seemed to be covering Merilon in heavy, white silence. The parchment rustling in the Priest's hands sounded unnaturally loud and jarring. Cringing, he stopped.

Then Prince Garald said, very softly, "My lord, they are here, in your home."

Lord Samuels raised his head. "Here? My Gwen . . ."

Lady Rosamund clasped her hands together with an eager cry.

"They are waiting in the hall. I want to make certain you are strong, my lord," Garald continued earnestly, holding onto Lord Samuels's arm, restraining him as it seemed he was about to fly from his chair. "Remember! It has been ten years for them! She is not the girl you knew! She is changed—"

"She is my daughter, Your Grace," Lord Samuels said hoarsely, thrusting the Prince aside. "And she has come home!"

"Yes, my lord," replied the Prince quietly, sadly. "She has come home. Father Saryon—"

The catalyst left without a word. Lady Rosamund, with Marie at her side, came to stand by her husband. He put his arm around her; she clung to him, hastily wiping away all traces of her tears from her face and smoothing her hair. Then she caught hold of Marie, holding the catalyst's arm with one hand, her husband's with the other.

Saryon returned, accompanied by Joram and Gwen, who stood waiting in the doorway, hesitant to enter. Both were muffled in heavy fur cloaks and hoods that they had retained, not wanting to reveal their identity to the servants. On entering, Joram cast his hood back from his head, revealing a face that was—at first glimpse—cold and impassive as stone. At the sight of Lord Samuels and Lady Rosamund, however, the man's stern facade crumbled. Tears glimmered in the brown eyes. He seemed to try to say something to them, but he could not speak. Gently, turning to his wife, he helped Gwen remove the hood from her head.

Gwen's golden hair gleamed in the firelight. Her pale, sweet face with the bright blue eyes glanced curiously around the room.

"My child!" Lady Rosamund attempted to float through the air to her daughter's side, but her magical energy failed her. Bereft of Life, she stumbled across the floor. "My child! My Gwendolyn!" Reaching out, she clasped her daughter in her arms and held her close, laughing and crying at the same time.

Gently pushing her mother away, Gwen stared at the woman in amazement. Then recognition gleamed eerily in her blue eyes. But it was not the recognition for which her parents hungered.

"Ah, Count Devon," Gwendolyn said, turning from Lady Rosamund to talk—it appeared—to an empty chair. "*These* must be the people you were telling me about!"

3

Of Salt Cellars And
Teapots

Though it was only late afternoon, the snowfall in Merilon brought premature night to the city. The House Magi's magic caused the lights in Lord Samuels's elegant mansion to glow softly, bringing cheerful light into the cheerless parlor where Lady Rosamund sat with Marie and her daughter. Globes of light brightened guest rooms that had been long closed up as the servants aired out linen and warmed beds, scattering rose petals about to drive out the musty odor of long disuse. As they worked, the servants repeated to each other whispered tales of people returned from the dead.

The only room in the house that remained dark was milord's study. The gentlemen who met in there preferred the shadows that seemed conducive to the nature of their dark conversation.

"And that is the situation we face, Lord Samuels," concluded Joram, staring out the window, watching the snow that continued to fall. "The enemy is intent on conquering

our world and releasing the magic into the universe. We have
convinced them that such a goal will be difficult to attain and
will cost them dearly."

He had spent the past hour describing as best he could
the battle on the Field of Glory. Lord Samuels listened in
dazed silence. Life Beyond. Creatures made of iron who kill
with a glance. Humans with metal skin. Gazing from Joram
to Lord Samuels, Saryon saw that milord was apparently
struggling to get a firm grip on the situation, but it was obvious from the bemused expression on his face that he felt as
if he were trying to catch hold of fog.

"What . . . what do we do now?" he asked helplessly.

"We wait," replied Joram. "There is a saying in Beyond.
We must hope for the best and prepare for the worst."

"What is the best?"

"According to the *Duuk-tsarith* who have been watching
them, the invaders fled in panic. It was a rout, something
better than I had hoped. They appear to be — from what the
warlocks can tell — divided and unorganized. I know the officer they chose to lead this expedition, a Major James Boris.
In any other situation he would be a good officer, he is rooted
in logic and common sense. But that makes him a poor choice
to send to this world. He is out of his depth, over his head.
He won't be able to cope with a war that — to him — must
come straight out of a horror novel. I am betting he will retreat, take his men off-world."

"And then?"

"Then, we must find a way to seal the Border once and
for all. That shouldn't be too difficult —"

"The *Duuk-tsarith* are already working on it," Garald said.
"But it will take an extraordinary amount of Life. Some from
each Living person in Thimhallan — or so they speculate."

"And what about the worst?" Lord Samuels asked, after
a pause.

Joram's lips tightened. "Boris will send for help. We don't
have the time or the energy now to stop them on the Border.
We must fortify Merilon. We must wake this city from its
enchanted sleep and prepare its people to defend it."

"First someone must wrest control from that quivering
mass of jelly who huddles in his Crystal Cathedral and

whines to the Almin to protect him," Garald pointed out. "Begging your pardon, Father Saryon."

The catalyst smiled wanly and shook his head.

"You're right, of course, Your Grace, but who will the people follow?" Lord Samuels shifted in his chair, sitting forward. This was politics, something he could understand. "There are some — like d'Chambrey — who are intelligent enough to put aside differences and come together to fight this common enemy. But there are others — like Sir Chesney, that thick-headed, stubborn mule. I doubt he'll believe any of this about other worlds. Merciful Almin!" Lord Samuels ran his hand through his graying hair. "I'm not sure I believe it and I have proof before my own eyes. . . ."

His gaze left the study where the men sat talking and turned toward the adjoining parlor. From within the cold, formal room with its elegant furnishings, barely seen through the half-open door, Saryon could hear Gwen's voice. Its sad, haunting music was a fitting accompaniment — so it seemed to him — to this talk of war and death.

"Please don't misunderstand," Gwendolyn was telling her confused and distraught mother. "Count Devon is pleased with most of the changes you have made in his house. It's just that he finds it so confusing, what with the new furniture and all. Then there's so *much* furniture! He wonders if it's all necessary. Particularly these little tables." Gwendolyn fluttered a hand. "Everywhere he turns there's another little table. He keeps blundering into them in the night. And just when he thought he was growing used to the tables, you moved the china cabinet. It has stood in the same place for years — on the north wall of the dining room, wasn't it?"

"It — it . . . blocked the morning light . . . from the east windows . . ." murmured Lady Rosamund faintly.

"The poor man ran smack into it during the night," said Gwen. "He broke a salt cellar — quite by accident, he assures you. But the Count was wondering if it would be too much trouble to move it back."

"My poor child!" said Lord Samuels. With an abrupt motion of his hand, he caused the door between his study and the parlor to shut itself quietly. "What is she talking about?" he demanded in a low, anguished voice. "She doesn't recognize us, yet she knows about the . . . the china cabinet and . . . the salt cellar! The salt cellar! My god! We assumed one of the servants broke it!"

"What was the name of the previous owner of this estate?" Joram asked. He, too, had been listening to his wife, his eyes shadowed with pain that echoed in his voice.

Saryon started to offer comfort, but Lord Samuels was answering Joram's question and the catalyst clamped his lips shut. Shifting restlessly in his chair, the Priest began to rub his misshapen fingers, as though they ached. What comfort could he offer anyway? Empty words, that was all.

"The previous owner? He's dead. His name was . . ." Lord Samuels broke off, staring at Joram in horrified understanding. "Count Devon!"

"I tried to tell you," Joram said, sighing. "She talks to the dead. In this world, she would be known as a Necromancer."

"But the Necromancers are gone! Their kind was destroyed during the Iron Wars!" Lord Samuels turned his agonized gaze from Joram back to the parlor; his daughter's voice could still be heard faintly through the closed door.

Joram absently ran his fingers through his hair. "In the world Beyond they consider her to be insane. They do not believe in Necromancy. The healers theorize that the terrible trauma Gwendolyn underwent caused her to seek escape in a fantasy realm of her own imaginings, a realm where she feels safe from harm. I alone believe that there is a certain sanity in her madness, that she *can* truly communicate with the dead."

"Not you alone. . . ." Saryon corrected ominously.

Joram's dark brows came together. "No, you are right, Father," he said in a low voice. "I am not alone. Menju the Sorcerer — the man I mentioned in my document — also believes that she is a Necromancer. When he realized how valuable this ancient skill could prove to him, he tried to abduct her. That was when I first became aware of his true nature."

"Valuable?" Garald stirred in his chair. Sitting at Lord Samuels's desk, he'd been studying maps of Thimhallan, but it had grown too dark in the room to read them, and now he listened to the conversation. "How? What can the dead offer the living?"

"Have you never studied the work of the Necromancers, Your Grace?" asked Saryon.

"Not much," Garald admitted indifferently. "They propitiated the spirits of the dead—making amends for misdeeds, finishing tasks left undone, that sort of thing. According to the histories, their dying out after the Iron Wars was no great loss."

"I beg to differ with you, Your Grace," Saryon said earnestly. "When the Necromancers died out, the Church made it *appear* to be no great loss. But it seems to me that it was. I have spent many hours with Gwendolyn, listening to her talk with those only she can see and hear. The dead possess something of incomparable value—something that will forever be withheld from the living."

"And that is—" Garald said somewhat impatiently, obviously wanting to turn the conversation to more important matters but too polite to offend the catalyst.

"Complete understanding, Your Grace! When we die, we will become one with the Creator. We will know His plans for the universe. We will see, at last, the Cosmic Scheme!"

Garald suddenly appeared interested. "Do you believe this?" he asked.

"I—I'm not certain." Saryon flushed, averting his face, staring down at his shoes. "It is what we are taught," he added lamely. The old tormenting questioning of his faith— questioning he had thought answered by Joram's "death"— was being bandied about by his soul again.

"Say this is true," Garald persisted. "Could the dead grant this knowledge of the future to the living?"

"Whether or not I believed it, Your Grace"—Saryon smiled sadly—"that would seem to me to be impossible. The world the dead see is beyond our ability to comprehend, much as it is impossible for us to understand this world Joram has seen. We see time through a single window that faces only one direction. The dead see time through hundreds of windows facing all directions." The catalyst spread his scarred hands in an effort to express the enormity of this vision. "How, then, can they hope to describe what they see! But they can offer advice. And they did—through the Necromancers. In ancient days, the dead were granted the opportunity to counsel the living. People venerated their dead, they kept in contact with them, and they had the benefit of the dead's insight into the one Vast Mind. That is what has been lost, Your Grace."

"I see." Garald pondered, his eyes gazing thoughtfully at the closed door.

Saryon shook his head.

"No, Your Grace," he said quietly. "She cannot help us. For all we know, this unfortunate Count, talking of china cabinets and salt cellars, may be trying to get our attention to explain something much more important. But, if so, Gwendolyn could not impart that information to us. She can communicate with the dead, but not with the living."

The Prince appeared ready to pursue the subject, but Saryon — with a glance at Lord Samuels and another at Joram — shook his head slightly, reminding the Prince that — for two people at least — this was a painful subject. The father gazed through the closed door, the expression on his face one of perplexity and grief. The husband stared out into the dead, snow-shrouded garden in bitter resignation. Clearing his throat, Prince Garald abruptly changed the subject.

"We were discussing the fact that Merilon needs a leader, someone to rally the people," he said briskly. "I have stated before, I can think of only one person. . . ."

"No!" Joram turned from the window with an impatient gesture. "No, *Your Grace*," he added more gently, in a belated attempt to soften the harshness of his reply.

"Joram, listen to me!" Garald leaned forward to argue. "You are by far the —"

A Corridor gaped open suddenly in the center of the study, interrupting the Prince. Everyone in the room stared at it expectantly, but for a moment nothing was visible. Saryon could hear voices coming from within, however, and what sounded like a struggle.

"Take your hands off me! Lout! You've crushed the velvet. I'll have fingermarks on my sleeve for a week! I —"

Simkin, dressed in bright green hose, an orange hat, and a green velvet doublet tumbled out of the Corridor, landing in a heap on the floor. He was followed by Mosiah, still dressed in the uniform of an archer of Sharakan, and by two, black-robed and hooded *Duuk-tsarith*.

Apparently nonplussed at his less than graceful entrance, Simkin rose to his feet, bowed to the assembled gentlemen, and said grandly, with a flutter of orange silk and a graceful wave of his hand, "Your Grace, congratulate me. I have found them!"

Ignoring Simkin, who was preening himself on his latest triumph, Mosiah turned to the Prince. "Your Grace, *we* found *him*. He was in the enemy's camp. Acting on your orders, the *Thon-li*, the Corridor Masters, caught him and brought him to me. With their help" — he indicated the warlocks — "I managed to drag him here."

"Which is precisely where I was coming!" said Simkin with a pained expression. "Or I would have been if I'd known where *here* was. I've been searching everywhere, quite pining away for a glimpse of your handsome face, O Prince. You see, I have the most frightfully important information — "

"According to the *Thon-li*, he was on his way to the Cathedral," interrupted Mosiah caustically.

Simkin sniffed. "I presumed Your Grace was there, of course. Everyone who is anyone is at the Cathedral. The peasants are giving the most jolly riot — "

"Riot?" Prince Garald looked at the *Duuk-tsarith* for confirmation.

"Yes, Your Grace," said the black-robed warlock, hands folded before him. "We were coming to report this to you when Mosiah requested our assistance. The Field Magi have broken out of the Grove and are storming the Cathedral, demanding to see the Bishop." The black hood lowered slightly, one of the hands making a deprecating movement. "We could not stop them, Your Grace. Though they have few catalysts, they are still strong in magic, and our forces are weakened."

"I understand," Prince Garald said gravely, exchanging alarmed glances with Lord Samuels. Saryon saw both of them look toward Joram, who refused to meet their eyes, but stood with his back turned, staring into the garden that could now barely be seen through the gloom. "What is the Bishop doing?"

"He refuses to see them, Your Grace. He has ordered the doors to the Cathedral magically sealed. Those members of our Order with strength enough to cast spells are guarding it."

"So the Cathedral is safe for the time being?"

"Yes —"

"They won't attack it, Your Grace!" Mosiah cried. "They don't want to hurt anyone! They're frightened and they want answers."

"Is your father among them, Mosiah?" Prince Garald asked quietly.

"Yes, my lord," Mosiah said. His face flushed. "My father is their leader. He knows what really happened in the battle yesterday. I told him. Maybe it was wrong of me," he added with half-proud, half-shamed defiance, "but they have a right to know the truth!"

"They do indeed," Prince Garald said, "and hopefully we will be able to impart it to them." He glanced at Joram, who continued to stare into the night, his face stern and impassive. Shoving aside the maps, Prince Garald stood up and began pacing the room, his hands behind him. "So, Simkin," he said abruptly, turning to the green velvet clad young man, "you've been to see the enemy."

"E'gad! Of course!" said Simkin. With a wave of his hand, he conjured up a fainting-couch. "You will excuse me, I hope?" he asked languidly, stretching out on the couch that sat squarely in the center of the study, making it impossible for the Prince to continue pacing without running into it. "And do you mind if I change clothes? I've been wearing this same color of green for hours and I fear it does nothing for my complexion. Makes me look quite jaundiced."

As he spoke, the green hose and doublet transformed themselves into a red brocade dressing gown, trimmed with black fur cuffs and a thick fur collar. Red slippers with curled toes adorned his feet. Simkin appeared quite charmed with these and, lifting a foot, regarded it with delight.

"The enemy?" Garald reminded him.

"Oh, yes! Well, what else was I supposed to do, Your Grace? I trotted about the battlefield for a bit, but — while undeniably entertaining, it struck me that there was a chance that I might see the light, so to speak, in a most painful manner. Having a hole burned in one's skull is not my idea of an illuminating experience. However," continued Simkin, plucking the orange silk from the air and dabbing delicately at his nose, "I was determined to do something for my country. So, at great personal risk to myself, I decided" — dramatic flourish of the orange silk — "to become a spy!"

"Go on," ordered Gerald.

"Certainly. By the bye, Joram, dear fellow," said Simkin, reclining among an abundance of silk pillows, "did I say that I am delighted to see you?" He waved the orange silk. "You're looking well, though I must say you have *not* aged the least bit gracefully."

"*If* you were in the enemy's camp, tell us what you saw!" Joram persisted.

"Oh, I was there," said Simkin, smoothing his mustache with a slender finger. "Shall I prove it to you, my King? I am, after all, your fool. Do you remember? Two Death cards? You dying twice? They laughed at me then" — he glanced slyly at Mosiah and Saryon — "but I don't see them laughing now. I had a devil of a time getting into camp. Corridor is crawling with black and creepy things" — a scathing glance at the *Duuk-tsarith* — "all lurking about the enemy. . . .

"That's going to end, by the way," Simkin added nonchalantly. "An old friend of yours who calls himself Dog Doo the Sorcerer or something like that has sealed off the Corridors — "

Joram went white to the lips, becoming so pale that Saryon went to his side, resting a supportive hand on his arm. So this is it, Saryon thought. What he's feared all along has come to pass.

"Menju." Joram said in a barely audible voice.

"What did you say? Menju? That's it! Beastly name! Charming fellow, however. Travels about with a crude sort — a short, thick-necked military type who doesn't drink tea. Nevertheless, there I sat, a perfect teapot upon his desk. Crude fellow sent me out with a heavy-handed sergeant, a dim-witted man, fortunately. It was simplicity itself for me to return while he wasn't looking. I say, dear boy, are you listening?"

Joram didn't answer. Gently putting aside Saryon's hand, he walked blindly to the fireplace, his white robes brushing the floor. Gripping the edge of the mantelpiece, he stared into the embers of the dying fire, his face drawn and troubled.

"He is here!" he said at last. "Of course, I was expecting it. But how? Did he escape or did they free him?" He turned, staring at Simkin with eyes that burned more brightly than the smoldering coals. "Describe this man. What does he look like?"

"A handsome devil. Sixty if he's a day, though he pretends he's thirty-nine. Tall, broad-shouldered, gray hair, lovely teeth. I don't think the teeth are his, by the way. Dressed in the most fearfully drab clothes . . . ."

"It's him!" muttered Joram, slamming his fist into the mantel in sudden anger.

"And he's in charge, dear boy. It seems this Major Boris was all for clearing out and — Ha, ha! There was one highly amusing incident, must mention in passing. Sorcerer . . . ha, ha . . . mutated the Major's hand . . . turned it into a chicken foot! The look on the wretched man's face . . . priceless, I assure you! Ah, well," Simkin said, wiping his eyes, "I suppose you had to be there. Where was I? Oh, yes. Major was going to chuck it all and call it quits, but this — what did you say his name was? Menju? Yes. This Menju fellow changed poor old Boris's hand into a drumstick, causing the Major to "chicken" out if you'll forgive the expression."

Simkin appeared quite pleased with his joke.

"And?" persisted Joram.

"And what? Oh, that. The Major's not leaving."

"Joram —" Garald began sternly.

"What do they plan to do?" Joram asked, silencing the Prince.

"There was a word they used," Simkin said, stroking his mustache thoughtfully. "A word that described it quite aptly. Let me think. . . . Ah! I have it! Genocide!"

"Genocide?" Garald repeated in perplexity. "What does that mean?"

"Extermination of a race of people," Joram answered grimly. "Of course. It makes sense. Menju must kill us all."

4

The Almin Have Mercy

J oram, keep your voice
down!" Mosiah ordered.

It was too late. The door between the rooms opened, but
Lady Rosamund appeared. Her face was livid. She and
Marie had obviously both overheard Joram. Only Gwendolyn remained unaffected, sitting in the parlor and chatting
calmly with the late Count Devon.

"I'm certain they'll move the china cabinet back to the
north wall, since I've explained," she was saying. "Is there
anything else? Mice, you say, in the attic? They're eating
your portrait that's stored up there? I'll mention it, but —"

Distractedly, Lady Rosamund gazed from her daughter
to her husband. "Mice! China cabinets. . . . Now . . . what I
heard him say in here! They're going to kill us? Why? Why
is this happening?" Putting her head in her hands, she began
to sob.

"My dear, calm yourself," said Lord Samuels, hurrying to
his wife's side. Taking her in his arms, he laid her head upon

his chest, smoothing her hair with his hand. "Remember the children," he murmured, "and the servants."

"I know!" Biting on her handkerchief, Lady Rosamund sought to hush her weeping. "I'll be strong. I will!" she said, choking. "It's just . . . all too much! My poor child! My poor child!"

"Gentlemen, Your Grace," said Lord Samuels, looking back into the study, "please excuse me. Come, my dear," he said, helping his wife stand. "I'll take you to your room. Everything's going to be all right. Marie, stay with my daughter."

"Gwendolyn will be fine, my lord." Father Saryon intervened. "I will stay with her. Marie should be with her mistress."

Lord Samuels led his wife upstairs, Marie attending her. Father Saryon sat down in a chair near Gwendolyn, looking anxiously at her to see if this news disturbed her as well. Apparently not. Perfectly at home in the world of the dead, she was oblivious to anything transpiring in the world of the living.

"Father," said Joram abruptly, turning from where he stood beside the fireplace in milord's study, "please move closer, where you can hear us. I need your counsel."

What counsel can I offer? the catalyst wondered bitterly. Joram brought this doom upon the woman who loved him, upon her parents, upon the world. Upon himself.

Did he have a choice? Did we?

Patting Gwendolyn's hand, Saryon left her discussing the need for acquiring a cat with the Count. Moving his chair nearer the door that separated the parlor from milord's study, he sat down, his heart a burden almost too heavy to bear. What will he do now? Saryon asked himself, his eyes on Joram. What will he do?

Raising his head, almost as though he had heard the unspoken question, Joram faced him. The lead weight of Saryon's heart sank, his fears bearing it down. The pain-filled, anguished lines carved in the sculptured face had been ground out, leaving it smooth, hard, and unyielding. The bleeding soul had crept into its stone fortress and was hiding there, nursing its wounds.

"Genocide. This explains everything," Joram said coolly. "The murder of the civilians, the disappearance of the catalysts —"

"Joram, listen to me!" interrupted Prince Garald sternly. The Prince gestured at Simkin who was lounging, eyes closed, on the fainting-couch. "How did *he* know what they were saying?"

"By the Almin!" Joram swore softly. "That's true!" He turned from the mantelpiece. "How *did* you understand what they said, Simkin? You can't speak their language."

"I can't?" Simkin's eyes flared open wide. He appeared no end astonished. "By Jove, I wish someone had told me! Here I wasted all this time, sitting on the Major's desk, allowing that ham-fisted sergeant to run off with me, listening to them talk of sending for reinforcements, hearing that the reinforcements will be unable to get here for seventy-two hours. . . . Now you tell me that I didn't understand a single word they said? I'm quite put out!" Simkin glared round at them indignantly. "The least you could have done was tell a chap beforehand!"

Sniffing, wiping his nose with orange silk, Simkin flung himself back on the couch pillows and stared gloomily at the ceiling.

"Seventy-two hours," Joram muttered to himself. "That's the time from the nearest starbase. . . ."

"You believe him?" Garald demanded.

"I must!" Joram flashed back. "And so must you," he added grimly. "I don't know how to explain it, but he's seen the Sorcerer. He's described him *and* Major Boris! And what he claims he overheard makes sense. Boris *didn't* come here with orders to slaughter us! He came, undoubtedly, to intimidate us with a show of force, figuring we'd surrender. But Menju doesn't want that." Joram shifted his gaze from Garald back to the flickering embers. "He wants the magic. He is of this world. He wants to return to it and gain its power. And he wants everyone in it who could be a threat to him dead!"

"That's why he has taken the catalysts prisoner," said Saryon in sudden understanding. "He is using them to give him Life —"

" — and he is using that Life to intimidate Major Boris and to seal off the Corridor."

"I don't believe it! This is ridiculous!" Standing in the shadows of the study, practically forgotten, Mosiah had listened to Simkin's story in disbelief. Now, coming forward, he looked from the Prince to Joram to Saryon pleadingly. "Simkin's made this all up! They couldn't kill us all — *everyone* in Thimhallan! That's thousands, millions of people!"

"They can and they will," Joram said flatly. "They have committed genocide before on their own world, back in ancient times, and when they went forth into the stars and found life there, they did it again — slaughtering large numbers of beings whose only crime was that of being 'different.' They have developed highly efficient methods of killing — weapons that are capable of wiping out entire populations within minutes.

"They won't use those here on this world, however," Joram added thoughtfully. "Menju needs the magic in this world to remain intact, undisturbed. He couldn't risk using a high-energy weapon, one that might disrupt Life. . . ."

Garald shook his head, frustrated, obviously not understanding. "I agree with Mosiah. It's impossible!"

"No it isn't!" Joram cried angrily. "Get that out of your mind! Admit the danger! There are millions of people here, yes! But there are hundreds of thousands of millions in Beyond! Their armies are enormous. They can bring in soldiers numbering three times the population of Thimhallan if they choose!

"We fight. We defend our cities." Joram shrugged. "In the end we must lose, overwhelmed by sheer force of numbers alone. Those that survive the sieges and the battles will be systematically rounded up and put to death: man, woman, and child. The Sorcerer will keep a few hundred catalysts or so, to make certain their kind doesn't die out, but that will be all. He will gain control of this world, of its magic, and he and those few like him in the world Beyond will become invincible."

"The end of the world. . . ." Garald spoke before he thought. Saryon saw his face flush, and he cast a swift glance at Joram. "Damn it!" the Prince said suddenly, slamming his hands on the desk. "We've got to stop them! There must be a way!"

Joram did not immediately answer. The fire flared and, for an instant, Saryon saw by its light the man's lips twist in a dark half-smile and suddenly the catalyst was no longer in Lord Samuels's home, in the snow-bound city of Merilon. Once again, Saryon stood in the forge in the Sorcerer's village; he saw the fire of the hot coals shine in dark eyes; he saw a young man hammering a strangely glowing metal; once again, he saw the bitter, vengeful youth forging the Darksword. . . .

Someone else saw that youth, too. Someone else in the room saw and remembered. Mosiah looked at the man who had a year ago been his best, his only friend.

He looked at a man he no longer knew.

In the excitement and danger of the past day and night, Mosiah had been able to avoid looking at Joram — a Joram who had aged ten years to Mosiah's one, who had lived in another world, who had seen wonders that Mosiah could neither imagine nor comprehend. Now, in the hushed, fear-laden silence, Mosiah could no longer avoid studying the face that he knew so well, yet didn't know at all. His eyes misted with tears and he chided himself, knowing that he should be concerned with this larger tragedy, the impending destruction of his people, his world.

But that was too big, too awful to grasp. He focused on his smaller, personal tragedy, feeling selfish, but helpless to do otherwise. Hearing Joram's voice was like listening to one who was dead. It was — to Mosiah — the ghost of his friend speaking through this stranger.

Had it been the same for Saryon? Mosiah glanced at the Priest, whose eyes were fixed on Joram as well. Grief and sorrow mingled with pride and love on the catalyst's face, and it made Mosiah feel very lonely. No, the catalyst's love for the man is as strong and abiding as it was for the youth. And why shouldn't it be? After all, Saryon had sacrificed his life for that love.

And Garald? Mosiah's gaze turned toward the Prince. That was different. It had been easy for the Prince to find in

this man the admired comrade he had seen in the young
Joram. Differences in age and maturity had made friendship
difficult to establish then. Now at last they were equals. It
was Garald who had taken Mosiah's place.

As for Simkin, Mosiah cast him a bitter glance. Joram
could have come back a salamander and it wouldn't have
affected the fool's feelings one way or the other. There was no
one else who mattered. Lord Samuels and Lady Rosamund
were still in shock, unable to register any feelings at all except confusion and grief and fear.

That was how Mosiah had felt at first, but the initial fear
had been submerged in much greater fears, the shock had
worn itself out. Now he felt only empty and sad — a feeling
made worse whenever Joram looked at him. For Mosiah saw,
reflected in the man's eyes, his own sense of bitter loss. Neither could ever regain what they once had. For him, Joram
had died when he stepped across that Border. Mosiah had
lost his friend, never to find him again.

Long minutes passed. The only sound intruding on the
silence in milord's study was Gwendolyn's voice, rising and
falling, wandering in and out like a playful child. The voice
wasn't disturbing. In an odd way, Mosiah considered it as
much a part of the silence as the silence itself. If silence found
a tongue and could speak, it would talk with her voice. And
then, Gwen's voice could no longer be heard. Unnoticed by
Saryon, who was lost in a frightful dream of the past, she
glided silently from the parlor.

Now a waterclock, keeping track of the seconds, could be
heard, its drip, drip of passing time causing tiny ripples to
mar the surface of the silence. Outside, the snow changed to
rain. Drumming dismally upon the roof, it thudded into the
thick snow with dull, plopping splatters. A miniature ava-
lanche of snow, loosened by the rain, slid off the roof with a
rumbling, scraping sound, crashing down in the garden outside the window. So quiet was the room and so tense were
those inside that this caused everyone to start, including the
disciplined, unmoving *Duuk-tsarith*. Black hoods quivered,
fingers twitched.

At last, Joram spoke.

"We have seventy-two hours," he said, turning to face them, his voice firm, resolved. "Seventy-two hours to do to them what they intend to do to us."

"No, Joram!" Saryon rose from his chair. "You can't mean that!"

"I assure you I do mean it, Father. It is our only hope," Joram said coldly. His white robes, catching the light of the dying fire, gleamed faintly in the gray gloom of the room that was darkening with the coming of night. "We must destroy the enemy utterly, to the last man. There must be no one left alive to return to Beyond. Once we have wiped them out, we can repair the Border and seal ourselves off from the rest of the universe finally and forever."

"Yes!" said Garald decisively. "We'll strike them swiftly, take them by surprise!"

Walking to the desk, Joram bent over a map. "Here's where the enemy is located." He pointed, tracing a route with his fingers. "We'll bring in War Masters from Zith-el here. Centaurs and giants from the Outland. We can attack from these positions—" Impatiently, he glanced about. "I can't see. We need light. . . ."

Globes of flame burst into life, the *Duuk-tsarith* casting them into the air to dispel the shadows.

"The Field Magi will fight!" Mosiah said eagerly, hurrying over to the table to join Joram and the Prince.

"We'll present this plan to the nobles at the meeting tonight." The Prince hurriedly began rolling up the map. "Speaking of that, it's time we were going."

"How soon can we be ready?"

"Tomorrow night. Our people will be rested by then. We can strike tomorrow night."

"And we kill them all, every one! No survivors!"

"I say, how jolly!" Simkin woke up. "I have just the ensemble. I call it *Blood and Guts*!"

"May the Almin have mercy on their souls!" Prince Garald said coolly, motioning for the *Duuk-tsarith* to bring his sword and his cloak.

"Almin have mercy!" Saryon's hoarse cry startled them all. Joram and Mosiah turned, Prince Garald looked around.

"I beg your pardon, Father," the Prince said apologetically, "I meant no sacrilege."

"Sacrilege? Don't you fools see? How can you be so blind? There *is* no Almin! There will be no mercy! I couldn't admit it to myself until now." Saryon spoke feverishly, his gaze not on them but abstracted, staring far away. "But I've known for a long, long time.

"I knew it as I watched Vanya carry that tiny baby to its death. I knew it as I watched Joram step into Beyond. I knew it as I watched the endless mist day after day while they chopped at my flesh with their tools and broke my fingers, trying to take the weapon forged of darkness! I knew it as I watched the creatures of iron rumble across our world."

Saryon clasped his deformed hands together as if he would pray, but his twisted fingers turned the gesture into a pitiful mockery. "And now I hear you talk of more killing, of more slaughter. The Almin doesn't exist! He doesn't care! We have been left here alone to play this senseless game!"

"Father!" Mosiah, appalled, hurried over to lay his hand remonstratingly on Saryon's arm. "Don't say such things!"

Angrily Saryon shook himself free. "No Almin! No mercy!" he cried bitterly.

A crash, sounding from another room, interrupted the catalyst's tirade. A shout from the servants caused everyone —including the *Duuk-tsarith*—to run from the study to the dining room. Everyone, that is, except Simkin, who took advantage of the confusion to quickly and quietly disappear.

"Gwendolyn!" Joram caught hold of his wife. "Are you all right? Father, come quickly! She's hurt herself!"

The china cabinet was in ruins, its wood shattered; the fragile porcelain and glass it contained were nothing but splintered fragments scattered about the floor. In the midst of the wreckage knelt Gwendolyn, holding a fragment of broken glass in her hand. Blood dripped from her fingers.

"He's sorry, he truly is," Gwen said, looking around at them with her bright blue eyes. "But you've changed things so much, he doesn't recognize his own home anymore."

5

The Emperor's Son

The muttering of the crowd outside could be heard within the walls of Crystal Cathedral, an ocean of sound surging up from the street and breaking in rolling waves upon their transparent surface.

Standing beside his chair, staring out at the hundreds of people who hovered in the rain-soaked twilight outside, Bishop Vanya's right hand clenched in impotent fury. His left hand would have clenched as well, except that it hung limp at his side. Moodily Vanya reached over to massage the limb that refused to obey his commands, his eyes glaring at the crowd below with increasing frustration.

"What do they want of me?" he demanded, turning his glare upon the Cardinal, who recoiled from the baleful gaze. "What do they expect *me* to do?"

"Perhaps talk to them, say a few words. . . . Let them know the Almin is with them," suggested the Cardinal in mollifying tones.

The Bishop snorted, the explosive discharge so loud that it startled the Cardinal, already trembling with nervous dread. The Bishop was about to tell his minister what he thought of *that* idea when a hush fell over the people below, catching the attention of both men.

"Now what?" Vanya muttered, turning to look back through the crystal wall, the Cardinal hurrying to his side. "See?" The Bishop snorted again. "What did I tell you?"

Prince Garald had appeared above the crowd, riding upon a black swan. Accompanying him was Joram. At the first sight of the man in the white robes, a ripple of excitement ran through the multitude. The Bishop, pressed against the crystal wall, could hear their shouts.

"Angel of Death!" he repeated bitterly. He glanced at his quaking minister. "You want me to tell them the Almin is with them, Cardinal? Hah! They are being led by the Prince of Sorcerers, the devil incarnate, allied with a Dead man! He is marching them straight to their doom! And they, not content to follow like sheep, rush toward it, hurling themselves off the cliff!"

Pursing his lips angrily, the Bishop turned back to watch the scene outside his walls.

Prince Garald, descending from the swan's back, walked onto a marble platform that floated in the air above the heads of the crowd. Throwing back the hood of his cloak, he stood bareheaded in the rain, holding up his hands to call for silence. Joram followed more slowly. He appeared uneasy, standing on the platform's rain-slick surface so far above the ground.

"Citizens of Thimhallan, listen to me!" Prince Garald cried.

The crowd's shouting ceased, but the silence that replaced it was an angry silence, almost louder than the noise preceding it.

"I know," Garald spoke to the silence. "I am your enemy. Say, rather, I *was* your enemy, for I am your enemy no longer!"

Vanya muttered something at this.

"Holiness?" asked the Cardinal, who didn't catch it.

The Bishop, attending closely to the Prince's words that could just barely be heard through the crystal walls, motioned irritably for his minister to keep quiet.

"You have all heard the rumors about the battle," the Prince was saying. "You have heard about creatures of iron that can kill with a glance of their blazing eyes. You have heard of strange humans who carry death in their hands."

The silence remained unbroken, but there was a shifting and rustling in the crowd as each man glanced at his neighbor, nodding in confirmation.

"It is all true," Prince Garald continued in a low, grim voice. Low as it was, it could be heard quite plainly by the hushed crowd. It could be heard quite plainly by the Bishop and his Cardinal, standing in the Bishop's chambers above them.

"It is true!" Garald raised his voice. "It is also true that Emperor Xavier is dead."

Now the silence broke. The crowd cried out in anger, scowling and shaking their heads and occasionally their fists.

"If you don't believe me," Prince Garald called out, "look up there and you will see the truth!" He pointed — not to heaven as some supposed at first, but to Bishop Vanya.

Standing near the transparent wall, illuminated by the lights in his office, the Bishop was plainly visible to the crowd below. Too late, he tried to move, but he could not. Although his left leg wasn't paralyzed as was his arm, it was weak and he could not maneuver his great bulk about as easily as before. He could do nothing, therefore, except stand in his chambers, staring down at the people, his face contorted by an outer struggle to appear calm and an inner struggle with his fury. There was no mistaking the truth in the pallor of the man's jowls, the sagging face, the writhing grimace of the mouth. The rain sliding down the wall made the Bishop appear as if he were melting. Glancing at one another, muttering, the people turned away from the Bishop to listen to the Prince.

"An enemy is out there," Prince Garald continued relentlessly, shouting above the growing restless voice of the crowd, "an enemy more terrifying than you can imagine. This enemy has penetrated the Border! It has come from Beyond, from the realm of Death! This enemy seeks to bring death to our world!"

The crowd shouted loudly, drowning out the Prince's words.

Bishop Vanya shook his head, a sneer curled his lip. *"There will be born to the Royal House one who is dead yet will live, who will die again and live again. And when he returns, he will hold in his hand the destruction of the world,"* Vanya repeated softly. "Follow him, you fools. Follow him. . . ."

"We must join together against this enemy!" Garald cried out, and the crowd cheered. "I have been meeting with the nobles of your city-state. They have agreed with me. Will you fight?"

"Aye, but who'll lead us?"

This voice came from the front of the crowd, spoken by a man dressed in the plain, shabby clothes of a Field Magus. He flew forward hesitantly, as though being shoved from behind. Snatching off a bedraggled hat, he held it awkwardly in his hand and appeared at first abashed to be standing before the Prince. But once there, hovering in the air in front of the platform, he straightened his shoulders, facing the Prince and the white-robed man with quiet dignity.

At this moment, a young man who had been sitting — quiet and unobserved — on the back of the black swan rose into the air and came drifting down beside the Field Magus.

"Prince Garald," said the young man, "allow me to present my father."

"I am honored, sir," the Prince said, bowing in his graceful manner. "Your son is a valiant warrior who fought the enemy at my side yesterday."

The Field Magus flushed in pleasure at hearing this praise of his boy, but it did not deter him from his purpose. Clearing his throat in embarrassment, he glanced around at his followers, then continued.

"Begging your pardon, Your Grace. You say you aren't our enemy anymore. You say that there's an enemy out there bigger'n we can imagine. I guess we know that's true. We've all heard the tales told by my boy here, and others who were out there with you. An' we're willin' to fight this enemy, whoever he is or wherever he comes from."

The murmuring grew louder, and there were calls of support from the crowd.

"But," the Field Magus continued, nervously smoothing the hat with his callused, work-hardened hands, "no matter how honorable or noble a man you are, Prince Garald — and

I've heard good things told of you, I admit — you're a stranger to us. I think I speak not only for us field workers but for the people who work in this city as well"—cries of assent from the crowd—"when I say that we would feel better goin' into battle, led by someone who was one of us, so to speak. Someone we could count on to think of us as people he knew, not cattle bein' led to slaughter."

Joram stepped forward, watching his footing carefully on the slippery platform. "I know you, Jacobias. And you know me, though you may find that difficult to believe. I swear to you—" extending his hands, he looked out at the crowd—"I swear to all of you," he shouted, "that you can trust this man, Prince Garald, with your lives! We have just come from a gathering of the *Albanara*! They have chosen Prince Garald as their leader. I pledge him my support and I ask you—"

"No, no! We won't follow Sharakan!"

"One of our own!"

Mosiah, flushing in embarrassment, was arguing with his father. Garald glanced at Joram, as much as to say "I told you so." Joram, avoiding his gaze, was trying to make himself heard when one single voice, coming from the center of the crowd, rose above the clamor.

"*You* lead them, my son!"

The crowd hushed. The voice was familiar. The words, though quietly spoken, were said with such pride, mingled with a deep sorrow, that they echoed in the heart louder than a shout.

"Who said that?" People hovering in the air peered down beneath their feet, for the voice had seemed to come from below.

"He did! The old man! Stand aside and let him speak!"

Several people, floating above an old man, pointed at him. Backing away, they left him to stand alone in an ever-widening circle. The old man remained on the ground; he did not rise into the air with the others. No catalyst was with him, no friends, no family. His clothes were shabby and tattered, nearly falling from his body in rags. He was so bent and stooped that it was difficult for him to raise his head to peer upward toward the platform, blinking as the raindrops fell into his eyes.

A few of those in the crowd who had descended to get a better view suddenly sprang back up to join their fellows. An awed whisper began to circulate.

"The Emperor! The old Emperor!"

The circle around the old man grew larger, people craning their heads to see. Bishop Vanya, recognizing him, flushed red, then went white in anger. The Cardinal gasped audibly.

Prince Garald looked swiftly at Joram to see his reaction. There was none. Joram regarded the old man silently, without expression. The Prince gestured to the *Duuk-tsarith*, and the platform on which they stood sank slowly to the ground, the people swirling around it like leaves in a whirlwind.

As the platform came to rest on the stone pavement, the Prince motioned to the old man, who walked haltingly forward.

Looking intently into the old man's face, Prince Garald bowed. "Your Majesty," he said softly.

The Emperor nodded absently. He hadn't even looked at the Prince. Coming to stand in front of Joram, the old man reached out to touch him, but Joram — his face impassive, his eyes focused above his father's head — took a step backward. The Emperor, smiling sadly, nodded and slowly withdrew his hand.

"I don't blame you," he said softly. "Once, many years ago, I turned my back on you and they took you away to die." He glanced up at Joram. Though he was level with him, his bent body forced him to twist his head to look into the face of the tall man standing on the platform. "This makes the fifth time I have seen you, my son. My son . . ." The Emperor's voice lingered over the words. "Gamaliel. That was to have been your name. It is a word of the ancient days. It means 'reward of God.' You were to have been our reward, your mother's and mine." The Emperor sighed heavily. "Instead, the mad woman named you Joram — 'a vessel.' It was a fitting name. In our pride and fear, we cast you from us. The poor mad woman caught you up, and poured into you the sorrows of this world."

The Emperor gazed into the face of his son, who still did not look at him.

"I remember the day they took you from me. I remember the tears your mother shed, the crystal tears that shattered on your body. Tiny streams of blood ran down your skin. I turned my back on you, and they took you away to die. My fault, you say? The Church's fault?"

Straightening suddenly, rising almost to his full height, the Emperor cast a stern glance about the crowd. For an instant, the wan face was regal again, the crooked old man a proud and noble ruler. "My fault?" the Emperor questioned loudly. "What would you have done, people of Merilon, if you knew that a Dead child was destined to rule over you?"

The people drew away from him, looking askance at one another. The word *mad* was whispered about, and there was much nodding of heads. Yet there was not one among them who could meet the old man's accusing eyes.

Unconsciously, Joram's hand moved to touch his chest as though it pained him.

"Yes, my son" — the Emperor noticed the gesture — "they tell me you bear the scars of your mother's tears. They tell me that those scars helped prove your identity. I knew you long before that! I didn't have to see the scars on your chest. I saw the scars on your soul. Do you remember? It was the day at the house of Lord Samuels, the day I came to rescue Simkin the Fool from his latest folly. I saw your face in the sunlight, I saw your hair." The Emperor's eyes went to Joram's black hair, glistening in the rain. "I knew then that the son I'd fathered eighteen years ago lived! Yet I did nothing. I said nothing. I was afraid! Afraid for myself, but more afraid for you! Can you believe that?"

Joram's lips tightened, the hand on his breast twitched spasmodically; the only outward signs that he even heard his father's words.

"The next time I saw you was at the Crystal Palace, the night of the anniversary of your Death. Gamaliel. My reward! Your name burned my heart. I watched you meet your mother. Your mother — a corpse, the Life flowing through her veins a mockery. And you — alive but Dead. Yes, you were my reward."

Joram averted his face, a low strangled cry in his throat. "Take him away!"

The *Duuk-tsarith* glanced at Prince Garald, who shook his head. Garald put a hand upon his friend's shoulder, but Joram tore himself free. Gesturing furiously, he tried to say something but choked on his words. The Emperor gazed up at him pleadingly.

"The last time I saw you was at the Turning," he said in a voice as soft as the steady fall of the raindrops. "I saw the hope dawn in your eyes when you recognized me. I knew what you were thinking—"

"You could have acknowledged me!" Joram looked at his father directly for the first time, his eyes burning with the fire of the forge. "Vanya could not have put me to living death if you had claimed me for your own! You could have saved me!"

"No, my son," the Emperor said gently. "How could I save you when I could not save myself?" He bowed his head and his body bent again, crumpling back into the slumped, broken old man dressed in rags.

"I can't stay! I can't . . . breathe!" Clutching his chest, gasping for air, Joram turned to leave the platform.

"My son!" The old man reached out a trembling hand. "My son! Gamaliel!" the Emperor cried. "I cannot ask you to forgive me." He stared at Joram's back. "But perhaps you can forgive them. They need you now. . . . You will be *their* reward. . . ."

"Don't say that!" Once again Joram tried to leave but it was too late. People surged around him, asking questions, demanding answers, elbowing the old man out of the way. The Emperor's last words went unheard, drowned in the growing clamor of the crowd.

"The doddering old idiot," snarled Bishop Vanya from on high. "Xavier was right. We should have hastened his death—"

The Cardinal uttered a shocked reproof.

Bishop Vanya, rolling his head on its layers of paunchy skin, fixed his minister with a scornful gaze. "Don't give me that sanctimonious drivel. You know what's been done in the Almin's holy name. You've been able to close your eyes as you mumble your prayers, but you'll be quick enough to open them and snatch the rewards when I'm gone!"

Turning back again to observe the crowd, Bishop Vanya missed the glance of enmity and loathing bestowed upon him by his loyal minister.

It was growing dark. Night, hastened by the storm, was closing its fingers over Merilon. Here and there amid the crowd, the wizards caused magical lights to flare. Illuminated by their multicolored flames, Mosiah's father — now apparently the unofficial spokesman — stepped forward.

"Is what he says true, milord?" the Field Magus asked the Prince.

"Yes," Prince Garald replied. Lifting his voice so that all could hear, he repeated, "Yes, what you have heard is true — to the shame of every one of us in Thimhallan, not just Merilon. It was our fear that caused this man" — he laid his hand on Joram's shoulder — "to be sentenced to death, once as a child and again as a man. Joram is the son of the former Empress and Emperor of Merilon. Xavier, his uncle, knew of his existence and tried to destroy him. In this, he had the cooperation of Bishop Vanya."

The eyes of everyone in the crowd raised to the office in the Cathedral. Vanya, glaring at them all, reached out his good hand and, with a swift yank at the pull rope, dropped down the tapestry that covered the crystal wall.

He could shut out the eyes but not the sounds.

"The Almin has sent Joram to us in our hour of need!" It was Prince Garald's voice. "This proves that He is with us! Will you follow Joram — the son of your Emperor and the rightful ruler of Merilon — into battle?"

The crowd responded with a mighty shout.

Bishop Vanya, peeping through a chink in the curtain, saw that Joram did not turn to look at the people, but remained standing with his back to them, his head lowered, his face averted. Prince Garald leaned near, talking earnestly to him, and at last, Joram lifted his head and slowly faced the crowd, his white robes glimmering in the magical torchlight.

The crowd roared its approval. Surging forward, people surrounded their new Emperor, trying to touch him, begging for his blessing. Instantly, the *Duuk-tsarith* closed ranks around Joram. Prince Garald caused the platform to rise up into the air. The people spiraled upward with it, cheering and applauding.

The old man did not have the magical strength to join them, and so was left standing alone on the ground in the drizzling rain, forgotten.

"The Prophecy!" Vanya muttered in a hollow voice. "It is upon us! There is no escape!" Fear stood out in beads of perspiration on his forehead and trickled down the neck of his elegant robes. With faltering footsteps, he lurched backward, sinking into his chair, assisted by the Cardinal.

"E'gad! No escape? What a defeatist attitude! Quite a touching little reunion, wouldn't you say, Eminence? What with my tears and the rain, I'm half-drowned!"

The voice came from behind His Holiness. The Bishop, with a fearful start, squirmed around in his chair to see who had entered his private chambers unannounced and uninvited.

"What is the meaning of this outrage?" the Cardinal was sputtering.

A young man—chin and upper lip adorned by a soft, well-trimmed beard—stepped casually from the Corridor. He was dressed in a bright red brocade dressing gown, decorated in black fur. The long, pointed toes of his red shoes curled up and in upon themselves, a bit of orange silk fluttered from one hand like a flame.

"Sink me, Your Tubbiness," said the bearded young man, strolling across the rug toward the Bishop and tripping over his curly-tipped shoes, "you don't look at all well! You there"—this to the stunned Cardinal "—a glass of brandy. Look lively. Thank you." Lifting the snifter, the young man remarked, "To your health, Holiness," and drained it at a gulp. "Thank you." The young man handed the Cardinal the glass. "I'll have another."

"Ah, Bishop," he continued gaily, "you're looking better already. One more drink and you'll seem almost human. Who am I? You know me, my dear Vanya. The name's Simkin. Why am I here? Because, O Rotund and Flabby One, I have two new friends who are longing to meet you. I think you'll find them interesting. They are—quite literally—out of this world."

6

Dona Nobis Pacem

We came to this world in peace, Bishop Vanya," said Menju the Sorcerer in a smooth, melancholy voice. "We made the mistake — as is apparent to us now — of stumbling in upon your . . . um . . . war games. We were attacked, entirely by accident, according to you." This spoken reassuringly as Vanya appeared about to make some remonstrance. "But, not knowing this, we could only assume that Joram, a known criminal who is fleeing the law in our world, had discovered our plans and was lying in wait to destroy us." The Sorcerer sighed heavily. "It is truly a most regrettable incident. The waste of lives on both sides, deplorable. Isn't that so, Major Boris?"

Bishop Vanya glanced at the military man, who had been sitting stiff-backed on the edge of a soft, cushioned chair, staring fixedly before him. Simkin had removed the disguises the two men wore through the Corridor and the Major was once again dressed in what Vanya assumed was the military uniform of his kind.

"Isn't that so, Major?" the Sorcerer repeated.

The Major did not reply. He had not spoken a word the entire time that he, Simkin, and this man who called himself the Sorcerer had been in the room. Vanya watched closely for his reaction to the magician's repeated call for confirmation and did not miss the swift glimmer of hatred and defiance that flickered in the blond Major's light eyes. The man's strong, bulldog jaw was clenched so tightly that cords in the thick neck were plainly visible.

Vanya looked to see the Sorcerer's response. It was an odd one. Raising his right hand in the air, the magician flexed it several times, absently forming the fingers into a semblance of a bird's claw. Vanya was considerably interested to note that the Major blanched at the sight. The hate-filled glance was watered down by fear, the massive shoulders slumped, and the man appeared to shrink visibly into his ugly uniform.

"Isn't that true, Major?" the Sorcerer repeated the question.

"Yes," said Major Boris briefly, quietly. The lips closed tightly once more.

"The Major is extremely uncomfortable in this magical world and, of course, feels very strange here," Menju said in apology to Vanya. "Though he has been studying the language for several months and understands what we have been saying quite well, he does not feel confident of conversing yet. I hope you will forgive him his deficiencies in conversation."

"Certainly, certainly," the Bishop said, waving a pudgy hand, the hand that functioned. The other remained hidden beneath the massive desk at which His Holiness sat.

The Bishop had quickly recovered from his initial shock of receiving guests from a world that until an hour ago had not existed for him. Despite his stroke, Vanya retained all the shrewd observation and knowledge of mankind that had kept him in power so many years. While he began to chat idly with the Sorcerer about the differences and similarities in the languages of the two worlds — both of which had their roots in ancient times — he was in reality mentally summing up his two visitors, endeavoring to guess their motives for coming.

These two men were similar to anyone in Thimhallan, Vanya realized, with the exception that the Major was quite Dead and that the Sorcerer — having been bereft of magic for a number of years — was crude and clumsy at the art.

Studying the Major, Vanya almost immediately dismissed Boris from consideration. The Major, a blunt and honest military man, was obviously completely out of his depth and drowning in these deep waters. He was overawed by this world; he feared the Sorcerer. Boris was under the magician's control, which meant that the Sorcerer was the only true player in the game.

Menju the Sorcerer was lying when he claimed that he came here with peaceful intent. Of that, Vanya had no doubt. Menju did not remember Vanya, but Vanya knew and remembered Menju. The Bishop recalled something of the man's history. A secret practitioner of the Dark Arts of Technology, Menju had attempted to use his arts to seize control of a dukedom near Zith-el. Captured by the *Duuk-tsarith*, he had been summarily tried and sentenced by their tribunal to be cast into Beyond. The execution had been handled quickly and quietly; most of the people in Thimhallan probably never knew anything about it. That had been what — four years ago? Menju had been twenty then, he appeared to be about sixty now, and had spent, he told Vanya, forty years in the world Beyond.

The Bishop didn't understand that at all, although the Sorcerer had patiently attempted to explain — something to do with the speed of light and dimension doors. The Almin works in mysterious ways, the Bishop told himself, dismissing the matter as unimportant. What *was* important was the fact that this powerful man was here now and he wanted something. What did he want? And what was he willing to give up in return? Those were the urgent questions.

As for what he wanted, that at first seemed obvious to the Bishop. Menju wanted the magic. Forty years without Life had gnawed at this Sorcerer. Vanya could see the hunger in Menju's eyes. Now, back on his home world, the Sorcerer had once more partaken of Life. He had dined sumptuously, and the Bishop saw Menju's firm resolve that he would never go hungry again.

He's lying about coming here in peace, Vanya repeated inwardly, outwardly speaking of nouns, gerund phrases, and verbs. The attack upon our forces was no accident. It was too swift, too organized. That much I know from Xavier's early reports. According to the *Duuk-tsarith*, the strange human army is in serious trouble now. Our magi inflicted heavy casualties, forced them to retreat. Why is the Sorcerer here? What is his plan?

How can I make use of him . . . ?

"Speaking of language, I am amazed that Simkin was able to speak ours so quickly," said the Sorcerer.

"Nothing about Simkin amazes me," growled Vanya, glaring at the red-clad figure. Reclining leisurely on a couch in the Bishop's luxurious office, the young man had apparently dozed off during a discussion of prepositional phrases and was snoring loudly.

"Joram has a theory about him, you know," said the Sorcerer casually, though the Bishop thought he detected a glint in the man's eyes, the look of a card player endeavoring to calculate what his opponent holds. "He claims that Simkin is the personification of this world — magic in its purest form."

"An ugly thought and one typical of Joram," Vanya said sourly, not liking this sudden interest in Simkin. The Fool was a wild card in any deck, and the Bishop had been trying for well over an hour to consider how best to toss him away. "I trust that we as a people are better represented than by this undisciplined, amoral, unfeeling —"

"I say!" Simkin sat up, blinking and peering around in a dazed state. "Did I hear my name?"

Vanya snorted. "If you are bored, why don't you leave us?"

"E'gad!" Simkin yawned, slumping back down on the couch. "Is there going to be much more vocabulary? Because, if so, I think I *will* go dangle my participle in more entertaining and interesting surroundings. . . ."

"No, no," said Menju, his teeth flashing in a charming smile. "I beg your pardon, Simkin, my good friend, for putting you to sleep. Linguistics is a hobby of mine," he added, turning back to Bishop Vanya, "and I find this discussion of our language with one so knowledgeable as yourself a true treat. I hope that in the future we will spend many pleasant hours in such discussions, if that is agreeable to Your Eminence?" Vanya nodded coolly "But Simkin quite properly reminds us that time is short. We must exchange these pleasant topics for others of a serious nature."

Menju's handsome face grew grave. "I know you will concur with our earnest desire that this tragic and accidental war come to an end before irreparable damage is done to any relations that might be established between our two worlds, Holiness."

"Amen!" said the Cardinal fervently.

Vanya started, having forgotten his minister's presence, and, with an icy glance, silently rebuked him for speaking out of turn. The Cardinal cringed. Simkin, with a prodigious yawn, propped his feet up on the arm of the sofa and lay there admiring the curled toes of his shoes, humming a tune on a shrill, off-key note that had the effect of instantly irritating everyone present.

"I concur in your desire for peace," Bishop Vanya said cautiously, feeling his way ahead, his pudgy hand crawling over the desk, "but as you said there were, tragically, many lives lost. Not the least of which was the life of our beloved Emperor Xavier. The people feel his loss quite keenly — Will you stop that!" This to Simkin, who had launched into a funeral dirge.

"Beg pardon," Simkin said meekly. "Got carried away by my feelings for the deceased!" Covering his face with a sofa cushion, he began to weep loudly.

Vanya sucked in a quantity of air through his nose and shifted his great bulk in his chair, keeping his mouth tightly shut so that he would not say something he might later regret. He noticed the flutter of a knowing smile on the Sorcerer's lips. Obviously, the magician knew Simkin. . . .

But why should that surprise me? Vanya thought resignedly, letting out the air with a whoosh, like a deflating bladder. *Everyone* knows Simkin.

"I truly understand your people's grief," Menju was saying, "and I am certain that, although there is nothing we can do to bring back their beloved leader, some sort of reparation can be made."

"Perhaps, perhaps." Vanya sighed heavily. "But much as I agree with you, sir, I fear the matter is out of my hands.

Joram, that notorious criminal, has hoodwinked not only your people but ours as well. There are even rumors to the effect," the Bishop added casually, "that it was Joram who was responsible for Xavier's death. . . ."

Menju smiled, understanding Vanya's plan instantly.

The Bishop turned over his fat hand, reluctantly showing all his cards. "Be that as it may, Joram caused himself to be proclaimed Emperor of Merilon. He and a vainglorious man — one Garald, Prince of the city-state of Sharakan — are going to pursue this terrible war."

The magician and the Major exchanged glances at this — the cold and wary glances of reluctant allies, but allies nonetheless.

"I know that we are technically enemies, Bishop Vanya," the Sorcerer said hesitantly, "but in the name of peace if you could tell us what you know about their plans, perhaps we could find some way of forestalling them, of keeping more lives from being lost. . . ."

Bishop Vanya frowned, his hand closed into a fist. "I am no traitor, sir —"

"They're attacking you tomorrow night," interposed Simkin languidly. Casting aside the sofa cushion, he blew his nose on the orange silk. "Joram and Garald plan on wiping you out. Obliterating you from the face of this world. Not even a trace of your bodies will be left behind," he continued cheerfully, tossing the orange silk away into the air.

"It was Joram's idea. When your world doesn't hear the tiniest little peep from you, they will, hopefully, presume the worst has happened. The shell crushed, the chick dead; the cuckoo will think twice about laying eggs in this nest again. By which time, of course, we will have the henhouse repaired, the magical Border firmly intact once more. Lovely, isn't it?"

"Traitor! Why have you told them!" Bishop Vanya cried with a great show of anger, slamming his good hand down on his desk.

"It's only fair," Simkin returned, glancing at the Bishop in astonishment. "After all," he continued, raising a foot in the air and causing the toe of the shoe to uncurl, "I told Joram all *their* plans — the reinforcements coming. . . . Just as I was instructed. . . ."

"Reinforcements! Simkin instructed! What is the meaning of this?" Vanya demanded. "You said you came here in peace! Now I find that you are apparently adding to your military might. Not only that"—he waved a fat hand at Simkin—"but you are using this young man as a spy! Perhaps that is why you are here now! I will call for the *Duuk-tsarith*."

The Sorcerer's composure slipped the tiniest bit. The Bishop did not miss the swift, intense flare of anger in Menju's eyes, or the look he cast at Simkin. If this Sorcerer were *Duuk-tsarith*, Simkin would be a smudge of grease upon the sofa. So, Vanya thought smugly, Menju doesn't know the Fool that well, after all.

"Please do nothing in haste, Holiness," Menju said in mollifying tones. "Surely you can understand that we have to act to protect ourselves! The additional troops we called for are to be used only if we are attacked again by your people."

Major Boris's boot scraped against the floor. Vanya, darting a swift glance at him, saw the man shift nervously in his seat.

"As for spies, we stumbled upon this fellow spying on *our* headquarters and—"

Simkin, with a smile, caused the toe of his shoes to curl back up. "What can I say?" he responded modestly. "I was bored."

"—and finding that he took a sensible view of this situation," the Sorcerer continued, somewhat irritated at the interruption, "we sent him back to Joram, hoping, I confess, to frighten him into suing for peace."

Menju paused, then leaned forward, laying his hand upon Vanya's desk. When he spoke, his voice was low and earnest. "Let us be candid with each other, Holiness. Joram is the cause of this dreadful war. A dark and passionate nature such as his, combined with a keen intelligence, must make him a criminal, an outcast in any society." The Sorcerer's handsome face grew shadowed. "I understand he committed murder on this world. He has done that and worse in ours."

Bishop Vanya was appearing carefully dubious.

"Joram was gone for ten years from Thimhallan! Why do you think he bothered to return? Because of his great love for it?" The Sorcerer scoffed at the idea. "You and I both

know better than that! Often Joram has bragged to me how
he escaped the punishment he so richly deserved. In the same
way, he escaped punishment to which he was sentenced in
our world. He came back here because he is being hunted,
pursued! He came back here, so he has told me, to have his
revenge! To fulfill the Prophecy!"

Major Boris sprang to his feet. Shoving his hands in his
pockets, he walked rapidly to the end of the room. Vanya
could see a red flush spreading up the back of the man's thick
neck, just above the collar of his shirt. Arriving at the transparent wall, the major stretched forth a hand to push aside
the tapestry.

"I would not touch that if I were you, Major," Bishop
Vanya said coolly. "The *Duuk-tsarith* are standing guard outside the Cathedral. Should they catch a glimpse of you, I
could do nothing to protect you."

"It's too damn hot in here!" the Major said hoarsely, tugging at his collar.

"The Major is somewhat claustrophobic," began the Sorcerer.

"There is no need to apologize for the Major," interrupted
Bishop Vanya. "I know his type."

Menju, leaning back in his chair, regarded the Bishop
with a narrow-eyed, speculative gaze. Standing at the opposite end of the room, Major Boris wiped his sweat-covered
head with a handkerchief and tugged at his collar. The Cardinal, responding to a swift gesture from his Bishop, rose
noiselessly from his chair and went to keep the Major company. Coming up beside the Major, he began a desultory,
one-sided conversation.

Bishop Vanya glanced toward Simkin, but a snore from
the sofa indicated that the young man had, once again, fallen
asleep.

His Holiness, having appeared to allow himself to be persuaded, regarded Menju with due seriousness. "I will, for the
sake of the world, listen to what you have to offer. I do not
think it necessary to concern the military in these matters, do
you? They have so little understanding of the arts of negotiation and diplomacy."

The Sorcerer made an assenting motion with his graceful
hand. "I couldn't agree with you more, Holiness."

"Very well. My only desire is that we end this tragic war. As you say, I, too, believe Joram to be the cause. What is it, then, that you want of me?"

"Joram . . . *and* his wife. Alive."

"Impossible."

"Why?" the Sorcerer shrugged. "Surely you—"

Vanya cut him off. "Joram is protected by the *Duuk-tsarith*. You have been gone a long time, but you *do* remember them, don't you?"

It was obvious that the Sorcerer did. His face a shade paler, he glared at Vanya irritably. "I recall that you catalysts have a member of the *Duuk-tsarith* who acts for you alone."

"Ah, the Executioner." The Bishop nodded.

The Sorcerer became paler still, his breathing labored.

"I trust you are not claustrophobic, yourself?" the Bishop asked.

"No," the Sorcerer answered with a ghastly smile. "I am troubled by . . . old memories." Nervously, he adjusted the cuffs of his shirt.

"The Executioner might serve our purpose," began Vanya, frowning, though he saw the discomfiture of the magician with satisfaction. "However, the Font has ears and eyes and a mouth. Joram is now the mob's darling. I cannot be involved in any incident—"

"I say," came a fatigued voice, "just what do you intend doing with Joram anyway?"

The Bishop looked sharply at the magician, who looked sharply back at the Bishop. Both glanced warily at Simkin. Still lying on the couch, his head propped up on his hand, he was regarding them with bored curiosity.

"He will be returned to my world for his just punishment," said Menju.

"And his mad wife?"

"She will be given the care she needs!" the Sorcerer said sternly. "There are people on my world who are trained in treating insanity. Joram has refused to allow them near her—"

"So Joram is to go back to *your world*," Simkin continued, with a dreamy emphasis on the words, "while everyone on this world—"

"— remains here to live in peace and safety, secure from the machinations of Joram the archfiend, just as we discussed earlier," Sorcerer interjected smoothly, his gaze fixed unwaveringly on Simkin.

"Quite," said Simkin, and rolled over on his back.

"In fact," Menju continued, turning to face the Bishop after watching Simkin one final moment longer, "I can make arrangements for Joram's trial to be broadcast to this planet. It will be a bond between our worlds. I think you will find it quite fascinating, Eminence. We have large metal boxes that we can set up right here in your office. By attaching some wires and cable, you can look into this box and see images of what is transpiring in our world millions of miles away —"

"Metal boxes! Wires and cable! Tools of the Dark Arts!" thundered Vanya. "Take Joram from this world, then leave us in peace!"

Menju smiled, shrugging. "As you will, Holiness. All of which brings us back to the question of Joram. . . ."

"Oh, bosh!" said Simkin irritably, sitting up. "Do you realize that it's past dinner time? And I haven't had a thing to eat all day! All this talk of *Duuk-tsarith* and Executioners. Not conducive to whetting the appetite." The orange silk came fluttering out of the air to land in Simkin's hand. "You want Joram? Nothing simpler. You, O Toothy One"— he waved the silk at the Sorcerer — "are, I assume, capable of capturing him."

"Yes, of course. But he must be taken unawares — he and his wife. He mustn't suspect —"

"Nothing simpler! *I* have a plan," interposed Simkin loftily. "Leave everything to me."

Both Sorcerer and Vanya eyed Simkin warily.

"Begging your pardon, friend Simkin," Menju said, "if I appear hesitant to accept your generous offer. But I know very little of you, except what Joram has told me, and we know him to be capable of any falsehood or deceit. Should I trust you?"

"I wouldn't," Simkin remarked frankly, smoothing his mustache. "There isn't a soul who does — except one." Humming to himself again, he formed the orange silk into a loop.

"And this is?"

"Joram."

"Joram! Why should *he* trust you?"

"Because his is a perverse nature." Simkin knotted the orange silk above the loop. "Because I have never given him any reason to trust me. Quite the contrary. Yet trust me he does. I find it a constant source of amusement."

Thrusting his head through the noose he had made in the orange silk, Simkin looked at the Sorcerer and winked.

Menju frowned. "I must protest, Holiness. I don't like this scheme."

Simkin yawned. "Oh, come now! Be honest. It's not the scheme you don't like. It's me!" He sniffed. "I'm highly insulted. Or I would be," he added after reflection, "if I weren't so frightfully hungry."

Bishop Vanya made a noise that might have been a laugh at the Sorcerer's expense. Turning to confront him, the magician saw the sneer on the Bishop's face and flushed.

"He admits we can't trust him!" Menju said with some asperity.

"That is just his way," Vanya said crisply. "Simkin has done work for us before and has proven satisfactory. From what you say, he has done work for you as well. Time is short. Do you have an alternate proposal?"

Menju regarded the Bishop coolly and thoughtfully. "No," he replied.

"Ah!" Simkin laughed gaily. "As the Duchess d'Longville cried when her sixth husband dropped dead at her feet: 'At last! At last!' Now, down to business." He rubbed his hands together excitedly. "This is going to be an incredible lark! When shall we do the deed?"

"It must be tomorrow," the Sorcerer said. "If, according to you, he plans to attack us at nightfall, he must be stopped before then. After his capture, we can begin the peace negotiations."

"There is just one small thing." The Bishop hedged. "You may keep Joram and do what you like to him, but we want the Darksword returned."

"I'm afraid that is quite out of the question," the Sorcerer responded smoothly.

Vanya glared at him, scowling. "Then there is no further point in negotiating! Your terms are unacceptable!"

"Come, come, Holiness! After all, we are the ones threatened by your forces! We must protect ourselves from attack! *We* will keep the Darksword."

The Bishop's scowl became more pronounced — a difficult matter to achieve, with one side of his face hanging limp as his useless arm. "Why? What can it possibly matter to you?"

The Sorcerer shrugged. "The Darksword has become a symbol to your people. Losing it — and discovering that their 'Emperor' is, in reality, a murderer — will demoralize them. You hesitate over this trifle, Eminence! It's just a sword, isn't it?" he asked blandly.

"It is a weapon of evil!" Vanya replied in stern tones. "A tool of the devil!"

"Then you should welcome the opportunity to be rid of it!" Stretching his arms, the Sorcerer adjusted the cuffs of his shirt-sleeves. This time, however, his air was confident, his composure restored. "In return for this token of goodwill from your world, I will have Major Boris send a message to my world, canceling the reinforcements. Then your people and mine may begin serious peace negotiations. Do you agree?"

The Bishop's nostrils flared. Glaring at the Sorcerer, he sucked air into his nose, the pudgy hand suddenly ceasing its spiderlike crawl over the desk, its fingers curling up like the toes of Simkin's shoes. "It appears I have little choice."

"Now, have you any suggestions regarding where and how we capture Joram?"

The Bishop shifted his body in his chair, causing the paralyzed left arm to slide off his lap. Surreptitiously, he caught hold of it, giving a sidelong look to see if the magician was watching. *What a fool he takes me for!* Vanya said to himself, settling the arm back in its place once more. *So it's the sword he's after! Why? What does* he *know of it?*

The Bishop appeared indifferent. "Capturing Joram must be up to you and Simkin, I'm afraid. I know nothing of sordid matters. I am a churchman, after all."

"Oh, really!" Simkin heaved an exasperated sigh. "This has gone on quite long enough! Which was something else the Duchess said, her sixth taking an interminable length of time over dying. I told you I have it all planned."

Spreading the orange silk out upon Vanya's desk, Simkin waved his hand over it and letters appeared on its surface.

"Shh—" he hissed as Menju was about to read it aloud. "The Font has ears and eyes, you know. Meet me here"—he indicated the name of the place written on the silk scarf— "tomorrow at noon. You will have Joram and his wife, both completely at your mercy and unsuspecting as babes."

Bishop Vanya, his lips pursed, his eyes practically buried in rolls of fat, took one look at the name of the location written on the silk and grew extremely pale. "This place is out of the question!"

"Why?" Menju asked coldly.

"Surely you know its history!" Vanya said, regarding the Sorcerer incredulously.

"Pah! I have not believed in ghosts since I was five! From descriptions I vaguely recall reading of this place, it will suit our purposes admirably. Plus I begin to see the inklings of Simkin's plan to get Joram there without suspicion. Most ingenuous, my friend." The magician glanced down his elegant nose at the Bishop. "You are not using this pretense to wriggle out of our agreement, are you, Holiness?"

"Far from it!" Vanya protested earnestly. "I am concerned only for your safety, Menju."

"Thank you, Eminence." The Sorcerer rose from his chair.

"Remember, you have been warned. You will handle everything?" The Bishop remained seated, concealing his handicap.

"Certainly, Holiness."

"Then I believe that it is all we have to say to each other."

"Yes, although there *is* one more matter we need settled." The Sorcerer turned to Simkin. "You are entitled to a handsome reward for your services, Simkin. That is, I assume, why you're doing this, after all. . . ."

"No, no!" protested Simkin, looking deeply offended. "Patriotic. I regret that I have but one friend to give for my country."

"I insist that you accept something!"

"I couldn't possibly," said Simkin loftily, but with a glance at Menju from beneath half-shut eyelids.

"My world, and this one"—Menju gestured at Vanya—
"will be eternally grateful."

"Well, perhaps there *is* one small favor you can do for me,
now that you mention it." Simkin drew the orange silk slowly
between his fingers.

"Name it! Jewels? Gold?"

"Bah! What do I need with filthy lucre? I ask only one
thing—take me back to your world."

The Sorcerer appeared considerably astonished at this
request. "Are you serious?" he asked.

"As serious as I generally am about anything," Simkin
replied offhandedly. "No, wait. I take that back. I fancy I'm
more serious about this than usual."

"Well, well. Is that all? Take you with me?" Menju
laughed expansively. "Nothing easier! It's quite a brilliant
idea, in fact! The hit you will make as part of my act! You
will be the toast of the universe without doubt, my friend! I
can see the marquee now!" The magician waved his hand.
"*THE SORCERER* and Simkin!"

"Mmmm. . . ." The young man smoothed his mustache
thoughtfully. "Well, well. We can discuss *that* later. For now,
we really must be going. Collect the Major, don our disguises, and return to those remarkably ugly buildings in
which you odd people choose to dwell."

Rising slowly up into the air, his red brocade dressing
gown flashing like flame in the bright lights of the Bishop's
chambers, Simkin drifted over to the tapestry-covered wall.

As he passed by Menju, muttered words came floating
back. "*SIMKIN* and the Sorcerer . . ."

7

Eye In The Sky

The sun sank down into the horizon hurriedly, without calling attention to itself. Night came quickly to Thimhallan, therefore, and a new moon rose. Curved in a malicious grin, it might well have been laughing at the follies of mankind that met its eyes. . . .

"The magician takes me for a fool!"

Left alone with the Cardinal after the departure of Simkin and his "friends," Bishop Vanya sat behind his desk, glaring at the empty chair the Sorcerer had lately occupied.

The Bishop had been all pleasant smiles — or at least the half of his face that could smile had been smiling — until his guests left. But once they were gone — Simkin's voice prattling away merrily the while, its irritating tones the last sound Vanya heard as the Corridor closed about them — the smiling side of the face became as cold and frozen as its paralyzed other half.

"The Darksword! That is what he wants," Vanya snarled, the pudgy hand crawling over the desk, the Cardinal staring at it in a horrible kind of fascination. "A token of goodwill! Bah! He knows the truth about it, about its powers. Joram must have told him. Menju knew about Simkin, after all. He knew about the Turning, he knew about Joram crossing into Beyond. Yes! He knows about the sword!

"*You* are the fool, Menju, to think I would give it up!" Vanya muttered, his plans bubbling and fermenting, coming to a frothing head. It appeared, from the perspiration on his brow, that his mental cup was overflowing.

"You Sorcerer! You devil of the Dark Arts! No wonder you have no fear of demons in that cursed place you have chosen to do your foul deed. You are one yourself, no doubt. But you might as well serve me as serve a Darker Master. Rid me of the Prophecy. Rid me of Joram. I'll make of *him* a martyr and throw *you* to Prince Garald and the mob that will be howling for your blood. They'll have you and your pitiful army to crucify. *I'll* have the Darksword. . . ."

With the heat of his emotions, the ice thawed, the smile returned to half the face.

"Send for the Executioner," ordered the Bishop.

"The fat Priest takes me for a fool," the Sorcerer said complacently.

Staring into a mirror he had conjured up, he carefully straightened his tie and smoothed nonexistent wrinkles from his lapels. He and the Major were back at their headquarters seated in the Major's office. He had divested himself of his disguise—though Simkin had assured him, before leaving, that the red brocade dressing gown "is *you*!"

"*I* think you are mad!" Major Boris muttered in hollow tones.

"What did you say, James?" the Sorcerer asked, though he had heard well enough.

"I said I don't understand!" the Major returned heavily. "What have you done except put us in a more desperate situation than ever! Why did you reveal our plans to Joram! You knew it would force him to attack us before the reinforcements arrive—"

"Assuredly," the Sorcerer said coolly, combing his thick, wavy hair.

"But why?"

"Major"—the magician continued to look critically into the mirror—"consider this. We have sent a frantic message for reinforcements back to our world. They arrive and find us seated calmly in the midst of this enchanged realm, not a shot being fired. Then we regale them with tales of giants and dragons, whimpering that we don't dare fight because the bad bogeymen are going to get us! They will double up with laughter!" His usual suave and unruffled appearance restored, the Sorcerer banished the mirror with a clap of his hands. Turning, he faced the Major. "Instead, they find us battling for our lives against monsters and crazed wizards! They'll enter the fight, kill without mercy, and be only too glad to wipe out this demonic populace."

"And by provoking Joram to attack, you've forced me to fight as well," Major Boris said, staring out into the night with glazed, unseeing eyes.

"It isn't that I don't trust you, Major." Reaching across the table, the Sorcerer patted James Boris's right hand. Shuddering at the touch, the Major snatched his hand away, thrusting it protectively in his pocket. "It was just that I needed . . . insurance. I think it a bit naive of you to believe that Joram would have let you escape this world unharmed anyway. You saw them mobilizing Merilon for war. . . ."

Major Boris had seen, and he remembered. Darkening the room, Bishop Vanya had invited his guests, before they left, to look upon Merilon the Beautiful.

Preparing for war, Merilon's twilight had been changed into day—its streets lit by countless angry, flaring suns. The Major's grim face grew grimmer still as he gazed upon nightmare monsters flying through the air, legions of skeletons marching down the street. He could repeat the Bishop's scornful words, tell himself that they were illusions, incapable of harm. But who would tell his men, facing these things on the field of battle? And if he did tell them, why would they believe him? Especially if they had just seen their comrades torn to shreds by the beaks of real cockatrice, their invincible tanks crushed beneath the feet of real giants. There was no separating illusion from reality in this awful world.

Fear chewed at Boris, like centaurs devouring the flesh of their living victims. His right hand, hidden in the pocket of his fatigues, shook. It was all he could do to keep from bringing it out to examine it, to see if it still *was* a hand. . . .

"My men may be hunks of meat in your trap," he told the Sorcerer bitterly, "but we're not going to wait for the wizards to fall on us like ravening wolves. I'm going to attack their city tomorrow. Take them by surprise."

The Sorcerer shrugged. "I don't care what you do, Major, as long as you do not interfere with my plans for acquiring the Darksword."

"I won't," James Boris returned heavily. "I need the damn sword, remember? I'll launch the attack at noon. You're certain Joram will be out of the way by then?"

"Absolutely," Menju said, rising and preparing to take his departure. "And now, if you'll excuse me, Major, I have plans of my own to make for tomorrow."

The Major continued to look glum.

"What about this . . . Simkin? I don't trust him."

"That fop?" The Sorcerer shrugged. "He'll do what he's promised. He wants his reward, after all."

"But you've no intention of taking him back with us, have you, Sorcerer?" Major Boris stood up as well, keeping his hands in his pockets. "He may be a fop, but he's a dangerous one. From what I've seen, he's a better magician than you can ever hope to be!"

The Sorcerer regarded the Major with a cool, unfaltering gaze. "I trust that shot made you feel better, James. Now you can go to your bed with some shreds of dignity clinging to you. Not that I have to explain, but to be quite honest I *had* considered taking him. He would be an undoubted asset to my act. But you are right. He is too powerful. He would — so to speak — demand top billing. Once he has given me Joram, Simkin will meet the same fate as everyone else in this world."

"And what about Joram?"

"I want him alive. He will be useful to me. He'll tell me of the powers of the Darksword and how to construct more of these weapons — "

"He won't, you know."

"He'll have no choice. I'll have his wife. . . ."

The moon roamed across the sky, perhaps in search of new diversion. If so, it found little.

Following a highly satisfactory meeting with the Executioner, the Bishop retired to his bedchamber. Here, assisted by a novitiate, he was engulfed in a voluminous nightshirt and helped to his bed. Once there, Vanya realized he had forgotten, in the excitement of the evening, his nightly prayers. He did not get back up. Surely this once the Almin could make do without receiving instruction and advice from his minister.

In another part of the world, Major Boris, too, went to his bed. Lying on his regulation cot, he was ostensibly trying to rest, although he didn't know which alternative he feared worse — that he wouldn't fall asleep . . . or that he would. Either way, he knew his dreams were likely to be extremely unpleasant.

Two men were still awake — the Sorcerer and the Executioner, both planning how to take their prey upon the morrow.

The moon, finding nothing interesting in that, was about to set when, after all, it did run across something amusing.

A bucket with a bright orange handle sat in a corner of the geodesic dome that served as the headquarters for the army from another world. This was by no means an ordinary bucket. Having worked itself into a state of indignation, it was, literally, coming apart at the seams.

"Menju, you cheat! You're not playing at all fair! Taking Joram back to a brave, new world and not me!" The bucket flipped its handle about quite savagely. "Well, we'll see about that!" the bucket predicted ominously. "We'll see. . . ."

Per Istam ——
Sanctam. . . .

Count Devon is truly sorry about the china cabinet, but it happened, he thinks, because he is uneasy in his mind about the mice nibbling his portrait. The painting would be glad to return to its old place upon the wall if only someone would so instruct it. He has tried, but it doesn't hear his voice.

"He doesn't want the portrait destroyed, for without it he can't recall what he looks like.

"The mice concern him. He says there are far too many. It comes with being shut up in a closed, comfortable attic without any predators; his late wife being terrified of cats. The mice have had a comfortable life and are now fat and sleek with a decided taste for art. Yet he has discovered in his solitary, wakeful ramblings (for the dead who can sleep do so, never to wake, while those who can't find sleep roam constantly in search of rest) many small corpses in the attic.

"The mice are dying, and he can't understand why. Their tiny bodies litter the floor, more each day. And here is a very strange thing. He has heard from a woman who once lived across the street and who, it seems, died from lack of attention and it took three days for somebody to notice, that the mice in her attic are suffering the very same fate.

"Sealed up, safe and secure, they are, she says, suffocating."

BOOK THREE

I

Emperor Of Merilon

Night attempted to lull Merilon to sleep, but its soothing hand was thrust away by those preparing for war. Joram took command of the city, naming Prince Garald his military leader. He and the Prince immediately began to mobilize the population.

Joram met with his people in the Grove. Gathering around the ancient tomb of the wizard who had brought them to this world, many of the citizens of Merilon wondered if that almost forgotten spirit stirred restlessly in his centuries-old sleep. Was his dream about to end and yet another enchanted kingdom fall to ruin?

"This is a fight to the death," Joram told the people grimly. "The enemy intends to wipe out our entire race, to destroy us utterly. We have seen proof of this in the wanton attack upon innocent civilians on the Field of Glory. They have shown no mercy. We will show none." He paused. The silence that flowed through the crowd grew deeper, until

they might have been drowned in it. Looking at them from
where he stood on the platform above the tomb, Joram said
slowly, emphasizing each word, "Every one of them must
die."

No one cheered when Joram left the Grove. Instead,
they turned quickly and quietly to their duties. Women
trained alongside the men; the very old and the infirm staying behind to mind the children — many of whom might be
orphans when night fell again on Thimhallan.

"Better that," Mosiah's father said to his wife as they both
prepared to practice for battle, "than dead."

A call went forth for War Masters, who came to Merilon
through the Corridors from all parts of the world. Under
their tutelage, the civilians, including the Field Magi, were
given hasty instruction in fighting the enemy, aided by their
own catalysts.

Mosiah's parents took their places beside old Father
Tolban, the Priest who had served the village of Walren for
so many years. Due to his advanced age, the meek, dried-up
Field Catalyst could have remained behind with the children.
But he insisted on going to battle with his people.

"I have never done a worthwhile thing in my entire life,"
he told Jacobias. "I have never known a proud moment. Let
this be it."

Though the outside world was dark and slumbering, the
city of Merilon burned with light. It might have been day
beneath the dome — a terrible, fear-laced day whose sun was
the fiery glow of the forge. The *Pron-alban* had hastily conjured up a workplace for the blacksmith. He and his sons and
apprentices like Mosiah worked to repair weapons damaged
in the previous battle or create new ones. Though many in
Merilon looked with horror upon the Sorcerers, practicing
their Dark Art of Technology, the citizens swallowed their
fears and did what they could to assist.

The *Theldara* tended the injured, buried the dead, and
hastily began working on enlarging both the Houses of Healing and the Burial Catacombs. The druids knew that, by the
rising of the moon tomorrow night, they would need many
more beds . . . and graves.

City Below was thronged with people: War Masters arriving continually from all over Thimhallan, catalysts coming

from the Font, refugees pouring in from the Outland, fleeing the nameless terror. The streets were so crowded it was difficult to either fly or walk. University students filled the cafes and taverns, singing martial songs and thirsting for the glories of battle. Moving through the crowd, the *Duuk-tsarith* walked the streets like death personified, keeping order, quelling panic, and quietly whisking away those of the students whose eagerness in practicing their spell-casting seemed likely to prove more dangerous to themselves than the enemy.

City Above was wide awake as well. Like the Field Magi, many of the nobles were also practicing for battle. Sometimes their wives, too, stood beside them. But more often the noble ladies could be found opening their large houses to the refugees or tending the injured. A Countess might be seen brewing herbal tea with her own hands. A Duchess played at Swan's Doom with a group of peasant children, keeping them amused while their parents prepared for war.

Joram watched over everything. Everywhere he went, people greeted him with cheers. He was their savior. Taking the romantic half-truths Garald had woven around the true story of Joram's lineage, the people further embroidered it and decorated it until it was practically unrecognizable. Joram tried to protest, but the Prince silenced him.

"The people need a hero right now — a handsome king to lead them into battle with his bright and shining sword! Even Bishop Vanya doesn't dare denounce you. What would *you* give them?" Garald asked scornfully. "A Dead man with a weapon of the Dark Arts who is going to bring about the end of the world? Win this battle. Drive the enemy from the land. Prove the Prophecy wrong! *Then* go before the people and tell them the truth, if you must."

Joram agreed reluctantly. Surely Garald knew what was right. *I can afford honor,* the Prince had once told him. *You cannot.*

No, I suppose I can't, Joram thought. Not with the lives of thousands in my hands.

"The truth shall make you free!" he repeated to himself bitterly. "I am destined, it seems, to spend my life in shackles!"

It was nearly midnight. Joram walked by himself in the garden of Lord Samuels's home. Leaving the city, he had come back — at Father Saryon's insistence — to get what rest he could before the morrow.

He could have moved into the Crystal Palace. Glancing up above him, through the leaves of a myrtle tree, Joram could see the Palace hanging over him like a dark star. Its lights extinguished, it was barely visible, shining in the pale light of a new moon.

Shaking his head, Joram looked hastily away. He would never go back there. The Palace held too many bitter memories. There he had first seen his dead mother. There he had heard the story of the death of Anja's child. There he had believed himself nameless, abandoned, unwanted.

Nameless. . . .

"I wish to the Almin that fate had been mine!" Pausing beneath the snow-laden boughs of a drooping lilac bush, Joram leaned against it for support, ignoring the chill water that dripped from the leaves, soaking his white robes. "Better to be nameless than to have one name too many!"

Gamaliel. Reward of God. The name haunted him. The memory of his father haunted him. He could still see the old man's eyes. . . . Realizing, he was shivering violently, Joram began to walk the dark paths again, trying to warm himself.

At least the rain had stopped. Several *Sif-Hanar*, arriving through the Corridors this evening from other city-states, brought an end to the deluge. A few of the nobility demanded that the magi change the weather to spring again immediately, but Prince Garald refused. The *Sif-Hanar* would be needed for the upcoming battle. They could end the rain and keep the temperature moderate in Merilon this night, but that was all. The nobles grumbled, but Joram — their new Emperor — agreed with Garald, and there was nothing the nobles could do.

But Joram supposed he could look forward to future arguments like that. He stumbled as he walked. He was tired almost to the point of exhaustion, having slept fitfully last night after the battle, troubled by dreams of two worlds, neither of which wanted him — the real him.

Nor do I want either of them, he realized wearily. Both have betrayed me. Both hold nothing for me but lies, deceit, treachery.

"I won't be Emperor," he said to himself in sudden resolve. "When this is ended, I'll turn Merilon over to Prince Garald to rule. He is a good man; he will help change it to a better place."

But would he? Could he? Good and honorable and noble as he was, the Prince was *Albanara*, those born with the magical gifts needed to rule. He was accustomed to diplomacy and compromise; he reveled in the intrigues of court. Change, if it came at all, might be long in the coming.

"I don't care," Joram said tiredly. "I'll leave. I'll take Gwendolyn and Father Saryon and we'll live quietly by ourselves someplace where it won't matter to anyone what my name is."

Moodily pacing the garden, hoping to wear himself out so that sleep — deep and dreamless — would claim him at last, Joram found himself walking near the house. Hearing voices, he glanced up at a window.

He stood outside a downstairs room that had been made into a bedchamber for Gwendolyn. Clad in a rose-colored nightgown with long, flowing sleeves, his wife sat in a chair at her dressing table, allowing Marie to brush out her lovely, golden hair. All the while, she talked animatedly to the dead Count and a few other deceased who had apparently joined the party.

Lord Samuels and Lady Rosamund were in their daughter's room as well. It was the sound of their voices that had attracted Joram's attention. They stood close to the window, talking to a person Joram recognized as the *Theldara* who had treated Father Saryon during his illness in the Samuels's house.

Taking care that he didn't allow any of the light shining from inside the house to fall upon him, Joram crept softly through the wet foliage and, hidden by the shadows of the dark garden, drew near the window to hear their conversation.

"There is nothing, then, you can do for her?" Lady Rosamund asked in pleading tones.

"I'm afraid not, milady," the *Theldara* said bluntly. "I've seen madness in many forms in my life, but nothing to equal this. If it *is* madness, about which I have my doubts."

Shaking her head, the druidess poked and picked at various packets of powders and bunches of seeds and herbs that she carried in a large wooden container that hovered obediently in the air beside her.

"What do you mean? Not madness?" Lord Samuels demanded. "Talking to dead Counts, going on about mice in the attic —"

"Madness is a state into which the subject falls whether he or she wills it or not," said the *Theldara*, thrusting out her jaw and glaring at Lord Samuels. "Sometimes it's brought on by upsets in the body's harmonies, sometimes by upsets in the soul's. And I tell you, milord and milady, that there is nothing wrong with your daughter. If she talks to the dead, it's because she obviously prefers their company to that of the living. And from the way I gather some of the living have treated her, I don't much blame her."

Having fussed over and arranged her medicines to her satisfaction, the *Theldara* called briskly for her cloak.

"I've got to get back to the Houses of Healing and tend those who were wounded in that terrible battle," she said as the servant assisted her with her wrap. "You were lucky I happened to be making another call out near here or I wouldn't have had time to look in on this case. Too many others are dependent on me for life itself."

"We're very grateful, I'm sure," said Lady Rosamund, twisting the rings on her fingers, "but I don't understand! Surely there must be *something* you can do!"

They followed the *Theldara* to the door of Gwen's bedchamber, and Joram, moving close to the window, was forced to press his face against the pane in order to hear the druidess's reply. He might have spared himself the trouble, however, for the *Theldara* spoke in a loud, clear voice.

"Madam," she said, raising a finger in the air as though it were a flagpole and she was going to hoist her words on it, "your daughter chooses to be *who* she is and *where* she is. She may live her entire life in this manner. She may decide at breakfast tomorrow that she doesn't want to anymore. I can't say and I can't force her to come out of that world into one that doesn't appear to me to be much better. Now I must get back to those who truly need me. If you want my advice, you'll do as your daughter says—hang up that painting of Count Whosit and buy a cat."

The Corridor opened wide, swallowing the druidess at a gulp. Lord Samuels and his lady stared bleakly after her. Turning listlessly, they looked back into the bedchamber where Marie was endeavoring to persuade Gwen to go to bed. But Gwendolyn, blithely ignoring the catalyst, continued to talk to her unseen companions.

"My friends, you are all so agitated! I can't understand why. You say dreadful things are going to happen tomorrow. But dreadful things are *always* happening tomorrow. I don't see why this should make tonight any different. I will sit with you tonight, however, if you think it will help. . . . Now, Count Devon, tell us more about the mice. Dead, you say, with no trace of blood. . . ."

"Dead mice!" Lady Rosamund laid her head on her husband's chest. "I wish she were dead herself, poor child!"

"Hush, don't say such a thing!" said Lord Samuels, holding his wife close.

"It's true!" Lady Rosamund cried. "What kind of life is she leading?"

His arm around his wife, Lord Samuels led her from her daughter's room. Marie remained with her charge, sitting in a chair near the bed. Gwen, relaxing, propped up among her pillows, chatted with the air.

Though he was chilled to the bone, Joram remained standing in the dark garden, his head pressed against the glass.

Your groom's gift to her will be grief. . . .

The catalyst's words echoed mournfully in his soul. Once long ago Joram had dreamed of being a Baron. Everything would be right with his life when he had wealth and power. Now he was Emperor of Merilon. Now he had wealth, but there was nothing he wanted to buy. He had squandered the only thing he'd ever had of value. Now he had power. And he was using it to fight a war—a war that would cost countless lives.

Dead bodies lying in the scorched grass. . . .

Tiny, furry bodies littering the attic. . . .

My fault! *My* doing! The Prophecy is coming to fulfillment despite everything I do! Maybe there's nothing I *can* do to stop it! Maybe I don't have a choice. Maybe I'm being dragged inexorably to the edge of the cliff. . . .

"Damn You!" He swore at the dark and cheerless heavens. "Why have You done this to me?"

In despairing, bitter anger, he slammed his fist against the trunk of a young spruce tree.

"Oooof!" gasped the spruce. With a painful cry, it toppled over. Branches writhing, leaves rustling, the tree lay moaning at Joram's feet.

2

Simkin's Bark

I say!" gasped the spruce. "You've killed me!"

The air shimmered around the tree, eventually coalescing, somewhat weakly, into the prostrate form of Simkin. Clutching his stomach, he rolled on the ground, his clothes every which way, leaves stuck in his hair and beard, the orange silk wrapped around his neck.

"Simkin! I'm sorry!" Fighting a wild desire to laugh, Joram helped the young man stagger to his feet. "Forgive me. I — I didn't know that tree . . . was you."

A chuckle escaped him. Recognizing in it a note of hysteria, Joram firmly forced himself to swallow it. His lips twitched, however, as he assisted the weak-kneed, doubled-over Simkin inside the house.

"Blessed Almin!" Lady Rosamund cried, meeting them in the hallway. "What has happened? Simkin! Are you all right? Oh, dear! The *Theldara*'s just left!"

Wheezing pathetically, Simkin gazed at Lady Rosamund with pain-filled eyes, mouthed the word *brandy*, and fainted dead away, collapsing in a pitiful heap on the floor.

Between Joram, Mosiah, and Prince Garald, they carried the comatose Simkin — red brocade dressing gown, fur-trimmed collar, curly shoes, and all — into the sitting room. Lady Rosamund, her hands fluttering helplessly, hurried along behind, calling distractedly for Marie and generally alarming the entire household.

"What happened to him?" Garald asked, dumping Simkin rather unceremoniously on a sofa.

"I hit him," Joram said grimly.

"About time!" Mosiah muttered.

"I didn't mean to. He was standing in the garden, disguised —"

"Ohhhhhh!" groaned Simkin, lolling back on the sofa and flinging an arm over his head. "I'm dying, Egypt, dying!"

"You're not dying!" said Garald disgustedly, leaning down to examine the patient. "You've just had the breath knocked out of you. Sit up. You'll feel better."

Thrusting the Prince aside with a feeble gesture, Simkin motioned weakly for Joram to come nearer.

"I forgive you!" Simkin murmured pitifully, gasping for breath like a freshly caught trout. "After all, what's murder between friends?" He gazed dimly around the room. "Dear lady! Lady Rosamund. Where are you? My vision's fading. I can't see you! I'm going fast!"

He held out a groping hand to Lady Rosamund, who was standing next to him. Glancing uncertainly from Prince Garald to her husband, Lady Rosamund took Simkin's hand in hers.

"Ah!" he breathed, placing her hand on his forehead. "To be speeded heavenward by a woman's gentle touch! Bless you, Lady Rosamund. My last apologies . . . for littering your sitting room . . . with my corpse. Farewell."

His eyes closed, his arm sagged, his head fell back upon the sofa cushions.

"Dear me!" Lady Rosamund became extremely pale, dropping the hand she held.

Opening his eyes, Simkin lifted his head.

"Don't bother about . . . last rites." He grabbed hold of Lady Rosamund's hand again. "Not necessary. I've led . . . life of a saint. . . . Most likely . . . I'll be canonized. Farewell."

The eyes rolled up. The head fell back. The hand went limp.

"I have the brandy, milady," said Marie gently, entering the room.

An eye opened. The hand fluttered. A voice whispered faintly from the depths of the sofa cushions.

"Domestic . . . or imported?"

"Quite a shock, I assure you!" Simkin said feelingly an hour later. "There I was standing in the garden, taking a deep whiff of the fine evening air when — wham! I am struck painfully and unexpectedly in the midriff."

Covered with Lady Rosamund's own silk shawl, his fourth glass of brandy — imported — hovering within reach, Simkin sat propped up among innumerable pillows, apparently fully recovered from his "brush with death."

"I've said I was sorry," Joram remarked, not bothering to hide the smile whose warm glow actually touched the brooding eyes. Grinning ruefully, he held up his hand, exhibiting knuckles that were scratched and bruised from having slammed into the tree trunk. "I hurt myself as much as I hurt you."

"One might say my bark is worse than my bite!" Simkin replied, sipping brandy.

Joram laughed, such an unexpected sound that Father Saryon, entering the room from having visited Gwen, stared at his friend in amazement. Seated in a chair near the sofa on which Simkin lay in luxury, Joram appeared — for the first time since his return — to forget his troubles and relax.

"Forgive the fool his sins," muttered the catalyst, who could never quite break himself of the habit of communicating with a deity in which he didn't believe.

"And I accept your apology, dear boy," said Simkin, reaching out to pat Joram on the knee. "But it *was* rather a shock," he added, wincing and consoling himself with another brandy. "Especially considering that I'd come here with the express purpose of bringing you good news!"

"What's that?" Joram asked lazily, winking at Prince Garald, who shook his head in amused forbearance and shrugged.

It was now either very late at night or very early in the morning, depending on one's viewpoint. Lady Rosamund, exhausted from the day's events, had been assisted to her bed by Marie. Lord Samuels suggested that the gentlemen gather in the sitting room with Simkin (so as not to be forced to move the invalid) and partake of a brandy themselves before going to bed, each putting off, for a few moments, the thoughts of what tomorrow might bring.

"What news?" Joram repeated, feeling the brandy warm his blood as the fire warmed his body. Sleep was stealing up on him, putting soft hands over his eyes, whispering soothing words.

"I've discovered a way to cure Gwendolyn," Simkin announced.

Starting, Joram sat up straight, spilling his brandy.

"That isn't funny, Simkin!" he said quietly.

"I had no intention of being funny—"

"I think you had best drop the subject, Simkin," Prince Garald interposed sternly, his gaze going from Joram to Lord Samuels, who had pushed his brandy glass aside with a trembling hand. "I was about to suggest we retire for the night anyway. Some of us, it seems, already have." He glanced at Mosiah, asleep in his chair.

"I am perfectly serious!" Simkin retorted, injured.

Garald lost patience. "We have put up with your nonsense long enough. Father, would you—"

"It isn't nonsense."

Tossing the blanket aside, Simkin sat up on the sofa. Though he answered Garald, he wasn't looking at the Prince. His gaze rested on Joram with a strange, half-serious, half-mocking expression, as though daring Joram to refuse to believe in him.

"Explain yourself then," Joram said briefly, toying with the brandy glass in his hand.

"Gwendolyn talks to the dead. She's obviously a throwback to the old Necromancers." Simkin squirmed into a more comfortable position. "Now, by purest coincidence, this was an affliction suffered by my little brother, Nate. Or was it Nat? At any rate, he used to entertain assorted ghost-ies and ghoulies nightly, causing my mother no end of worry, not to mention the tedium of being constantly wakened by clanking chains, snapping whips, and unearthly shrieks and howls. Or was that the time Aunt Betsy and Uncle Ernest came to spend their honeymoon with us?"

"Anyway, to continue," Simkin hurried on, seeing Joram's face grow darker, "one of the neighbors suggested that we take poor little Nat . . . Nate? Nat," he muttered, "I'm positive that's it. . . . Where was I? Oh, yes. Well, what-ever his name, we took the tyke to the Temple of the Necro-mancers."

Joram, who had been staring into his brandy glass impa-tiently, only half-listening, turned his gaze full upon Simkin.

"What did you say?"

"See there, no one ever pays attention to me," Simkin complained in aggrieved tones. "I was mentioning the fact that we took little Nate to the Temple of the Necromancers. It's located above the Font, on the very top of the mountain. It's not used anymore, of course. But it was once the center of the Order of Necromancy in the ancient days. The dead used to come from miles around, so I've heard, to catch up on all the gossip."

Ignoring Simkin, Joram turned to look at Father Saryon, hope burning in the dark eyes so brightly that the catalyst hated himself for being forced to quench the flame.

"You must put this thought out of your mind, my son," he answered reluctantly. "Yes, the Temple is there, but it is nothing more than pillars and walls of stone, lying in ruins. Even the altar is broken."

"So?" Joram said, eagerly sitting forward.

"Let me finish!" Saryon said with unaccustomed stern-ness. "It has degenerated into an evil, unhallowed place, Joram! The catalysts attempted to restore its sanctity, but they were driven away, according to report, and returned to tell fearsome tales. Or worse, some never returned at all! The Bishop finally declared that the Temple was cursed and pro-hibited all from going there!"

Joram brushed aside his words. "The Temple is on top of the Font, on top of the Well of Life — the source of magic in this world! Its power must have once been great."

"Once!" Saryon repeated with emphasis. He laid his hand on Joram's arm, feeling his excited tension. "My son," he said earnestly, "I would give anything to be able to say that, yes, in this ancient and holy place, Gwendolyn could find the help she needs. But it cannot be! If there ever was a power there, it died with the Necromancers!"

"And now a Necromancer has returned!" Gently but firmly, Joram withdrew from the catalyst's touch.

"One who is undisciplined, untrained!" Saryon argued in frustration. "One who is — forgive me, Joram — insane!"

"It is rumored to be a dreadful place," said Lord Samuels slowly, his eyes reflecting the light of Joram's hope. "But I must admit that this seems a good idea! We could take the *Duuk-tsarith* for protection."

"No, no!" said Simkin, shaking his head. "Wouldn't do at all, I'm afraid. Those creepy warlocks are spookier than the spooks. Joram and Gwen must go alone, or perhaps with the bald Father here, who might be useful in intervening with the Powers of Darkness, should any be lurking about. It will be quite all right, I assure you. It was with poor little Nate. Cured him completely." Simkin heaved a heart-rending sigh. "At least we supposed it did. We never knew for certain. He was dancing for joy among the rocks when his foot slipped and he tumbled over the side of the mountain!"

Wiping his eyes with the orange silk, Simkin made a manly struggle to fight back the tears. "Don't offer to comfort me," he choked. "It's all right. I can bear it. You must go at noon tomorrow when the sun is right above the mountain."

"Joram, I am opposed to this!" Saryon pursued his argument. "The danger is —"

"Pish-tosh!" Simkin sniffed, lying back on the sofa cushions with a yawn. "Joram *does* have the Darksword to protect himself, after all."

"Of course! The Darksword!" Joram glanced at the catalyst in triumph. "If there is any evil magic about this place, Father, the sword will protect us!"

"Absolutely. Go tomorrow, before the battle," Simkin repeated, casually toying with the blanket.

"Why this insistence on tomorrow?" Garald asked suspiciously.

Simkin shrugged. "Makes sense. If Gwen should happen to get rid of the mice in *her* attic — no offense intended, dear boy — she might be able to establish contact with the long departed. The dead could be of help to us in the forthcoming altercation. Then, too, Joram, think what a comfort it would be to go into battle knowing that you will be greeted on your return by a loving spouse who does *not*, as a general rule, smash china cabinets."

Joram bit his lip to silence his tongue during this last tirade, his face the face of one undergoing the torments of the damned. Nor did anyone else speak, and the room filled with quiet — an uneasy, restless quiet, a quiet loud with unspoken words.

Gazing intently at Simkin, brows furrowed, as though he longed to pierce the lolling head with his eyes, Prince Garald opened his mouth, then changed his mind, clamping his lips firmly shut. Father Saryon knew what the Prince wanted to say, he wanted to say it himself — What game is Simkin playing now? What are the stakes? Above all, what cards does he hold that none of us can see?

But much as he obviously longed to, the Prince couldn't say a word. This was an intensely personal matter, not only to Joram, but to the poor girl's father. It would be all very well for the Prince to remind Joram of his responsibilities as Emperor, his duty to his people. But Father Saryon knew, as did Garald, that Joram would throw all of that away in order both to cure his wife and to assuage his own guilt.

The catalyst looked at Lord Samuels. His face carefully expressionless, he sat with his head lowered, his brandy untouched in his hand.

Reading milord's thoughts, Saryon was not surprised when Lord Samuels lifted his head and looked at him, breaking the silence at last. "You seem to know something about this place, Father. Do you believe there is a danger?"

"Most certainly," replied Saryon emphatically. He knew what Lord Samuels was going to ask next and he was prepared with his answer.

"Is there . . . hope?" milord asked through trembling lips.

"No!" Saryon fully intended to reply. Aware of Joram's intense, unwavering gaze upon him, he meant to say it firmly, whether he believed it or not.

But as the catalyst opened his mouth to douse their hopes with cold logic, a strange sensation swept over him. His heart jolted painfully in his chest. When he tried to speak, his throat swelled, his lungs suddenly had no air. The frightening sensation of being turned to stone crept over him again. This time, however, it was no magic spell that froze him. Saryon had the terrifying impression that a great Hand had reached into his body, strangling him, choking off his lie. The catalyst struggled against it, but to no avail. The Hand gripped him fast, he could not answer.

"There *is* hope then, Father!" Joram said, his unwavering gaze never leaving Saryon's face. "You cannot deny that! I see it plainly!"

The catalyst stared at him pleadingly and even made a strangled sound, but it was too late.

"I will go," Joram said resolutely. "If you and Lady Rosamund agree with me, milord," he added belatedly, hearing Lord Samuels draw a shaking breath.

Milord faltered, his voice broke. But when he spoke it was with quiet dignity. "My daughter lives among the dead now. What worse fate could befall her, except to join them. If you will excuse me, I will go talk to my wife." Bowing, he hurriedly left the room.

"Then it is settled," Joram said, standing up. The brown eyes gleamed with inner flame; the dark, grim lines of grief and suffering on his face smoothed out. "Will you come with us, Father?"

Of that there was no question, no doubt. His life was bound up in Joram's; it had been since he first held the tiny, doomed child. . . . The Hand released Saryon. Gasping from the suddenness of his freedom, shaken by the inexplicable experience, the catalyst could only nod in reply.

"Tomorrow," Simkin repeated a third time. "At noon."

This was too much for Prince Garald to swallow in silence. Glancing at Simkin sharply, he rose to his feet, stopping Joram as he was about to leave the room. "You have every right to tell me that it is not my place to interfere."

"Then don't," Joram said coolly.

"I'm afraid I have to," Garald continued sternly. "I must remind you, Joram, that you have a responsibility to our world. My god, man, we're going to war tomorrow! I insist you reconsider!"

A slight sneer twisted Joram's lip. "This world can go to the devil —" he began.

"—and fulfill the Prophecy!" Garald finished.

The thrust hit home. There was a sharp intake of breath. Joram's face went livid, the brown eyes blazed. Saryon was reminded again, chillingly, of the youth who had forged the Darksword. He hurried forward to intervene, fearing that Joram might strike the Prince, but it was Simkin who ended the matter.

"Oh, for pity's sake, if you two are going to fight, please do it somewhere else." His jaw cracked with another yawn. "It's been an extremely fatiguing — not to mention gut-wrenching — day. I'm quite done in. I'll extinguish the lights." Every light in the room winked out, plunging them into semidarkness, lit only by the flickering coals of the dying fire. "Keep the noise of saber-rattling down to a minimum."

An orange silk night cap appeared out of nowhere and floated through the air, settling upon Simkin's head. Curling up comfortably amid the sofa cushions, the young man fell instantly, to all appearances, fast asleep.

Turning abruptly, Joram walked toward the door.

Garald stood a moment, staring at Joram's back, obviously wanting to say something, yet undecided. He glanced at Father Saryon, who made an urgent gesture with his hand. Garald hurried after Joram, interposing his body between his friend and the door.

"Forgive me for pursuing this matter, Joram. I can only imagine what torture you undergo daily."

Laying his hand on the Prince's arm, Joram started to shove Garald aside.

"Joram, listen to me!" Garald demanded, and Joram stopped, caught and held by the caring and compassion he heard in the man's voice more than by the restraining hand laid upon him.

"Think about this carefully!" the Prince continued. "Why is Simkin suddenly so interested in Gwen's welfare or in yours either, for that matter? He's never given a damn about anyone before. Why is he so insistent about you going and why tomorrow?"

"It's just his way!" Joram said impatiently. "And he *has* helped me before this. Maybe even saved my life. . . ."

"Joram," interrupted Garald firmly, "it could be a trap. There could be more waiting for you there than ghosts. Think about this. I've been thinking about it all day. How *did* Simkin understand what the enemy said? That's impossible, even for one of his 'talents.' How did he understand unless they *told* him what to say."

It was dark in the hall. Before retiring for the night, the servants had dimmed the magical lights. The globes in the lofty cobwebby corners of the hallway gleamed with a white, cold light, making it appear as if stars, flying through the house like insects, had been captured in the webs of the house spiders. Far away — it sounded as if it came from the morning room — could be heard a thud and a crash. Father Saryon wondered briefly if poor Count Devon was roaming the halls.

Joram did not reply. Saryon — looking at his face, seeing it white and cold as the face of the moon — could tell by the brooding expression that this last argument had at least made an impression. Prince Garald, noting this as well, wisely took his leave.

Saryon said nothing either. He was, he admitted to himself, afraid to speak. Still unsettled by his recent unnerving experience, the catalyst dared not add anything. He could only trust that Garald's seed of doubt, planted in Joram's soul, would take root and grow.

It appeared to have fallen on fertile soil at least. Sighing heavily, Joram started to turn away when a voice — muffled and slightly fluff-filled — came out of the depths of the sofa.

"Trust your fool. . . ."

3

Falling

There was a family chapel in the house of Lord Samuels, as in almost all the houses of the nobility and the upper middle class in Thimhallan. Although all the chapels are generally similar in appearance, some were vastly different, a difference that rose higher than vaulted ceilings and gleamed more brightly than polished rosewood. In some households, the chapel was obviously the heart of the dwelling. Here everyone — master and mistress, children and servants (all being considered one in the sight of the Almin, if nowhere else) — gathered daily for prayer, led by the House Catalyst. These chapels breathed with Life. The wood glowed from much use. The stained glass windows, with their symbols of the Almin and of the Nine Mysteries, glistened in the morning sun. At night, tiny, magical lights filled the chapel with a soft radiance, relaxing to the spirit, conducive to private prayer and meditation. It was easy to believe that the Almin dwelt in such peaceful, beautiful surroundings. It was easy to talk to Him in such a place. It was easy to hear His answers.

The late Count Devon, who had owned the house prior to Lord Samuels, had been a deeply religious man. In his day, the chapel was filled with light and Life. Upon the Count's death, the chapel, like the rest of the house, was sealed shut; its lights put out, its furniture draped in black cloth, its beautiful stained glass windows shuttered. When Lord Samuels moved in, he opened the rest of the house to the outside world, but the chapel remained closed and locked. He did not do this out of anger or bitterness over the loss of his beloved daughter. Lord Samuels was not the type of man to shake his fist at the Almin and vow that he "would never speak to You again!" Rather, something within his soul had died. Asked by the servants if he wanted the chapel restored to service, he caught himself answering, "What's the use?"

And so the chapel remained shut, its ornately carved rosewood doors closed, its windows dark and lifeless. The magical seal laid over the door was an unusually strong one, and it took Father Saryon a considerable amount of mental effort to remove it. Finally succeeding, he made his way inside and collapsed in the nearest pew, unaccustomed to the strain of using so much of his own Life force.

The pews were slick with a fine film of dust. So were the floors. Everything in the chapel was covered with dust, Saryon noted, wondering where it came from. It felt soft to the touch. Holding his small globe of flame close, he saw that it was reddish-colored and sweet smelling. Saryon's analytical mind instantly began to work, delighted in this bit of irrelevancy to banish the tension. Holding the small globe high, Saryon could barely make out wood beams in the ceiling far above him. These, he deduced, must be magically shaped of cedar. Unlike the rest of the wood in the chapel, the beams remained rough and unpolished, probably to enhance their smell. Hence, the wood dust.

That problem solved, Saryon sighed and reflexively rubbed his tired eyes, instantly regretting that he had done so when he realized from the sudden gritty feeling that he had rubbed wood dust into them. Blinking, he wiped his tearing eyes on his sleeve.

You should be in bed, he told himself. He was exhausted and he knew — recalling past warnings from the *Theldara* — that he should not tax his strength. But he also knew he could not sleep. He was *afraid* to sleep. Fear was slowly creeping over him, chilling and immobilizing as the dreadful spell that had been cast upon him, the spell that had changed his flesh to stone. It had all started tonight, with that awful sensation of the Hand laying hold of him, preventing him from telling Joram not to go to the Temple.

It was foolish, dangerous. There was no hope for Gwen. The Necromancers were gone. Saryon doubted if they could have helped her anyway. He would have been able to convince Joram of this. His arguments added to Garald's would have undoubtedly persuaded Joram not to go, not to risk his wife's life as well as his own in this foolhardy endeavor.

Surely he won't go! Surely!

Laying his head upon the hand that rested upon the back of the pew in front of him, Saryon shivered in a paroxysm of fear. As he had analyzed the wood dust, he attempted to analyze his fear, seeking its source in order to deal with it on a rational basis. But he could not find it. It was a faceless, nameless terror and the more he concentrated on dragging it to light, the darker it grew. Saryon had lived through many frightening experiences. He could still remember — horribly — the fear he'd experienced when he first felt the numbing blast of the spell hit him and he knew his living body was slowly turning to stone.

But that was nothing — *nothing* — compared to the fear that gripped him now. He had not experienced this overwhelming sense of loss and despair. No, he recalled, staring into the sweet-smelling, softly lit darkness of the chapel. When the first wave of terror had begun to recede, he had felt imbued with peace and joy. He had done what was right. He had seen his sacrifice touch Joram deeply, the light of his love drive away the darkness of the boy's soul. That knowledge sustained the catalyst in the days and nights of his endless vigil. Though he had not made peace with his god, he had found it within himself.

Or thought he had. The Darksword that shattered his stone flesh shattered his peace as well.

Saryon's hands hurt him and, looking down, he realized that he was hanging onto the edge of the pew for dear life. He tried to relax. The feeling of fear did not leave, however.

"It's the battle tomorrow night," he muttered to himself. "So much depends on the outcome. Our lives! The existence of our world! How dreadful it will be if we lose!"

"How dreadful it will be if you win."

Who spoke? Saryon heard the words as clearly as he'd ever heard anything in his entire life, yet he could swear he was alone. Shuddering, he looked around. "Who's there?" he called out tremulously.

There was no answer. Perhaps he hadn't heard anything. There was certainly no one in the room, probably no one awake in the house.

"I am exhausted," Saryon said to himself, mopping chill drops of perspiration from his head with the sleeve of his robe. "My mind is playing tricks."

He tried to stand, he instructed his body to rise, but the body remained seated, the Hand holding him down. Then, beckoning to him, it pointed.

Before his horrified eyes, Saryon saw clearly the aftermath of the fighting: All — *all* of the strange humans lying dead. The *Pron-Alban* using their magic to dig a huge grave. The bodies — those that could be found and had not been devoured by centaurs — tumbled into it, the earth shoveled over them. All traces of their existence as humans — as husbands, fathers, brothers, friends wiped out. After a hundred years, no one in their world remembered them.

But Thimhallan did. No tree, no flower, no grass grew on that mass grave. Weeds, noxious and poisonous, sprang up. It was a diseased blemish upon the land. And the sickness from it spread slowly and surely through the world until everything died.

"But what is the alternative?" Saryon cried aloud. "Death? That's it, isn't it? We have no choice! The Prophecy! The Prophecy is fulfilled! You have given us no choice!"

The Hand that gripped him suddenly opened wide, and Saryon became conscious of a Presence. Vast and powerful, it filled the chapel so that the walls must surely burst from the strain. Yet it was tiny and minute, existing within each small grain of dust that drifted down from the ceiling. It was fire and water, burning and cooling him. It was awful and he cowered from its sight. It was loving and he longed to rest his weary head in its palm, begging for forgiveness.

Forgiveness for what?

For being a card in a great cosmic game played for the amusement of one player?

For being tormented and persecuted, for being shoved over the edge of a cliff.

The voice spoke again, sternly. "You do not understand. You cannot understand the mind of God."

"No!" Saryon gasped. "I don't understand! And I will not amuse You further. I renounce You! I deny You!"

Rising unsteadily to his feet, Saryon stumbled from the chapel. Once outside, he slammed the door shut and stood leaning against it, his breath coming in shuddering sobs. But as he stood there, holding the door shut with his body, he knew he could never keep the Presence locked up within that room. He could no more deny it than he could deny his own existence. It was everywhere. Around him. . . .

Within him. . . .

Saryon pressed his hand over his heart, digging his fingers into his flesh.

4

The Blink Of An Eye

Saryon struggled frantically to escape a deep chasm in which he was trapped. Sheer walls, rising on either side of him, blocked his view of the sky. A raging river that cut through the rock cliffs threatened to engulf him in its white, foaming water. Vines wrapped around his feet; tree limbs stretched out their clawlike fingers to drag him back. Lost and alone he wandered, seeking a way out. Suddenly, there it was! A cut in the sheer rock face, a glimpse of sunlight and blue sky. It seemed an easy climb and, strength renewed, he hurried toward it.

At first it *was* easy and he soon left the chasm floor behind. Unfortunately, he drew no nearer the blue sky. Then he realized that the higher he climbed, the taller rose the cliff. The side of the wall became more difficult to negotiate. Black bats swooped out of caves, darting at him, causing him to lose his footing, threatening to send him sliding back down into the chasm. Still he struggled on and, at last, he reached the top. With a final effort, he pulled himself over the edge and stared into a huge, unblinking eye.

Pressing his face down on the rock, Saryon cowered away from the eye. But he knew he could not hide anywhere that it did not see him.

"Up, Catalyst!" called a voice.

Saryon lifted his head. Beside him stood a tree. Gathering his robes about him, Saryon scrambled up the trunk. Sheltered by the green leaves, he breathed a sigh of relief. The Eye could not see him here. Just as he said this, the leaves turned brown and, one by one, began to drop off. The Eye found him again. Then a branch broke beneath his feet. And another.

"Father!" A hand was shaking his shoulder. "Time to get up."

Waking with a start, Saryon clutched at the hand as the world fell away beneath him. The hand's grip was strong and firm and he clung to it thankfully. The hand let loose of him, however, and the catalyst fell back among his pillows, feeling as exhausted and bruised as if he had — in reality — spent the night climbing cliffs.

Joram walked over to the window and drew back the shutters. Cold, bleak light from a chill, white sun streamed into the room, causing Saryon to wince.

"What time is it?" he asked, blinking in the bright light.

"It lacks an hour until noon. You have slept away the morning, Catalyst, and there is much to be done this day."

"Have I? I'm . . . I'm sorry," said Saryon, sitting up dazedly. He kept his face averted from the sun. Was that the Eye? Watching him?

What nonsense! It was only a dream.

Leaving his bed, Saryon bathed his face in cold water and dressed hurriedly, conscious of Joram's mounting impatience. Pacing the room, a tense, eager look on his usually stern, impassive face, Joram was dressed for travel, Saryon noted uneasily. Over his white robes was thrown a gray cloak. Though Saryon could not see it, he knew that beneath this cloak Joram wore the Darksword, strapped to his back.

"You have decided to go to the Temple," Saryon said in a low voice. Sitting down on the edge of the bed, he started to draw on his shoes. Dizziness assailed him as he bent over, however, and he was forced to pause a moment until the weakness passed.

"There was never any decision to be made. It was a foregone conclusion." Joram noticed Saryon resting, doing nothing. "Hurry, Catalyst!" He made an irritated gesture with his hand toward the window and the sunlight. "We must arrive there at noon today, not noon tomorrow! You said you would go with us. Did you mean that? Or are these dawdlings a priestly trick to try to keep me from going?"

"I will go with you," Saryon said slowly, looking up from his shoes to Joram. "You should know that without asking, my son. What cause have I given you to doubt me?"

"You're a Priest. Isn't that cause enough!" Joram sneered and started for the door.

Rising to his feet, Saryon followed. "Joram, what is wrong?" he asked, gently touching him on the sleeve of his white robes. "You are not yourself."

"I'm certain I don't know who else I would be this morning, Catalyst!" Joram retorted, jerking his arm away from Saryon's hand. Seeing the Priest's look of concern, Joram hesitated, the stern face relaxed. Running his fingers through his thick, black hair, he shook his head. "Forgive me, Father," he said with a sigh. "I have not slept well. And I do not foresee any sleep this night or perhaps many nights to come. I want only to go to this place and find help for Gwendolyn! Are you ready?"

"Yes, and I understand how you feel, Joram," Saryon began, "but—"

Joram impatiently broke off his words. "No time for that now, Father! We must find Gwen and leave before Garald or any of the rest of those fools attempt to stop me!"

His face hardened. Saryon stared at Joram, wondering at this change. Yet why should it amaze me? he asked himself sadly. I've seen it coming. I've seen the light of the forge fires shine in his eyes. It is as if all the intervening years, the suffering and hardship that taught him compassion, have been stripped from him, *his* warm flesh changed to stone.

The chasm Saryon had just escaped yawned before him. Each step drew him nearer its edge. Surely, surely there is a path away from it! Let me turn around and find it.

A hand gripped his arm painfully. "Where are you going, Catalyst? It is time to leave!"

"Please reconsider!" Saryon faltered. "There must be another way, Joram!"

The forge fire flared, scorching the Priest. "You have a choice, Father," Joram said bitingly. "Either come with me or stay behind. Which will it be?"

A choice! Saryon almost laughed. He could see the path leading away from the cliff. It was blocked by boulders that had fallen years before. He could not go back.

"I will come," the catalyst said, bowing his head.

The white sun filled Lord Samuels's house with light for the first time in many days. Glinting blindingly off the surface of the melting snow, it was not a warm light or a cheerful one. The garden was lovely beneath its white shroud, but it was a lethal loveliness. The plants were frozen solid, encased in snow. The weight of the ice broke off huge tree limbs. Giant trees split in two.

Despite the discomfort of the cold weather, the streets outside Lord Samuels's house were packed with people, milling around, hoping to catch a glimpse of Joram, begging those that came out for news. A continual stream of War Masters, Ariels, Guildmasters, *Albanara*, and others had been flowing into and out of the house since dawn. The preparations for war were well underway.

Inside, Lord Samuels, the Prince, Cardinal Radisovik, several members of the nobility, and the War Masters were assembled in one of the upstairs ballrooms that had been hastily converted into a War Room.

Prince Garald, maps spread out on a large table, began explaining his plans to the assembled leaders. If he noticed that the atmosphere within the ballroom was nearly as chill as the atmosphere without, he ignored it.

"We'll strike at night, come at them out of the darkness while they're asleep. They'll be confused and unorganized. We should seem like a continuation of some terrible nightdream for them, so we'll use the Illusionists first. Count Marat, you'll lead your forces in here" — Garald pointed to a grouping of geodesic domes that sprang up magically beneath his fingertips — "and you'll — "

"Begging your pardon, Prince Garald," interrupted Count Marat in a smooth voice. "These plans of yours are all very well, but the Emperor is our leader. I came here this morning expecting to discuss matters with him. Where is he?"

Prince Garald glanced swiftly at one of the *Duuk-tsarith*, hovering like a shadow in the corner. The hood shivered slightly in answer. Frowning, Garald turned back to the Count. Marat was not alone in his demands. Many others of the *Albanara* of Merilon were nodding agreement.

"The Emperor has not had any sleep in the past two nights," Prince Garald returned coolly. "Since these are his plans, which I am attempting to discuss with you, I did not feel that his presence was required. I have, however," he added, seeing the Count about to speak, "sent Mosiah after him. The Emperor should be here — "

A pounding on the sealed door to the War Room interrupted him.

Garald nodded and one of the *Duuk-tsarith* removed the magical seal from the door. Everyone turned to look, the nobles prepared to bow before their Emperor. But they saw only Mosiah . . . alone.

"Where is Jor — the Emperor?" Garald demanded.

"He's . . . he's sent me with a message," Mosiah stammered, giving Garald a swift glance.

"He's sent me with a message, *Your Grace*," rebuked Cardinal Radisovik, but Mosiah didn't hear him. He continued to look intently at Prince Garald.

"It's . . . uh . . . confidential, Your Grace." He made a motion with his hand, indicating that they step near the window.

Prince Garald straightened from bending over the map. "A message?" he repeated irritably. "Did you tell him we have been needing him this past half-hour? Isn't he — Oh, very well. Excuse me, milords."

Ignoring the nobles, who were muttering among themselves, Mosiah walked swiftly over to the large glass windows. Prince Garald and Lord Samuels went with him, the *Albanara* suspiciously watching every move they made.

"Your Grace!" Mosiah said softly. "It's nearly noon!"

"I don't need to know the time," Garald snapped. Then, realization slowly dawning, he fell abruptly silent, his gaze drawn reluctantly to the magical timeglass that stood on one of the mantelpieces in the elegant ballroom. The tiny sun trapped inside had nearly reached its topmost point and was blinking brightly in its arc halfway above a tiny world.

"Damn!" the Prince swore softly, turning from the nobles to face the window, his hands clasped behind his back. "I thought I had convinced him not to go!"

"Perhaps he's just walking in the garden." Lord Samuels suggested.

"I've looked! He isn't! And Father Saryon and Gwendolyn are gone, too!" Moving nearer Prince Garald, Mosiah pretended to be studying the garden with interest. "There's worse news!" he murmured. "Simkin's disappeared as well!"

"Lord Samuels, question the servants," ordered Garald quietly. "Ask if any of them have seen Joram or Father Saryon this morning. Try to do it without alarming anyone," he added, but it was too late. Before he could stop him, the distraught lord dashed across the length of the ballroom and ran out into the hallway, shouting for the servants. The nobles watched him go, their faces growing increasingly grim and cold.

"Prince Garald!" called out Count Marat loudly. "I insist on knowing what is going on? Where is the Emperor?"

"Where is the Emperor?" The cry was taken up. Chaos erupted, everyone talking at once and no one making himself heard.

"Silence!" Garald roared finally, and the clamor died away. "You'd think we were faeriefolk gone mad!" he added sternly. "Mosiah has just told me that the Emperor's wife is extremely ill this morning and he does not want to leave her. Lord Samuels has just sent the servants for the *Theldara*. Lord Samuels also informs me that luncheon is being served. I suggest that you take this opportunity to dine. The Emperor will be meeting with you after dinner. My lords, this way. The servants will show you. Thank you, go ahead without me. I will join you presently."

Exchanging dark glances and continuing to grumble among themselves, the nobles and the War Masters of Merilon slowly left the room. Those with a mind to stay were assisted politely but firmly on their way by Prince Garald's warlocks. Once everyone was gone, the Prince gestured to the *Duuk-tsarith* to seal the door.

"Wait outside," Garald instructed the warlock. "Admit Lord Samuels, but no one else."

The *Duuk-tsarith* vanished, leaving the Prince, Cardinal Radisovik, and Mosiah alone in the room. Sunlight glared through the many windows, streaming down upon the marble floor, illuminating the maps rolled up on the table. No one spoke. Radisovik looked questioningly at the Prince, but Garald, toying with the maps, refused to meet his minister's eyes. Mosiah endeavored to stand calmly and wait, but he shifted nervously from one foot to the other, wiping his sweating palms upon his archer's uniform. Everyone looked up in relief when Lord Samuels reappeared, bringing a flustered maid with him.

Abashed at being in the presence of the Prince, the maid was at first incoherent. It took some time for Garald's gentle, courteous manner to calm her and enable her to answer his questions.

Yes, she had seen the Emperor. She was changing the bed linens that morning when she saw Joram, dressed in a traveling cloak, going into Father Saryon's room. Sometime later, she saw them emerge from that room and walk down the hall. She overheard them talking of Lady Gwendolyn.

Yes, the Emperor appeared tense and nervous, but so was everyone else in the house. She was that upset herself it was a wonder she didn't faint dead away.

Yes, now that she thought of it, Father Saryon had seemed nervous as well. He was very pale and walked as though he was being cast into Beyond. These were terrible times, as she'd been saying to Cook only this morning.

No, she couldn't recall having seen the gaudy young man with the beard and that suited her fine, due to certain shocking things he'd said to her last night, which she hoped she was never to be put in the way of hearing again or she would be forced to give notice.

"Thank you, my girl," said Prince Garald abruptly. With a curtsey and a sly smile for Mosiah, the maid departed. The *Duuk-tsarith* once more sealed the door shut. "Well, that seems clear enough," Garald continued with a heavy sigh. "Joram's gone to the Temple, and he's taken Father Saryon and Gwen with him."

"Temple? What temple, Your Grace?" asked Cardinal Radisovik, mystified.

"The Temple of the Necromancers."

"The Almin go with them!" the Cardinal said fervently, making the sign against evil.

"Begging your pardon, Holiness, but I don't think the Almin's going to be enough," Mosiah said. "I think we should be there, too. This is some kind of trap, isn't it, Your Grace?"

"I don't know!" Garald snapped, moodily pacing the length of the room. "Simkin's story about Nat or Nate is obviously a lie, yet there was enough truth in it to lure Joram into believing him. And others, too, I might add." He glanced at Lord Samuels, who stood apart from them, staring unseeing into the garden.

"If my daughter *is* a Necromancer, this Temple could be the only place in this world where she might find help!" Milord turned an agonized face toward the Prince. "If we go blundering in, Your Grace, we might ruin everything."

"Or we might save their lives!" Mosiah interjected. "We could take the Corridor, Your Grace, just check to make certain everything is all right. Simkin *was* with the enemy, after all!"

"I know! I know! I know!" Garald shouted impatiently, striking his hand down upon the table. "I know Simkin! I know he'd gamble away his soul, Joram's soul, and the souls of everyone in this world for anything from a dancing chicken to a boiled potato if it caught his fancy!"

"In which case," Cardinal Radisovik said softly, "Joram is in real danger. Perhaps, Garald, Mosiah is right. . . ."

A black form appeared in the center of the War Room, coming upon them with the suddenness of a thunder clap. The hands of the *Duuk-tsarith* were clasped tightly before him as was proper — only they were clasped too tightly, the fingers twisting with the strain. His voice, when he spoke, was tighter still.

"Your Grace, the enemy is on the move!"

"What?" Garald demanded in astonishment. "Are they leaving?"

"No, Your Grace. They are —"

A brilliant, blinding light exploded in their eyes. The huge glass windows imploded. The room was swept by a storm of shattered crystal. Paintings fell from the walls; the walls themselves cracked and buckled. A large ceiling beam split and sagged. The walls, the ceiling, the very foundation of the house shook and trembled.

Nearby explosions completed the message that the warlock, lying dead, his body riddled by shards of glass, was unable to deliver.

Merilon was under attack.

The house of Lord Samuels gave a final shudder. The timeglass, which had withstood the initial shock wave, tumbled from the mantelpiece, the glass case breaking into a hundred glittering fragments. Free from its confines, the tiny sun rolled under the carpet. The tiny world bounced into the ashes of the fireplace.

5

The Temple Of
The Necromancers

The Temple of the Necromancers held an honored place in the world — it stood on the very top of the Font, the tallest mountain in Thimhallan. The foundation on which it had been built had been magically leveled, but the Temple had more the appearance of perching on a rocky crag than resting firmly on solid bedrock. This was undoubtedly due to a trick of the eye, as the saying went, enhanced by the fact that the Temple and its Garden occupied the only level ground that existed at that dizzying height.

According to legend, the Temple of the Necromancers had been raised up from the stone of the mountain by the hands of the dead themselves. The summit of the mountain formed the Temple's cavelike back wall, the magically altered peak that spiraled gracefully into the clouds was the Temple's roof. The two side walls, facing east and west, were built out from the back. Following the natural lines of the mountain, they each rose up from the tops of sheer cliffs. Bishop

Vanya's Garden — referred to in these days as the "top" of the mountain — was actually five hundred feet below.

The columned portico of the Temple, facing north, opened onto a large, circular expanse of level ground. Here, paving stones had been laid out in the shape of a wheel. Nine sidewalks formed nine spokes that led from the outer walkway to a huge altar stone in the hub of the wheel. One symbol of each of the Nine Mysteries was engraved at the end of each walkway. All nine symbols were repeated, carved into the altar stone.

This area had once been well kept. Comfortable wooden benches stood at intervals around the wheel's hub. Between each of the nine spokes, beds of flowers had bloomed, coaxed by the hands of the druids to grow at this high altitude.

In this once lovely Garden, in this magnificent setting, people came from all over Thimhallan to counsel with, ask advice of, or merely pay a cordial visit to their dead. The Necromancers — born to the Mystery of Spirit and permitted by the Almin to dwell in both worlds, that of the living and that of the dead — acted as interpreters, carrying messages from one world to the next and back again.

The Necromancers had been a powerful Order, the most powerful in Thimhallan at the time of the Iron Wars, or so it was whispered. A word from the dead had been known to topple thrones and bring down royal houses. The *Duuktsarith*, who feared nothing living, reportedly had trembled when they approached the Gardens of the Necromancers. There had been those, particularly among the rulers of the land, their warlocks, and their catalysts, who had looked upon this power with a jealous eye.

No one knew exactly how the Necromancers perished during the Iron Wars. It was a confused time. Countless numbers of people lost their lives during that bloody conflict. The Necromancers had always been a very small sect; few people were born to the Mystery of Spirit, and fewer still had the discipline to enable them to endure a life of death. It is easy to understand how a small group might have perished and their passing gone unnoticed.

Suffice it to say that at war's end the catalysts announced that the Necromancers had been wiped out. The practicers of the Dark Arts, the Technologists, were blamed for the murders, as they were blamed for every evil that had befallen the land during the past century.

Few missed the Necromancers. The dead of the land — and there were many — had generally died bitter deaths. The living were only too happy to put their grief out of their minds and get on with living, which, in many cases, was difficult enough.

If any thought to wonder why no more children were born to the Mystery of the Spirit, they might have asked the catalysts or the *Duuk-tsarith* or the parents of children who occasionally heard voices not audible to others or talked to friends that were not there. In these instances, the children either outgrew this strange phase or, if the "phase" persisted, the children disappeared.

What Father Saryon said about the Temple was true — people *were* prohibited from setting foot on Temple grounds. But — and this is not to disparage the word of the catalyst, who was undoubtedly repeating the gossip of the Font — it was *not* true that the Temple had fallen under a curse. It was *not* true that certain powerful catalysts had tried to lift the curse and had never returned.

The truth of the matter was very simple — no one had ever bothered. The only curse the Temple of the Necromancers lay under was the curse of being forgotten.

The red robes of his disguise rustling about his ankles, Menju the Sorcerer stepped cautiously out of the Corridor onto the long neglected grounds of the Temple. The *Thon-li* who brought him here were shocked beyond measure at his traveling to this place and had earnestly tried to dissuade him. Only by stating that this was a wartime emergency had the Sorcerer been able to convince them to send him to his destination.

Their fears, however, had done nothing to bolster his confidence. His hand clasping the phaser gun kept concealed in his pocket, words of a spell for repelling the dead on his lips, Menju looked swiftly around and instantly sensed the true nature of the place. Relaxing, he breathed a sigh of relief.

Though the sun beamed from a cloudless sky, an aura of sadness and melancholy hung over the Temple like thick fog, casting an almost perceptible shadow on the broken walls and the crumbling stone. There was an eerie stillness about the place, too; an unnatural quiet, as if countless numbers of unseen people were standing about, each holding his or her breath, waiting for something to happen.

Shivering in the still, cold mountain air, the Sorcerer put his phaser away, grinning over his fears. But it was a weak grin at best and he sat down upon one of the decaying stone benches with an unintended suddenness, resulting from his knees giving way.

What had he expected, after all? he scolded himself. Legions of howling dead, leaping, shrieking, out of the darkness to protest this trespass? Skeletal hands touching his? Figures in white winding sheets and chains stalking about, bewailing the degenerate state of his mind and promising him three ghostly visitors before morning?

"Bah! Humbug!" he said aloud and was able to laugh — with only a slight shudder — at his own little joke.

Wiping the chill sweat from his brow, Menju took a moment to regain his composure and to investigate his surroundings. He had come here purposefully early to do just this. The sun was even with his left shoulder. He had over an hour until noon.

Phaser in hand, he carefully and coolly began to examine every rock and boulder around the perimeter of the Temple grounds. He checked out his surroundings with elaborate care. Despite his immediate observation that there was no one here, Menju had the strangest impression that someone was examining *him*. Finding nothing and no one, however, he firmly banished the thought, considering it to come from the same childish source as the clanking chains and white sheets.

Leaving the cliff's edge, the Sorcerer walked down one of the paths through the dead Garden, desiring a closer look at the altar stone. The path he selected was the one of his own Mystery — that of Technology. Whether he chose this path out of superstition, a feeling of homesickness, or because it merely suited his humor, Menju didn't bother to analyze.

Stalks of dead plants that had not decayed in the cold, dry air of the high mountain elevation stuck up out of the frozen dirt on either side of the path. Small, dead, ornamental saplings lay with their roots in the air, having been blown over by the winter winds. The Sorcerer glanced without interest at the remnants of the Garden. Arriving at the altar stone, he stared at it curiously, running his fingers over the symbols of the Nine Mysteries carved into the rock. It was an unusual type of rock, he saw. Some sort of ore. Perhaps darkstone! he thought, feeling a tremor of excitement.

Examining it closely, he tried to recall legends he had heard about the altar stone. How it had been raised out of the Well of Life far below, at the base of the Font. How it had been a sort of plug in the Well and how, once the stone was removed, the magic gushed forth like magma, flowing out over the world.

That made sense, he realized suddenly. The darkstone had capped the Well! It was an exhilarating thought.

Standing at the center of the world, directly above the source of the magic, Menju could feel Life pulsing around him, surging through him. He reveled in the sensation. He couldn't believe he had forgotten how exciting it was, possessing the magic again.

The Sorcerer studied the boulder critically. It was huge! It must stand at least seven feet tall. His arms would not even go halfway around it. It weighed — what — a ton? If it *was* darkstone, its value would be incalculable! His hand, touching it, shook with anticipation.

"Joram will know if it is darkstone or it isn't," the Sorcerer murmured, smiling to himself. "I must try to keep him conscious when I capture him, at least until he's had a chance to tell me."

Patting the altar stone fondly and longingly with his hand, the Sorcerer continued his inspection, finally reaching the Temple itself.

Nine stairs shaped out of stone led up to the porch. Nine crumbling columns supported a broken roof that jutted out from beneath the spiraling summit of the mountain. Drawing nearer, the Sorcerer saw that parts of the ceiling had collapsed beneath the weight of rock and years. Large chunks of stone littered the floor. The altar, barely seen through the shadows, appeared to have been crushed by a ceiling beam. Climbing the crumbling stairs, Menju noted with satisfaction that the darkness inside the Temple was thick and impenetrable.

Menju nodded to himself. Taking one final look around, he glanced out over the plains far to the north, to where the city of Merilon stood glittering in the sun. Squinting, he stared intently at the city, thinking he saw the glint of metal. Was it Major Boris's tanks taking up position to bombard the magical dome? Or was it the sunlight, flashing off an ice-bound lake? He couldn't be certain.

Shrugging, the Sorcerer turned away. Once he had the Darksword, it wouldn't matter anyway. Meanwhile Boris and his men could have their fun. It kept the Major occupied, kept him from brooding. And it would heat up the blood of the soldiers, filling them with the fear and hatred necessary to exterminate the people of this world.

The sun was high above his head. It was nearly time. Returning to his selected hiding place, Menju mulled over matters in his mind. The fighting on this world was likely to be long and costly, even with the Darksword. These people wouldn't go to their deaths without a struggle. A pity he couldn't use some of those depopulation bombs that killed without damaging buildings and such. Would those disrupt the magic? Possibly not. He'd have to consult the physicists. Come to think of it, Joram might know.

What about Joram? Would he cooperate? Entering the Temple, the Sorcerer allowed himself a smile of satisfaction. His plan was foolproof. Joram was known to be devoted to his mad wife. Once realizing that Menju had Gwendolyn captive, Joram would be only too happy to cooperate. Insane though the woman may be, at least she was capable of some form of rational thought. Better that than seeing her mental capacity reduced to the level of a rotting tomato.

Menju switched the setting on his phaser from "kill" to "stun." Crouching down in the darkness behind a column of the ruined Temple, conscious of a breathless hush that had settled over the top of the world, the Sorcerer waited.

6

The Executioner

Menju's instincts were right. He *was* being watched. And though most of the eyes watching him belonged to the dead, one pair did not. One pair belonged to the living. Someone else had arrived at the Temple of the Necromancer. Someone else was waiting.

The presence of the humans disturbed the dead, who had not seen living bodies on their hallowed ground in centuries. But it was not just the presence alone of these two men that caused the spirit's restless agitation. Clustered about their Temple, they watched with unseeing eyes, listened with deaf ears, spoke with dumb mouths. For there was no one to understand them, no one to hear them, and their sense of frustration was great. The dead—who were one with the mind of Almin—knew the danger but were helpless to act. All they could do was watch with those watching and wait with those waiting.

This second Watcher was, in reality, the first. He had arrived at the Temple of the Necromancer very early in the morning, just as the pale, cold sun was struggling up over the mountain peaks, creeping sluggishly into the sky as if wondering why it bothered to rise at all. Even the eyes of the dead — who see time moving not second by second as do the living, but as one vast, everchanging ocean — nearly missed noticing this man. Emerging from the Corridor, he vanished again instantly, disappearing almost in the second of his appearance.

It took some doing, but the dead located him, or at least part of him, for this man was good at his calling. No human eye could pierce his shield of invisibility, and it was all the spirits could do to keep his image in their minds. The man they saw was dressed formally for the commission of Justice, wearing gray robes decorated with the symbols of the Nine Mysteries. Many of the dead recognized him — the Executioner — and they either trembled or cursed him.

One of the most powerful warlocks in Thimhallan, the Executioner dwelled within the Font. His services belonged exclusively to the catalysts in general, and Bishop Vanya in particular. In return for performing such deeds for them as the Turning to Stone and the Banishment to Beyond, the Executioner was given unlimited Life and freedom to use that Life as he chose. Thus he had been able to develop his skills in the discipline of magic far beyond those of his peers.

This day, however, the Executioner was not going to rely upon magic. As did the other Watcher in the Temple, he carried in the pocket of his gray robes a Tool, a demonic device created by the Dark Arts of Technology.

Intrigued by the device, which he had spent the night studying, the Executioner withdrew it and examined it intently. The dead, drawn by curiosity, crowded around, gazing at the device in shock and horror. What it was and what it did they had some idea, since they were one with the Creator of All. They found the terrible device difficult to understand, however, as perhaps did the Creator, who must have, on occasion, regretted giving mankind intelligence that was turned so often to malevolent pursuits.

The night previous, Bishop Vanya had called the Executioner to his office. Giving him his orders, he had made certain that the warlock knew exactly what was required of him.

"For returning to this realm and bringing upon it untold danger, the sentence of death is placed upon this man Joram," pronounced the Bishop's sonorous voice. "He has tricked the people into naming him Emperor; therefore, the rest of the *Duuk-tsarith* are bound by strict oaths to protect him. You — the Executioner — are to consider yourself above these laws, since the Church — the highest authority in the land, existing by the blessing of the Almin — has decreed Joram's death. Once the sentence has been carried out, you will retrieve the Darksword and bring it immediately to me to prevent its presence in the world from causing further harm."

The Bishop had stopped here for breath and to carefully scrutinize the Executioner in order to make certain that he understood what he was meant to understand and didn't what he wasn't.

"Further," the Bishop had continued, sucking in a noseful of air, "although the execution of Joram is undeniably justified, we consider that it will be best — the people being in a nervous and unsettled state — to allow the populace to believe that their Emperor has met his death at the hands of the enemy. A man called Menju the Sorcerer, a criminal you yourself cast into Beyond, is meeting with Joram at the Temple of the Necromancers — clear proof, by the way, that our Emperor intends to betray his people. It would be quite beneficial to all concerned if the two, Joram and this Sorcerer, were to have a falling out that would result in the Emperor's death. . . ."

The Executioner, understanding perfectly, had bowed in acquiescence and removed himself from the Bishop's presence without uttering a word.

Entering a Corridor, the warlock left the Font, traveling through time and space until he arrived at the secret, subterranean chambers of the Order of *Duuk-tsarith*. Making his needs known to those in charge, the Executioner was immediately given access to certain rooms kept sealed off from the rest. In these rooms, the personal effects confiscated from the bodies of the strange humans were being studied.

Various members of *Duuk-tsarith*, engaged in sorting and cataloging the effects, bowed in homage to one so high-ranking in their Order, and stood aside from their work to allow him to examine the objects. He was not interested in the remarkable timekeeping devices or the ugly jewelry or the pieces of parchment that had captured images of other strange humans, mostly females and children. The Executioner passed over these without a glance. He was interested only in the weapons.

Although not born to the Ninth Mystery himself, the Executioner was familiar with the tools of the Dark Arts, having studied them as he had studied much else in this world. Carefully he went over the cache of weapons, examining each one he came to, being careful not to touch any of them. Occasionally he asked a question of one of the *Duuk-tsarith* standing respectfully nearby. The Executioner discovered, however, that he knew as much, or in some cases more, about these weapons than they did.

Although he had not participated in the battle, he had watched it with interest, noting the lethal swiftness with which the weapons casting the beams of light could kill. He studied these first. Small enough to fit in the palm of the hand, the metal devices gave absolutely no indication, at least outwardly, of how they were operated.

The Executioner was just beginning to think he might have to trust his luck to one of these anyway, hoping he would not accidentally incinerate himself while endeavoring to figure out how it worked, when he came to something that suited him much better.

A projectile weapon.

He had read of these in the ancient texts of the Dark Arts. Although as far as anyone knew, none of these devices had ever been constructed on Thimhallan, they had been theorized and a few crude renderings of how they might work still existed. This weapon was, of course, much more complex than any of the drawings the Executioner had seen, but he assumed it operated along the same principles.

Wrapping it gingerly in a cloth, the Executioner placed the weapon and a large number of what appeared to be its projectiles in a box. He sealed the box with strong runes of protection against fire and explosion, then, carrying the box carefully, he left the dark and secret chambers of the *Duuk-tsarith*, and traveled the Corridors to Merilon.

The blacksmith, nearly on the verge of collapse from exhaustion, was considerably startled to see a gray-robed figure emerge from the Corridor outside his makeshift forge in Merilon. Everyone on Thimhallan knew of the Executioner, by legend if not by sight. Strong and stalwart man though he was, the blacksmith could not help shuddering with fear when the warlock approached him.

A panicked thought entered the smith's weary mind. "I'm going to be blamed for the enemy's attack and executed without benefit of a trial." Lifting a hammer, the smith prepared to sell his life dear.

But the Executioner, speaking in his cool, deep voice, assured the smith at once that it was his brains the warlock sought, not his head.

Bringing the box out of the folds of his robes, the Executioner rubbed out the runes, unwrapped the cloth, and exhibited the weapon to the blacksmith.

Sighing in awe, the smith lifted the weapon and ran his hands over it lovingly. The ingenuity and perfection of its workmanship and design caused his eyes to mist over with tears. The Executioner abruptly cut short the smith's rapturizing, however, by demanding to know how the thing worked.

It is possible that the Executioner cringed slightly when the smith began to dismantle the weapon. Possible . . . but doubtful. The Executioner was a highly disciplined individual who, if he had emotions, never revealed them to anyone. To all outward appearance, he stood unmoved and unmoving, his face concealed by his gray hood the entire time the smith worked on the weapon.

The blacksmith spent an hour in intense examination of the tool and, at last, after reverently reassembling the components, announced bluntly, "I know *how* it works, my lord, though how they captured all that power is beyond me."

"That," answered the Executioner, "is more than sufficient."

The blacksmith, holding the weapon in his hands and stroking it fondly, explained matters clearly and concisely.

"Aim the weapon at your target. When you press against this small lever with your finger" — the blacksmith pointed —

"the weapon will shoot forth the projectile with such force that it should go through damn near anything."

"Flesh?" asked the Executioner offhandedly.

"Flesh, rock, iron." The blacksmith looked at the weapon with wistful longing. "I don't suppose you'd care to see it demonstrated, my lord?"

"No," the warlock replied. "Your explanation is satisfactory."

Retrieving the weapon, the Executioner stepped into the Corridor and vanished. With a heavy sigh, the smith hefted his hammer and began pounding on a crude spear tip, all the joy having gone out of his work.

Returning to the safety and privacy of his own chambers in the Font — chambers far underground, studiously avoided by everyone, and the only place where, it was said, the eyes of the Font were blind and the ears stopped up — the Executioner demonstrated the weapon himself. Pointing it at a wall, he wrapped his finger around the small lever as the blacksmith had indicated and squeezed.

The concussive blast nearly deafened him, the weapon's recoil staggered him. He all but dropped the thing and his hand stung with the shock for minutes afterward. Going to examine the target on the wall, once he had recovered himself, the Executioner was frustrated to find no trace of the projectile. The wall was smooth and undamaged. Further investigation revealed, however, that this was not the fault of the tool but the fault of the one using the tool. The Executioner had missed his target by, if not the proverbial mile, then certainly a city block.

Undaunted, the Executioner cast a temporary spell of deafness over himself. Holding the weapon with both hands, he finally managed, after an hour, to at least come close to hitting his target. Measuring the holes he had made in the wall, the Executioner saw that they fit well within a space large enough to accommodate a human's upper body. This was good enough. It was nearly dawn anyway and he had to make certain he took up his position unseen and unsuspected.

When he arrived at the Temple, the Executioner stationed himself near the altar stone, protected from all eyes except those of the dead by his shield of invisibility. From this vantage point, he observed the Sorcerer's arrival (the Executioner could have reached out and touched the man) and watched with keen interest as Menju selected his own hiding place.

The Executioner glanced at the sun. Not too much longer. Standing in the bright sunlight, conscious of a breathless hush that had settled over the top of the world, the Executioner waited.

7

Watching, Waiting

Father Saryon peered cautiously at the Temple of the Necromancer, intending to investigate this place of rumored evil before setting foot upon its grounds.

"Come on, will you?"

Pushing past the reluctant catalyst, Joram stepped out of the Corridor onto the crumbling white marble walkway. His intense, eager gaze scanned the area swiftly: the ruined Temple behind him; the altar stone in the center of the wheel; the vast vista of the world spread out before him, Merilon shining in the distance like a teardrop upon the face of the land.

Saryon followed, every nerve fiber tense and alert. Reaching out with his being, as he did when he drew Life into his body, he felt about him with mental fingers as a blind man feels about him with his hands. He sensed Life — the magic was extremely strong here, but that was not unusual. They were, after all, standing directly above the Well of Life itself. He sensed death, too, but that may have been his overwrought imagination.

His fears were apparently groundless. The Temple appeared to be empty. Nothing moved, not even the air. No sounds of the living world below drifted upward to disturb the solitude. The silence was absolute, complete, unbroken.

Why, then, was he afraid?

"We are here in good time," Joram remarked, glancing up at the sun and nodding in satisfaction. He rubbed his hands together to remove the chill of the mountain air. "It is almost noon." Turning and looking around curiously, he walked past his wife, who was just stepping out of the Corridor, without a word or a glance.

"I see no legions of ghouls thirsting for our blood, do you, Catalyst?" Joram continued caustically, going over to investigate the altar stone.

"No, but that doesn't mean. . . ."

Saryon's words died, he stared in perplexity.

Joram's back was turned to him. The folds of the long traveling cloak swept the ground as he walked. Concealed beneath that cloak, encased in the magical scabbard, was the Darksword. The weapon was well hidden. No one glancing at Joram casually would have noted anything unusual or out of the ordinary about him. But Saryon, who had traveled with Joram for so long, had come to notice a difference in the way he walked when he wore the sword. Perhaps it was the weapon's weight, or a peculiar construction of the scabbard, but Joram always appeared slightly stoop-shouldered when he wore the Darksword, as though bowed down by an invisible burden.

He bore no burden now. His back was straight, his walk free and easy.

He's not carrying the sword. . . . We are defenseless! Saryon's first thought was to keep near the Corridor and he reached out to catch hold of Gwendolyn as she started to wander off.

Placidly, she allowed him to detain her and, standing beside the catalyst, she gazed about the Temple grounds, her blue eyes calm, seeing nothing in this world, caring nothing about what happened. And here was Joram, acting the same way! What could he have been thinking, to leave his sword behind?

Certainly, Joram didn't appear worried or nervous. He stood by the altar stone, lounging against it as though waiting for someone. Why was he acting so strangely? Perhaps it had something to do with this terrible place.

Although Saryon neither saw nor felt any evil about the Temple of the Necromancers, his fear was growing. Maybe it was the oppressive sadness that hung over the Temple — the terrible sadness of those who have been long forgotten. Or maybe it was the breathless hush in the air. Everything seemed to be watching, waiting. Even the sun itself appeared to have come to a stop directly above them.

We must leave, go back through the Corridor. Somehow, he must convince Joram of the danger. That wouldn't be easy, since it was a danger he himself could not define, but he had to try. Marshalling his arguments, Saryon started toward his friend, when Gwendolyn suddenly broke free of his grasp.

"No! No! There are too many of you!" she cried, backing away from him. "Don't touch me!" She was not looking at the catalyst, but beyond him. Stretching out her arms, she warded off unseen hands. "There are too many of you! I can't understand you! Stop shouting! Leave me alone! Leave me alone!"

Gwen clasped her hands over her ears, as if shutting out a tumult. Saryon stared at her helplessly. The only sounds that could be heard in the still, unmoving air were her own cries. He reached out to her, but, turning from him, she ran down the path, retreating as before an onslaught. Dodging first one way and then another, her erratic movements looked like some macabre dance performed with nonexistent partners.

"I can't help! Why do you plead with me? I can do nothing, I tell you! Nothing!"

Her palms covering her ears, her golden hair gleaming pale and unlovely in the chill light, Gwen began to run toward the Temple in a desperate effort to escape the unseen mob. She made it as far as the altar stone. Tripping over the long hem of her gown, she fell to her knees, and knelt there, cowering from her tormentors.

Hastening after her, Saryon saw that Joram stood not ten paces from his terrified wife. But he made no move to go to her. Instead, he leaned against the altar stone, watching her with amused interest, as if grateful to her for providing him with entertainment to pass the time.

Anger surged through Saryon. He didn't know what had come over Joram. He didn't care, not anymore. Let him sink back into the darkness! Hurrying to Gwen's side, Saryon bent down and gently took hold of her hand.

A sharp, distinct crack split the air.

Then another.

And another.

And one more.

Saryon's heart froze, his blood froze, his feet and legs, his hands. He could not move. He could only crouch on the pavement, holding onto Gwen, listening to the mind-numbing sounds careen among the rocks and reverberate from the Temple walls.

And then, the cracks stopped.

Fearfully, Saryon waited for the dreadful noise to come again. All he heard were the hollow echoes rattling down the mountainside. These, too, finally dwindled, swallowed up by the vastness of space.

Nothing moved, nothing stirred. Even Gwen's cries hushed. It was as if the sounds had torn the air asunder and now silence rushed in to fill the void.

The catalyst had only one clear thought in his mind — to get out of this place. It was obvious to him that nothing in this accursed Temple was going to help Gwendolyn, who huddled, shivering in his arms. There was every possibility, in fact, that this Temple and the dead who dwelt here might drive her deeper into her madness.

"I'm taking your wife home —" Saryon began in a shaking voice, looking up at Joram. The catalyst's breath caught in his throat. "Joram?" he whispered, letting loose of Gwendolyn and rising slowly to a standing position. "My son, what's wrong?"

Joram leaned weakly against the altar stone, staring at Saryon in the most profound astonishment. The brown eyes were open wide. His lips parted to speak, but no words came. One hand was pressed against his breast and beneath the hand, Saryon saw a crimson stain grow like a living thing, spreading out slowly over the white robes. Three more stains appeared on his body, bursting into bloom like lurid red blossoms.

Lifting the crimson-stained hand slowly, Joram stared at it in the same bemused amazement. Puzzled, he looked back at Saryon and, shoving himself away from the altar stone, he took a step toward the catalyst. Staggering, he fell before he reached him.

Saryon caught him in his arms. Touching the fabric of the crimson-stained robes, the catalyst felt the warm wetness of life's blood draining from Joram's body, falling through Saryon's fingers like the petals of a shattered tulip.

8

My Poor Fool . . .

The sound came from behind them, a low, muffled curse.

"What was that?" Saryon raised his head. "Who spoke? Is someone there? Help! Will you help me?"

It had seemed to come from the Temple.

"Who is there?" Saryon called desperately. Being careful not to disturb the injured man he held in his arms, he twisted around to look. But the shadows inside the Temple of the Necromancers remained unmoving, dark and silent as the realm they guarded.

Nothing but my imagination. Who would be there? Saryon asked himself bitterly. His gaze went to Gwendolyn, crouched on the pathway near him. She was looking around her expectantly, as though waiting.

Had it been her voice? Had she spoken? She loved Joram! Loves him still, for all Saryon knew.

"Gwendolyn!" He spoke softly and gently, fearful of startling her. "Come to me! Stay with Joram while I get help."

Hearing Saryon's voice, she turned to him. Her gaze went to her husband and flitted over him like butterfly wings, darting here and there over the stalks of the lifeless plants. The dead must have been shocked into silence, because Gwen's fear of them appeared to have vanished. Slowly, she started to rise to her feet.

Suddenly it occurred to Saryon that they themselves might be in danger! Whatever had struck down Joram in this mysterious and horrifying manner might be waiting to lash out again with its whiplike cracks!

"No! Gwen! Stay down!" Saryon cried frantically, and either the terror and urgency in his voice penetrated the mists of Beyond that clouded her mind or unseen hands caught hold of her and kept her from rising. Saryon, in his agitated state, had the distinct impression it was the latter.

He scanned the Temple once again, then the Garden, the pathways, the jagged edges of the summit, searching frantically for their enemy.

"Not that I care for myself," the old Priest muttered, lowering his head over the body he held in his arms, tears dimming his eyes. Although still breathing, Joram had lost consciousness. Gently, Saryon stroked the thick, black hair back from the deathly white face. "I am tired of this life, tired of the fear, tired of the killing and the dying. If Joram must die here, then I can find no better resting place."

Shaking his head angrily, Saryon fought back his tears. Give way to despair and you *are* dead, and so is Joram and so is Gwendolyn! She must get to a place of safety. If there was such a place. . . . The Temple! It had once been sacred ground. Perhaps the Almin's blessing lingered there still.

"Gwen, run to the Temple," instructed Saryon, forcing himself to speak calmly and quietly, "Quickly, my child! Run to the Temple."

Gwendolyn made no move to go. Gazing around with that same expectant look, she gave no indication that she had even heard him.

"Take her there!" Saryon cried urgently to the shadows in the empty Garden. "Take her to the Temple! Guard her there!"

It was a cry born of desperation, and no one was more astonished than the catalyst to see Gwen lifted to her feet by unseen arms, unseen hands helping her stand.

"Hurry!" he breathed, waiting in fear for that sharp crack.

Bearing Gwen along, the dead swept past him. He could feel the soft whisper of their presence upon his cheek; he saw it flutter Gwen's gown and stir her golden hair as they bore her to the Temple. When she stumbled, she was caught and supported. When she started to falter, she was hurried forward. Saryon saw her stumble up the nine stairs leading into the Temple, and he saw her vanish into the shadows.

The catalyst sighed in relief, one care off his mind. And now, he repeated to himself stubbornly, I must get help for Joram, for all of us. He looked back at the man in his arms, and his heart sank within him, the cold, logical part of his mind telling him that, for Joram at least, there *was* no help.

"There must be a chance to save him!" Saryon shouted fiercely, defiantly at the heavens.

In mocking answer, the body in his arms shuddered, a groan of pain escaped the lips. The catalyst clasped Joram tightly, trying to keep hold of the spirit that was seeping away with every drop of blood. "If only I knew what had happened to him!" he cried to the cold empty sky.

"Sink me!" came a weak voice. "That makes two of us!"

Startled, Saryon lowered his eyes from the heavens back to earth, to the man he held in his arms. Gone was the stern face with its high cheekbones and firm jaw. Gone was the luxuriant black hair with its shock of white. Gone were the dark, lowering brows, the brown eyes, burning with a deep, inner flame. Instead he saw a face of indeterminate age with a pointed chin, a soft beard and mustache; the eyes regarding him with an almost comical expression of puzzled indignation.

"Simkin!" Saryon gasped.

"In the flesh," remarked Simkin, struggling for breath. "Though . . . that particular part of me . . . is . . . rather ventilated. I'm feeling . . . a distinct draft . . . about the kidneys. . . ."

"But where . . . where's Joram?" stammered Saryon, mystified.

"Here," came the stern reply.

A figure in white robes, its head covered with a white hood, stood above them. In its hand was the Darksword.

Joram knelt at Simkin's side and, though his voice was stern, the hand that reached out to the injured young man was gentle. From Joram's fingers fluttered a bit of orange silk that appeared to have been cut in two by a sharp blade.

"Ah, clever boy!" Simkin choked, a small stream of blood trickling from the corner of his mouth. "You . . . escaped . . . my cunning knot." His head lolled back, his eyes closed.

"What's happened to him?" Saryon asked in a low voice.

Laying the sword down upon the pavement, Joram carefully peeled aside the blood-soaked fabric of Simkin's white robes, examining the wounds in his chest. He glanced down at the other wounds in the stomach and shook his head.

Simkin moaned, shuddering convulsively.

Joram's stern expression softened. Taking the orange silk, he dabbed gently at the sweat-covered forehead. "My poor fool," he said softly.

"Isn't there anything we can do?" asked Saryon.

"Nothing. I don't know what's kept him alive this long, unless it's his magic," Joram replied.

I should pray. I should say something, Saryon thought confusedly, although the idea of sending Simkin heavenward on the wings of prayer was, somehow, ludicrous.

Easing the shivering body to the ground, the catalyst placed his hand upon the young man's forehead. Bowing his head, he murmured, "Per istam Sanctam Unctionem indúlgeat tibi Dominus quidquid—"

"I say, Bald One," came a weak, peevish voice, "could you quidquid somewhere else? Damnably annoying!"

"Why did you do this, Simkin?" Joram asked softly.

"E'gad!" Simkin stared up at Joram with fevered eyes. "You've . . . gone all fuzzy." He grimaced. "Beastly sort of game this. Don't much . . . fancy it . . . at all. Where are you, dear boy? Everything . . . dark. . . . Frightened of . . . dark. Where? Where are you . . . ?" He gasped, his hand twitched feebly.

Clasping the bloodstained hand in his, Joram held it tightly. "I'm here," he said. "And it's dark because you've got that stupid helm over your head, the one that makes you look like a bucket."

Simkin smiled, relaxing. "I was . . . fond of being a . . . bucket. Damn good one . . . too. They . . . never suspected, in fact. That's how I knew. . . ."

"Knew what?"

The eyes became unfocused, wandering off to stare far away into the pale, cold sun.

"'Brave, new world. . . .' Take *you*! Not Simkin." A glimmer of life, of spirit flickered in the eyes. Slowly, their gaze came back, focusing on Joram. "So I . . . became *you*! Would have been . . . grand trick. I would have won . . . the game." A spasm of pain contorted his face. Gripping Joram's hand with his last strength, Simkin pulled him near. "Still, it's been a jolly time . . . hasn't it?" he whispered. "Jolly time — as . . . Duchess d'Longville said. . . . Final words before . . . her last husband hanged her. . . ."

A smile fluttered on his lips, then became fixed and rigid. The voice died away, the hand went limp. Gently, Joram placed it over Simkin's breast, tucking the bit of orange silk in the lifeless fingers.

"— *deliqústi. Amen.*" Saryon murmured.

Reaching out, he closed the empty eyes.

9

There Will Be Born . . .
One Who Is Dead

Joram, I don't understand!"
Saryon, bewildered, gazed at
Simkin pityingly. "What happened to him?"

"Did you hear sharp, cracking sounds right before he
fell?"

"Yes! It was dreadful—"

"Exploding powder, like we read of in the texts of the
ancient practicers of the Dark Arts. It fires lead projectiles."
Joram's eyes scanned the area, squinting in the sunlight.
"Did you see anyone? Where did the sound come from?"

"From over there, I think," Saryon said hesitantly, pointing toward the edge of the mountain's summit. "It was . . .
difficult to tell. And I saw nothing." He paused, licking his
dry lips. "Joram, whoever did this to Simkin was trying to
kill you."

"Yes. And I think we both know who it is."

"The Sorcerer?"

"Of course. He's probably hiding among the rocks there
on the edge of the cliff. Though why would he use a re-

volver? It's not his style. . . ." Joram's brows came together, frowning thoughtfully. "Why indeed?" he muttered. "Unless it isn't him."

"Who else?"

"Someone who fears not only me as Emperor but the Prophecy as well. Someone cunning enough to make it *appear* to be the work of the enemy."

"Vanya!" Saryon paled.

Swiftly, Joram glanced around, keeping his hood pulled over his face. "Don't move," he cautioned, placing his hand firmly over the catalyst's wrist. "We've got to think this out and right now, while whoever's out there is confused, wondering who *I* am."

"Perhaps the killer's gone," Saryon suggested. "If he thinks he succeeded. . . ."

"I doubt it. After all, he didn't get what he came for."

Joram and the catalyst both glanced at the Darksword, lying near the base of the altar stone.

"He'll realize his mistake and try again," Saryon said coolly. His fear was gone. In its place was an unconcerned emptiness. As in the battle with the warlock, he was detached, an observer, watching himself perform his role in this tragic farce.

"He won't try for a while. He saw me fall, then saw someone else arrive with the sword. This is unexpected. His plan has gone awry. He must rethink it!" Joram yanked Saryon down, huddling over Simkin's body. "Keep low!"

"Why doesn't he just kill us anyway? Use that . . . weapon on us?"

"He will — eventually. But he hasn't a very good aim. He fired four shots, after all, to kill one man. He'll run out of bullets — projectiles — soon and then he'll have to reload, if he even brought any more than what the gun holds. He's probably *Duuk-tsarith*. This gives us a chance."

"It's the Executioner then," Saryon guessed. "He's the only person Vanya would trust. But I don't understand how you can be sure it's a warlock!"

"Because the Sorcerer wants me alive!" Joram hissed, gripping the catalyst's wrist with painful intensity. "Simkin was hidden in the Sorcerer's headquarters. He heard them say they were going to take *me* to the brave, new world — *not*

Simkin! He had to believe they were planning to capture me *alive*, otherwise he would never have dreamed up this fool scheme! This morning he came to me and tricked me into entering a Corridor. He took me to some godforsaken place, bound my hands with that wretched orange silk of his, and then he became me!"

"He planned to go back to the Sorcerer's world disguised as you. But why didn't Simkin take the Darksword?"

"He couldn't! It disrupts his magic. The Sorcerer wants me alive — to teach him about the sword and show him where he can find more darkstone. Vanya's the one who wants me dead. *He's* the one who's sent the killer."

Moving slowly and cautiously, Joram picked up the Darksword.

"What are you doing?" Saryon asked fearfully.

"If it *is* a warlock, he's hiding behind an invisibility spell. I've got to drain his magic, force him out where we can see him. If I don't, he can come at us from any direction, get as close as he wants. Then it won't matter how well he can shoot."

"But if you're wrong!" Saryon caught hold of Joram. "If it isn't a warlock. If it is the Sorcerer trying to kill you—"

"*Per istam Sanctam*, Father," Joram answered grimly. Twisting to his feet, he raised the Darksword.

Thirsting for Life, the weapon instantly began to drink up the magic. Saryon felt himself weaken but only slightly; as a catalyst he possessed little magic to feed the sword's hunger. His Life was enough, however, to send tiny flickers of blue light dancing up the crude, ugly blade.

The sword's power grew as it absorbed more and more of the magic. The blade began to burn brighter, taking on a hot, whitish blue glow. Suddenly a streak of light arced past Saryon, coming from somewhere behind him. Striking the sword, the light sizzled, a ball of blue flame shot from the hilt to the tip of the blade. Turning, amazed, Saryon saw that the light had come from the altar stone! The rock itself was beginning to glow a luminescent blue; the symbols of the Nine Mysteries gleamed white against it. Another arc of light shot from the stone, followed by another.

Saryon looked to Joram, to see if he noticed, but the man had his back to the altar stone. Holding the sword before him, Joram turned this way and that, staring intently into the empty air around him, searching for his enemy.

And then the air was empty no longer. It shimmered and darkened, and a man appeared, enveloped in long gray robes. He was walking down the pathway, moving toward them under the cover of his magical spell of invisibility, and he stood no more than ten feet from them. Seeing Joram's eyes focus on him, he realized he had been discovered. The Executioner raised his hand.

"Father, look out!" Joram cried.

Saryon had no time to move or even blink. The air cracked. Dropping the Darksword, Joram staggered backward, gasping in pain. A crimson stain darkened the white sleeve of his right arm.

The warlock made a dive for the sword, but Joram was quicker. Catching hold of it, he leaped at the Executioner, but the warlock, with the coolness and quick thinking of that highly disciplined class, resorted to his magic. Using what Life remained to him, he soared into the air, flying with windlike speed to the jumble of boulders that stood near the edge of the mountain and vanishing among them.

Grabbing hold of Saryon, Joram hurried the catalyst to the opposite side of the altar stone, forcing him to lie flat upon the broken pavement.

"Stay down!" he ordered.

"You're hurt!"

"The man's a better shot than I gave him credit for," Joram said grimly. Dropping the sword, he clasped his hand over the wound. Dark red blood welled up through his fingers. "The bastard must have been up practicing all night! The bullet's lodged in my arm!" Groaning, he swore softly. "I can't move my hand."

"Let me look at it —" Saryon started to sit up.

"Damn it, Father! Keep your head down!" Joram ordered furiously. "Hold still!" He glanced back around the rock, looking toward the direction in which their foe had disappeared. "We're safe enough for now, but we can't stay here. He'll circle around, using those boulders for cover, and try to pick us off from another angle."

Joram nodded toward the Temple. "We'd be safer in here."

"And Gwen's inside!" Saryon said suddenly, realizing remorsefully that in the confusion and danger he had forgotten all about her.

"Gwen!" Joram glared at the catalyst. "You brought my wife here? You let Simkin bring her?"

"What would you have had me do, Joram?" Saryon asked. "He was *you*! He was you ten years ago! Bitter, arrogant, determined to have your own way."

"And you forgot that I have changed —"

"Forgive me, Joram," Saryon faltered, "but I have seen you changing back. I've seen the darkness growing on you every day."

Leaning back against the blue-glowing altar stone, Joram sighed. Sweat broke out on his forehead, his face paled, and his jaw muscles clenched. Drawing a deep, shuddering breath, he glanced at Saryon, the bitter half-smile on his lips. "You are right, Father. It wasn't your fault. I brought it on myself. After all, Simkin was only imitating what he knew best. And I *am* changing . . . for the worst, perhaps." His face darkened, the forge fire flickered to life within his eyes. "But it seems I must become what I was — to save this wretched world."

His voice died, and he sank back against the stone.

"Joram!" Saryon shook him, fearing he had fainted. The catalyst felt eyes watching them. Any moment he expected to hear that terrible crack. "Joram!" he said urgently. "We can't stay here! We must reach shelter!"

Dazedly, Joram lifted his head and nodded wearily. "You'll have to carry the sword, Father."

If we left it here, perhaps the Executioner would take it and go away, was Saryon's first, unspoken thought. The words were on his lips, but he swallowed them. No, the sword is my responsibility. I gave it Life.

Saryon picked up the weapon.

Slowly, Joram rose to his feet, propping himself up against the stone. "I will go first and draw his fire. Don't argue, Father. You'll be burdened with the sword." The dark and pain-filled eyes turned intently upon the catalyst. "If I fall, you must promise me you'll go on, without stopping. No, listen, my old friend. If anything happens to me, it will be left up to you. You must destroy the Darksword."

"Destroy it? How?" Saryon asked involuntarily.

"How should I know!" Joram flashed impatiently. Pain made him catch his breath. He closed his eyes, pressing back against the rock. "I don't know," he said more calmly through ashen lips. "Cast it from the mountain, melt it down." He smiled the dark and twisted half-smile again. "It's what you've wanted to do since I first made it anyway. If I fall, go on. Do you swear? By the Almin?"

"I swear . . . by the Almin," Saryon mumbled. Making a show of gathering his robes about him so that he could run more easily, he did not have to look at Joram as he spoke the vow.

"Good!" Joram sighed. "And now," he said, drawing a deep breath, "we run. Keep low. Ready?"

Joram looked questioningly at Saryon. The catalyst nodded once, reluctantly, and Joram broke into a staggering run.

Despite his agreement to let Joram go first, Saryon was not far behind him. He had only a dim notion of what was meant by "drawing fire" and it felt more natural to stay near his friend.

As for not stopping to help Joram if he fell?

Well, that had been a promise sworn to the Almin. A hollow vow, as far as Saryon was concerned, keeping his eyes on the white-robed figure stumbling over the uneven ground ahead of him.

The distance from the altar stone located in the center of the wheel to the Temple, which stood on the southern edge of the wheel's rim, had seemed minute to the catalyst — until he knew his life depended on covering that distance as swiftly as possible. Suddenly the Temple and its sheltering walls appeared to have taken a gigantic leap backward.

Saryon ran as fast as he could, but that wasn't very fast. He had never fully recovered his strength following his illness. Encumbered by the heavy sword and the long robes flapping around his ankles, he took only a few steps before he heard his breath wheeze in his lungs. The pavement was broken, uneven, and made running that much more difficult. More than once, Saryon felt a paving stone twist beneath his feet, causing him to slow for fear of losing his balance and falling. All the while, he kept his eyes upon his friend.

And then Joram *did* fall. Tripping over a slab of broken marble, he instinctively reached out his injured arm to catch himself. It collapsed beneath his weight and he tumbled to the ground, writhing in pain.

Grasping Joram, ignoring his snarled commands to leave him be, Saryon dragged him to his feet with a strength the catalyst couldn't believe was left in his old, tired body. Together they kept running, reaching the nine stairs.

A high, whining sound like the buzz of an angry hornet passed so close to Saryon's ear that he almost swore he could feel its wings. A fraction of a second later, a part of a Temple column exploded, sending fragments of rock flying everywhere. The catalyst, in his dazed and exhausted state, didn't comprehend what it was.

Struggling up the stairs, the two dove thankfully into the cool, shadowy confines of the Temple walls. Joram fell to the floor like one dead. Rolling over on his back, he lay with his eyes closed, his breathing quick and shallow. His right sleeve was soaked with blood. Saryon, dropping the heavy sword, sank down next to him. Only then did it occur to the catalyst that the buzzing sound had been one of the deadly projectiles. Saryon was past caring. His blood pounded in his ears. He was so dizzy he could barely see.

Gasping for breath, he glanced around the Temple confines.

"Gwen?" Saryon called softly.

There was no answer, but the catalyst soon found her. Barely visible in the shifting shadows, she was sitting calmly on a broken altar at the back of the Temple, watching them with — for her — unusual interest.

Seeing that she was apparently unharmed and thinking Joram had fainted, Saryon bent over him to examine the wound. At his touch, Joram flinched.

"I'm all right!" Shoving Saryon's hand away, he managed to sit up.

"I think the bleeding's stopped," Saryon said hesitantly.

"The cloth's stuck to the wound. Don't touch it! Where's Gwen? Is she all right?"

Saryon started to reply, but another voice — a strange one — answered instead.

"Your charming wife is safe, Joram. Looney as ever, but safe. And you are safe yourself, at least for the time being.

"Really, Joram," the strange voice continued, speaking the language of Thimhallan, "I am impressed. Once again you have returned from the dead. Have you ever considered anything in the Messiah line?"

10

And In His Hand
He Holds

Atall man in black robes stepped out of the shadows of the Temple. He was handsome, Saryon saw, with gray hair and a prepossessing smile. That smile, however, was false, the work of a well-trained illusionist. Tense and strained, the lips and facial muscles were being hard pressed to hold it in place. And though the tone of the man's voice was glib, an undercurrent of awe and fear marred the smooth surface.

"I truly believed you were killed, my friend," the man said, coming to stand beside Joram, staring down at him intently. "I can see the theater billing now: *Back from the Dead by Popular Demand!*"

Joram did not even look at the man, much less bother to reply. The man smiled.

"Come, come, old friend. You survived four bullet wounds, any one of which could have proved fatal. I would appreciate knowing how you performed that trick. Was it done with a bullet-proof vest? Or perhaps. . . ."

He glanced at Saryon as he spoke, and the catalyst was aware of being intently studied, identified, and stored away for future use all by one quick look of the intelligent eyes.

". . . perhaps it was you who brought our friend back to life, Father Saryon. Yes, I know you. Joram has told me a great deal about you and I imagine that he has, in turn, told you a great deal about me. I am Menju the Sorcerer — a rather dramatic appellation, I admit, but it looks well on a theater marquee. And if it *was* you who resurrected Joram, Father, I will buy you a tent and all the folding chairs your evangelistic heart desires!"

"If you mean did I heal Joram, I am a catalyst, not a druid." Saryon saw the chasm of his dream yawn dark and deadly before him. He must walk carefully, cautiously. "If what you told Joram is true, you lived in this world long enough to know that catalysts have very limited powers of healing and that even druids cannot raise people from the —"

"Don't let him badger you, Father," Joram interrupted coldly. "He knows well enough you didn't heal me."

Menju made a graceful gesture of supplication. "Take pity on me. Satisfy my curiosity. I swear I was truly grieved to see you die. It was quite a shock."

"I'll bet it was," Joram said dryly. "Help me stand," he instructed the catalyst. Ignoring Saryon's remonstrations, he struggled to his feet. Leaning back against a broken column, he regarded Menju warily. "That wasn't I who died out there. You saw me arrive through the Corridor."

"Perhaps I did," Menju remarked casually, his gaze fixed on Joram. "Uncanny resemblance. Who —"

"Simkin." Joram's breathing was too fast, too shallow. Saryon moved nearer.

Menju nodded. "Ah, I begin to understand. The teapot. I underestimated you, my friend. Quite a clever ploy, sending this fellow up here, masquerading as yourself. Did you guess it was a trap? Or did he tell you? I thought him an untrustworthy bastard, just like that fat priest, Vanya, who sent his assassin to try to snatch the prize from me. But the Bishop will pay for his treachery." The magician shrugged. "They all will pay."

Joram staggered, nearly falling. Catching himself, he refused Saryon's proffered assistance with an angry shake of his head.

"You need medical attention, Joram," Menju said, appraising him coolly. "Fortunately, it is near at hand, thanks to the Corridors. A word from the Father will return us to my headquarters. Catalyst, open a Corridor."

"I can't —" Saryon began when he was interrupted by a glad cry.

"Come inside! Don't be afraid!" Springing up from the broken altar where she had been sitting, Gwendolyn ran toward the portico, her bright eyes glittering with their eerie light even in the shadowy confines of the Temple.

"Gwen, no!" Joram caught hold of her. "You can't go out there —"

Gwendolyn easily broke free of her husband's weak grasp, but it was not to run outdoors. Stopping just inside the portico, she held out her hands. "Come in! Come in!" she repeated, a hostess welcoming long-awaited guests.

"Don't be frightened," she continued, her voice tinged now with sadness. "Are you in pain, still? It will pass in time. It is only a phantom pain, remembered by the part of you that clings to your life. Let it go. It will be easier. For you, the battle has ended."

"Battle? What battle is she talking about?" Joram demanded, turning to the Sorcerer.

"Gettysburg?" The Sorcerer shrugged. "Waterloo? Perhaps she fancies she's Napoleon today."

"You know better than that!" Joram replied. His eyes gleamed feverishly, sweat trickling down his pale face. "You know her power. She's talking to dead who are. . . . My god!" he whispered in sudden realization. "You've attacked Merilon!"

"Don't be hard on Major Boris, Joram. He is a soldier, after all, and you couldn't expect him to stay penned up like a steer in the slaughterhouse."

"It won't do any good. You can't penetrate the city's magical shield."

"Ah, that's where you are wrong, my friend. The thickheaded Major actually came up with an ingenious idea. He converted the flying troop carriers into assault ships. He plans to use their laser fire to destroy the magical dome. It may not pierce the magic, but it will drain the Life of those who keep that magic in place. The shield will soon disintegrate. The Crystal Palace will fall out of the skies, taking with it those huge marble slabs — what do they call them, the Three Sisters? Poor ladies. They, too, will crash to the ground."

"Thousands will die!" Saryon cried, aghast. Staring out across the plains, he saw a brilliant flaring of light, the glinting of the sun shining off the metal bodies of the creatures that were crawling, antlike, around the perimeter of the city. That was all he could see with his eyes; mentally he saw much, much more.

Prince Garald — if he were still alive — fighting courageously but bewildered and unnerved over this unexpected attack. Lord and Lady Samuels, their little children, and the countless other noble families whose homes were built upon those floating marble slabs dying horribly, crushed in the falling wreckage. The Crystal Palace, smashing to the ground, exploding into millions of shards of knife-sharp glass fragments. . . .

"Let go of your life," repeated Gwendolyn sadly.

"If only I could get there!" Joram cried in a low voice. "I could help — What am I saying?" He laughed bitterly. "I brought this on them!" Slumping back against the column, he covered his eyes with his bloodstained hand.

"The time of the Prophecy is accomplished, Joram," the Sorcerer said. "Leave them to their fate. How did that charming little quotation run? 'And in his hand he holds the destruction of the world — '"

" — or its salvation," said Gwendolyn.

Lost in his despair, Joram didn't even appear to hear her. Saryon did, however. Turning, he stared at her intently. She, too, was gazing out at the beleaguered city, her eyes wide and unfocused, a sweet, sad smile on her lips. Moving slowly and quietly, so he would not startle her, the catalyst laid his hand upon her shoulder.

"What did you say, my dear?"

"She is raving!" the Sorcerer snapped impatiently. "Enough of this. In case you have forgotten, there is an assassin out there. Catalyst, open a Corridor — "

A Hand was outstretched, trying to help Saryon back from the edge of the cliff. He had only to reach out, take hold of it. . . .

"Continue, my dear," he said urgently, his voice trembling, trying to contain his excitement so as not to frighten the woman.

Gwendolyn gazed about her with a dreamy expression. "There is someone here — an old, old man — a Bishop. Where are you? Oh, yes. There, in the back." She pointed vaguely. "He's been waiting for centuries for someone to listen to him. It was all a mistake, he says, running away from our home like spoiled, angry children. Then came the Iron War and everything was falling apart. He prayed to find out how to change the world. The Almin granted his prayers, hoping that mankind would turn back from the dangerous path on which he trod. But the Bishop was too weak. He saw the future. He saw the terrible danger. He saw the promised redemption. Dazzled by his vision, he perished. The words of the Almin that were meant to be a warning remained unspoken, unfinished. And mankind, in his fear, made of that warning a prophecy."

"Fear. . . . A warning. . . ." murmured Saryon, light filling his soul. "Joram, don't you understand?"

Joram did not even look up. His head lowered, his face was hidden by the mat of tangled black hair. "Drop it, Father," he muttered harshly. "It is senseless to go on fighting!"

"No, it isn't!" Ecstatic, Saryon lifted his hands to heaven. "My God! My Creator! Can You forgive me? Joram, there is a way — "

A crack, a whine. Fragments of stone burst around them. Joram knocked Saryon to the floor. Menju flattened himself against a column.

"Gwen!" Joram cried, trying to reach his wife. Bewildered by the noise, she stood in the open, staring around in confusion. Before Joram could reach her, however, unseen hands snatched her back out of danger and whisked her away, hurrying her to the rear of the Temple.

"It's all right, Joram! The dead will protect her!" Saryon cried.

Another crack ricocheted through the Temple, smashing into a wall behind them.

"We've got to get out of here!" Reaching into the pocket of his robes, Menju drew his phaser, adjusted it, and fired a burst of light at a glimpse of movement he caught near the

altar stone. A puff of smoke and rock dust erupted from the
stone, leaving behind a charred streak.

Taking advantage of the covering fire, Joram grabbed
hold of the Darksword, and ducked behind a column beside
the Sorcerer.

"Over here, Father! Keep down!"

Wriggling across the chill stone floor on his stomach,
Saryon reached the columns. Leaning against one, Joram
peered out into the Garden. Their enemy was nowhere to be
seen. Menju fired again, missing again.

"Open a Corridor, Father!" he snarled.

"I can't!" Saryon gasped.

Another crack split the air. Menju flung himself back
against his column. Saryon shrank down, huddling near the
floor. Joram appeared too weak to move, perhaps even to
care. He held the Darksword in a limp grasp. His wound was
bleeding again; the stain on his sleeve was growing larger.

Worriedly, the catalyst looked from Joram back to Gwen.
He could barely see her. Somehow the dead had managed to
persuade her to find shelter behind the crumbling altar. A
dusty beam of sunlight pouring through a crack in the ceiling
shone upon her golden hair and lit her bright blue eyes.

Menju followed his gaze. "Take us out of here, Catalyst,
or by the gods I'll use this on her!" He pointed the weapon at
Gwendolyn. "Unless you can move faster than the speed of
light, Joram, don't try anything."

"Joram, stop!" Laying a restraining hand on his friend's
arm, Saryon turned to face the magician. "I cannot open a
Corridor in here because there is none to open!"

"You're lying!" The Sorcerer kept the phaser aimed at
Gwen.

"I would to the Almin I were!" Saryon said fervently.
"There is no Corridor within the Temple of the Necromancer! This was sanctified ground, a holy place; the Necromancers alone were permitted to enter it. They never allowed
a Corridor to be opened here. The only one is out there"—
Saryon nodded—"near the altar stone."

"And the Executioner knows it!" Joram said grimly.
Sweat covered his forehead, his damp hair curled around his
pale face. "That's why he's taken up his position there."

Glancing at Saryon, Menju studied the catalyst's face intently, then — with a curse — lowered his weapon. "So we are trapped in here!"

Another sharp crack blasted into the stone column near the Sorcerer, a chip of rock grazing his face. Cursing, he wiped blood from his cheek with the back of his hand and started to fire again. Then he stopped, staring thoughtfully out across the plains. "We are trapped," he repeated, reaching into the pocket of his robes, "but not for long."

Bringing out a second small metal device, he pressed his thumb against it. A light blinked on and a scratching noise came from within it, sounding to Saryon like an animal with long claws struggling to escape.

Lifting the device to his mouth, the Sorcerer spoke to it. "Major Boris! Major Boris!"

A voice came back, but it was accompanied by so much scratching that it was difficult to understand the words. The Sorcerer, scowling, shook the metal device slightly. "Major Boris!" he called again angrily.

Saryon stared at the device in horror.

"Blessed Almin!" he whispered to Joram. "Does he have this Major Boris trapped in there?"

"No," Joram answered wearily, almost smiling. He remained standing, but only, it seemed, by sheer force of will. "The Major is in Merilon. He carries a device like that one. Through it, the two men can communicate with each other. No, hush! Let me hear!" He motioned Saryon to silence.

Saryon could not understand what Menju was saying; the man was speaking in his own language. He watched Joram's face for a clue as to what was happening.

Seeing his friend's lips press together in a straight, grim line, Saryon asked softly, "What is it?"

"He's called for an air strike. They're diverting one of the assault ships from the attack on Merilon and sending it here."

"Yes, a simple way out, really" said the Sorcerer complacently, shutting off the device and returning it to his robes. "The ship's lasers will sweep the entire Garden, effectively incinerating our friend with the gun. Then the ship will land and transport us away from here. There will be a medic on board, Joram. He will give you a stimulant to keep you going so that you can assist me in winning the battle of Merilon with the Darksword. Always keeping in mind, of course, that I'll have your lovely wife close at hand, not to mention the catalyst, both of whom will suffer if you should attempt to — how shall I put it? — upstage me."

Thrusting back the sleeve of his robe, Menju glanced at a device he wore on his wrist. "It will arrive in a matter of minutes."

If Saryon didn't understand the unfamiliar words, he understood their import. He looked at Joram. His face was expressionless, his eyes closed. Was he so despairing, so defeated, so hurt that he would give in? Was it, as he said, senseless to keep fighting?

Saryon tried to pray to the Almin, tried to summon that Presence, tried desperately to grab hold of the Hand held out to him. But fear caught hold of the catalyst instead. Clutching his throat with fingers of stone, it choked off Saryon's faith. The Hand wavered, then disappeared, and the catalyst realized bitterly that it had all been just a delusion.

II

The Destruction Of The World

Alow humming sound grew gradually louder and louder. Saryon, starting, saw a look of satisfaction on Menju's face. The magician's gaze was fixed expectantly on the sky and Saryon risked peeping out past the column. It occurred to him, as he did so, that there had been no more projectiles hurled at them in the last few minutes. Perhaps the Executioner had given up.

"A fool's dream!" Saryon muttered to himself bitterly. He scanned the clear blue sky, seeing nothing, although the humming sound was becoming increasingly loud. The Executioner would never give up, never admit he had failed in his assigned task. His Order considered death the only excuse for failure, and the Executioner would not be an easy man to kill. Although Joram had drained him of some of his magical Life, he was still a threat, still a danger. He was, after all, one of the most powerful warlocks in Thimhallan.

Does this Sorcerer from another world realize what he's up against? Saryon wondered, glancing at Menju speculatively. Noting the man's calm demeanor, his smile of self-assurance, Saryon doubted it. After all, Menju had been young when he was cast out of this world — only twenty, so Joram had said. He probably knew little of the *Duuk-tsarith*, knew little about the many powers of their Order: the acute sense of hearing that allowed them to detect the approach of a butterfly by the fluttering of its wings, the keen powers of sight that let them see through a man's skull into his thoughts.

Menju was pleased with his newly recovered abilities in magic, but he had forgotten its true power. He regarded it as a toy, an amusement, nothing more. When the crisis came, he preferred to trust in his Technology.

"There is the strike ship," he said crisply. "It won't be long now." He flicked a glance at Joram. "Is our friend able to walk, Father? You'll have to help him. I've got to direct the ship's fire."

He spoke into the device again. This time the scratching sound was considerably lessened; the voices speaking back from within the contraption he held in his hand were clearer and Saryon judged — from the intent manner in which Menju stared into the heavens as he talked — that he was communicating with whatever monster he had summoned to do his bidding.

Following the magician's gaze, Saryon could still see nothing and was just wondering if the creature was invisible when a flaring glint caught his eye. He gasped, having been unprepared for the tremendous swiftness with which the thing traveled. At one instant it was very small, a brightly shining star that had gotten mixed up and burst out during the day instead of night. The next instant, the thing was larger than the sun; then larger than ten suns. He could see it clearly now, and he stared in shock.

The catalyst had not been present at the battle at the Field of Glory. He had only heard descriptions of the great creatures of iron, the strange humans with silver skin and metal heads. This was the first time he had seen one of these creations of the Dark Arts, and his soul trembled with fear and awe.

The monster was made of silver, its body glistening in the sun. It had wings, but they were stiff and unmoving, and Saryon was at a loss to understand how it flew so rapidly.

The monster had no head or neck. Blinking, multicolored eyes sprouted on the top of its body. The only sound it made was the humming noise, now so loud that it practically drowned out Menju's voice.

Saryon felt Joram's hand, warm and reassuring, on his arm.

"Steady, Father," Joram said softly. Drawing him near, he added in a low voice, "Make it appear as though you are tending my wound."

Glancing at the magician, who was absorbed in his monster summoning, Saryon leaned closer to Joram.

"We can't allow him to take us on board that ship. When he moves us out there, watch for my signal." Joram paused, then said softly, "When it comes, get Gwen out of the way."

Saryon was silent for a moment, unable to reply. When he did, it was in a husky voice. "My son, even with the Darksword you can't fight them all! Do you know what you are saying?" He kept his head lowered, pretending to concern himself with the wound. Joram's hand, touching his face, made him look up and he saw the answer in Joram's clear, brown eyes.

"It will be better this way, Father," he said simply.

"What about your wife?" Saryon asked, when he could speak for the burning ache in his chest.

Joram looked toward the back of the Temple, where Gwendolyn sat amid the shadows, the single bright ray of light glistening in her hair. "She fell in love with a Dead man, who brought her nothing but grief." The dark, ironic smile twisted his lips. "It seems I can be of more use to her dead than alive. And at least" — he breathed a sigh, half-bitter, half-wistful — "perhaps she will talk to me then." His hand tightened around Saryon's arm. "I leave her in your care, Father."

My son, I will not live through this! were the words in Saryon's heart and they very nearly burst out. But he checked them, swallowing them with his tears. No, it was better that Joram find peace in his last moments.

I will hold him in my arms as I held him when he was a baby. And when the brown eyes close forever and he is at rest, when the struggle that has been his life is finally ended,

then I will rise up and, in my clumsy, fumbling way, I will
strike out at the cold and uncaring Presence until I, too, fall.

A blinding flash followed by an explosion jolted Saryon
from his bleak imaginings. A beam of light from the monster
struck the ground near the altar stone, blowing a gigantic
hole in the dirt not far from where Simkin's body lay. Wisps
of smoke curled into the air. The metal creature, hovering
overhead, was slowly sinking down toward the ground.

Menju shouted into the device, his voice questioning.

"What is he saying?" Saryon whispered.

"He's asking if they destroyed the warlock." Joram
paused, listening, then he looked up at the catalyst with grim
amusement. "They say they did. At least, no life registers on
their screens."

"No life! Fools," Saryon muttered, but — catching a
warning glance from Joram — he fell silent. Menju drew near
them, keeping a wary eye on the Garden.

"Our gun-toting friend is finished apparently," the magician said. "Let's get ready to move out." He gestured toward
the rear of the Temple. "Unless you want your wife to remain
here, Joram, and become a permanent member of her own
fan club, you had better get her away from those ghoulish
bodyguards."

"I will bring her," offered Saryon.

The catalyst moved slowly, a prey to despair that clutched
at his footsteps and caught at the skirts of his robes, threatening to drag him down.

Gwendolyn sat on the dusty floor behind the broken
altar, her head resting against a large stone urn. She did not
look up as Saryon approached, but stared straight ahead into
nothing. The catalyst gazed at her pityingly. Her golden hair
was bedraggled, her gown torn and dirty. She had no care for
where she was or what was happening, no care for Joram, no
care for herself.

"Hurry up, Father!" Menju ordered peremptorily, "or we
will leave her behind. You will serve me as hostage just as
well."

Maybe that would be kinder, Saryon thought, reaching
out his hand. Gwen glanced up at him. Docile as always, she
appeared perfectly willing to come with him and started to

rise up from her hiding place behind the altar. But invisible hands, catching hold of her, held her back.

In the one shaft of sunlight filtering through the dust, Saryon could almost see the unseen eyes staring at him suspiciously, the mouths silently shouting to him to leave the sacred ground he was violating. So vivid was this impression that he very nearly put his hands over his ears to blot out the sound he couldn't hear, closing his eyes to the sight of the anger and distress he couldn't see. This is madness! he thought, panicking.

"Father!" Menju said warningly.

Saryon took hold of Gwen's hand firmly. "I am grateful for what you have done," he called out to the empty air. "But she is among the living still. She does not belong to you. You must let her go."

For an instant it seemed he failed. Gwen's chill fingers closed over his, but when he tried to pull her toward him, he met a resistance so strong that he might well have tried to pull the Temple from the side of the mountain.

"Please!" he begged urgently, tugging Gwendolyn forward, the dead pulling her back. A wild impulse to laugh hysterically at this absurd situation overtook him. He choked on it, knowing that his laughter must end in him breaking down and sobbing like a frightened child. The shouts of the silent voices around him reverberated in his ears, though he couldn't hear a word.

Then, suddenly, the unheard tumult ceased as though it had been silenced by a single word.

Gwen was free, so unexpectedly that she tumbled forward into the catalyst's arms, nearly upsetting them both. He caught her, helped her to stand, brushing back the golden hair that veiled her face. She did not appear the least bit disturbed by anything that had occurred, but continued to look around her with detached interest, as if all this were happening to some other person.

"Aren't you coming?" she asked, twisting her head to talk to the shadows as Saryon hurried her forward.

The catalyst had the eerie impression that legions of ghosts were crowding around them, their unheard footfalls resounding loudly through the silence of the Temple.

Menju stood waiting impatiently for them near the head of the Temple stairs, his weapon trained on both Gwen and the catalyst. Standing beside him, leaning against a pillar, Joram watched silently. He appeared at first glance almost too weak to stand, let alone fight. Saryon alone saw the fire burning deep in the dark eyes, the unyielding purpose taking shape, being forged into a blade of iron.

"We all go together," instructed Menju, motioning Saryon and Gwen out of the Temple with a gesture of his weapon. In his other hand, he held the speaking device. "Joram, I am keeping the catalyst and your wife between us. Try anything—anything at all—and one of them dies instantly."

"What about the Executioner?" Saryon asked, hesitating at the top of the stairs, wanting desperately to drag time to a halt.

"That pile of ash?" Smiling, Menju indicated the hole in the ground near the altar stone, the few wisps of smoke rising from it. "I don't think you have anything to fear from him anymore, Father. Now move!" He gestured with the weapon.

There was no choice, no hope. Bowing his head, Saryon drew Gwendolyn nearer him and stepped outside. After the shadowy confines of the Temple, the sunlight was blinding. Putting her hand to her eyes, unable to see, Gwen stumbled at the top of the nine stairs. Saryon held onto her, guiding her footsteps, noticing as he did so that Joram had descended the stairs ahead of them.

Joram moved slowly, weakly, his breathing labored as though merely drawing each breath was a struggle. But Saryon saw his hand clenched firmly over the hilt of the Darksword.

Despite his self-assured demeanor, Menju was clearly nervous. Occasionally he prodded Saryon and Gwen, impatiently ordering them to hurry up, and he kept a wary eye on Joram. But most of Menju's attention was focused on the silver creature that—from what Saryon could make out of Menju's mutterings—was apparently not landing fast enough to suit the magician. Irritably, the Sorcerer shouted into the speaking device.

Turning slightly, ostensibly to see what had become of his wife, Joram looked at Saryon intently and silently mouthed the words, "Keep back!"

The bitter pain in Saryon was so unbearable that he was almost thankful it would end soon. Following Joram's orders, he slowed his steps — an easy matter since Gwendolyn was gazing around in vague curiosity, completely oblivious to everything. Menju was now a step or two ahead of them. Intent on staring at his winged monster, he had not noticed that they had stopped walking. The magician was lifting the device to his mouth to talk at it again when voices, coming out of the device, interrupted him. Startled, cursing beneath his breath, Menju turned, looking into the sky behind him.

A dark shadow swept over them, a shadow cast by gigantic green wings sprouting from a huge reptilian body. The Executioner appeared out of nowhere. Standing beside the altar stone, he coolly ordered the dragon to attack. The dragon dove straight down on the silver creature, screaming shrilly in hatred, its huge, taloned feet extending to strike.

Garbled cries came out of the speaking device in Menju's hand. Immediately, the silver monster performed an evasive maneuver, veering sideways in a frantic attempt to avoid its enemy. The dragon's claws clipped the edge of a silver wing, sending the monster rolling through the air. The dragon soared upward on the air currents and veered around for another attack. The silver creature nearly crashed into the side of the mountain, saving itself at the last instant. A burst of flame shot from its tail, and it pulled straight up out of the dive.

The dragon flew at it again, and this time the silver creature was ready for the attack, shooting a single beam of light at the glittering green and gold enemy. The tip of the dragon's wing burst into flame. Screaming in pain and rage, the dragon unleashed its fiery breath. A ball of flame enveloped the silver creature. The cries emanating from the listening device grew shrill and panic-stricken and then Saryon heard no more, for suddenly *his* world burst into flame around him.

A wall of magical fire, created by the Executioner, sprang up out of solid rock. Burning green and gold, its intense heat blistered Saryon's hands and face, the super-heated air seared his lungs. He pulled Gwendolyn close to him, trying to shield her with his body, but she was wrenched from his arms and he could not see what became of her for the blazing light and thick smoke.

A horrible cry burst out of the smoke and fire ahead of him. Trying to avoid the flames that licked the steps at his feet. Saryon peered frantically into the smoke through watering, stinging eyes. A figure emerged — a figure clothed in flame! It was Menju, his gray robes ablaze with the magical green fire. His yells were terrifying as he flailed about in agony. The catalyst had a swift, indistinct impression of the magician's wide-open, screaming mouth, the flesh of his face blackening in the fire, and then the Sorcerer sank down out of sight into the smoke swirling upon the stairs.

I am next! Saryon thought, watching the green flames flow up the steps toward him. Then Joram, wielding the Darksword, leaped in front of Saryon, standing between him and the fire.

As soon as Joram raised the sword the fire jumped from the rock straight for the blade and Saryon had a sudden vision of Joram engulfed in the magical blaze. But the sword greedily drank up the flame. The fire diminished, the blue flame of the Darksword burned brighter and brighter as the green flame died, and Saryon saw, standing before them, the Executioner.

The warlock had discarded the projectile weapon, relying instead upon his magic. The Darksword was draining the Life from him very quickly. He had faced it before, however, and knew what to expect. Looking up at the top of the mountain above the Temple, the warlock made a gesture. At his command, a chunk of the mountain wrenched itself free. The gigantic boulder bounded down the mountainside, hurtling straight for Joram.

His attention focused upon the Executioner, Joram could not see his danger. There was no time to warn him. Flinging himself forward, Saryon knocked Joram off his feet. The two tumbled down the stairs; the Darksword flying as Joram lost his grip on it.

Saryon had a confused impression of the boulder smashing into the stairs, of rock striking his body, of pain bursting in his head. Then he was slipping away into a vast darkness. . . .

But I can't die. Joram! I can't leave Joram. . . .

Struggling against the darkness and the pain, Saryon opened his eyes. The Temple crawled and writhed in his vision. Shaking his head to clear it, he winced in sudden agony and was very nearly sick.

"Joram!" he repeated groggily, submerging his pain in his fear for his friend. Lifting his head to look around, he discovered he was lying at the foot of the stairs, amidst the rubble of the shattered boulder. Joram lay near him, his eyes closed, his face white, smooth, calm . . . at peace at last.

"Farewell, my son!" Saryon murmured. He could feel no grief. It was better this way, so much better. Reaching out to touch the tousled black hair, he caught a glimpse of movement out of the corner of his eye.

The Executioner appeared, standing over them. From somewhere above, Saryon heard an explosion. Debris fell from the skies. He paid no attention to it. After a brief glance at the Executioner, he paid no attention to his enemy either. The catalyst's hand closed over Joram's. Kill me, Saryon thought. Kill me now. End it swiftly.

But the Executioner, after studying Joram intently, turned away. Saryon glanced after him without much interest. The warlock was leaving, his task finished. Then the catalyst froze, a cold wind of fear blowing away the fog of pain. The warlock *hadn't* completed his task! Not yet. Leaning down, the Executioner picked up the sword that lay dark and lifeless upon the steps.

If anything happens to me, it will be left up to you. You must destroy the Darksword.

There was only one thing Saryon could do. Barely able to recall the words of the prayer through the throbbing pain in his head, the catalyst began to drain Life from the warlock.

It was an attempt born of desperation. Draining Life is a slow process. Saryon hoped the Darksword had already drawn off most of the warlock's magic. If so, the catalyst could cripple him immediately.

The warlock instantly felt the catalyst's attack. Dropping the sword on the broken steps, the Executioner turned to face Saryon. The catalyst could not see the Executioner's face, hidden as it was by the hood of his gray robe. But he could almost sense the man smiling, and Saryon knew he had failed. The warlock was still strong in Life. Raising his hand, the Executioner prepared to cast a spell that would destroy the catalyst.

At least, Saryon prayed, bowing his head, the end will be swift.

Light flared, blinding him. He heard a sizzling sound and braced himself, waiting for the firestorm, the last terrible agony.

A hoarse cry of pain and anger sounded near him.

Startled, Saryon opened his eyes. The Executioner stood before him, but he was not looking at the catalyst. He had whirled to face a new enemy.

Menju lay upon the flame-swept stairs of the Temple. His body badly burned, the magician lifted a bloody and blackened hand. Aiming his weapon, he fired at the Executioner again.

At the same instant, the warlock shrieked out words. Knives of ice, flashing in the sunlight, flew from the Executioner's fingers. Speeding through the air, the blades thudded into Menju's body, impaling it upon the stairs. The Sorcerer fell without a cry. He might well have been dead already.

Saryon was aware, suddenly, of warm liquid trickling down his neck. The throbbing pain in his head increased, as did his dizziness. A red-tinged mist clouded his vision, and he could barely see the Executioner's hooded head, turning in his direction once more.

Saryon could do nothing. He could not even continue draining the man's Life, for he himself was teetering on the edge of consciousness. He watched the warlock turn . . . and saw the gaping hole blown through the Executioner's chest. The warlock made a spasmodic motion with his hand, then pitched forward on his face, dead. Saryon felt nothing, not elation, not relief. Nothing except bitter pain and despair.

He sank down upon the pavement, the stone cool beneath his cheek. Saryon closed his eyes. He was lost in a thick mist, stumbling blindly along the edge of a cliff, knowing that a single misstep must plunge him into the chasm. He had a vague impression that the Hand was there, wanting to help him.

Around him, beyond him, above him, he could hear the world dying.

"I can never forgive You for what You have done," Saryon whispered. Spurning the Hand, he stepped over the edge.

The Hand caught and gently held him.

12

The Triumph Of The Darksword

ather?" A sense of danger beat at Joram, pounding like the hammers of the forge, making sleep impossible. He was back in the smith's shop, creating the Darksword. Saryon was giving it Life. Then, suddenly, everything went wrong. Before his eyes, the catalyst was turning to stone. . . .

"Father!" Joram cried.

He woke up, his body drenched in sweat. The sound of hammering ceased.

All was silent around him, a terrible, unnatural silence; the world holding its breath like a drowning man, knowing that it would not be able to draw another.

Looking into the sunlit, blue sky above him, Joram remembered where he was, but he couldn't, for a moment, recall what had happened. He saw in his mind a blazing magical fire, felt its intense heat, and he remembered raising the Darksword against it, stopping it. He heard Gwen scream, Saryon cry out. A weight struck him from behind. The sword flew from his grasp . . . and . . . nothing.

"Saryon," he mumbled thickly, trying to sit up. "Saryon, I —"

Turning, he saw the catalyst.

Saryon lay in the midst of a pile of shattered stone. Dust and blood from a jagged gash on the side of his head covered his face. His eyes were closed, his expression peaceful. He might have been asleep.

"Father?" Joram said, touching him gently.

Saryon's skin was cold, his pulse weak and irregular. Concussion, shock. He needed treatment. Joram started to look around for something to cover the injured catalyst, but he stopped, staring, immobilized by the terrible sight.

The body of the Executioner lay on the pavement near the altar stone, a hole burned through the warlock's back. Menju's blackened body was sprawled on the Temple stairs. Rivulets of blood ran from it, twining together, breaking apart, merging again to form small pools on the sidewalk below.

"Gwen?" he called fearfully, looking up the stairs toward the Temple. Her name died on his lips. The portico of the Temple was smashed, the mangled fragments of the silver strike ship gleamed from among the broken stones. The body of the ship's pilot hung at a grotesque angle from the crushed cockpit. The dragon's twisted corpse lay huddled nearby.

"Gwen!" Joram shouted. Rising to his feet, fear giving him strength, he made his way up the rubble-strewn stairs, calling out his wife's name. There was no answer. Reaching the porch, he tried to shove aside a piece of wreckage to reach her in case she was trapped inside. Sudden dizziness and a wrenching pain in his arm reminded him of his injury. He staggered, almost falling.

The distant sound of an explosion, like a muffled thud, caught his attention, penetrating his despair. Turning, Joram looked out from the top of the mountain onto the plains below. Sunlight glinted off hundreds of metallic surfaces — tanks crawling around Merilon. White flashes of laser fire bombarded the magical dome. He thought he saw — though it might have been his imagination from this distance — one of the gleaming crystal spires of the Palace topple.

Everything, everyone around him was dead. Now Merilon was dying. The Prophecy was coming to fulfillment.

"Why didn't *I* die?" Joram cried in anguish. Bitter tears stung his eyes. Then, suddenly, blinking them back, he looked out again across the plains. "Perhaps that's why . . ." he murmured.

He would die, but not here. He would die in Merilon, fighting. The Prophecy *wasn't* fulfilled. Not yet.

Looking hastily around, Joram caught a glimpse of dark metal almost buried beneath the crushed stone. Setting his teeth against the agony that each move caused, he made his way through the wreckage, back down the stairs. The Darksword lay near the body of the Executioner. One of the dead warlock's hands was stretched out, almost touching it.

Joram leaned down to lift the sword. His legs gave way and he ended up falling to his knees beside it. Reaching out his hand, he hesitated. "I can save them," he said, "but for what? For this?" Lifting his head, he looked on nothing but death.

He will hold in his hand the destruction of the world —

Joram looked back at the Darksword. The sun shone bright upon it, but it did not reflect the light. Its metal, dark and cold as death. . . .

And Joram understood.

Going to Merilon, dealing death to its foes. *That* fulfilled the Prophecy. This war would end, but there would come another and another. Fear and mistrust would grow. Each world sealing itself off from the other. At the end, each would believe that the only way to survive was to destroy the other totally, never realizing that, in so doing, it would destroy itself.

"Open the window. Set the Life free," came a clear, sweet voice behind him.

Turning, he saw Gwendolyn sitting calmly amid the wreckage at the top of the Temple stairs. Her bright blue eyes were on her husband. There was no sign of recognition, yet she was speaking to him.

"How?" Joram cried out from where he knelt beside the sword. Raising his arms to the heavens, he shouted in frustration. "How do I stop this? Tell me how."

His voice came echoing back. Bounding off the columns of the Temple, reverberating from the mountainside, it cried louder and louder, "How?" Thousands of dead voices took up the cry, each voice softer than the softest whisper. "How?"

Gwendolyn motioned for silence and the echoes hushed. Everything in the world hushed, waiting. . . .

Clasping her hands around her knees, Gwendolyn regarded her husband with a serene smile that pierced him to the heart, for he saw that she still did not know him.

"Return to the world that which you took from it," she said.

Return to the world that which you took from it. He looked at the weapon in his hand. The Darksword, of course. He had made it of the stone of the world. But how to return it? He had no forge fire to melt it. He might cast it off the mountain peak, but it would only fall to the rocks below and lie there until someone else found it.

His eyes went to the altar stone. Looking at it closely for the first time, he realized what Menju had suspected earlier—it was made of darkstone.

Turning back to Gwen, he saw her smiling at him.

"What will happen?" he asked.

"The end," she said. "Then the beginning."

He nodded, thinking he understood. Lifting the sword, he walked over to Saryon. Kneeling down beside the catalyst, he kissed the mild, gentle face.

"Good-bye, my friend . . . my father," he whispered.

He noticed that, strangely, his weakness was gone, the pain had disappeared. Rising to his feet, he walked to the altar stone with firm, unfaltering steps.

He raised the sword as he drew near the altar, and the blade began to burn with blue flame. The altar stone responded, the symbols of the Nine Mysteries starting to shine with a white-blue light. He touched each symbol carved into the rock, tracing them with his fingers: Earth, Air, Fire, and Water. Time, Spirit, and Shadow. Life. Death.

Turning to his wife, he held out his hand. "Will you come stand beside me?"

He might have asked her to dance. "Of course!" she answered with a laugh. Jumping to her feet, she ran lightly down the stairs, her gown trailing in the blood.

Drawing near her husband, he saw her gaze curiously at his injured arm. Her blue eyes glanced at Saryon, then at the dead Executioner, then at Simkin's body, and an expression of sad, puzzled wonder shadowed her face. Looking back at Joram, she reached out and touched his blood-soaked sleeve with the tips of her fingers. He flinched, and she drew her hand away quickly, putting it behind her, staring at him shyly.

"You did not hurt me. Not my arm, at least," he amended, for he knew she must have seen the pain on his face. "I was remembering . . . long ago, when you first touched me like that." He gazed at her searchingly. "Have they truly found peace in death? Are they happy?"

"They will be, when you free them," she answered.

That was not the answer he wanted, but then, he realized, he had not asked the question that was in his heart. *Will I find peace in death? Will I find you once again?* He could never ask that question, he realized, for it would have no meaning for her.

She was watching him expectantly. "They are waiting," she said, a touch of impatience in her clear voice.

Waiting. . . . It seemed the whole world was waiting, had waited, perhaps, ever since the moment of his birth.

Turning from her, Joram grasped the hilt of the Darksword with both hands. Lifting the weapon high over his head, he braced his feet firmly in the soil of the dead Garden. He drew in a deep breath, then — with all his strength and might — he plunged the Darksword straight into the heart of the altar stone.

The sword entered the rock easily, so easily that it astonished him. The altar stone flared a brilliant white-blue and shivered. He felt the tremor beneath his hands, as though he had thrust the sword through living flesh. The tremor extended out from the stone, traveling farther and farther.

Beneath his feet, the mountain itself shuddered. The ground quivered and heaved like a live thing, splitting apart. The Temple tottered on its foundations; cracks split the walls; the roof caved in. Joram lost his footing and fell to his hands and knees. Gwendolyn crouched near him, staring around her, wide-eyed and fascinated.

Then, suddenly, the shaking ceased. Everything was still and quiet once more. The flaming light of the altar stone faded. Nothing about the stone appeared changed, except that the sword had vanished. No trace of it remained.

Joram tried to stand, but he was too weak. It was as if the sword — taking its last victim — had drained the life from his body. Leaning wearily against the altar stone, he looked out across the plains, wondering vaguely why it was beginning to grow dark when it was still noonday.

Perhaps it was his own sight failing, the first shadows of death. Joram blinked rapidly, and the shadows did not diminish. Staring at the sky more intently, he realized that it was not his failing vision. It was truly growing darker.

But such an odd, eerie darkness. It came from the ground, rising up over the land like a fast-flowing tide, fighting the sun that still lit the land from above. In this strange battle of darkness and light, objects stood out with unnatural clarity, every line sharply delineated and defined. Each dead plant stalk was touched with a radiance that made it seem almost alive. Tiny drops of blood upon the pavement glistened a brilliant red. The gray hairs on the catalyst's head, the lines on his face, the broken fingers of his hands were so clear in Joram's sight that he knew they must be visible from the heavens.

So, too, must heaven see the flaring lights of the attacking tanks, the jagged lightning bolts of the defending wizards. As the darkness continued to deepen and the wind began to rise, Joram watched the battle around Merilon rage ever more furiously.

Glancing up into the heavens to see if Anyone was watching, he saw the reason for the darkness. The sun was disappearing. A solar eclipse. He had seen them before. Saryon had explained their cause. The moon, passing between Thimhallan and the sun, cast its shadow on the world. But Joram had never seen an eclipse like this. The moon was sweeping across the sun, devouring it. Not content with nibbling at it a small bite at a time, the moon was feasting on entire chunks, leaving no crumb or scrap behind.

The darkness grew deeper. At the edges of the world, along the horizon, it was night. Stars appeared, flashing into life for a brief instant, then vanishing as another darkness, deeper than night, engulfed them. The edges of this darkness flickered with lightning, and thunder rolled across the land.

The sky grew darker and darker. The shadows rose up slowly around Joram. It was still light upon the mountain peak — a tiny fragment of sun shone down on them, desperately clinging to life. Watching the darkness rise up from the land below, Joram had the strange feeling that he and Gwen were adrift on an ocean of night.

Eventually, however, the darkness must overtake them as well, the storm-tossed seas capsizing their fragile craft. Part of him was afraid, part begged him to find shelter from the coming storm. He knew he should, but he couldn't move. It was like the paralysis of deep sleep; he watched what was happening as in a dream. His pain was gone, and he no longer had feeling in his arm. His right hand might have belonged to someone else's body.

The wind grew stronger, lashing at him from all directions. Stinging bits of rock bit into his flesh. Gwendolyn's golden hair enveloped her in a bright cloud.

Joram drew his wife near, and she huddled beside him in the shelter of the altar stone. She was not afraid but stared eagerly into the approaching storm; her eyes reflecting the jagged lightning, her lips parted to drink the wind.

And because she was not afraid, Joram's last fears left him. He could no longer see Merilon now. The fragment of sun shone down on the mountain peak alone; the rest of the world was dark.

The dying light gleamed softly on Saryon's peaceful face, touching him like a benediction. Then the darkness covered him. A last tiny ray formed a halo around Gwendolyn's hair, and Joram kept his eyes fixed upon her. He would take this vision of her with him from this world and keep it, he knew, in the next. There she would recognize him. There she would call him by name.

The darkness surged closer. Joram could see only Gwen, her bright eyes on the storm. And he noticed, studying her face, that it had changed. Her expression was calm, there was no fear. But before it had been the calm of madness. Now it was the calm, beautiful face of the woman who had looked into his eyes once, so long ago, when he had supposed himself alone and nameless. The calm, beautiful face of the woman who had stretched out her hand to him in love and trust.

"Come with me." He murmured the words he had spoken to her then.

Gwendolyn turned her blue eyes upon him. The darkness gathered thickly about him. The sun, it seemed, shone only in her eyes.

"I will, Joram," she said, smiling at him through her tears. "I will, my husband, for I am free now — as the dead are free, as the magic is finally free!" Reaching out, she took him in her arms and held him tightly, cradling his head against her breast. With her gentle hand, she smoothed his hair, her soft lips touched his forehead.

His eyes closed, and she bent over him, shielding him.

The sun vanished, darkness covered them, and the terrible storm broke over the world.

13

Requiem Aeternam

One by one, blown down by the blasting winds, the Watchers on the Border toppled. The spell holding them prisoner — some for centuries — broke apart like their own stone bodies. The very last to fall, the one that withstood the fury of the storm to the end, was the statue with the clenched hand.

Long after the oldest oaks had been uprooted and tumbled across the land like twigs, long after the tidal waves had smashed upon the shores, long after city walls were crushed and burning and the armies of the battling forces of Merilon scattered in all directions, this one statue braved the storm, and — had anyone been near — they might have heard hollow laughter.

Time and again the wind slammed into it, the sand stung its stone flesh. Lightning burst over it, thunder hammered on it with its mighty fist. Finally, when the darkness was deepest, the statue fell. Crashing to the shore, its stone shattered, bursting into millions of tiny fragments that were gleefully caught up by the howling winds and strewn over the land.

His spirit freed, the catalyst joined the dead of Thimhallan to watch, with sightless eyes, the end.

The storm raged a day and a night, then — when the world had been swept clean by wind, cauterized by fire, and purified by water — the storm ceased.

All was very quiet, very still.

Nothing moved. Nothing could.

The Well of Life was empty.

Epilogue

Huddled in the shadow of their broken city Gate, their meager possessions gathered around them in crude bundles, the last inhabitants of Merilon stood in line, waiting.

They waited in silence for the most part. Bereft of their magic, forced to walk upon the ground in bodies that felt clumsy and heavy and difficult to control without the grace of Life, the magi had little energy left to expend in speech. They had nothing to talk about that was not depressing and despairing anyway.

Occasionally a baby whimpered, and then could be heard the soft reassuring murmur of a mother's voice. And once three small brothers, too young to understand what was happening, began playing at war in the rubble-strewn street. Pelting each other with rocks and screaming in glee, their voices resounded shrill and unnerving in the lifeless streets. Others, standing or sitting in line, glanced at them in irritation, and their father stopped their play with a sharp word of reprimand, his bitter tone flicking across their innocence, inflicting wounds they never forgot.

Silence fell, and the line of people settled back to grim waiting. Most tried to keep within the shadows of the wall; though the air was chill — especially for those of Merilon who had never known winter — the sun beat down upon them unmercifully. Accustomed as they were to the meek sun that had shone over Merilon decorously for centuries, this new and fiery sun frightened them. But though the bright sunlight was unbearable, the people glanced up in fear and apprehension whenever a shadow darkened the sky. Dreadful storms, the like of which had never been known in the world until now, periodically ravaged the land.

At intervals here and there along the line of people, strange humans with silver skin and metal heads stood guard, watching the magi closely. In the guards' hands were metal devices which, the people of Merilon knew, fired a beam of light that could either cast one into the sleep of unconsciousness or the deeper, dreamless sleep of death. The magi were careful to keep their eyes averted from the strange humans or, if they did look at them, it was with swift, furtive glances of hatred and fear.

For their part, the strange humans — though attentive to their duty — did not appear overly nervous or ill at ease. These magi they were guarding were families, generally of the lower- and middle-class workers, and were not considered dangerous. A vast difference from the long line of black-robed warlocks who were being marched down the street. Their hoods cast aside, their faces grim and expressionless, they walked with heads bowed. The glint of steel manacles could be seen gleaming beneath the long sleeves of the tattered black robes. They moved with a shuffling step, their feet chained together at the ankles. The warlocks and witches were under heavy guard; the strange humans outnumbering them nearly two to one and watching each of them with a nervous intentness that quickly stopped the slightest movement of a hand.

The *Duuk-tsarith* prisoners were hustled rapidly out of the Gate, the waiting people of Merilon barely glancing at them as they passed by. Wrapped up in their own misery, the people of Merilon had little sympathy for the misery of others.

This same lack of interest applied to a person being carried out of the broken Gates on a stretcher. A heavy, rotund man, he was borne by six stout catalysts who sweated and staggered beneath their burden. Although gravely ill and unable to walk, the man was regally attired in his rich red robes of office, his miter carefully balanced on his head. He even managed to weakly raise his right hand, extending his blessing over the crowd as he passed. A few people bowed their heads or removed their hats, but for the most part they watched their Bishop leaving their city in mute despair.

A few university students, standing near the Gate, peered out into the plains, attempting to see what was happening; rumors having spread among the students that the warlocks were going to be exterminated. The captive, black-robed *Duuk-tsarith* were, however, loaded into the body of one of the silver creatures along with Bishop Vanya's pathetic entourage. Seeing that the prisoners hadn't been lined up and set on fire, the students — somewhat disappointed — lounged back against the crumbling, charred walls, muttering imprecations at the guards and whispering plans for rebellion that would never come to fruition.

The rest of the people of Merilon avoided looking out onto the wind-swept plains. It had become an all-too familiar sight in the past week — the gigantic silver-bodied creatures that the strange humans called "air ships" opening their maws, swallowing up thousands of people, then rising into the sky and disappearing into the heavens. It would be their turn to enter one of the creatures' bellies soon enough.

The people had been reassured, time and again, that they were not being taken to their deaths. They were being relocated, removed from a world that was now unsafe. They had even been able to talk — through some demonic means of the Dark Arts — with friends and relatives who had been carried off to this other "brave, new world." Still, they remained huddled inside their shattered city to the bitter end. Though few could bear looking on the wreckage of Merilon without tears blurring their vision, they sought desperately to cling to its memory as long as possible.

The street was empty following the Bishop's departure, and the crowd began to stir around in anticipation of its being their turn to go; people gathering up their bundles or hunting about for children. There was some comment, particularly among the watching students, when a figure was seen emerging from the silver creature and walking across the plains toward Merilon. The figure drew nearer, and the students — seeing that it was only a catalyst, a stooped, middle-aged man whose brown robes were too short for his height, showing his bony ankles — lost interest.

A strange silver-skinned human stopped the catalyst as he entered the Gate. The catalyst pointed to a man under heavy guard, a man being kept apart from the rest of the people. Like the *Duuk-tsarith*, this man's hands were manacled. He was not dressed in black robes, however. He wore velvet and silk. But the clothes that had once been elegant and rich were now torn, dirty, and stained with blood.

The guard nodded and the catalyst entered the Gate, walking up to the man, who did not notice him. The prisoner's head was bowed, he stared at the ground in despair so dark and bitter that the people standing in line looked at him with pity and respect, finding comfort in his presence, knowing that he shared their sorrow.

"Your Grace," said the catalyst softly, coming up to stand beside him.

Raising his head, Prince Garald looked at the catalyst and a wan smile of recognition lightened his face. "Father Saryon. I wondered where you had gone." He glanced at the catalyst's neatly bandaged head. "I feared perhaps your injury —"

"No, I am fine," Saryon said, reaching up to touch the bandage and wincing slightly. "The pain comes and goes, but that is to be expected, so they tell me, with what they call a 'concussion.' I *have* been to the healing rooms in the ship, but it was to visit our young patient."

"How is Mosiah?" Garald asked gravely, his smile disappearing.

"He is improving . . . finally," Saryon said with a sigh. "I have been with him most of the night and we came very near losing him. But we finally persuaded him to take the treatment offered by the . . . the healers of their kind" — he gestured toward the strange humans — "since the *Theldara* have lost their power. Eventually, Mosiah listened to me. He accepted their help at last, and he will live. I left him in the care of Lord and Lady Samuels to come tell you."

Prince Garald's face darkened. "I don't blame Mosiah. I would not have taken their treatment," he said with a bitter oath. "I would sooner have died!"

Angry tears filled his eyes. He shook his manacled hands, fists clenched, his wrists straining against his bonds. Seeing this, one of the guards raised his weapon and said something in a sharp voice that sounded inhuman and mechanical through the metal helm.

"I would sooner have died!" Garald repeated in a choked voice, glaring at the guard.

Saryon laid his hand upon the Prince's arm, about to offer what words of comfort he could, when a stirring among the waiting crowd caught their attention and that of their guard as well.

Three figures walked down the ruined street of Merilon. Picking their way carefully among the rubble that littered the streets, they passed the still-smoldering, fire-blackened trees of the Grove, and approached the Gate. One of the three — a short-statured, muscular man in a plain, neat uniform — did not pay much attention to the wreckage, but regarded it with the grim face of one who has seen this kind of thing all too often. The two accompanying him, however, appeared genuinely moved and distressed by it.

One in particular — a golden-haired woman with a gentle, lovely face — gestured here and there, speaking to her companion in a low voice, shaking her head as though recalling happier times. The companion — a dark-haired man dressed in white robes, his right arm in a sling — bent close to hear her; the man's face, though stern and dark, was marked by a grief the depths of which few could know or understand.

One person watching saw, one person understood. Saryon brushed his hand swiftly across his eyes.

The three people were accompanied by at least a dozen silver-skinned, weapon-carrying humans, who kept their eyes and weapons trained on the crowd.

The silence of the people of Merilon broke. The crowd surged to its feet. Shaking their fists at the white-robed man, they screamed curses and threats. They threw rocks. People lunged out of line, trying to attack the man. The silver-skinned humans closed around their commander and the man and the woman, while other guards shoved the worst offenders back against the wall or turned their stunning light beams on them, causing them to crumple to the ground. The most violent were taken into custody and hustled away to the makeshift guardhouse within what was left of the *Kan-Hanar*'s office.

The black-haired man in the white robes did not appear angry or frightened. He even stopped a guard from apprehending a young woman who had darted out of the crowd to spit upon him. His concern appeared to be for the golden-haired woman, for he put his arm around her and held her close, protectively. She was pale but composed and looked at the people with a sad sympathy, all the while appearing to speak words of comfort to the man.

The shouting and the rock-throwing continued as the three moved along the line of people standing near the Gate. The curses were bitter, the threats vile and ugly, and Prince Garald, his brows contracted in a frown, glanced at Father Saryon. The catalyst was pale and shaken.

"I am sorry you had to witness this, Father," Garald said abruptly, his scowling gaze on the white-robed man. "But he shouldn't have come. He brings it on himself."

Saryon kept silent, knowing that nothing he could say would alleviate the Prince's bitter anger. His heart ached with sorrow — sorrow for the people, for Garald, for Joram.

Major Boris snapped a command and the guards began herding the people out of the Gate, marching them toward the waiting air ship. This distraction helped restore order, the people being forced to gather up their belongings. Slowly they filed out of the ruins of their city. All cast narrow-eyed glances at Joram as they left, shouting a final imprecation, shaking clenched fists.

Joram continued walking. Accompanied by Gwendolyn and Major Boris, surrounded by bodyguards, he was seemingly oblivious to the people's screams of hatred; his face so cold it might have been carved of stone. But Saryon — who knew that face so well — saw the deep pain burning in the brown eyes, the jaw muscles clenched tight against it.

"If *he* is to travel with us, I refuse to go! You can do what you like to me!" Garald cried out harshly to the Major, as the three came near him.

Standing tall and straight, holding his manacled hands before him with a grimly noble air as if he wore bracelets of rare jewels instead of strong steel, the Prince cast Joram one dark look — a look so expressive of contempt, anger, and betrayal that it was far worse than the vilest curse and cut into Joram's flesh more deeply than the sharpest rock.

Joram did not falter. He met Garald's gaze unflinchingly, facing him with pride tempered only by sadness.

Watching the two, Saryon was reminded vividly of the time Garald and Joram had first met, when the Prince had mistaken the young man for a bandit and held him prisoner. There was the same pride in the set of Joram's shoulders, the same air of nobility. But the fire of arrogance and defiance that had flared in the eyes of the boy was gone, leaving behind ashes of grief and sorrow.

The same memories might have stirred within Garald, or perhaps it was Joram's steadfast, unfaltering gaze that met his without shame or apology, for the Prince was the first to avert his eyes. His face flushed, he looked out over the wrecked city of Merilon into the storm-ravaged lands beyond.

Major Boris spoke at some length in his own language. Joram listened, then turned to Garald to translate.

"Your Grace," Joram began.

Garald sneered. "Not Your Grace!" he said bitingly. "Say 'prisoner' instead!"

"Your Grace — " Joram repeated, and now it was Garald who flinched, hearing in those two words a deep respect and a deeper sadness, sorrow over something precious lost, never to be regained. The Prince did not look at Joram, but continued staring off into the distance. His eyes blinked rapidly, however, and pressing his lips together, he swallowed the tears his pride would not permit him to show.

" — Major Boris extends his wish that you will consider yourself his guest aboard the transport," Joram said. "He says it will be an honor to share his quarters with so brave and noble a soldier as yourself. He hopes that you will do him the favor of spending the long hours of the journey in teaching him more about our people — "

"*Our* people?" Garald's lip curled.

"—and our ways and customs so that he might better serve them when you arrive at your destination," Joram said, ignoring the interruption.

"When we arrive at the slave camps, you mean!" Garald spit the words. "*Some* of us, that is!" he added bitterly, refusing to look at Joram. "I suppose, traitor, that *you* will go back to your friends—"

It was clear that Major Boris understood Garald's bitter words. Shaking his head in regret over an apparent misunderstanding, he said something to Joram, then—with a gesture—motioned for the guard to remove the manacles.

Jerking his hands back, Garald rebuffed him. "I will remain chained as long as my people are chained!" he cried furiously.

"Your Grace," interposed Father Saryon, speaking in a low, firm voice, "I ask you to remember that *you* are the leader of your people, now that your father is dead. The people have put their trust in you and—as their leader in exile— you must keep their best interests in mind. You cannot give way to hatred. That will accomplish nothing except breed more hatred and bring us back to this—" The catalyst gestured with his misshapen hand to the ruins around them.

Prince Garald struggled within himself. Standing beside him, Saryon could feel the strong body tremble and see the proud lips quiver as the Prince fought to conquer his pride, his rage, and his pain.

"I realize I don't know much about politics, Your Grace," Saryon added. "But I speak to you as a man who has suffered much and seen others suffer. I want this suffering to end. Remember, too, that I act—by your request—in the capacity of your advisor. I am, I know, a poor substitute for that wise man who commended me to you with his dying breath, but I believe Cardinal Radisovik would have offered this same counsel."

Garald bowed his head, the tears coursing unchecked and unheeded down his cheeks. He bit his lip, either unable or unwilling to answer. Major Boris, watching him anxiously, spoke again to Joram and it was obvious from the tone of the Major's voice that he was earnest and sincere in what he said.

Joram, listening, nodded and translated. "The Major reiterates to you his pledge that our people are not slaves. You are being taken to relocation camps where you can adapt to the new worlds in which you will be living. Eventually, when it is deemed wise, you will be free to go where you choose, live where you will in whatever manner that you see fit. There is only one restriction, of course — that you do not return to this world. This is solely for your own good. The violent nature of the frequent storms sweeping the land make it virtually impossible for anyone to live here."

At this statement, Saryon thought he saw Gwendolyn smile sadly and press nearer her husband. Joram's arm around her tightened as he continued speaking, his steady, unwavering gaze never leaving Garald's face.

"Although your powers in magic appear gone now, because there is no longer a concentration of magic within this world, the wise rulers of the worlds Beyond know that, in time, Life will return to you. Since the magic has been dispersed once again throughout the universe, it is believed that your powers will conceivably grow as strong as they were in ancient times. Our people could be a tremendous asset for the worlds Beyond."

"We could also be tremendously dangerous," Garald muttered darkly.

Major Boris answered, emphasizing his words with a pronounced movement of his hand.

"The Major admits that this is true," Joram said. "He knows that it is the nature of some men to abuse power and attempt to use it for their own selfish interests. Such a man was Menju the Sorcerer. But he also knows that it is the nature of others to sacrifice themselves for the good of the people and to do what they can to make the world — all worlds — a better place."

It seemed Saryon would have spoken here, but Joram, with a glance, shook his head and continued.

"The Major has received word that the other magicians who were in the plot with Menju have not been deterred by the death of their leader or the fact that he meant — all along — to betray them as well. They have fled to secret locations and are planning to continue their fight, using the new strength that they will acquire now that the magic is back in the universe.

"James Boris does not say, but I will add," Joram remarked quietly, "that these evil magi are our responsibility in a way, since it was we who cast them out of our society. The magi out there will, of course, consider you and all like you a threat and will do what they can to destroy you. The rulers of the worlds Beyond hope that our people will help find and defeat them."

"And, of course, Your Grace," Saryon said with fine irony, "there are those among us like Bishop Vanya who will, undoubtedly, try to establish their own stranglehold over these new worlds. We need strong and honorable people like yourself and like Major Boris. Working together, you can accomplish much that is good."

Stepping forward, Gwendolyn laid her gentle hand upon Garald's arm. "Hatred is a poisonous soil in which nothing can grow," she said. "A tree — no matter how strong — planted in such soil will only wither and die."

Garald stared straight ahead beneath his lowered brow, his face grim and implacable. The Major motioned again to undo the manacles and, once more, the guard stepped forward. The Prince kept his hands close to his body, concealing them beneath his torn, bloody robes. Then, slowly, reluctantly, he extended his arms. The guard removed the manacles, and Garald's proud gaze turned unwillingly to Major Boris.

Though the short, sturdy Major did not even come up to Garald's chest, his shoulders were equal in breadth to the strong Prince's. The two men were near the same age, both in their thirties, and — though one was dressed in red velvet, silken doublet, and hose, and the other in drab khaki — there was a similarity between the two that showed itself in the upright stance of each, and in their honest, forthright demeanor.

"I will accept your offer, Major Boris," Garald said stiffly. "I will do what I can to help you . . . understand my people and, in turn, I . . . will" — he swallowed, then continued gruffly — "learn to speak your language. I have the following conditions, however."

Major Boris listened attentively, his face slightly shadowed.

"First, that my advisor, Father Saryon, be permitted to remain with me." Garald looked at Saryon gravely. "If you will, Father?"

"Thank you, Your Grace," Saryon said simply.

Nothing was easier to arrange. Major Boris had been about to suggest it himself.

"Second, that the chains and manacles be removed from my people," Garald said firmly. "I will talk to them," he added, seeing the Major frown, "and I will pledge my word that — if we are treated well as you promise — we will give you and your rulers no cause for alarm. I also ask that we be allowed — for the time being — to govern ourselves."

After a moment's hesitation, Major Boris nodded, speaking to Joram.

"He agrees for his part," said Joram, "but he cannot answer for his superiors. He believes, however, that both of you, acting together, can help persuade the rulers of the worlds Beyond that this is in the best interests of all concerned."

"Your hand, sir?" Major James Boris said clumsily, stumbling over the words that he spoke in Garald's language. He held out his hand.

Slowly, Garald extended his own. As he did so, the marks of the manacles could be seen plainly upon his wrists. Remembering his anguish, Garald hesitated, and his hand shook. He appeared about to refuse the Major's courtesy, and Saryon held his breath, a prayer in his heart.

His lips setting in an even, firm line, Garald pulled the tattered sleeve of his shirt down over the scars, then accepted the Major's hand. James Boris grasped the Prince's hand firmly in turn, shaking it heartily, his own lips widening in a grin.

Gwendolyn inclined her head to listen to some voice only she could hear, then looked at the two of them with a smile. "The dead tell me that this friendship you have forged today will become legend in the history of the worlds Beyond. Many are the times when each of you will be willing to lay down his life for the other as you fight to bring order to your universe. As the potential for good grows now in the worlds with the return of magic, so too the potential for evil, beyond even what you can now imagine. But with your faith in each other and in your God"—she glanced at Father Saryon—"you will triumph."

Major Boris, embarrassed and seemingly a little non-plussed at being lectured by the dead, hurriedly cleared his throat and barked out orders to the guards. Saluting the Prince, Father Saryon, and—last and most respectfully—Joram, Major James Boris turned and left, stomping off to attend to other duties.

Looking after him, apparently favorably impressed by the firmness of his handshake and his straight, military posture, Garald smiled slightly to himself. The smile vanished, however, as he caught sight of Joram watching him.

With an angry, abrupt motion of his hand, the Prince checked Joram as he started to speak.

"No words between us." The Prince's cold eyes stared somewhere above Joram's shoulder. "You admitted to me that you had the power to save my world and you did not. Instead, you deliberately chose to destroy it. Oh, I know!" he said harshly, forestalling Saryon's attempt to intervene. "I have heard your reasons! Father Saryon has explained your decision to release the magic into the universe. Perhaps, in time, I can come to understand. But I will never forgive you, Joram. Never."

With a cool bow to Gwendolyn, Prince Garald turned on his heel. He would have walked away had not Joram caught hold of his arm.

"Your Grace, hear me. I do not beg for your forgiveness," Joram said, seeing Garald's face grow cold and stern. "I am finding it difficult to forgive myself. It seems that the prophecy was fulfilled. Was I destined to do it? Or did I have a choice? I believe I had a choice, as did others. It was because of the choices we all made that this happened. I have learned, you see, that it was not so much a Prophecy as a Warning. And we ignored it. What would have happened to me, to this world, if fear hadn't overthrown love and compassion? What would have happened if my father and mother had kept me instead of casting me off? What would have happened if I had listened to Saryon and destroyed the Darksword, instead of using it to seek power? Perhaps we could have discovered the world Beyond through peaceful means. Perhaps we would have opened the Borders, released the magic freely. . . ."

Garald's expression did not change; he remained standing stiffly, tensely, staring straight ahead.

Sighing, Joram clasped the Prince's arm more firmly. "But we did not," he said softly. "This world was becoming like my mother — a corpse, rotting and decaying, maintaining a semblance of life by the magic alone. Our world itself is dead, except in the hearts of its people. You will carry Life with you, my friend, wherever you go. May your journey be blessed . . . Your Grace."

Garald's head bowed, his eyes closed in anguish. His own hand, its wrist scarred and bleeding, rested for a brief instant on Joram's. Storm clouds massed on the horizon, lightning flickering on their fringes. Tiny whirlwinds surged about the ruins of Merilon, sucking up bits of dust and rock and tossing them into the air. Shaking himself free of Joram's grip, the Prince turned away.

His tattered cape whipped around him, and debris scattered beneath his booted feet. Without a backward glance, Prince Garald exited the crumbling Gate and began the long walk across the barren plains to where the air ship waited.

Sighing, Saryon drew his hood up around his head to protect him from the stinging sand.

"We should be going along as well, Joram," he said. "Another storm will break soon. We must be on our way to the ship."

To the catalyst's astonishment, Joram shook his head.

"We are not going with you, Father."

"We only came to say good-bye," Gwendolyn added.

"What?" Saryon stared at them in perplexity. "This is the last ship! You must take it —" Suddenly, their meaning became clear. "But you can't!" he cried, looking around at the ruins of Merilon; the lowering, swiftly moving storm clouds. "You can't stay here!"

"My friend" — reaching out, Joram clasped Saryon's broken hand in his own — "where else can I go? You see them, you hear them." He gestured toward the refugees being herded out the Gate toward the waiting ship. "They will never forgive me. No matter where they go or what happens

to them, my name will always be spoken with a curse. They
will tell their children about me. I will be reviled throughout
time as the one who fulfilled the Prophecy, the one who destroyed the world. My life and the lives of those I love would
be in constant danger. Far better for my wife and me and for
our children that we remain here, in peace."

"But alone!" Saryon looked at Joram in despair. "On a
dead world! Swept by storms! The earth itself shakes.
Where will you live? The cities lie in rubble. . . ."

"The mountain fortress of the Font stands unharmed,"
Joram said. "We will make our home there."

"Then I will stay here with you!"

"No, Father." Joram glanced again at Garald's tall, upright figure as it made its lonely way across the plains.
"Others need you now."

"We will not be alone, Father," Gwendolyn said, placing
her soft hand over her husband's. "The dead will inherit this
world. We will be company for them and they will be company for us."

Saryon saw — standing behind Gwen — indistinct shapes
and ghostly forms, staring at him with intense, knowing eyes.
He even thought he saw, though it vanished when he looked
at it directly, a fluttering of orange silk.

"Farewell, Father," Gwen said, kissing his wrinkled
cheek. "When our son is of age, we will send him to you to
teach as you taught Joram."

She smiled so sweetly and cheerfully, looking at her husband with so much love in her face, that Saryon could not
find it in his heart to pity her.

"Good-bye, Father," Joram said, grasping the catalyst's
trembling hand tightly. "You *are* my father, the only true one I
ever knew."

Clasping Joram in his arms, Saryon held him close, remembering the baby whose small head once rested upon his
shoulder. "Something tells me, my son, that I will never see
you again, and I must say this to you before we part. When I
was near death, I saw — I understood, at last." His voice
breaking, he whispered huskily, "What you did was right, my
son! Always believe that! And always know that I love you! I
love you and honor you —" His words failed, he could not go
on.

Joram's tears, mingling with Saryon's, fell into the black hair that curled upon his shoulders. The two clung to each other as the storm winds blew about them more fiercely. One of the guards, with a nervous glance at the swirling clouds, moved forward to tap the catalyst respectfully on the shoulder.

"It is time for you to go. May the Almin be with you, Father," Joram said quietly.

Saryon smiled through his tears.

"He is, my son," he said, placing his hand over his heart. "He is."

APPENDIX:

The Game Of Tarok

Tarok is one of the earliest known games utilizing the tarot cards, whose appearance in Europe around the fourteenth or fifteenth century still remains shrouded in mystery. Many theories exist concerning the origin of the allegorical and mystical cards, relating them to everything from the Egyptian Book of Thoth to the Hebrew Kabbalah to roving bands of Christian dissenters who may have used the symbolic pictures on the cards to teach their lessons to an illiterate populace.

Most scholars credit gypsies with introducing the cards into Europe. Since most Europeans of the time believed — erroneously — that the gypsies came from Egypt (hence the name *gypsy*), it is easy to see how the theory arose that the cards were Egyptian in origin, a theory that is open to debate. It is doubtful that the gypsies themselves invented the cards. They used them merely for crude forms of divination, without any apparent understanding of the cards' complex symbolism.

The cards gained popularity in Europe despite the fac that they were frowned upon by the Church. Many of ou earliest references to the tarot cards are edicts banning thei use. The cards were popular among the wealthy nobility however, and this kept them in existence. Hand-painte decks decorated with gold leaf, crushed lapis lazuli, an other substances with such exotic names as "dragon's blood and "mummy dust" appeared in royal courts.

It is speculated that since fortune telling was prohibite by the Church, games utilizing the cards were invented. Th introduction of movable type made the cards available to th general populace, and eventually the tarot decks were soo too popular and widespread for the Church and politicians t continue fighting. Christian symbolism even came to be use on the cards, perhaps in an effort to try to make them mor palatable to Church officials.

In general, the tarot decks that exist today have change little over the past five hundred years. The tarot deck in cludes the twenty-two cards of the Major Arcana and th fifty-six cards of the Minor Arcana, or suit cards. The firs twenty-two cards are known as trump cards, the word *trum* deriving from the Latin *triumphi*, or triumph. The word *tarc* comes from the sixteenth-century Italian term *tarocchi*, th plural of *tarocco*, which was used to refer to the Major Arcana cards and later to the entire deck. *Arcana* is a Latin wor meaning mysterious or secret. *Tarot* is the French derivativ of *tarocchi*, and it was this term for the cards that becam popular in the English language.

Throughout the centuries, scholars have attempted t analyze the allegorical and mystical meanings of the taro cards, particularly those of the Major Arcana. Beginnin with the first card (numbered either 0 or 22), known as th Fool card, the deck also includes cards picturing the Magi cian, the Sun, the Moon, Death, the Hermit, the Hange Man, the Lightning-Struck Tower, the Devil, and the World among others.

A favorite theory concerning the allegorical meaning o the tarot is that the cards represent the Fool's (man's) journe through life. The Fool is generally represented as a yout walking heedlessly along the edge of a cliff. His eyes are o the sun; he is not watching where he is going and appears t be in imminent danger of falling. A small dog (man's base, physical nature) barking at his feet appears to be either trying to warn the Fool away from the cliff's edge or drive him over. The people the Fool meets — such as the Magician, the Hermit — and the experiences he undergoes in his journey through life will provide him with the self-understanding he must acquire in order to complete his journey successfully.

Our fascination with the cards and our enjoyment of the games that were developed using them continues to this day. Most modern card games use a revised version of the tarot deck, retaining almost all the cards of the Minor Arana, or the suit cards, plus the joker, or the Fool card. Among the Minor Arcana are the court cards: kings, queens, knights, and pages, plus cards of each suit numbering from one (the ace) to ten. The suits of the early Minor Arcana were swords, cups, coins, and staves, now known as spades, hearts, diamonds, and clubs.

The game of tarok — still popular in some places in Europe — is unusual in that it retains use of the cards of the Major Arcana as well as the Minor Arcana. It can be played by two or three players, although later rules include up to four players.

There are many different versions of the rules of tarok. The following comes from *The Encyclopedia of the Tarot* by Stuart Kaplan, and was the basis for the game played by our characters. It uses the seventy-eight card deck; the dealer deals three hands of twenty-five cards each, leaving three cards facedown on the table. The players sort their hands and the dealer discards his three most useless cards, exchanging them for the three on the table.

Points are scored before play begins. The twenty-two trump cards vary in value, and points scored are determined by which trump the players hold and how many. Players then score additional points by taking "tricks" — high cards taking low cards. One hundred points wins the game.

The Fool card is the lowest card in the deck. It cannot take a card of any suit, but it may be played to any suit that is led. The fascinating aspect about the Fool card as far as we are concerned is that it may be substituted to protect a card of greater value. If, for example, a king of cups is led and the player following holds the queen of cups, that player may substitute the Fool in order to save his queen.

For those interested in learning more about the tarot cards or the game of tarok, the following are recommended reading:

The Encyclopedia of Tarot, Volume 1, by Stuart R. Kaplan, U.S. Games Systems, Inc., New York, 1978.

A Complete Guide to the Tarot by Eden Gray, Bantam Books, New York, 1981.

About the Authors

Born in Independence, Missouri, Margaret Weis graduated from the University of Missouri and worked as a book editor before teaming up with Tracy Hickman to develop the *Dragonlance* novels. Margaret lives in a renovated barn in Wisconsin with her teen-aged daughter, Elizabeth Baldwin, and several pets. She enjoys reading (especially Charles Dickens), opera, and rollerskating.

Born in Salt Lake City, Tracy Hickman resides in Wisconsin in a 100-year-old Victorian home with his wife and four children. When he isn't reading or writing, he is eating or sleeping. On Sundays, he conducts the hymns at the local Mormon church.

The Darksword Trilogy marked Margaret and Tracy's first appearance as Bantam Spectra authors. They followed up with *Darksword Adventures*, a companion volume and game book set in the same world, then, the **Rose of the Prophet** trilogy. **The Death Gate Cycle**, a seven book series being published in hardcover and paperback, is their most inventive fantasy fiction yet. In addition to their collaborations, each is working on solo series. The first of these is *Star of the Guardians* by Margaret Weis.

Two Special Previews—

DRAGON WING, Volume One of
The Death Gate Cycle
by Margaret Weis and Tracy Hickman

and

THE LOST KING, Volume One of
Star of the Guardians
by Margaret Weis

On the following pages are two exciting previews of upcoming novels by premier science fiction and fantasy storytellers, Margaret Weis and Tracy Hickman.

THE DEATH GATE CYCLE

— ■ —

Known for their innovation, Margaret Weis and Tracy Hickman reach an entirely new level with The Death Gate Cycle. *For this seven-book extravaganza they have developed four completely realized worlds. In the first four novels, a new adventure with both continuing and new characters will be set on each of the four worlds. In later volumes, the realms begin to interact, with the supreme battle for control of all the worlds in the final novel.*

The following sceene gives us an irresistible taste of the world of DRAGON WING, the first novel in *The Death Gate Cycle*, and the plots surrounding even the most knowledgeable of men who live there.

Coming close to Hugh the Hand, the courier raised his lantern and stared quizzically into the assassin's face, inviting question or comment. The Hand saw no need to waste his breath in asking questions he knew would not be answered and so stared back at the courier in silence.

The courier, slightly nonplussed, started to say something, changed his mind, and softly exhaled the breath he had drawn in to speak.

Abruptly, he turned on his heel and gestured to the assassin to follow. Hugh fell into step behind his guide. The courier led the way to a place that Hugh soon came to recognize, from early and dark childhood memories, as a Kir monastery.

It was ancient and had obviously been long abandoned. The flagstones of the courtyard were cracked and in many cases missing entirely. Coralite had grown over much of the standing outer structures that had been formed of the rare granite the Kir favored over the more common coralite. A chill wind whistled through the abandoned dwellings where no light shone and had probably not shone for centuries. Bare trees creaked and dry leaves crunched beneath Hugh's boots.

Having been raised by the grim and dour order of Kir monks, the Hand knew the location of every monastery on the Volkaran Isles. He could not remember hearing of any that had ever been abandoned and the mystery of where he was and why he had been brought here deepened.

The courier came to a baked clay door that stood at the

bottom of a tall turret. An iron key, worn on a ribbon around the courier's neck, unlocked the door. The Hand peered upward, but could not see a glimmer of light in any of the windows. The door swung open silently—an indication that someone was accustomed to coming here frequently. Gliding inside, the courier indicated with a wave of his hand that Hugh was to follow. When both were in the cold and drafty building, the courier once again locked the door, tucking the key back inside the bosom of his tunic.

"This way," said the courier. The direction was not necessary—there was only one possible way for them to go and that was up. A spiral staircase led them round and round the interior of the turret. Hugh counted three levels, each marked by a clay door. The Hand, surreptitiously testing each as they ascended, noted all were locked.

On the fourth level, at another clay door, the iron key again made an appearance. A long narrow corridor, darker than the Lords of Night, ran straight and true before them. The courier's booted footsteps rang on the stone. Hugh, accustomed by habit to treading silently in his soft-soled, supple leather boots, made no more noise than if he had been the man's shadow.

They passed six doors by Hugh's count—three on his left and three on his right—before the courier raised a warning hand and they stopped at the seventh. Once again, the iron key was produced. It grated in the lock and the door slid open.

"Enter," said the courier, standing to one side.

Hugh did as he was told. He was not surprised to hear the door shut behind him. No sound of a key turning in the lock, however. There was no light in the room but the soft glow given off by the coralite-outside. The faint shimmer illuminated the room well enough for the Hand's sharp eyes. He stood still a moment, closely inspecting his surroundings. He was, he discovered, not alone.

The Hand felt no fear. His fingers, beneath his cloak, were clasped around the hilt of his dagger, but that was only common sense in a situation like this. Hugh was a businessman and he recognized the setting of a business discussion when he saw it.

The other person in the room was adept at hiding. He was silent and kept himself concealed in the shadows. Hugh didn't see the person or hear him, but he knew with every instinct that had kept him alive through forty harsh and bitter cycles that there was someone else present. The Hand sniffed the air.

"Are you an animal? Can you smell me?" queried the voice—a male voice, deep and resonant. "Is that how you knew I was in the room?"

"Yeah, an animal," said Hugh shortly.

"And what if I had attacked you?" The figure moved over to stand by the window. He was outlined in Hugh's vision by the faint radiance of the coralite. The Hand saw that his interrogator was a tall man clad in a cape whose hem he could hear dragging across the floor. The man's head and face were covered by chain mail; only the eyes were visible. But the Hand knew his suspicions had been correct. He knew to whom he was talking.

Hugh drew forth his dagger. "A hand's breadth of steel in your heart, Your Majesty."

"I am wearing a mail vest," said Stephen, King of the Volkaran Isles and the Uylandia Cluster. He was, seemingly, not surprised that Hugh recognized him.

A corner of the assassin's thin lips twitched. "The chain mail does not cover your armpit, Majesty. Lift your elbow." Stepping forward, Hugh placed thin, long fingers in the gap between the body armor and that covering the arm. "One thrust of my dagger, there—" Hugh shrugged.

Stephen did not flinch at the touch. "I must mention that to my armorer."

Hugh shook his head. "Do what you will, Majesty, if a man's determined to kill you then you're dead. And if that's why you've brought me here, I can only offer you this advice: Decide whether you want your corpse burned or buried."

"This from an expert," said Stephen, and Hugh could hear the sneer if he could not see it on the man's helmed face.

"I assume Your Majesty requires an expert since you've gone to all this trouble."

The king turned to face the window. He had seen almost fifty cycles, but he was well-built and strong and able to withstand incredible hardships. Some whispered he slept in his armor, to keep his body hard. Certainly, considering his wife's reputed character, he might also welcome the protection.

"Yes, you are an expert. The best in the kingdom, I am told."

Stephen fell silent. The Hand was adept at reading the words men speak with their bodies, not with their tongues. Though the king might have thought he was masking his turbulent inner emotions quite well, Hugh saw the fingers of the left hand close in upon themselves, heard the silvery clinking of the chain mail as a tremor shook the man's body.

So it often was with men making their minds up to murder.

"You also have a peculiar conceit, Hugh the Hand," said Stephen, abruptly breaking his long pause. "You advertise yourself as a Hand of Justice, of Retribution. You kill those who allegedly have wronged others, those who are above the law, those whom—supposedly—my law cannot touch."

There was anger in the voice, and a challenge. Stephen was obviously piqued, but Hugh knew that the warring clans of Volkaran and Uylandia were currently being held together only by a mortar composed of fear and greed and he did not figure it worth his while to argue the point with a king who undoubtedly knew it as well.

"Why do you do this?" Stephen persisted. "Is it some sort of attempt at honor?"

"Honor? Your Majesty talks like an elflord! Honor won't buy you a cheap meal at a bad inn in Therpes."

"Ah, the money?"

"The money. Any knife-in-the-back killer can be had for the price of a plate of stew. That's fine for those who just want their man dead. But those who've been wronged, those who've suffered at the hands of another—they want the one who brought them grief to suffer himself. They want him to know, before he dies, who brought about his destruction. They want him to experience the pain and the terror of his victim. And for this satisfaction, they're willing to pay a high price."

"I am told the risks you take are quite extraordinary; that you even challenge your victim to fair combat."

"If the customer wants it."

"And is willing to pay."

Hugh shrugged. The statement was too obvious for comment. The conversation was pointless; meaningless. The Hand knew his own reputation, his own worth. He didn't need to hear it recited back to him. But he was used to it. It was all part of business. Like any other customer, Stephen was trying to talk his way into committing this act. It amused the Hand to note that a king in this situation behaved no differently from his humblest subject.

Stephen had turned and was staring out the window, his gloved hand—fist clenched—resting on the ledge. Hugh waited patiently, in silence.

"I don't understand. Why should those who hire you want to give a person who had wronged them the chance to fight for his life?"

"Because in this they're doubly revenged. For then, it's not my hand that strikes the killer down, Your Majesty, but the hands of his ancestors, who no longer protect him."

"Do you believe this?" Stephen turned to face him; Hugh could see the moonlight flash on the chain mail covering the man's head and shoulders.

Hugh raised an eyebrow. His hand moved to stroke the braided, silky strands of beard that hung from his chin. The question had never before been asked of him. It proved, so he supposed, that kings *were* different from their subjects—at least this one was. The Hand moved to the window to stand next to Stephen. The assassin's gaze was drawn to a small courtyard below them. Covered over by coralite, it glowed eerily in the darkness and he could see, by the soft blue light, the figure of a man standing in the center. The man wore a black hood. He held in his hand a sharp-edged sword. At his feet stood a block of stone.

"The only things I believe in, Your Majesty, are my wits and my skill." Twisting the ends of his beard, Hugh smiled. "So I'm to have no choice. I either accept this job or else, is that it?"

"You have a choice. When I have described the job to you, you may either take it or refuse to do so."

"At which point my head parts company from my shoulders."

"The man you see is the Royal Executioner. He is skilled in his work. Death will be quick, clean. Far better than what you were facing. That much, at least, I owe you for your time." Stephen turned to face Hugh, the eyes in the shadow of the chain mail helm were dark and empty, lit by nothing within, reflecting no light from without. "I must take precautions. I cannot expect you to accept this task without knowing its nature, yet to reveal it to you is to place myself at your mercy.

I dare not permit you to remain alive, knowing what you will shortly know."

"If I refuse, I'm disposed of by night, in the dark, no witnesses. If I accept, I'm entangled in the same web in which Your Majesty currently finds himself twisting."

"What more do you expect? You are, after all, nothing but a murderer," Stephen said coldly.

"And you, Your Majesty, are nothing more than a man who wants to hire a murderer." Bowing with an ironic flourish, Hugh turned on his heel.

"Where are you going?" Stephen demanded.

"If Your Majesty will excuse me, I'm late for an engagement. I should've been in hell an hour previous." The Hand walked toward the door.

"Damn you! I've offered you your life!"

Hugh didn't even bother to turn around. He sounded weary and exasperated. "The price is too low. My life's worth nothing. I don't value it. In exchange, you want me to accept a job so dangerous you've got to trap me to force me to take it? Better to meet death on my own terms than Your Majesty's."

Hugh flung open the door. The king's courier stood facing him, blocking his way out. At his feet stood the glowlamp and it cast its radiance upward, illuminating a face that was ethereal in its delicacy and beauty.

He's a courier? And I'm a Sartan, thought Hugh.

"Ten thousand barls," said the young man.

Hugh's hand went to the braided beard, twisting it thoughtfully. His eyes glanced sideways at Stephen, who had come up behind him.

"Douse that light," commanded the king. "Is this necessary, Trian?"

"Your Majesty"—Trian spoke with respect and patience, but it was the tone of one friend advising another, not the tone of a servant deferring to a master—"he is the best. There is no one else to whom we can entrust this. We have gone to considerable trouble to acquire him. We can't afford to lose him. If Your Majesty will remember, I warned you from the beginning—"

"Yes, I remember!" Stephen snapped. He stood silent, inwardly fuming. He would undoubtedly like nothing better than to order his "courier" to march the assassin to the block. The king would probably, at this moment, enjoy wielding the executioner's blade himself. The courier gently drew an iron screen over the light, leaving them in darkness "Very well!" the king snarled.

"Ten thousand barls?" Hugh couldn't believe it.

"Yes," answered Trian. "When the job is done."

"Half now. Half when the job is done."

"Your life now! The barls then!" Stephen hissed through clenched teeth.

Hugh took a step forward toward the door. The young man, still blocking his way, shot a warning glance at the king.

"Half now!" Stephen's words were a gasp.

Hugh, bowing in acquiescence, turned back to face the king. "Who's the victim?"

Stephen drew a deep breath. Hugh heard a clicking, catching choke in the king's throat, a sound vaguely similar to the rattle in the throats of the dying.

"My ten-year-old son," said the king.

STAR OF THE GUARDIANS

———————■———————

Volume One
The Lost King
by Margaret Weis

*Even before Margaret Weis teamed up with Tracy Hickman,
she had several writing projects in the works. Now, more
than ten years in the making.* **Star of the Guardians** *is
finally published. It's the page-turning tale of the man
known as the Warlord and his search for the lost heir to the
galactic throne.*

"Ah, Dr. Giesk. I was beginning to think you might fail
me."

The deep baritone voice was emotionless, almost pleasant
and conversational. But Dr. Giesk shuddered. *Failure* was a
word the Warlord never spoke twice to any man. The doctor
could not remove his hands from the controls of his delicate
equipment, but he managed to give the Warlord a beseeching
look.

"The subject proved unusually resistant," Giesk quavered. "Three days, my lord! I realize he was a Guardian, but none of the others held out that long. I can't understand—"

"Of course you can't understand." The Warlord stared down impassively at the man on the table. He laid a gauntleted hand upon the quivering chest of the man with as little regard as he would have laid that same hand upon the man's coffin. Yet, when the Warlord spoke, his voice was soft, tinged with a sadness and, it seemed, regret.

"Who is there left now who understands, Stavros?"

The gloved fingers touched a jewel the man wore around his neck. Hanging from a silver chain, the jewel was extraordinarily beautiful. Carved into the shape of an eight-pointed star, the gleaming jewel was the only object worn by the naked man, and it had been left around his neck by the Warlord's expressed command.

"Who knows of the training, the discipline, Stavros? Who remembers? And you. One of my best."

The man on the table moaned. His head moved feverishly from side to side. The Warlord watched a moment in silence, then bent close to speak softly into the man's ear.

"I saved your life once, Stavros. Do you remember? It was at the Royal Academy. On a dare, you had climbed that ridiculous thirty-foot statue of the king. You were what—nine? I was thirteen and she . . ." the Warlord paused, "she would have been six. Yes, it was soon after she came to the Academy. Only six. All eyes and hair, wild and lonely as a catamount." His voice softened further, almost to a whisper. The man on the table began to shiver uncontrollably.

"Fascinating," murmured Giesk with professional interest, monitoring his instruments. "I haven't been able to illicit a response that strong in three days."

The Warlord moved his hand up to the man's head, the

gauntleted fingers stroking back the graying hair almost caressingly. "Stavros," commanded the Warlord, his helmeted visage bending over the man. "Stavros, can you hear me?"

The man made a slight moaning sound. A froth of blood appeared on his ashen lips.

"Be quick, my lord!" cried Dr. Giesk, "or you will lose him!"

The Warlord brought his face so near to that of his victim that his breath touched the man's skin, displacing the bubbles of blood and saliva on the gaping mouth.

"Where is the boy?"

The man shivered, fighting with himself. But it was useless. The Warlord regarded him intently. The gauntleted hand moved to rest upon the cold white forehead.

"Stavros?"

In a wild, tortured shriek, the man screamed out words that made no sense to Giesk. He glanced at the Warlord uncertainly.

The Warlord slowly rose and straightened. "Well done, Dr. Giesk. You may now terminate."